REBEL HEIR

JAINE DIAMOND

DREAM WARP
PUBLISHING Ltd.

Rebel Heir
Jaine Diamond

Published by DreamWarp Publishing Ltd.
www.jainediamond.com

Cover Design: DreamWarp Publishing Ltd.
Cover Photo: Michelle Lancaster @lanefotograf
Cover Model: J.J. Michaels
Back cover image: Gastown Steam Clock, Vancouver

Rebel Heir

To every reader who's ever written to me to tell me how my books and characters have impacted your life and your heart, I humbly thank you.

villain
noun
A dangerous or harmful person; a criminal.

Prologue

Talia

When I was ten years old, I made a deal with the Devil. Sort of. Technically I made a deal with the Devil's son. But it really just amounts to the same damn thing.

Poor life choices.

In my defense, I was *ten*. I really didn't know what I was getting into. Plus, he was sneaky about it. And very, very cute.

"You can't," he drawled lazily, dangling a leg off the side of the dock. He lay on his back with one arm tucked behind his head and the sun blazing off his white tennis shirt, and even squinting up at me he looked cute. He'd lured me over here with promises of chocolates, but failed to mention that we had to steal them first.

Typical.

His name was Lexington, but everyone called him Lex. Except his dad, who called him "boy." As far as I was concerned, he was the most aggravating boy in the whole world. He knew I was already grounded, so I'd get in extra crap if I got caught.

Lex, on the other hand, would only get in crap *for* getting caught. His parents were way different than mine.

But even so…

"Yes, I can," I insisted.

"You won't."

I would. I already was.

I hopped to my feet and tiptoed up the dock like a thief-in-the-making before he could utter another word. Then I stole through the bushes, poised to sneak into the fancy backyard pavilion where his parents were hosting a party, and swipe us the coveted chocolates. They had a sweet filling of hazelnut or vanilla cream. Lex's house-keeper made them; her specialty was dark chocolate ones with real liquor in them. We weren't even supposed to eat those ones, but we did.

Why did *I* have to steal them, though?

Because Lex dared me to, and I was a sucker for Lex's dares. The second he uttered *You can't* something flipped inside me. It was my stupid switch. Once flipped, it was hard to unflip. Especially when Lex was watching.

Plus, I really wanted those chocolates.

I could hear him sneaking up behind me. He wanted a front row seat to the crime, but if I got caught he wouldn't want to miss that either.

My heart drummed in my chest as I crept up to the stone pavil-ion's half-wall. I was supposed to be next-door, at my family's summer house, not here, thieving liquor filled desserts, and defi-nitely not hanging out with Lex. But also, something happened to me when I did stuff that impressed Lex. It made my stomach tingle in a weird, good way.

Luckily, when I peeked into the pavilion and eyed the dessert table, my parents were nowhere to be seen. And pulling off the theft really wasn't that hard. It was like taking candy from—well, a bunch of drunk adults. They were all drinking and mingling and stuff, and all I had to do was wait for a moment when no one was looking, dart out and hunker down behind the dessert table, then snatch as many chocolates as I could hold. I stuffed them in the pockets of my sundress and snuck back behind the wall, where Lex was waiting.

We scurried back down through the trees to the dock, snuck into the boathouse and flopped on one of the daybeds in the sun. I dumped my score on the mattress between us and watched Lex's eyes light up.

Ha. *Victory.*

Since we'd met three summers before, Lex and I had been friendly(ish) enemies. Frenemies. Competitive, argumentative, and drawn to each other like flies to poop. If we spent more time together than we did, we'd probably end up getting arrested or dead.

Good thing whatever relationship we had was limited to a few weeks over summer holidays, when we were temporary next-door neighbors on this little island off the coast. The rest of the year, I lived in Vancouver and he lived a world away in Toronto, where I liked to pretend he didn't exist.

Bummer for me, there really wasn't anyone else to hang out with on the island all summer but a few toddlers and the old people, so I usually just ended up sneaking around with Lex. (There was Keri Kerrington, who only came for a couple of weeks, and since she was twelve, already had boobs, and she told me she kissed Lex—twice—in the boathouse, I really didn't want her to come back. It wasn't that *I* wanted to kiss Lex. But she couldn't just sweep in here and turn my summer nemesis into her summer boyfriend and kiss him—with tongue—in the boathouse. Gross.)

I eyed Lex as he handed me a chocolate. He seemed happy. I didn't trust it. He'd been grouchy lately, like he always got towards the end of summer, before he had to fly back to Toronto. And usually the grouchier he got, the more diabolical his dares got.

I figured the chocolates would at least get him off my back for a bit.

But then he said, "You and me, we're gonna get married." He rolled onto his back, sucking on a melting chocolate. The sun poured over his face and he gazed up at me with his melted-caramel eyes, the picture of innocence, which he was not.

I wrinkled my nose at him. "We are not."

"You have to marry someone, Natalia," he said with exaggerated patience, like he was speaking to a baby or something. He always spoke to me like that, using my full name, like my parents did when I was in trouble.

I eyed him suspiciously. "Why would I marry you?"

"Why wouldn't you?"

I rolled my eyes. Lex and his stupid dares. He thought he could get me to do *anything*.

"You can't trick me," I informed him, even though he tricked me all the time. And this definitely smelled like some kind of trick.

The first time I met Lex, my dad sat me down afterwards and told me to stay away from him. That his father was "a very bad man." From that day on, I was definitely scared of him—not Lex, but his dad. But maybe I would've been scared of the man anyway. He always seemed to be in a bad mood. He swore a lot. And he always wore a suit, even in summer. Another man in a suit drove him around in a big black car and other men in suits were always visiting him. My parents visited, too, bringing food and dragging me along while they drank coffee, our moms gossiped and my dad was fake polite to Lex's dad.

I'd even overheard my dad call Lex's dad *Satan* behind his back, but he was still nice to his face.

Meanwhile, I was supposed to be steering clear of Lex. But it wasn't that easy. All summer long he just kept goading me into yet another one of his diabolical dares. Dares that usually ended with one of us—usually me—getting in crap.

I tried, I really did, but it was hard to best him when he was almost two-and-a-half years older than me, bigger, stronger, and way the hell sneakier. He wasn't smarter, only because I would never admit that he was. But sometimes I had to wonder.

I knew I shouldn't have fallen for his dares, but they were just so irresistible—right up until they got me in crap.

That's the thing about the son of Satan. He's fun, but dangerous. Dangerous but fun.

"It's not a trick," he informed me. "I'm a good catch."

"How would you know?"

"I know more about marriage than you do."

Maybe. But his dad was cheating on his mom with his actual wife, who lived back in Toronto, so I wasn't sure about that. (I overheard Mom telling Dad so.)

"I'll be inheriting a sizable fortune from my grandparents," he went on, "and Mom says that Helena says I need to be married before I turn thirty. So, when I turn twenty-nine, if neither of us has gotten married yet, you can marry me. Then we get the money." He said it like it was the simplest thing in the world. He used phrases like "sizable fortune" and called his rich grandmother, Helena, by her first name. He also checked the time on his watch very seriously, like he knew I had somewhere to be.

He wasn't serious, though. How could he be serious?

I was pretty sure the part about the inheritance was true. But by the time he was twenty-nine, which was a million years away, someone else would marry him anyway.

When we'd arrived on the island that summer, I'd discovered that my summer nemesis was cute. This was news to me. He didn't look much different than the summers before, but for some reason his super light dusting of freckles, tangle of caramel-brown hair and sun chapped lips were kind of fascinating, when before they'd always just been *there* and maybe mildly irritating, like everything else attached to Lex.

My cousin had a poster on her bedroom wall of Nick Carter with his shirt off, and every time I looked at it I got a melty feeling in my stomach. I got that same feeling whenever Lex rolled his caramel eyes at me.

I didn't like it.

"Come on," I said, stuffing another chocolate in my mouth. "I've gotta get home before Dad checks and finds me gone. Take your half of the chocolates."

"Fine." He rolled over and started splitting the loot into two piles, taking forever to choose the ones he wanted.

I grabbed his watch arm and twisted it, checking the time and sighing impatiently. Dad rarely got angry with me, but he'd already given me crap for several stunts this summer. The worst was when I jumped off our boat last week and tried to swim to shore, which was way farther away than it looked. Luckily, Dad came to the rescue on a jet ski and fished me out. Which was how I almost drowned—and got grounded for the rest of the summer.

(Yes, I took all the blame. I was hardly gonna admit that Lex dared me to do it.)

"Look, if you'd just agree to it…" he said, laser focused on chocolate sorting.

"Agree to what?"

"Marry me." His eyes met mine, and my stomach did that weird melty thing. Shirtless Nick Carter really had nothing on those caramel eyes.

"Fine," I muttered through chocolate, "I'll marry you. Hurry up."

"You will?"

"Whatever."

Lex pulled out the black leather notebook he carried in his back pocket at all times and opened it to the bookmark. Then he pulled the pen from his shirt pocket. It said *Davenport* in gold script, his mom's last name. (His mom's family had even more money than his dad's; that's where the giant inheritance was coming from. Mom gossiped a lot.)

I licked chocolate off my fingers as he started writing carefully in the notebook. "What are you doing?"

"Getting it in writing. Then we can both sign it."

"Gimme that." I pulled the book from his hand. I'd always

wanted to know what he kept in this thing. I read his neat, boyish handwriting.

I, Natalia De Santis, agree to marry Lexington when he turns 29.

I flipped back one page.

I, Keri Kerrington, agree to marry Lexington when he turns 29.

"Keri's in here?!" I flipped back another page. "Who the heck is Jasmine?"

"It's just insurance." Lex took the book back with a shrug. "They'll probably grow up to be ugly anyway."

My jaw dropped. I didn't know exactly what "insurance" was. I was ten. But I was simultaneously appalled and flattered.

"You can wait and see if you get a better offer," he added casually. "But you won't."

"Maybe I will!"

"Maybe you won't."

"What if I do?"

"Then it doesn't matter. If you're already married when I turn twenty-nine, the deal will be null and void."

"I don't trust you."

He rolled his eyes again. "It's a simple legal contract, Natalia. I'm not messing with you."

I narrowed my eyes at him. Lex was always messing with me.

"I mean, who knows..." He brushed his melty chocolates into his hand and stuffed them into his pocket. "Maybe someone else will ask you, and he won't even be old and mean and smell bad." He met my eyes again and I caved.

"Gimme that book again." I grabbed his notebook and pen, a rush of heat exploding in my chest that had nothing to do with the thrill of stealing chocolates. I knew I wasn't supposed to do this. That if Dad saw my name in Lex's book, he'd freak out and ground me for the rest of my life.

But I signed my name carefully on the page, my heartbeat thumping through me so hard, my hand kinda shook.

Natalia De Santis

There. No biggie. It was just a piece of paper.

It wasn't like he asked me to sign my name in blood or anything.

Though I did let him prick my fingertip with a pin. (Never asking myself, at the time, why he'd conveniently brought a pin with him.)

It hurt, a lot, but I pretended it didn't. I pressed my bloody fingerprint to the paper, and he pressed his next to mine. I could smell his sweet, chocolatey breath as he leaned in next to me to do it, his hair falling over his eyes.

I also never asked myself, at the time, why the other girls who signed their names in his book didn't have to seal their agreements with blood.

Maybe I should've been just a tiny bit worried that this blood pact might go sour on me. Lex's schemes always did. Unfortunately, the boat incident wasn't the first time he'd said "jump" and I jumped. And I got screwed.

But it wouldn't matter anyway, right? His twenty-ninth birthday was years away. I'd already be married by then.

And if I wasn't, so what? Daddy wouldn't really be mad. I'd be old enough to choose whoever I wanted to marry.

And who knew? Maybe I would marry Lex.

Any girl could tell Lex Davenport wasn't going to grow up to be ugly.

———

He didn't grow up to be ugly.

But he was, after all, the son of Satan.

And as it turned out, both of the above were a real fucking problem.

Chapter One

Talia

16 years later…

I dissolved into the trees along the backyard fence like a shadow. Maybe it was those two delicious peach Bellinis I'd just sucked back with the girls that made me feel extra nimble, but I was kind of impressed with myself.

Under the dark of the trees, pause, make sure no one's noticed you just slipped out the back door…

Nope. They're drunk. *You're good.*

Then, poof. Gone. Like a ninja, around the side of the house to the gate in the fence that no one used.

Ease it open, and you're free and clear.

I was a solid ninety-nine-point-nine percent sure that I'd just made a clean getaway from the party as I shut the gate behind me. Then my phone dinged in my purse. I paused in the shadows to dig it out and check. If it was someone at the party, I'd tell them I was in the bathroom or something, and later I'd make some excuse that I was tired and had to go home. Lame but plausible.

Sure enough, I had a text from Roni, one of my best friends and the party host: *Where you at?*

Shit. I texted her back: *Peeing.* Then I stashed my phone. I wondered if I should try to grab an Uber now or put some distance between myself and the property first, when I heard something rustling above me. And not like a delicate bird in the tree boughs.

More like a large panther scaling the fence, but less graceful.

"Ouch. *Shit*," snarled a voice above me. Not a panther.

A man.

I looked up—and screamed as a black-clad figure descended on me in the dark. "Fuck!" he shout-grumbled as he landed on me. Then he hissed: "*Shhh!*"

He *shushed* me.

I'd stopped screaming anyway as his entire grown-man body weight knocked the air from my lungs. I managed to wheeze out something that was supposed to be *Get the fuck off me*, but he was already getting off. I gasped for air as he sprang to his feet—in a pair of scuffed black motorcycle boots.

I peered up.

Ripped black jeans molded to long, manly legs… black sweater poured over a sinfully hot upper bod… black leather vest… *ugh,* I knew where this was headed. Yup. Biker patches all over the leather vest.

And that *face.*

He leaned back down into the shadows to see me better. I saw dreamy-thick brown hair with the most stupidly perfect natural caramel-blond highlights, and caramel-brown eyes to match. "Talia?"

"Lex," I wheezed.

He offered me a hand up and I slapped my hand into his. He pulled me to my feet. Then I plucked my hand back.

"What are you doing here?" he said dubiously. And by *here* I was pretty sure he meant *under me in the dark*, not *at this party.*

"Uh, what am I doing here?" I stalled, studiously brushing grass off the butt of my jeans like *that's* what I was doing here, instead of sneaking out of this party because I'd just seen *him* arrive. "Nothing," I lied. "Just going into the party. You?"

"Uh… perimeter sweep," he mumbled, avoiding my eyes. "You know, security."

Right. He worked security for Roni's man, Jude; true. But scaling a fence in the dark when there was a gate, right there? That was a panic move if I ever saw one.

"There's a gate," I informed him.

"What?"

I pointed past him into the shadows.

He glanced at it and muttered, "Motherfucker."

Uh-huh. Security, my ass.

He looked at me, eyelids lowering. "Were you sneaking out?"

"No." *Busted.* "Were you?"

"No."

Lies!

Wait. Why would he be sneaking out of Jude and Roni's party?

Was *he* sneaking out because he heard *I* was here?

"Well, then." I drew my shoulders back and tried to look like I was on my way *in* when he fell out of the sky and landed on top of me. Because that totally wasn't a sign from the universe or anything. "I guess I'll see you around."

I strode past him and through the gate, scooting my ass back into the party I'd just tried to leave. I went in through the back door off the kitchen, tossed off my jacket, spotted Roni at the bar in the living room and headed straight for it. I needed more Bellinis to get me through this night. Many more Bellinis.

I didn't even look back to see if Lex followed me in.

He totally followed me in. Then he proceeded to watch me from across the crowded room while pretending not to.

So that's how it's gonna be.

Fine with me.

I helped myself to another Bellini and planted myself by the bar with Roni and some of our friends. Roni and Jude had thrown this "welcome home" party for us all because we'd just come home to Vancouver off of a nineteen-month world tour. Me, Roni and Jude, the two rock bands we worked for—Dirty and the Players—and all the local staff and crew.

I'd started out working with Dirty while I was in college, as an assistant on their management team, but now I worked for the Players as their assistant manager. It was better this way.

Lex worked for Dirty, on Jude's security team.

Ever since I'd been promoted to my position with the Players two years ago, I'd crossed paths with Lex a lot less. Thank God he didn't come on this tour. If he did, we'd be working together, traveling together, partying in one another's vicinity all the damn time... and it... would... *suck.*

So, why was I standing here, pretending to listen to Roni's story about... something? While doing absolutely nothing but thinking about Lex, and trying to sneak glimpses of him across the room?

I mean, obviously if someone's staring at you, you want to know, right? I was just checking.

Yup. He was still staring.

I turned my back to him decisively, just as Carl strolled up.

"Hey, baby!" I cried, and several people turned to look. The party was loud, music was rocking and the house was packed with people, but apparently my jubilant, desperate squeal cut through everything for a decent radius. Even my boyfriend looked surprised. Carl's eyebrows rose as his arms opened. I was already throwing myself into them.

We hugged, kind of awkwardly kissed—Carl had always been weird about PDAs—and he released me. "Whoa. You're happy to see me."

"Obviously." I grasped his hand and shoved my fingers through his.

"Sorry I couldn't get here earlier. Dinner went late."

"Sure, sure. It's fine."

Weirdly, I'd actually forgotten he was coming.

His gaze drifted down the front of my low-cut blouse. It was tucked into my tight, high-waisted jeans, and he took those in too, with a long, slow drink of his dark eyes... as I bounced on my toes with restless energy. But it wasn't his gaze that had me all flustered. It was the feeling of Lex Davenport checking me out across the room.

I held up my drink. "Bellini?" Then I pounded back the rest of it.

Carl chuckled and Roni, who'd been eavesdropping, passed one from the bar to his hand.

"I see you've had a few." My boyfriend's dark eyes crinkled as he tasted his Bellini.

"Just a few." I set my empty champagne flute on the bar and Roni promptly offered me another.

I took it. "Thanks. Do I look thirsty?"

"You look..." She looked me over. "Sweaty."

I laughed, too loudly, and took a generous swig of my cocktail as Roni gave me a curious half-smile.

Out of the corner of my eye, I swore to God I could feel Lex coming closer. I had no idea if he was coming this way on purpose or if the space between us was just diminishing as he mingled his way through the party. But either way, I needed more distance.

"Lex mingle. I mean—*let's*," I stammered, "uh, *let's* mingle." I tucked Carl's hand into my ribs like a football and towed him along as I plunged into the crowd.

I could *not* handle talking to Lex tonight. Not with the vivid memory of his whole body sprawled on top of mine permeating my system, cell by cell, bringing awareness of his proximity to every nerve. *Yup. That happened. He was all over you. All six-feet, lean muscle and long limbs of him, pressed against you in the dirt.*

Why was that so *hot*?

Because you'd love to fuck him in the dirt.

Shit. Where the hell did that come from? My thoughts were going haywire and my senses were snap-crackling to attention in that strange, uncontrollable way they did whenever he was near.

Nope, I did not need to talk to him. Or keep looking at him across the room. I'd stop doing that, right now.

I looked over. He was talking to some guy and not looking at me.

Okay, I'd stop looking at him *now*.

I introduced Carl to various people he hadn't met yet, hoping to keep him occupied, and it worked. Carl was a business manager. He quickly got talking business with my boss, Brody Mason, manager of Dirty and the Players—a conversation I would've normally been interested in—and I took the opportunity to make sure Lex wasn't venturing any closer.

He wasn't.

I wasn't sure why I felt… disappointed?

Or why his mere presence made me so damn uncomfortable.

I'd gotten pretty accustomed to all the other bad boys who showed up at these work parties—from the rock stars to the crew members to the music biz execs, to the bikers on Jude's security team. I'd gotten accustomed to the rough dudes. The famous dudes. The richer than God dudes.

The hotter than sin dudes.

I'd never gotten accustomed to Lex, though.

Kinda awkward when the boy you spent three summer holidays with as a kid, thought you hated but really fell stupidly in puppy love with and promised to marry but then never saw again past ten years old, suddenly showed up in your life again. And when you happened to see him outside your friend's place one night, straddling a giant Harley-Davidson motorcycle, he flashed you his teeth and touched his tongue to one of his silver upper canines—and you realized with horror that while bad boys, bikers definitely included, were so not your thing, this particular biker made your clit throb.

That was four years ago, and in all fairness to me, at the time, I had no idea who the mysterious, hot, random biker with the creepy, sexy teeth was. Because Lex Davenport had grown up. He'd changed. That cute but aggravating boy I used to know, who wore a Bvlgari watch and white tennis shirts, had grown into a badass man.

I didn't discover who he was until weeks later, when I ran into him again at a band party, we were officially introduced, and I heard his name. And he heard mine. Time seemed to freeze as his eyes met mine—and it all hit me when I looked into his caramel-brown irises, like a lightning bolt to the crotch.

Summers on the island. Melted chocolates.

A marriage pact sealed in blood in his little leather bound notebook.

And I died of equal parts embarrassment and lust.

The next time I saw him, not two weeks later, both of us were leaving on a world tour with Dirty that lasted for a year-and-a-half —the Hell & Back tour, which could not have been more appropriately named, if you asked me.

Lex Davenport and I were coworkers.

On the very first night of that tour, while partying at a bar with the band and a bunch of the crew, I succumbed to peer pressure and did a blow job shooter out of Lex's lap in front of many witnesses. And the way he'd looked at me, the way he gently held back my hair while I sucked that shooter from between his thighs... I thought he wanted me. And I felt drawn to him, even though I didn't fully understand it. I knew he was a biker and so not my type.

Turned out, I wasn't his type, either. Because he never. Once. Made a move on me.

Quite the opposite.

As a result, I'd never touched him, and let me be clear about this: I was never going to.

After we came home off the Hell & Back tour, things between

us didn't get any better. Every time we ran into one another at some event, the heat was still there. The silent avoidance and denial of one another, even as the attraction smoldered in the silence.

At least, my side of it smoldered.

Luckily, I'd barely seen him in the last two years. I'd avoided him wherever I could. I hadn't even laid eyes on him since a party here at Roni and Jude's house a few months ago, on a tour break. It was a barbecue, on a hot summer day—and Lex had peeled his shirt off. And yeah, I fucking noticed.

A lot of guys took their shirt off at that party. But Lex? I'd never seen him shirtless, other than when he was twelve. The man's body could only be described by any rational, heterosexual woman as a weapon of instantaneous mass destruction. My brain completely detonated at the sight of it, leaving me irrationally in pieces.

Lean, sculpted muscles you could get totally lost in trying to navigate with your imagination (and I did). Naturally tanned-looking olive skin. And tattoos, just a few of them, scattered across his torso in the exactly sexiest spots. A small motorcycle across one pec, right above his golden-brown nipple. A dagger wrapped in barbed wire, plunging down the side of the leanly muscular V that disappeared into his low-slung jeans. And across his back, holding court above the most perfect, round male ass I'd ever seen so artfully swathed in ripped denim, the logo of his motorcycle club, the West Coast Kings MC, in all-black: the skeletal king of spades, like from a playing card, but much, much deadlier. The King's broken crown crept up the back of Lex's neck, just visible above the neckline of his shirts.

Not that I'd been staring for years and wondering what it was, and what lay below his clothes or anything.

Now, I knew. And I wanted to etch that tattoo into his back with my fingernails and my teeth.

At that barbecue, I'd indulged in a few too many Fuzzy Navels and, when he seemed to notice I couldn't stop staring at his naked nipples, Lex and I had engaged in a passionate staring contest across the yard for like two hours. Which ended in absolutely nothing except me going home, early and alone, to test run my newest vibrator (a solid three stars for getting the job done but seriously lacking in caramel eyes, biker tattoos and danger vibes), and a holy vow to myself to get over Lex Davenport.

The man was all eyes and zero follow through. And he'd had *four years* to follow through.

So why was he still checking me out across the room, right now?

He was, wasn't he?

As Carl and I mingled on, I made damn sure we were headed in the opposite direction from wherever *he* was. But this party really wasn't big enough. Because suddenly, our mingling brought us face to face with him.

Lex loomed right in front of us, his broad shoulders blocking our way, his caramel eyes drifting from my face to Carl's. But just before they did, when he met my eyes, he touched his tongue to one of his silver canines; his lips parted slightly and I saw it.

It made me drool. And not from my mouth.

I squeezed Carl's hand tighter.

In the years that had passed since we were kids, Lex Davenport had not only swapped out his tennis shirts for a biker vest, several tattoos and an assortment of tantalizing muscles, but a set of pearly white veneers and platinum canine teeth.

Not that that was irrationally hot or anything.

"Hey. I'm Lex." He offered his hand to my boyfriend.

"Carl." They shook hands while I clung to Carl's free hand.

"Lex works with Dirty," I supplied. "Sometimes. Not right now. Well, not right today. I mean, maybe he is. I don't know." I swallowed as both men looked at me. I was starting to babble, and once that got started it would be harder than a herd of drunken horses to rein in. I took a breath, reminding myself that I was not drunk. Yet. "We don't work together," I summarized, then pressed my lips shut.

Lex's eyes held mine. "We used to. Still could, any day."

I laughed unnecessarily. "Not likely."

"West Coast Kings," Carl read the patches on Lex's leather vest. "You work with Jude?"

"Uh-huh." Lex looked my boyfriend over. Carl was wearing unripped jeans and a blazer over his sweater, with a tie. "How about you?"

"I'm a business—"

"He's a business manager," I cut in. "In Toronto. He runs several businesses. Very successful."

Lex's eyes met mine again.

"So," I went on, and yes, I could feel the babble rising up, like prosecco bubbles doused with peach liquor, but hey, I really couldn't stop myself, "we met on tour. When I was in Toronto with the bands. We hit it off, and then we had this kind of long distance thing, you know, I was on tour and he was always traveling. But then I'd fly out to see him all the time and he'd fly out to see me. It was…" I felt Carl looking at me, so I turned to him.

"Awesome," he finished for me. He smiled.

I smiled.

"Sounds romantic." Lex almost sounded happy for us, and my smile died. I didn't trust anything that came out of his mouth. I never had. "So, how was the tour, Tal?" He was still staring at me. "You know, since I missed this one. Maybe you can give me the highlights."

Highlights. Right.

Like the fact that I didn't have to see *him* every damn day, like I did on the Hell & Back tour. I didn't have to watch him drinking, partying and talking everyone's ear off, cracking jokes with the guys, making everyone laugh and having a grand old time—all while ignoring me.

And then staring at me, mute, from the shadows every time he was on duty.

(Not that he never talked to me at all. There was that really fun time when he snuck onto my tour bus to bluntly ask me about one of my coworkers, something about her being his 'flavor,' and basically brutally rejecting me before I even had a chance to make a move on him. It was painful, yet a healthy reminder of exactly why he was so perfectly wrong for me. *Bad boy.* Also, he'd reamed me out for flirting with Jimmy, one of the guitar techs—as if his security job extended to securing my pussy. Apparently it did. Jimmy and every other male in a several mile radius mysteriously found me repulsive from that day on, judging by how many times I managed to hook up on that tour. Spoiler alert: it was zero times.)

Oh, and this was nice. I didn't have to deal with the nonsensical physical cravings that racked my body while he just stared at me all the damn time like he wanted to eat me alive, but never, ever tried to do anything about it.

Those were definite highlights.

"Uh, how about I let you two catch up," Carl offered, when Lex and I just continued our staring contest. "I haven't seen Jude yet. I'll go say hi." He seemed to be looking at me, like, *Is this okay?*

I forced a smile. Could he not see that I was sweating here? Nope, apparently not. Because he was actually leaving me, his girlfriend, unattended, with the hot, badass biker.

Really, a dumbass move for any guy.

"Sure, babe," I said faintly.

He kissed me on the lips, right in front of Lex, and I could feel the full force of those caramel eyes burning down on us. Then Carl slipped away, our hands drifting apart as I released my death grip and let him have his blood flow back.

I turned back to Lex, dropping the happily in love routine.

"We don't have to do this," I told him. "He's just being polite, letting me catch up with a former coworker. Carl is courteous like that."

Lex stared at me, his eyelids going half-mast. Totally different look than he just gave me in front of my boyfriend.

"What?" I demanded, when he said nothing.

"Nothing," he said.

"*What?*"

"Nothing."

"Well, nice seeing you." I turned to depart, but stopped short. I turned back to him. He was still standing there, giving me that look. The one that contained an entire Shakespearean soliloquy. But he said nothing.

"Why do you say it like it's *something*, then?"

He smirked faintly. Then his lips parted and his tongue did that thing, drifting across his ganster-meets-movie-star-vampire teeth… and the pleasure system between my legs short circuited.

I swallowed.

He noticed.

His eyes fell to my lips, then my throat.

I turned on my heel and beelined through the crowd to Carl's side. I found him over by the entrance to the dining room with some people I didn't know, chatting. I slipped my hand into his, finished my forgotten Bellini, and snuck a look across the room.

Lex was looking at me. I mean, he was talking to some guys and not looking at me. But he was totally looking at me.

Our eyes met and I looked away.

Stop looking.

Just ignore him and act like a normal human.

Honestly, I had no idea what this whole confusion of impulses in my body was about, or why they insisted on assaulting me *every time* I ran into him. Lex Davenport was nothing if not wrong for me. But when he lowered his eyelids at me a minute ago and ran his tongue across his teeth, my pussy turned into a freaking water slide.

My heart was pounding in my chest, and it wasn't because my boyfriend was holding my hand and looking so handsome in his neat blazer, his dark hair curling at the nape of his neck.

It should've been.

But it wasn't.

Fuck me.

"Baby."

"Huh? What?" I whipped my head around to Carl so fast I was afraid I might've splashed him with drool. I touched the back of my wrist to my mouth. "What, hon?"

He smiled at me. "I thought you might like another." He held up a fresh champagne glass, half-filled with bubbly peach liquid. "Bellini. It's your favorite, right? Roni just dropped it off."

Really? Roni came by? And I didn't even see her?

Because I was lusting over Lex across the room?

Christ, did she see that shit? Roni wasn't one to miss that shit.

I took the drink Carl offered, guiltily, and took a sip, setting my empty glass aside. "Thank you."

"Come here." Carl tugged my hand and guided me to a quieter spot in the corner of the living room. "I wanted to talk to you. I'm so sorry I have to leave tomorrow. You deserve more than two quick days. I just can't get out of these meetings—"

"I know. It's okay." I ran my hand up his solid arm, giving him a squeeze. "We already went over this. I'll see you soon. I can't wait to come hang out at your place again. I feel like I could really use a break from Vancouver."

He smiled a little, bemused. "You just got home. You love it here."

"I know. But you're not here."

And Lex is.

Carl's eyes darkened with arousal, and he cleared his throat. "Talia..."

"Yes?"

From the corner of my eye, I noticed Lex moving through the room. And it pissed me off that I was letting him interrupt this. I only had a few more hours with Carl before he had to catch a plane home in the early morning. He was a busy, successful man. I owed him my attention for this little bit of time we had together until we saw each other again, at least.

"I know this is quick..." he was saying, as he slipped his hand around my lower back. "I just wanted to make this special and I figured doing it here, at your friends' house, surrounded by people who love you and who'll be happy for you, even when I can't be here, would be the right thing to do."

"Okay…" What was he talking about?

Did I miss something while I was sneaking glances across the room and trying to ignore Lex? I refocused my attention on the serious, almost nervous look on Carl's face as he held me against him.

"The thing is," he said softly, clearing his throat again, "I wanted to ask you—"

"Well, don't you look like you need a refill." Roni appeared next to us, holding up two liquor bottles with a smirk. Prosecco and peach schnapps. Apparently, we were doing Bellinis on the fly now.

"Yes, please," I gushed. She dumped a generous shot from each bottle into my half-filled glass until it almost overflowed.

"Bottoms up." She winked and sashayed along to find the next half-empty glass, as I brought mine to my lips before it could bubble over.

"Uh—" Carl opened his mouth to say something, but I thrust my *hold that thought* finger in the air and took a deep swig of my drink.

Something small and hard hit my molar and bounced *into my throat.*

I cough-sprayed liquor across the room. Something was *in my drink* and it was now sliding down my throat!

Oh my God. I was choking.

"Talia?" Carl peered at me. "Are you choking?"

I dropped my glass and it shattered on the hardwood floor. I grabbed at my throat.

Dumbass question, Carl!

"Oh, fuck." His eyes went wide, panicked. "I shouldn't have put it in there!"

He put something in my drink??

I made a creepy, dying sea creature sound as I tried to cough up my lungs, and he patted me on the back, in shock. People were starting to turn this way.

Then two big bodies came bowling through, pushing people aside. It was Jude. And *Lex.*

Because this wasn't horrifying enough.

I reached for them blindly as my eyes started to water and whatever had gotten stuck jabbed painfully into my throat tissue. At least it wasn't totally cutting off my air.

"She's breathing," I heard Carl say as the music stopped.

"Move," Lex growled as he pushed in behind me. He wrapped his arms around me, balled his fists together in the middle of my breastbone and heaved upward. He repeated the move as Jude encouraged me to cough. And while I was choking in Lex's arms, I realized his dick was pressed against me for the first time. I could feel the thick mass in his jeans, nestled into my ass crack.

Really, though?? That's what you're thinking about right now?

At least he wasn't hard. If this was making him hard, he'd really have to go.

He heaved again, and booze and spit and something hard ejected from my mouth, along with my pride and my last shred of dignity.

Luckily Jude had quick reflexes and managed to dodge out of the way. Would've been a shame to ruin his shirt.

Whatever that hard thing was, it bounced on the hardwood with a little metallic clink.

I blinked at it, gasping for air. It was gold and twinkly.

There was only one small, gold, twinkly thing that I could imagine a man slipping into his girlfriend's champagne glass.

Then I threw up.

Lex's hold on me slipped as maybe I startled him—because who wanted to hug the puking girl?—and I sagged to the floor like a soggy, slippery noodle before anyone could seem to catch me.

I lay on my back, covered in booze and barf, looking up at the man who just tried to propose to me and the guy I fell in love with when I was ten.

"Can someone please help me up," I croaked, "so I can die?"

Chapter Two

Talia

It was a ring.

My amazing boyfriend had dropped a 2.5 carat diamond ring into my champagne flute to surprise me. He was definitely trying to propose.

And I choked on the ring.

Obviously, he didn't expect me to shotgun my Bellini. He'd apologized about ten thousand times as Jude cleared a path and Roni steered us into their bedroom. She asked me if I was okay, and when I assured her I was now fine—physically—she shut the door behind us.

Carl and I were alone.

"Are you really okay?" he asked me immediately.

"Fine. My throat feels a little scratchy. I'll be okay. Just... mortified."

"Don't be." He blinked at me. He still looked halfway in shock. "That guy... Lex... who is he again?"

"No one." I turned to look at myself in the mirror over Roni's dresser. My long blonde hair was all over the place. Mascara had smeared under my eyes when they were watering, and I set about trying to fix it.

I could see Carl looking at me, trying to piece together what just happened. I was still processing it myself.

The ring.

The botched proposal.

The barfing.

And Lex, rushing to the rescue.

"But he…"

"He's just a guy on Jude's crew," I said quickly.

"He saved your life."

I turned to face him. "I wasn't going to die. It didn't cut off *all* my air."

"But if it went any farther down your throat…" Carl looked pale, worse than I did.

"Hey." I went over to comfort him, putting my hand on his chest. "I'm okay."

His unfocused gaze seemed to clear. His eyes locked with mine. "I need to thank him. I didn't act fast enough. It all happened so fast…"

"Really. You don't need to thank him. He works security with Jude. It's what they do. They're all reactive and protective like that." I tried to smile to make him feel better. "I told you when we met. You pick me, you pick the entire Dirty/Players circus. I'm never leaving them, unless they fire my ass and file a restraining order."

He smiled, a little, at my stupid joke. "I pick you," he said. And held up the ring.

The ring!

Jesus Christ, I forgot all about the ring.

"It's so… beautiful," I choked out, totally at a loss for words. It wasn't. It had an oval diamond, a yellow-gold band, and looked like something an old lady would wear. Though I had met his mom;

seemed like something *she* would wear, which was a clue to who took him shopping for it.

To his credit, however, it was probably expensive. He meant business.

"I notice that wasn't exactly a 'yes,'" he said gently.

I swallowed. "You didn't actually ask yet." I knew I sounded… unencouraging. Afraid. I wanted him to ask, because who wouldn't? He was handsome and successful and had great hair.

But I didn't want him to ask.

We'd only been together for a few months. And a lot of that time, we'd been apart.

My parents already loved him. That was important to me.

My friends didn't, for some reason I could never quite figure out. They wouldn't say so; I could just tell. Like, they were being polite and waiting for me to break up with him so they could tell me what they really thought. We were new; maybe they thought I'd end it anyway.

But I had no reason to end it.

Carl Caldwell had wined and dined me like a total gentleman. I mean, if anything, he was maybe too much of a gentleman. If that was a thing? We hadn't even had sex yet. And yeah, that was a problem.

I expected that any man I dated treated me with respect. But come on. We'd been on more than a dozen dates. Throw me down and pull my hair a little and put it in. I'm not gonna complain.

However, I wasn't holding my breath on that happening. He'd told me from day one that I was, quote, the woman of his dreams. And that he'd treat me accordingly. Right down to courting me, the old fashioned way. And all the nice dates and flowers weren't terrible.

I knew we could probably have an amazing life together. Carl checked off all the important boxes on my list. He had a career. He treated me like gold. He respected my family.

And maybe most importantly: he was not a bad boy.

While I suspected there was a red-blooded male under the sweater vests just waiting to be unleashed when he felt he'd courted me sufficiently, Carl was no outlaw biker. He was a solid, tax-paying, law-abiding dude. A catch. A keeper.

So why was I sweating again, and not in the good way?

"I'm asking," he said seriously.

I blew out a breath. "Okay. Um…"

"Talia." He tucked the ring into the palm of my hand, then took my hands in his. "That proposal didn't go well for you. I know. It didn't go so well for me either." He smiled, trying to make me smile. So I did. "So, take this." He pulled the ring box out of his blazer and pressed it into my other hand. "Keep it for now. Think about it. Okay?"

"Okay." I nodded, sniffing a little. My eyes were watering again.

"I just wanted it to be special for you. Here, at home, where your heart is. With the whole crazy circus. I know how much you love them."

He wrapped his arms around me. Giving me a hug, comforting me.

It was something Lex had never, ever done for me. Well, except when he was trying to save me from choking on the ring at my botched proposal.

Why was I even thinking about him, when Carl was holding me? What was wrong with me?

Why was I so damn confused about someone who only gave off *danger* vibes and *run the hell away and save your sanity* vibes?

Carl was the smart life choice. We'd had a perfect, storybook love. Boy meets girl. Boy and girl fall in love. Boy proposes. Girl says yes?

But.

I didn't say yes.

I didn't say yes at all.

"Can you just give me a minute? You know, to clean up and

compose myself?" I gazed up at him hopefully. "Before I have to go back out there and face everyone?"

"Of course." He kissed my forehead. "Take all the time you need."

"Just... go let people know I'm fine. That everything can go back to normal. And I'll slip out of here when I'm ready, okay?"

"Okay."

"And please ask Jude to make sure no one else gets in here. I need a moment alone."

"Of course, babe."

He gave me another kiss and a comforting squeeze, then slipped out the door.

I went straight into the en suite bathroom to clean up. Where, about five minutes later, Lex found me in the bathtub.

———

"It's really more effective if you fill it with water."

I looked up. I was sitting in the empty bathtub, fully dressed, with my knees pulled up to my chest.

Lex was standing in Jude and Roni's bathroom, staring down at me.

"How did you get in here?"

"I know a guy."

"Remind me to advise Roni to break up with Jude."

I slid the shower door shut in his face, which was ridiculously unsatisfying since it was on a smooth gliding system, didn't make a noise, and it was transparent glass. Lex just stared me down right through it.

I looked away, glaring at the faucet.

"Hey, don't be mad at Jude." He slid the glass door right back open. "I told him I wanted to check on you. Seeing as how I just saved your life, he felt inclined to let me pass."

I rolled my eyes. "You did *not* save my life."

He leaned casually on the shower door. "Carl seems to think so."

Oh, God. Did Carl actually go thank him?

I gave him a sharp look. "You better have been nice."

"Why wouldn't I be nice?" He smiled slightly, flashing his teeth, and I tried not to visibly shiver. Then he ordered, "Move over," as he stepped into the bathtub.

I squirmed farther back to avoid being stepped on—or touched by him at all—and squeaked in protest. "What are you doing?!"

"I'm coming in."

He was already in. Somehow, he managed to fold and wedge his entire man-body in and sit down, facing me. Except his long legs were kinda splayed out, one on my left side, the other one lifted up, his foot resting on the side of the tub to my right.

He was spread eagle, surrounding me like a bad dream.

Sweat broke out all over my body.

I pulled my arms and legs in tighter, balling up like a spider playing dead. He wasn't touching me, but I was *between his legs*.

He relaxed back, kind of awkwardly, next to the faucet. It was a big tub, but not that big.

"This is—" I sputtered. "Don't you—?"

"You know, when I walked into the bedroom and you weren't there," he said calmly, producing a silver cigarette case out of some inner pocket in his biker vest, "I knew exactly where you'd be."

I eyed him with annoyance. "How?"

He plucked out a fat joint, tucked it between his lips and lit up with a lighter he'd also produced from a pocket. His eyes narrowed at me. "Because when we were kids," he said, exhaling marijuana smoke into the air above us, "you hid in the bathtub that time. It's the only other time I've seen you this upset."

He held the joint out, ash up, offering it to me.

I shook my head. No way I needed to get high with him in a bathtub right now. This night was already enough of a disaster.

"What *time*?" I said suspiciously. True, I'd hidden in a few bath-

29

tubs in my life, both with and without water in them, when I wanted to be alone. But I didn't remember him ever climbing into one with me before.

"Keri Kerrington," he mused. "Remember that girl who showed up, what was it, our second summer?"

I bristled at the way he so casually referenced our few shared childhood summers. He'd never mentioned them to me before.

Kind of allowed me to hope he'd forgotten them.

"I don't remember," I muttered.

"You remember. Prissy redheaded chick. She had a nice rack. And attitude to go with it. You two hung out a lot. And then you didn't."

Because you kissed her and she wouldn't shut up about it.

"I don't know what you're talking about."

"I think you guys had a fight or something. That's what your mom said when I came looking for you."

Thanks, Mom. Thanks a lot.

"So?"

"So, your dad wasn't around, so she let me sneak in to see you. I found you in the bathtub, sulking."

"I wasn't sulking."

"So you do remember."

I blew out an annoyed breath. "Vaguely."

"You told me to go away. Maybe I shouldn't have."

He sucked on the joint, then ran his tongue slowly over his lip— and my uterus squeezed. I swore I could feel my ovaries throb. Everything the man did with his mouth was like a curious obsession for my reproductive parts.

I met his eyes. "Please do not recount childhood memories to me."

"Why?"

"Because I'm in yours. And you're in mine. It's disturbing."

He held my gaze. "I mean, you could've forgotten me."

No. I couldn't.

But what business did he have remembering me? And what the hell was he doing with me in this bathtub? Usually, he acted like he'd *rather* forget my existence.

Maybe my public mortification at this party amused him. Maybe, like when we were kids, I was an amusing plaything to pass the time with until something better came along.

Maybe it amused him to know that my love life hadn't turned out nearly as successful and... prolific... as his had. On that Dirty tour, I'd seen him with so many girls, it made my head spin. I got motion sickness, just watching them come and go.

His caramel eyes stared me down. "So, what got you so upset out there?"

"I wasn't upset."

"You didn't choke on that ring for nothing."

"I didn't know it was in my drink," I grit out. Did we really have to talk about this? It was hardly his business. Even *if* he saved my life.

He flicked the ash off his joint, into Roni and Jude's bathtub.

"I hope you plan on cleaning that up before you clear out of here."

"You're not seriously marrying that guy."

"Maybe I am."

He smiled at me and his silver canines glistened, shiny and wet. I swallowed. Why I found his stupid vicious teeth so hot, I'd never know. But the way my body responded... it was like he'd just whipped out his dick—and it was *glorious*.

"No, you're not," he said.

"He just proposed. I haven't even answered him yet."

"Because you choked on his ring."

"So?"

"So, you really think he's the one for you?"

"Maybe."

His smile faded and his eyes darkened. He put out what was left of his joint on the faucet. "So then why are you in this bathtub with me?" he said quietly.

"*You* got in with me."

"You didn't get out." His eyes met mine again, his eyelids low. He was done having his smoke. Maybe he was about to get up and leave.

Christ, there was something wrong with me. Because I didn't want him to leave.

But instead of leaving he said, "I once asked you to marry me, and you said yes."

"I was ten years old," I reminded him, my defenses and my annoyance level rising simultaneously.

"You signed a contract."

"It was a page in a notebook!"

"You sealed it with blood."

"Did I?" I tried to pretend I didn't remember. But I'd never forget.

It was a gorgeous summer day, I had blood and chocolate on my hands, and he had deep, caramel-brown eyes that I'd literally jumped off a boat and almost drowned for.

First love.

Lex Davenport was mine.

"Too bad my boyfriend just proposed," I said cooly.

"Yeah." His expression didn't change. "Too bad I have a girl-friend anyway."

I blinked at him, utterly fucking shell-shocked by that bomb.

WHAT?

And also *THE FUCK??*

My cheeks flushed with heat as my head spun with that unexpected plot twist.

Mkay, let me just get this fucking straight.

The untouchable, impossible to get, bachelor biker had a motherfucking whatnow? A *girlfriend?*

I instantly wanted to murder a bitch I didn't even know existed until three seconds ago.

"So unfortunate," I forced out.

"Guess that means you're off the hook. You know… I'm turning twenty-nine in two days." He studied my face, and I hoped to God I wasn't as transparent on this as I usually was on… everything. "Said you'd marry me when I turned twenty-nine."

"Phew. Guess I dodged that bullet."

"Guess so. You might've heard my mom's family disowned me anyway, so I'm never getting that inheritance."

"I heard."

"So, I have nothing to offer you."

"Not one thing."

He stared at me. I stared right back, sweating.

If he had a girlfriend, why the fuck was he still sitting here with me?

"There's gonna be a little party for my birthday. You should come."

What?

No.

Oh dear God, no. Not if all the wild, drunken horses on the planet dragged me there.

"Too bad I'm busy." I totally wasn't.

Carl was flying back to Toronto tomorrow and I had zero plans other than sleeping off the hangover that would inevitably follow a night such as this. Because I was about to get very, very drunk in an effort to block it out.

"Making wedding plans?" he ventured.

"Probably." I mean, if I was sane that's what I'd be doing tomorrow. And right now.

Instead of sitting in a bathtub with a guy I wasn't even supposed to be wasting my time thinking about. But he was still sitting here with me, and he wasn't leaving.

There was something in his eyes as he looked at me. Girlfriend or not, he was messing with me. Flirting with me. Bringing up the marriage pact we made as kids? Implying that Carl wasn't the one for me...

Was this the moment? The moment when the hot but totally wrong for you guy told you not to marry the awesome good guy, and you ended up marrying the hot bad boy instead?

Or at least fucking him at a party, and realizing that you couldn't marry either of them.

"I hope you're happy, Talia," he finally said, almost gently.

That totally wasn't what he was supposed to say.

His kindness was unsettling. I couldn't trust it.

In a weird way, I didn't even want him to be happy for me and Carl anyway.

Worse than that: it pissed me off.

Lex was all hot looks and cold goodbyes. He was married to his biker club. He probably didn't even want to get married. He wasn't that boy who made me sign my name in his little notebook, planning out his future. Now, he was somebody else.

Somebody even more wrong for me than he was back then.

But my arms and my legs unfolded on an exasperated groan. "You hope I'm *happy*?" I practically growled, pouring all the frustration and confusion and *what if?* I'd ever felt towards him into it.

Then I crawled forward, climbed over his spread thighs—and shoved myself into his lap.

His leg fell off the side of the tub as I straddled him. I landed, hard, on his groin—and he groaned. It was a low, rolling groan from deep inside, and it wasn't from pain.

His dick was hard in his jeans, and I'd just sat on it.

My whole system caught fire as I realized: he had an erection.

His eyes met mine, shifting from cool and impervious to lit the fuck on fire in a heartbeat. It was all the encouragement I needed. I grabbed his face and went in.

"Tal—"

I cut off the sound of my name on his lips as my mouth

slammed against his in a hungry, open-mouthed kiss. My tongue lapped deep into his mouth. And I ground myself against him, my whole body getting into it—my hips working in an automatic rhythm, desperate, lost, possessed... instantaneously drowning in how fucking *right* he felt.

Oh, *shit*. This was too, too good.

Which meant this was a bad, bad idea.

A moan spilled from my mouth into his as I kissed him harder.

His hands splayed across my back in a stunned, delayed response, and he growled, a low, primal noise in his throat.

But then he ripped his mouth away. "Natalia," he panted, his eyes glazed with lust as they entangled with mine.

"Lex," I whispered back.

"*Talia.*"

A familiar voice echoed off the tile above us, and I looked up in horror.

My boyfriend stood next to the bathtub, staring down at us.

Chapter Three

Lex

I woke up hungover as shit, to the sound of a gorilla pounding on the wall.

I lifted my head, blinked my eyes half-open in the dark.

Dead silence.

I flopped back into my pillow. My head was pounding.

The pillow stank of booze and sweat and the ghosts of pathetic, wavering promises to myself. I needed to change my pillowcase. And my sheets. And my entire fucking life, starting with the moment I heard Talia De Santis was at that party last night, decided to avoid a torturous repeat of the last time I saw her at a party—then failed to scale a fence properly and ended up falling on top of her.

And then wandering back into the party and staring at her across the room like a horny jackal crushing on a kitten.

And then climbing into a bathtub with her.

Sure, saving her from possibly choking to death wasn't exactly a regret. But the rest of it? A slow descent into liquid madness.

Roni and her fucking girlie drinks. Jude's woman really needed to calm the fuck down with all the sugary cocktails that went down like bubbly juice and made you feel like you needed to swiftly die the next day.

Of course, Roni didn't force me to drink like twenty of them after Talia left the party with her boyfriend. Fiancé?

Whatever he was, he must've cured childhood cancer in some alternate universe in order to end up with Talia De Santis in this one. The girl was all bright brown eyes and golden skin and cheer-leader pep, mixed with smart, determined and almost-annoyingly responsible—and some kind of curiosity about me that had crept into her blood, like a brain-cell-killing zombie virus that she couldn't purge, tame or kill, no matter how she tried. I saw it in her eyes whenever she looked at me.

Blinding. Starving. Maddening. *Lust.*

Knew exactly what that felt like myself. Unfortunately.

The girl had lost her mind, for sure. That was the only explana-tion for what she pulled last night. I could still feel the heat of her pussy through her jeans, through my jeans, as she straddled me and sat on my cock.

I'd never been that close to her before, that *almost in her* before.

Except in my nightmares.

I groaned and ground my hips into the mattress now, hard as fuck. I could smell her, her soft lips soaked in peach liquor. After what happened to her—choking on that goddamn ring, throwing up —she didn't even taste like vomit. She tasted like sweet innocence and soft, clean flesh and mistakes, and everything pure I wanted to pour myself into. Dick first.

"Wake up, hooker!"

The walls vibrated as Maddox hammered on my bedroom door with his fists, like a fucking gorilla.

Yeah, so I didn't imagine that.

"Get the fuuuuuck up!"

"I'm up," I muttered, not loudly enough. My voice broke.

I groaned and rolled over as he fist pummeled my door again. My dick was still hard, but Maddox's voice was starting to kill it.

"Are you up?" my club brother called through the door. "It's fuckin' gorgeous out!"

Was it? The one small, barred window in my room was covered with a black satin Corrosion of Conformity banner that was there when I moved in, years ago. I groped around for the lamp by my bed, knocking over a precarious tower of paperbacks before switching it on. "Fuck," I muttered as the books crashed on the floor.

What time was it?

Where the fuck was my phone?

"Get your ass up!" hollered the world's most annoying friend. Unfortunately, our rooms at the Kings' clubhouse shared the bathroom in between. Which meant I had to deal with Maddox's loud arguments with his girlfriend, their even louder sex, his hair all over the sink after he shaved, his fucking pubes on my soap, and his early morning wake-up calls.

According to Maddox, we were *best* friends. He'd informed me so over beers one night and never taken it back.

He hammered on the door again. The one to the hallway, not the shared bathroom. "C'mon! We're goin' for a ride!"

I forced myself up, otherwise he'd never fucking shut up. Naked, I shoved a pillow in front of my morning wood and opened the door a foot. I looked at him through one cracked eye. "You kidding me?" I rasped.

Maddox was fully dressed, leathers and all. His dark hair, shaved on one side, slicked back. Accessorizing with a grin. He'd obviously been up for a while, and he wasn't kidding. "Get dressed. King wants your ass on the road. Nomads are rollin' into Abbotsford, we're goin' for beers and pillow talk."

It took me a minute to catch up.

Pillow talk. That meant intel.

We had information for the Nomads, or they had some for us, or both, and King wanted Maddox to personally relay it. Maddox preferred to call it *pillow talk, words of endearment, sweet nothings.*

Anything but what it actually was. Because Maddox was paranoid. He talked in so much code I didn't know what the fuck he was going on about half the time.

I had no idea why King always had him relaying shit; must've been annoying as fuck trying to decode whatever intel he brought back. But if my club President was sending me on a run, I was going on a run. Even if I'd rather crawl back into bed, jerk off, and maybe die a quick, merciful death, courtesy of my own gun.

"Yeah. Just gimme a minute." I slammed the door in his face.

"I'll meet you downstairs!"

"Yeah." I yawned and stumbled through the room, getting dressed. Pulled on yesterday's jeans off the floor, an old but clean Motörhead shirt from the closet.

As the shitty facts of being *me* today sank in.

Not only was I stupidly fixated on a girl I was never gonna have —and now had to live with the memory that she sat on my dick and shoved her tongue in my mouth and I still couldn't have her—but my birthday was tomorrow and that posed a major fucking problem.

To be dealt with tomorrow.

First, wake the fuck up and do your job.

Maybe I'd die on the road today, get run over by a truck hauling bibles or something, and it wouldn't matter.

Poetic justice.

When I went to take a piss in the bathroom, I was slapped with a vivid flashback of sitting in Jude's bathtub last night, crotch to crotch with Talia. While she slammed her mouth down on mine and swiped her tongue so deep she almost hit tonsils.

All this time, I'd kinda hoped she didn't have it in her. But shit.

By the time I got my dick out of my jeans over the toilet, I was hard as fuck, so pissing was out of the question until the situation changed.

Fuck it.

I stepped into the bathtub, pressed a hand to the tile wall, licked the palm of my other hand, shut my eyes and went to town. Slid my dick through my fist as I punched my hips forward, slow, then faster and faster, as I thought about what I'd rather be doing right now.

Talia.

While her big brown eyes looked right at me.

Her soft, sweet lips opening for me, her tongue seeking mine.

God, she'd be so soft and clean and good. I needed something like that in my life. And in my mouth. And wrapped around my dick.

All I had to do was picture her straddling me like she did in that bathtub, but buck naked, and sliding her wet pussy up my hard shaft as she whimpered at me to fill her up…

I came so hard it was fucking stupid. It felt so good, it almost hurt.

I opened my eyes to watch my come hit the wall as it shot out of me in long, aching spurts.

Good thing Maddox wasn't in the next room to hear it, because pretty sure I made some embarrassing, desperate noise that he'd never let me live down as my balls emptied up Talia's imaginary pussy.

I looked down at the jizz at my feet. I had come on my bare toes.

I felt dizzy and leaned on my arm, catching my breath.

Fuck, I was hungover. Parched. I needed water.

I rinsed off my foot and the tub and stepped out, fucking woozy. That orgasm just about leveled me. But what else was new?

The truth was I'd been coming like that for Talia De Santis ever since she happened back into my life four years ago and invaded the pleasure center in my brain.

Sadly, she was never actually in the room when it happened.

Yeah. Fucking stupid.

I washed up, guzzled some water. Decided not to shave because I was seeing my father tomorrow and fuck him.

Then I instantly felt guilty for thinking of Talia and my father in such close succession. As if the very thought of him could somehow taint her goodness.

And that is why you stay away from girls like Talia De Santis.

Because she doesn't deserve to be in bed with the Devil.

She's innocent. Clean.

Leave her that way.

I should never have brought up all that shit last night about the marriage pact we made as kids. Embarrassing her. Confusing her, maybe. Because, what, I was annoyed that some smarmy guy in a V-neck sweater and tie gave her a diamond ring? And she choked on it?

I mean seriously, how big did that diamond need to be? I should've felt sorry for her. Dude must've had some small dick, giving her a ring like that. That was a definite dick size compensation diamond.

Whatever.

The best thing for her, really, was to marry some regular guy, small dick or not, who'd buy her a nice house in the suburbs where she could pick out paint colors and good silverware, get knocked up with triplets and forget I ever existed.

I shouldn't have let her climb into my lap. I shouldn't have let her kiss me. She'd surprised me, but I could've stopped her. The fact that I didn't was just gonna fuck with her head. I shouldn't have let any of it happen, starting with getting into that bathtub with her.

I really didn't give a shit that her boyfriend walked in on us. That was his mistake.

But it hurt Talia. That part sucked.

She went running after him when he turned and walked out. It felt like a slap in the face, but what did I expect?

Running after him, and away from me, was the right direction for her to be headed.

I dragged my hand through my hair, which was about as close as it was getting to styled right now, then staggered back into my room. I found my phone on the floor and pulled on my black-and-gray lumber jacket. Slipped on my Kings cut overtop. Shoved my wallet into a pocket and my knife into my boot sheath under the leg of my jeans, and headed downstairs, still trying to shake off what happened last night.

As long as I didn't see her again, it wouldn't happen again. Simple as that, right?

I just had to get better at planning my escape route so I didn't accidentally end up on top of her again. Because once that happened, I was locked into her orbit for the night.

Never. Happening. Again.

I shoved through the door into the clubhouse bar, and it was oddly quiet. Calm before the storm vibes. They hadn't said so, but I knew my club brothers had a birthday party planned for me tonight. Probably thought they were being all ninja about it, planning it behind my back and throwing the party the night *before* my actual birthday.

But they knew I wouldn't be around to celebrate with them tomorrow anyway.

Looked like there wasn't much going on here last night for a Saturday. But Saturdays weren't much different from Wednesdays when you lived your life as an outlaw.

Only the Old Man, Grim, was sitting at the bar, one of our last living OG members. He was talking to one of the prospects, Finn, who was working behind the bar. Probably setting up for tonight. I gave Grim a tap on the shoulder, nodded at Finn as I passed.

When I stepped out through the front door, the sunlight that hit my face was blinding. Big, clear blue sky stretched over the Kings' compound and beyond. Rare for October, this kind of day. It probably wouldn't even last. The clouds would roll in. It was inevitable.

Maddox was already on his Harley, itching to go.

"See? What'd I tell ya?" He grinned at me like a kid at Christmas. There wasn't much Maddox liked better than a clear day to ride. His woman's pussy, maybe, judging by those noises I heard through the wall.

But I understood the enthusiasm. There wouldn't be many more days to ride in full sunshine this season. I could probably get away with blaming my lackluster mood on the hangover, though.

Another prospect, Toad, opened the compound gate for us as I got on my bike and put on my helmet. I noticed my car was parked across the lot, and it took me a moment to remember why it was there. Toad had fetched it from Jude's place for me last night, after I got back here, drunk as shit.

I'd had to leave my car behind, catch a ride back with Maddox after I put back way too many of Roni's cocktails, courtesy of my wavering promises to myself. If I didn't drink enough, probably would've done something truly fucking stupid, like getting in my car to go chasing after Talia, shove that diamond ring up her boyfriend's ass. The smell of her all over me, her taste in my mouth, had to go, get drowned into oblivion, before I lost my will to remember why I couldn't have her in the first place.

I lifted my chin at Toad and he jogged over to me.

"Starter's acting up again."

"Yeah, I noticed that." He glanced over at my Chevelle. "I'll take care of it."

"I'll be out of town tomorrow," I told him. Soon as I could drag my ass out of bed, I'd be flying out to meet my father, but Toad didn't know that shit. No one did. "You can drop me at the airport sometime in the morning."

"For sure, Lex."

I started up. Maddox was already sitting at the edge of the road, motor rumbling, ready to hit the highway. Even he didn't know the real reason for my shitty mood. Definitely wasn't just the hangover, or what happened with Talia last night.

Some secrets were heavy. Some crushed the goodness out of you, bit by bit, year after year, until you wondered what you were keeping them for. But then, inevitably, you remembered.

So no one has to die.

Maddox bolted up the road and I took off after him. Might as well enjoy this ride. This day.

Who knew?

Might just be my last day on Earth.

———

When we rolled back into the compound that night, I could see why Maddox was so eager to get my ass out of town.

It wasn't just the weather or the run to Abbotsford, where we basically had lunch with some brothers from our Nomad chapter, including Jude. Then we went for a cruise, ended up back in Abbotsford at the shooting range owned by Maddox's big brother, Axel, where we met Axel and hung out for hours before the three of us finally rolled back to the clubhouse.

By the time we got back, it was dark out and there was definitely a party in full swing. They'd put some work into this. *Happy Birthday* banner over the clubhouse door and everything.

As soon as I parked and got off my bike, Toad handed me a beer. When we walked into the clubhouse bar, the place erupted. It was already loud with people, music. I was the guest of honor, but they'd hardly waited for me to get started.

Pretty much any excuse for a party was welcome at the clubhouse, sure, but a patched member's birthday was a big deal. We were family. A brotherhood.

And as of this year, I'd been patched in for ten years.

Several of my club brothers, mainly the officers, greeted me with a kiss on the lips. I didn't flinch. If a brother, especially a senior member, kissed you on the lips in greeting, you kissed him back. It was a club thing.

You got used to it.

Every member of the Vancouver chapter—the mother chapter—of the West Coast Kings MC who could possibly be here tonight would be here, along with members from the other local chapters, plus old ladies—the wives, or almost wives, of members. No kids; it wasn't that kind of party. But the women had brought food. There was a self-serve spread along the far end of the pool table area, between the bar and the kitchen.

Someone put a plate in my hands, potato salad and a burger. One of the old ladies. I kissed her on the cheek. Then people kept coming around to wish me a happy birthday, giving out kisses, hugs and slaps on the back. And shots of tequila.

By the time I was finished that burger I was half-blitzed. Between Jude's brother, Piper—our Vice President and my sponsor into the club all those years ago—basically ordering me to drink, and Maddox and Axel making sure there was a full beer in my hand at all times, I had no chance. Didn't particularly want to get wasted the night before a meeting with my father; I needed every brain cell I had alive and kicking tomorrow.

But too fucking late.

I was settled in at the bar with Maddox and his girlfriend, having a pretty damn good time, when Jude walked in with Roni.

And fucking Talia.

I blinked at them across the room, wondering if I was *that* drunk and just seeing things; wishful fucking things. Roni brought some other hot friend with her, right?

Wrong.

Definitely Talia.

Her long blonde hair was curled in soft, smooth waves. Her body, worthy of a centerfold in a hot-college-girls-edition smut mag was poured into tight, ripped jeans, pale blue, and a tight, white shirt, a hole in the front that showed off the swell of her tits. I watched her slip off her jacket, her light-blue bra showing through her almost see-through top.

Then I watched her look around the room with wide, interested eyes, like she was looking *for* something.

They landed on me.

I looked away, turning to Maddox's girl. Her name was Éloïse, but we were lazy fucks so we called her Élo (rhymes with J.Lo). Élo was beautiful, had a French accent from actual France, not Quebec, and had a biochemistry degree. In summary, no one could actually figure out how Maddox had landed her, and if he was gonna shoot himself when she had to go back to France or if he'd be trying to score her some forged residency papers or what.

"Hey, Élo," I said. "Where're your friends tonight? Who's that girl? The one you brought to the barbecue, few weeks ago?"

Élo smiled her wide, pretty smile at me. "Oh, Lexington. She has a man."

"So? Tell her to come down."

She laughed, and Maddox, who was sitting next to her, his arm wrapped around her, squeezed her hip. "Don't laugh at him, baby. He's desperate for attention. Lex doesn't go for these club bunnies." He flicked his chin at some girls who'd joined the party, and not the old lady variety.

Bunnies. Creative. He definitely didn't call them anything that cute when his girlfriend wasn't around to hear it.

"I like beautiful, high-class women," I informed her, trying not to slur as I kissed up a bit, "like you, Élo. Bring some friends around next time."

"Aww, *mon petit méchant*, my friends are all scared of you," she said sweetly, cupping Maddox's jaw and giving him a soft kiss on the lips when he gave her a fake pout. I was not bilingual and I'd never looked it up, but Maddox had told me her little term of endearment for him—for all of us—meant *my little villain.*

Of course, Maddox was far from little, but Élo could've called him *my little heap of dog shit* and as long as she did it in French, he'd eat it up.

"Tell them we're teddy bears," he growled.

"I've tried!" she squealed, as he yanked her right off her stool and into his lap. Then his eyes dropped to her ass, in his lap, and he made a hungry, throaty noise I heard even over the music as she shifted, getting comfy.

Sometimes, I could totally see the perks of having a girlfriend.

Wasn't happening, though. Not for me.

When I looked across the room, Talia was sneaking a look at me while she pretended to be talking to Roni and some other girls.

I was too drunk for this.

How was she even here? This was not supposed to be a thing.

Roni had been to the clubhouse before, sure. Rumor was she'd dated my club brother Blazer on and off, years ago, though I'd never met her back then. The last few years, she'd come to plenty of club parties with Jude when he wasn't on the road with Dirty. As a Nomad, Jude came to less of our parties than Vancouver members, but when he did show up, Roni was often with him.

Talia had never shown her face at any kind of Kings party or at the clubhouse, for any reason.

Then again, I'd never invited her before.

Did she really come because I invited her?

Did it not occur to her that maybe that invitation was a shit poor idea, after what went down last night?

Why would she even want to see me again? And why wasn't she cuddled up in her fiancé's arms right now, planning their wedding?

I watched them move through the room, Jude greeting brothers, Roni hugging some of the other old ladies, introducing Talia around. Making her feel at home.

I knew Jude, though. He'd let the girls stay for an hour so they felt welcome, then he'd whisk them out of here before things got too rowdy.

When Jude and Roni came over to wish me a happy birthday, Talia didn't come with them. She stayed by the food table with a couple of the old ladies who seemed to be keeping an eye on her, probably because Jude told them to. I watched her take a beer one of them handed her way. She wrapped her soft lips around the bottle and took a swig.

Then she looked over at me again.

I looked away.

I'd avoided Talia De Santis for four straight years. I'd avoided her for a year-and-a-half while we traveled together on a world tour.

I could avoid her for another hour.

———

Over an hour and three beers later—I was on at least beer six or something, and yes, I fucking counted her beers—Talia looked torn. And pretty drunk.

When she finished drink four and set her empty beer bottle aside, she seemed to make up her mind.

Maybe she knew her time was running out.

Some of the old ladies were starting to leave and the club sluts and mamas had been rolling in steady. Groupies; so-called girl-friends; friends of the club; friends of friends; strippers. Club sluts and mamas came in all forms. Straight up, club sluts provided sex; mamas also provided other niceties, like food and housekeeping and pretty much whatever else a guy might want from a woman he'd fuck but never planned to marry.

But they all had one thing in common: club sluts and mamas were available for any guy wearing Kings colors, any time.

Not my rule. Just the way it was.

There were only two types of old ladies, though. Those who stuck around for this part of the night and those who didn't.

You could feel the vibe shifting in the room. Even Talia had to feel it.

It was getting louder. More crowded. Food and drinks were spilling on the floor. The lights had gone down. People were making out, getting drunk and sloppy.

Clothes were coming off.

Talia walked straight through it all, right over to me. I'd barely moved. I was still sitting at the bar, Maddox and Élo on one side of me and Axel on the other. Axel had his back to me, talking to some guys on his other side as I watched Talia walk up. I could've gotten up and left. Instead, I sat right where I was, drinking.

She stood right in front of me but didn't look at me. And instead of saying anything to me, she said, "Hi, Maddox."

Maddox was drunk, and looked surprised to see her. "Hey. Talia. What's shakin'?"

"Oh, you know. Just here to celebrate Lex's birthday."

"Cool. Have a shot with us." Maddox reached over the bar to the lineup of tequila shots that we'd been putting back between beers. Okay, so technically I was on drink eleven or something.

I tried to give him a *The fuck are you doing?* look. A *Can't you see she doesn't belong here?* look.

He didn't notice.

"Hi, I'm Talia." She offered her hand to Élo.

"Éloïse," Élo said, looking Talia over and shaking her hand. "And how do you know my Maddox?"

"Oh, I work with the Players, but I used to work with Dirty. So I work with Maddox sometimes at events. He's always very helpful and professional."

Élo beamed, proud of her man. She pinched his bearded chin lightly in her fingers. "You hear that, my sweet? The prettiest girls always have the nicest things to say about you. I wonder why that is?"

Maddox grinned and Élo slapped him lightly on the cheek. He handed her and Talia each a shot. Then he raised his chin at me. "What's up? Where's your shot?"

I gave him a *You're a dumbass dick* look, which he also didn't seem to notice, and picked up a shot. We all drank. Talia snuck a look at me just before she sank hers. It was the first time she'd looked at me since coming over.

Then she reached between me and Élo, leaning way in to set her shot glass on the bar. Her arm brushed mine as she drew back, sending goosebumps ripping across my skin. I could smell her sweet smell. Peaches. She always smelled like peach candy or something. And chick shampoo.

My dick instantly started hardening.

I grit my teeth.

"Hey," Axel grunted beside me. "Did I miss one?"

"No," I said.

"Yup." Maddox handed his brother a shot.

"Who's drinkin' with me?" Axel demanded.

"I will." That was Talia.

Axel's gaze fell to her. He was drunk, too. Our Sergeant-at-Arms, Axel was huge, terrifying at a glance to any regular human, and Talia just smiled at him.

"Get the girl a drink, Dog." That was Axel's brotherly nickname for Maddox.

Maddox handed Talia a shot.

"Thanks!" She smiled at Axel again, clinked her shot glass to his, glanced sidelong at me, and put back another straight ounce of Cuervo Gold. She only squirmed a little as it went down.

This time, I took the empty shot glass from her hand myself and put it on the bar. I picked up my beer, met Axel's eyes, then took a swig.

Axel raised an eyebrow at me, got the message, chuckled, and turned away again.

Then I looked at Talia. The fact that I'd finally just acknowledged her seemed to make her happy. She buried her fingers in the little pockets of her tight jeans and bit her lip a little.

"So, I wanted to wish you a happy birthday," she said, when Élo got busy talking to Maddox, probably sensing Talia wanted to talk to me alone. I definitely wasn't trying to give off that vibe to anyone, that I wanted her alone.

Maybe to Axel.

"Thanks," I said flatly. Maybe now that she'd gotten that off her chest, she could go the fuck home.

She gnawed on her lip a little more, like she was working up the courage to say whatever came next. "Where's your girlfriend?"

I blinked at her. "What?"

"I wanted to meet her. She's here, right? It's your birthday party."

Right. Girlfriend.

The one I already forgot that I told her I had, last night when we were in a bathtub together.

"Yeah. She's… uh, up in my room," I improvised. "Waiting for me."

She squinted at me, smelling bullshit. "Is that true?"

"No. She just went to pick up pizza."

She actually brightened. Must've been the munchies kicking in from all the alcohol she'd consumed. "Oh. I like pizza."

"She went for beers."

She shot a skeptical look at the bar, then at me. "There's not enough beer here already?"

I rubbed my face, too drunk for this and annoyed at her perceptiveness. "Jesus Christ, Talia. She's not here. Why don't you head home?"

She gave me what she probably hoped was a leveling look and leaned in, but she lost her balance a little and put her hand on my thigh to steady herself.

Heat ripped through me as her fingernails dug into my jeans. My balls throbbed. My jeans felt way too tight, but I resisted the urge to do a major rearrangement of my rapidly swelling cock.

"Is she not here because she's not here, or because she doesn't exist?"

I picked up her hand by one finger and removed it from my thigh. "You think I'm making up a girlfriend to try to get rid of you?"

Her eyes narrowed. Yeah. That was exactly what she thought. Because it was true.

"What's her name?" she demanded.

"Sugar."

"How old is she?"

"Twenty-five."

"What color is her hair?"

"Brown."

"How tall is she?"

"Who cares?"

She frowned. "You're making her up."

"You're delusional."

She turned to Élo, tapping her on the shoulder. "Excuse me. Do you think you could introduce me to Sugar?"

"Who?"

"Sugar. She's Lex's friend."

"Is she, now?" Élo gave me a sly smile. "Well. Then he'll have to introduce us both. If Lex has a 'friend' named Sugar… I have never met her."

Talia turned back to me in triumph. "She doesn't exist. And you're a real dick for lying to me like that."

"Never said I wouldn't."

She frowned again, not expecting that.

But whatever the fuck she thought happened last night in that bathtub, it didn't.

I needed to make sure she knew it.

"See, you seem to think we have some kind of… relationship."

That threw her for a major loop. A frown rippled over her pretty face again. "Well, I mean… I know we're not exactly friends. We were kind of enemies when we were kids, but—"

"Friends. Enemies. Whatever the fuck you wanna call it, you think whatever relationship we have, or don't, is governed by fair rules of engagement, right? Societal norms. Standards of behavior. Fucking morals. That's just how you see the world. I get it. But look around you. There's a stripper pole behind you and a guy passed out on the floor. This isn't Kansas, Dorothy. *Go home.*"

With that, I downed the rest of my beer before taking a fresh one off the bar, got up and left her standing there with her mouth open.

I walked across the room and sat down next to Drea on a couch.

Drea was cute enough. But let's be real. She was also basically a cum dumpster for any guy in the club who'd have her, and I wouldn't have touched that with three rubbers on at once.

Talia didn't know that, though.

When she watched Drea slide her hand up my thigh and I didn't remove it, her face fell.

I almost felt bad for her.

Especially when I lifted Drea's hand off my thigh and put it on my dick.

Chapter Four

Lex

Talia still hadn't taken her ass the fuck home. Like an hour later, she was still drinking at the bar with Maddox, Élo, Roni, Jude, and fucking Axel.

I was standing by the pool tables with some brothers, drinking yet another beer. And telling myself that the only reason I hadn't tossed her out yet myself was because Jude and Roni were watching her back.

Lying to myself.

Unfortunately, letting Drea touch my dick through my jeans only worked so well to get my message across, the one that said *You aren't welcome here*. Mainly because Talia turned her back to me as soon as she saw it happen and never looked at me again.

The second she'd turned away, I'd removed Drea's hand and cleared out of there anyway. I was hard as fuck just staring at Talia's ass across the room, and I really didn't need to give Drea any more encouragement.

Also, that whole scene had given off some kind of signal that I was looking for action, because suddenly every available chick in the vicinity was all over me, wishing me a happy birthday with a hug and a kiss and a groping—chicks who should've known better because I'd never shown any interest in them before.

I brushed them all off while I watched Talia across the room. Now I just looked like a dick all around, and Talia was ignoring me.

This was probably all my fault.

If I'd known who she was the first moment I laid eyes on her four years ago, while I was on a surveillance gig for Jude outside Roni's apartment, I would've avoided her from the start.

I never would've let her see me, and given her that look—the one that said I wanted her to notice me, and maybe think about me later when she played with her clit, *that* look. I could've looked away, pretended not to notice when she stumbled in response, almost dropping the tray of takeout coffees she was holding. But I didn't. I made it clear I was looking at her.

She wore tight jeans and a fuzzy white sweater with a little purple puffer vest, her blonde hair in waves down her back, and she looked like something I could easily devour a few times in a night.

The kind of girl who pretended she didn't like bikers, had never been with a biker, but stared at the brothers when they rolled into a bar—and came like a waterfall when my dick was inside her, begging for more.

I hadn't had enough girls like that.

Pure, sweet girls. The kind of girl who didn't even know what a bad boy was until I crossed her path. And spread her open.

The next time I saw her outside Roni's place and she looked back at me, I touched my tongue to one of my platinum canine teeth.

Maybe I'd scared her, at first. Couldn't say. But it was amusing as hell the way she'd blushed and picked up speed, bolting into Roni's building.

I didn't actually find out who she was until weeks later, when she showed up at a band party. When I heard her name, fuck yeah, I knew who she was. I remembered Talia De Santis. Though she'd changed, a lot. Grown up. I never would've recognized her. The Talia I'd known was a ten-year-old girl.

But as soon as I knew who she was, I knew it was over before anything could ever start between us. There would never be any *us*.

No matter how much I wanted to, I didn't fuck around with good girls whose lives I could ruin. I might screw them and never see them again. Never tell them my last name. Strangers. But that was different. I didn't get *involved* with good girls whose lives I could ruin.

And Talia De Santis was nothing if not a good girl.

When we'd both ended up on the Hell & Back tour, it was an eighteen month exercise in denial, restraint, and fucking madness. Soon as I caught the vibe that she might be into me, I could see no other option but shooting her down. Hard.

I made it ugly. Made sure I hurt her to drive her away.

But since I wanted her and couldn't have her, some kind of primal caveman instinct took over. I got overprotective, always watching over her. Never mind that I was supposed to be watching over the band. I felt stupidly possessive of Talia when she wasn't mine. And I made it my business to make sure no one else messed around with her, because I was jealous like that.

There was no way I was going through all that shit again.

No more tours for me, so long as Talia was involved.

Soon enough, she'd be busy with the Players' next album and then she'd be off on another tour with them. Problem solved, right?

Although the next tour wasn't scheduled yet. It could take months or a fucking year 'til that happened.

I turned my back to the bar, to her, and tried to focus on the pool table in front of me. There was a bit of a drunken tournament going on, but it wasn't holding my attention.

Why the fuck did I invite her to this party?

Because you wanted her to come.

And apparently you're a fucking masochist.

I was drunk, very drunk, and she was right over there. I knew she was drunk, too. And I was getting less and less convinced that I'd be able to stop myself if I got any drunker.

If she came over here.

If she kissed me again, like she did last night.

But why would she kiss me when I'd just pulled that shit, putting another girl's hand on my junk right in front of her?

Because she likes you. You know she likes you.

And her boyfriend just proposed and she's obviously confused, and you're a very bad person for even thinking about it.

The thing was, I was a bad person.

So inevitably, I ended up back at the bar. Standing right in front of her. Staring at her as I drank my beer, eavesdropping as she talked to Roni and Élo.

"So basically, we're semi-engaged," she was telling them. "That's where we're at right now. He's been really romantic about the whole thing, though. And so patient."

"That's very sweet," Élo said.

"You think that's sweet," Roni said, "you should see the diamond. Ice that size could end global warming."

Talia beamed, ignoring me. But she knew I was standing right here.

What the hell was she still doing here? Just the thought of any of my club brothers thinking she might be up for grabs tonight made me see blood red dripping down the walls.

Talia was innocent, clueless about MC life, and meant for a nice, ordinary life with a Carl.

But since my previous tactics to get her ass to leave didn't work —and I couldn't stop thinking about how nice it would be if I lived in a world where I could drag her upstairs and fuck her without caring about the consequences—I took her by the elbow when Jude wasn't looking and steered her away, to a corner by the front door.

"Semi-engaged?" I growled. Sounded a lot more angry than I thought I would, but maybe that was because my balls felt so backed up ever since she'd walked into the bar, I could barely remember my name. "What the hell is that? You're either engaged or you're not."

She lifted her chin. "Then maybe I am."

"I don't see that ring on your finger."

She blinked at me with bleary, drunk eyes. "Because I'm still thinking it over."

"Uh-huh. Thinking. Here."

"Yup."

"Those last few shots with the boys help clear anything up for you?"

Her eyelids lowered a little. "Maybe they did."

I drew back and studied her. What the hell did that mean? Was she cruising for some excuse *not* to marry her semi-fiancé?

And maybe some guy at this party was supposed to be that excuse?

Nope. No fucking way.

I took her by the arm and walked her straight out the clubhouse door, grabbing her jacket on the way. As soon as we were outside, I shoved it at her.

"What's up your ass?" she muttered, but she pulled the jacket on. It was cold out. I could see her breath, pale in the air when she said, "You're really grumpy on your birthday."

"It's time for you to go home, Natalia." I looked around the dark parking lot. Where was a fucking prospect when you needed one?

"You used my full name," she said softly.

I looked at her.

She was standing too close, and she gazed up at me with big, brown, drunk eyes. So dark, kinda mesmerizing against her blonde hair.

"Just like you used to when we were kids..." she said, dreamily. Like I was some fairytale prince who'd just rolled up in his chariot to make all her glittering fantasies come true.

Shit. She was more drunk than I thought.

I blinked. I tried to look away but couldn't quite do it. Fuck, she was pretty. "I'm getting someone to drive you home."

But neither of us moved. And something shifted in her eyes. Softened. Like maybe she realized I didn't really want to send her home, even though I would.

Was it that obvious?

"Why did you bring up our pact?"

"What pact?" Playing dumb: the world's laziest defense, and I was going with it.

"You know what pact. The marriage thing."

"I didn't."

"You did, last night."

I dragged my hand over my face. Fuck, I was too wasted to have this conversation. Or any conversation with her, really. "That was a mistake. Can't a guy make a mistake?"

"So I'm a mistake?"

"That's not what I said."

"I am *not* marrying you," she informed me. "No matter what we wrote in that stupid notebook."

"Okay."

Silence.

"I'm marrying him."

"Okay."

We stared at each other.

Then she flattened her hands on my chest and pushed me back, up against the clubhouse wall. I mean, I let her. She was like half my size.

She pressed herself against me. Tits to chest, groin to groin and one knee wedged up between my legs. I was still kinda hard—and that did it. Now I was hard as fuck. Again.

I wondered, not for the first time, what godawful shit I must've done in some former life to deserve the pure torture that was Talia De Santis.

She made a soft, helpless sound of want as she rubbed her whole body against mine with a shudder.

Obviously, she was not in her right mind.

The girl just told me, point blank, that she wasn't marrying me. Then shoved me up against a wall and slammed her body against mine.

Message received.

My dick was already so on board with whatever she had in mind, it was already seeping pre-come, lubing up for action.

"Talia…"

She gripped my shirt with her little fists and moaned as she buried her face in my neck, inhaling. She was smelling me.

"Uhhh…" I was really trying to remember why I was supposed to resist this—when she licked my fucking neck and my eyes rolled back in my head. And I went mute.

Christ. Could I just let her have her way with me? Let her do whatever she wanted with my body until we both came, then pretend it didn't happen?

That was my dick asking the questions, as her little teeth closed on my earlobe and tugged.

No.

No, you can't.

Her hands slid down my chest, my stomach… and my dick flexed in my jeans. Her fingers shook a little with nerves or excitement as they flirted with the button, then popped it open.

I didn't stop her. My arms stayed locked at my sides, my hands pressed to the wall behind me as I started to sweat. Profusely.

Her fingers slid down, over the bulge in my jeans, and I held my breath. I turned to stone. It was either that or groan like a pig and ram my hips forward, cram my dick into her hand. Maybe make it pop out the top of my jeans so she could grab it?

Motherfucking Christ, she was sucking on my neck.

"Ta… augggrrghh…" There were no words, just senseless, grateful sounds coming out of my throat. She started massaging the shaft of my dick through my jeans, like the angel she was, and drool pooled in my mouth. My unbuttoned jeans slid down a bit as she worked.

Her soft, sucking kisses moved down my neck.

Her fingers slid lower. Drifted over my swollen ball sac through my jeans and squeezed, and I choked on my own spit.

She made a soft, hungry sound in her throat as she squeezed my balls again. Her tongue lapped my throat. She was playing with my balls, massaging them in her hand… and my cock was rumbling like a waking volcano about to overflow with lava.

I barely noticed her other hand as it stole up my shirt. Until her warm little fingertips found my nipple and squeezed.

My dick spasmed in her grip and she looked down. At my cockhead. Which had burst out the top of my jeans.

Then she whispered against my throat, almost shyly, "Do you like blow jobs, Lex?"

My heart was beating so hard, I swore to God I felt it skip an entire two beats when I entirely stopped breathing. If she decided to drop to her knees and suck my leaking cockhead into her mouth, right now, I was done for. I could not resist fucking her mouth. I was not that strong a man, and I'd never been that good.

I was bad.

Very, very bad.

The only reason I'd managed not to fuck her this long was because I stayed the hell away from her. I did not end up in bathtubs with her, or let her press me against a wall while my dick slid out of my jeans and she massaged my balls and sucked on my throat.

"Uhh—*can't*," I coughed out.

She didn't seem to hear me. Her hand slid up my shaft a bit, squeezing through my jeans. A couple more inches and her fingers would touch the naked head. She'd touch the wet slit in the crown and I would no longer be responsible for what I let her do to me.

Or what I did to her.

Please, just let her lick it a bit.

I wondered if she'd give great, enthusiastic head. Or if she'd be nervous and timid.

Didn't care. A few seconds in her sweet mouth, seeing her at my feet, her big brown eyes looking up at me as I stuffed her face with my cock… and I was gonna paint her throat with so much come she'd probably choke on it.

Holy fuck, that mental image turned me on.

Just let her do it. No one's watching.

It was her idea.

It's a birthday gift.

Holy shit. I really was a terrible person.

My hips stirred, restless. My balls throbbed. There was dirt under my fingernails. Or paint. Or something. I was digging them into the wall.

I was trying.

"We—*Tal*—we can't be seen together, like this…" One desperate last attempt, as she murmured sweet, hungry sounds against my throat between kisses. She kissed her way along my collarbone, still squeezing my nipple in her fingers, teasing. She lifted my shirt. "We—"

She dipped her head and flicked her little tongue over my rigid nipple, and all the breath went out of me. She licked it, suckled on it a little while I muttered something like, "Jesus, fuck." Then I managed to grit out her name. "*Talia.*"

She blinked up at me, those beautiful brown eyes of hers, and stopped sucking on me.

I wanted her to do it again.

I couldn't think.

Let her. Do it.

She wants to.

What incredible shit did I do to get this lucky? I was pretty sure I didn't. Ever.

Was this good or was this bad? I didn't even know anymore.

The lust was clouding out my control, like spray paint blacking out a window.

Talia was breathing in quick, excited breaths. But she looked around into the dark, unsure. "No one's even here."

Not true. Finn had appeared over by the gate, hopefully not overhearing all this. The guy was half-deaf to begin with, so here's hoping. But the rumbling sound of bikes was rising in the distance, and he was opening the gate.

We were about to be a lot less alone.

It was bringing me back to my senses.

Talia met my eyes again. Maybe she thought I was fighting this because she was "semi-engaged." Maybe I'd just let her think that.

The truth was I couldn't risk getting involved with her. I couldn't afford to have that kind of liability, something to be used against me.

Someone to be hurt because of me.

I couldn't just take a birthday blow job from Talia De Santis, then casually stroll away. She wouldn't be a quick, one time screw, either. It would never be that way between us.

She'd get under my skin.

Maybe I'd always known that about her.

Maybe I'd always known we'd be standing here one day, and I'd be telling her, "It can't happen, Talia."

"Why?" she breathed, pressing against me again. "You want it to happen."

Yes. Yes, I did.

Obviously, she'd felt my pulsing hard-on and assumed she knew where this was headed, despite whatever was coming out of my mouth. My body disagreed with my brain. My brain was pickled, anyway. I'd give in, eventually. Quickly, if her experiences with other men were any indication.

I wasn't other men.

Other men didn't have the Devil breathing down their necks.

I took a deep breath. Felt like the first one I'd taken since she pushed me against the wall. I put my hands on her shoulders and guided her back a few steps, detaching her from my body. Then I tucked my dick away, fast, doing up my jeans.

Talia watched me do it with big, questioning eyes.

Then a couple of my club brothers rolled in on Harleys, loud. With one of Maddox's vans right behind them. I couldn't see who was at the wheel. Connor brought up the rear on his bike, following the van as it disappeared into the dark on the far side of the clubhouse.

The two bikes in lead pulled up in front of the clubhouse and backed into their designated spots, close to the front door. It was Blazer.

And King.

I kinda hoped they wouldn't even notice us, but we were standing right next to the damn door. Why the hell didn't I clear her out of here?

Blazer got off his bike, giving Talia a once-over as he walked past. His eyes met mine just before he disappeared into the clubhouse. He didn't smile. He definitely didn't say *Happy birthday, brother*.

What the fuck?

When King took off his helmet, he shook out his dark curls and tossed it to Shifty, who'd materialized from the shadows to take it for him. It was Shifty's number one job as a prospect to make sure the President's bike, helmet, boots and everything else he so much as breathed on was gleamingly clean the next time he went to use it. It was a coveted position for a prospect. King wasn't just the President of the mother chapter of the West Coast Kings; he was our national President. All our support clubs, even our brothers out east, the Dead Kings, all answered to King.

He got off his bike and stalked toward the front door of the clubhouse. Boots, dark jeans, clean white shirt under his leather jacket. Dark beard, cold ash eyes. King looked like the offspring of James Dean and a plundering pirate, with tats, piercings, and pretty lips to boot, because girls didn't already love a badass enough. As he stalked past, he threw up his arm, his gloved finger pointed straight at me.

"Brother," he growled, in that bone rattling tone of his. "Get your ass inside."

His gaze flicked to Talia, briefly. Raked over her. Then he went in through the clubhouse door.

Right. Whatever the fuck was going on, I needed Talia out of here. Now.

When I looked down at her, she was hugging herself. "Who was that?" she said quietly, as the door slammed shut in King's wake.

"To you? No one."

I took her by the arm again and led her over to the gate, where Finn and Shifty were locking up. I was about to inform one of them —whoever seemed least likely to try to talk to her or flirt with her in any way—that he was driving Talia home, when I heard Jude's voice. "Lex. I'm takin' the girls home."

I turned to find Jude and Roni stepping out of the clubhouse, holding hands.

Thank Christ.

"You don't mind?" I asked him, because I was drunk. It didn't occur to me until the words were out and Jude's eyebrows furled that I'd made it sound, with three little words, that I thought Talia was more my responsibility to take care of, to protect, than his.

I dropped her arm.

Jude kinda scowled at that, too. "Let's go, Tal," he said shortly.

Talia looked at me, but I tried to pretend she didn't.

Roni came over to put an arm around Talia and steer her toward Jude's car. Talia looked back at me over Roni's shoulder.

Jude stood looking at me for a long moment.

When I met his eyes, dark, unreadable, I just couldn't keep my mouth shut. "She really engaged to that Carl guy?"

Jude's expression didn't change. The man could be stonier than a brick wall. I admired his poker face; I hadn't quite mastered it to that level myself.

I also tended to talk too much when I was drunk. Or stressed out. "You think he's good for her?"

Jude said nothing. Dark eyes sizing me up.

"We've had him checked out?" I assumed we had. "We" being Jude, Brody, and whoever they told to run a background on Talia's new boyfriend. They checked out anyone who came in close contact with Dirty or the Players, and Talia had worked for the bands for years. Doubtful they'd sit back and watch her get engaged to some random without a background check.

"Not your concern," he informed me evenly.

"I was getting her a ride," I said, to fill the silence.

"She has one."

"Yeah. Thanks."

His eyes narrowed a fraction. Why was I thanking him, when he just told me she wasn't my concern?

"She's drunk," I offered. "Wouldn't want anyone to make that a problem for her."

"Yeah." Jude stared me down. "Wouldn't want that."

"Don't be a dick."

He didn't smile, but he gave me a hug and a slap on the back.

"What's going on in there?" I asked him as he walked away. I nodded toward the clubhouse; the ominous vibe that lingered in King's wake. It didn't escape me that Jude had cleared out with his woman seconds after King and Blazer walked in.

Whatever was going on, Jude didn't want to be involved. Not when his woman was here.

But he didn't answer me. "Goodnight, brother. Happy birthday."

I watched him get into his black Bentley Bentayga and roll out. I waited until the gate was locked. Then I headed around the far side of the clubhouse, where Maddox's van had pulled in.

It wasn't one of the work vans with the logo from Axel's home security company on the side. It was the plain, battered black one.

Parked by the back door. One of my club brothers, Bane, was standing by the door. He raised his chin to me in greeting, but no smile.

The rear doors of the van stood open, but the harsh security lights over the back of the clubhouse cast the interior in shadow.

Bodies were rustling around inside the van.

As I got closer, a couple of my club brothers hopped out the back of the van. Connor, and Maddox's younger brother, Hendrix. They pulled two people along with them, stumbling, covered head to toe in black. Long black robes, or sheets or something, with black hoods pulled over their heads.

As Bane opened the back door of the clubhouse for them, I watched my brothers lead their captors over to the club and disappear inside.

I followed them, tossing Bane a look. *Who's in the hoods?*

But he said nothing. Just slapped me on the shoulder, then shoved me into the building.

Shit. I kinda hated being drunk in front of King; especially when he needed me alert.

Whatever was about to go down, I just hoped I wasn't too wasted to deal with it.

Chapter Five

Lex

I woke up to the sound of a door opening and a toilet flushing.

I was hungover as fuck, again. I knew it before my eyes were open. A long, aching groan rumbled up from the depths of my body as I tried to roll over.

Who the fuck was in my room? No way I brought anyone back here last night.

"Yo, hooker, get the hell out of bed."

Fuck. *Maddox.*

I shoved my face back into the pillow. Why the hell did I give up my apartment last year to live here full-time?

Oh, right. Because I was never there anyway. And throwing away that kind of money on rent was just stupid. Even if this place came with a bunch of annoying as shit roommates with boundary issues. Kinda like a frat house but with guns.

"It's your fucking birthday," he informed me, as if I didn't know. "The ladies are lined up around the block to suck that dick."

I lifted my arm just enough to give him the finger. Maddox was annoyingly impervious to the need for a decent night's sleep. He could survive, even thrive, off like four hours of shut-eye.

"Hate," I grumbled, "you."

He laughed and threw something at me. A shirt landed on my head. It stank of weed and perfume. And *puke*.

I tossed it away. Who the fuck threw up on my shirt? Not me. I'd remember that.

"Not hatin' me last night," he said jovially, and I groaned again, remembering allll the fucking tequila we'd put back together. And the body shots I'd done off that chick.

Those people in the black hoods that got hauled out of Maddox's van and into the club? Strippers.

Fuckers had me thinking my party had been cut short by an abduction. But the hoods, and everything else, came off as soon as I followed them inside. Underneath were two girls in pasties and not much else. One of them went straight to work on the pole in the bar and the other one hopped into King's lap.

It was my party, so she did offer to hop into my lap first, but I passed on that.

A lot of the wives had cleared out by then, there were still more than enough women in the room to go around, and around, but I'd parked myself with Maddox and Élo at the bar, where I was taken care of.

My brothers really went all out on my party.

Didn't help the fact that I was miserable. More than a little head-fucked over what happened with Talia. And, because it was my actual birthday today, that meant I had serious shit to take care of.

Shit with my father.

"Don't you have somewhere to be?" Maddox was lingering, leaning in the doorway to the bathroom as I rubbed my eyes and forced them open. "You headin' to Toronto?"

"Yup."

"Then get your ass up." He grinned at me. He was way too happy. Why wasn't he hungover as shit?

Because he was an asshole who poured three times as much tequila for me as for himself, so he could gloat about it right now. And he wasn't the only one who played that game last night.

"Please, go wake up Blazer." I dragged myself up to sitting, dropping my legs over the side of the bed. "Just piss on him or something."

He laughed again. "What'd he do to you?"

"Tequila," I croaked.

"Pussy. Get your ass up and go eat cake with the rich people already. And try not to forget about us."

"Uh-huh."

"See you back here tomorrow?"

I looked over at him. The guy was always halfway to legit worried I was gonna get wooed over to the billionaire side of life, start wearing sweater vests and combing my hair back, making people call me Lexington. And leaving the club behind.

"Tonight, if I can help it."

If I don't die first.

"Good." He strolled over, reaching out for a fist bump, and I grunted, tapping my elbow to his fist. How the hell did I know if he washed his hands after he used the toilet? He rolled his eyes and headed back through the bathroom. The door on his side closed and I dragged my ass out of bed.

When I yanked open a drawer, I was greeted with neat rows of clean socks and underwear. A little birthday gift from the mamas, because they knew I wouldn't take a birthday blow job from any of them. Been there, done that, and when all your friends have done that too, kinda lost its charm.

Call me an idealist, but I preferred girls who'd never touched a biker's dick, until mine. My cock knew what it liked, and who was I to argue?

I got dressed and staggered into the bathroom where the sounds of morning sex, or maybe it was an argument, came muffled through the wall from Maddox's room. I banged my fist on the wall to say good morning. Or maybe just to be an asshole.

Someone banged back. Then music went on, loud. Awolnation, "I'm No Good." I laughed under my breath; no idea if that was fighting music or fucking music. You never could tell with Maddox and Élo.

I pounded back a glass of water, took a year long piss, brushed my teeth. Raked my fingers through my hair, ran my hand over my unshaved jaw. Looked myself in the eyes for a sec. That moment of humanity, seeing yourself as a human; an animal capable of dying. It would take very little. Cut off the air. Open up a vein.

Fragile creatures, we were.

I walked back into my room, pulled on my lumber jacket and Kings cut, yanked on my boots, stashed my knife. Plucked a joint out of my cigarette case and lit up as I headed out the door.

Found Grim sitting at the bar on my way out, tapped him on the shoulder. There were a few bodies laid out around the bar, but I slipped past so I didn't wake anyone. The less people I had to lie directly to, the better.

I went outside, where Toad was hanging out, waiting on me. We got in my car and headed for the airport in Pitt Meadows. It was the closest one where my father's private jet could pick me up.

What the Kings didn't know—what no one knew—was that I went to see my father on my birthday. Every year.

What I told my club brothers, my official story, was that I was going to visit family in Ontario. Obligatory birthday bullshit. That part was true enough. They assumed I meant the Davenports; my rich grandmother or maybe some aunts and uncles who still gave a damn. The Davenports were my mom's side of the family but I rarely saw them, other than Mom and my half-brother, Dane, who lived in Vancouver.

Truth was, none of the Davenports in Ontario wanted to see me. They'd disowned me long ago. Before birth, actually.

The Kings knew that, but they thought I had more contact with them than I did. Like, at least this once a year contact.

It was only my father who wanted to see me, though.

The father I'd disowned myself.

For the last nine years, on my birthday, he'd summoned my ass out to Ontario. Not to Toronto exactly, but to the particular area of the GTHA where he held reign.

His turf.

The one place on Earth he could make a body disappear without consequence, guaranteed. The place where he owned so much and so many, he was like a deity.

Of course, the Kings had that kind of power, too—all across the country. And out here on the west coast, my father had not much power at all.

So, he summoned me to him. I'd already gotten the call, yesterday, from one of his captains.

What would he have to say to me this year?

What would I say to him?

If we were betting men, we'd probably get it right. Our meetings were nothing if not predictable. But he still called, every year. And every year, I hauled my ass out there to face him.

My father was a very *I brought you into this world, I can take you out of it* type of father. I had no doubt he might do it, if I didn't show up. That would be an inexcusable disrespect. Ignoring him, refusing to meet with him, would be a crime worse than leaving him in the first place.

When you were connected to the Mafia, you paid tribute to the boss. No exceptions. And my father, Joseph Montanari, was the boss of the Montanari crime family.

My family.

So every year I made this trip, this grim pilgrimage as I'd come to think of it, to pay my annual penance for my greatest sin in my father's eyes: the sin of wanting nothing to do with him.

As always, he would want something from me. Something I

refused to give. And maybe this time it would cost me my life. You never knew. The man was a coldhearted killer.

Just look what he did to Lola.

You couldn't roll over and play dead, though. You had to stand before him and show him you weren't afraid. If he thought you were afraid, if he thought you cared—about anything he could use against you—that was his leverage.

And all you really needed to break something was the right leverage.

———

When I walked out onto the tarmac, the jet was already there, waiting for me. The airstairs were open and two of my father's men, made men, stood waiting for me at the bottom. Just in case they needed the muscle. Or the Berettas in their holsters.

In case I posed a problem.

My father's underboss, a man named Vincenzo who was supposed to be like an uncle to me, stepped out of the jet. I'd always liked Vincenzo, which just made it harder. They weren't all bad guys.

Criminals, yes. (*Hey kettle, meet pot.*) Extortionists, yes. Murderers, yes. But not all bad guys.

Not like my father was.

At least, I didn't know the depths of their evil firsthand like I knew my father's. But there were some things you'd just rather not know. Vincenzo smiled at me, and I wondered what his sons would've said about him, if I'd ever stuck around to ask.

He came all the way down the stairs and greeted me with a hug. He ignored what I was wearing, while the other two stared me down from the shadows behind their sunglasses. I didn't know these guys. I didn't know most of my father's crew anymore. They wore dark, heavy overcoats. Italian suits, Brioni or Armani or Zegna. They didn't understand the way I dressed. They didn't understand the need for me, for this; that much was clear.

But worse, they didn't understand my disloyalty to my father.

Maybe they wanted me dead. But that was up to their boss.

On the jet I sat across from Vincenzo, listening to his stories about his kids, his nieces and nephews. Not all blood related. The children of his Mafia "brothers" were his nieces and nephews. The conversation was light, friendly even. He said nothing to me about my father, about my life, about the Kings colors I wore. But the insinuation was clear: I was his nephew, but I wasn't where I should be, doing what I should do. I was a lost sheep who needed to return to the herd.

I, Lexington Miller Davenport, was the black sheep of my Mafia family.

When I'd realized that, one day when I was seventeen, I was smoking weed with Dane in his dad's backyard, by the pool, and I'd laughed so fucking hard. Dane thought I was choking or dying or something. I fell off my lounge chair and laughed for like forty-five minutes. That was some good, strong sativa, but shit. *I* was the bad guy here. The one who needed straightening out.

That was what they called it in the Mafia, or *Cosa Nostra*, as they called themselves. I needed to get *straightened out*. Become a made man. Because, you know, then I'd be on the right path. According to my father and his *consigliere*; his advisor. His under-boss and captains, his made men.

I was unmade.

A failure.

Still, my father would rather have me alive, with the potential to come back to him, be the son he always wanted me to be, than dead. As long as I kept paying my penance and he believed I wasn't a threat.

Or maybe one day he'd get tired of this arrangement.

Or he'd get killed and Vincenzo would take over and have me put down. I was a loose end, that may one day need severing.

Who could say?

Only death could sever that blood bond, or convince them you wouldn't rat, even if you knew virtually nothing. They'd never believe you knew nothing. And they'd never let go of a valuable potential earner.

My father saw so much lost potential in me.

It was there in his eyes, every year when he looked at me, standing in front of him in my Kings cut.

———

When we touched down on my father's turf and Vincenzo's car delivered us to the Italian restaurant where my father was waiting, I walked into the place like I did this every day. Like I belonged here.

That was how you approached the boss. That was how you walked through the room, a connected business, filled with connected people who all had their eyes on you.

At least we weren't alone. Much worse, if we were alone. You never wanted to be alone with them. With any of them.

I learned that early.

When I was eighteen, I made the crucial mistake of being alone with my father and some of his men. For the very last time. He wanted me alone now, they'd have to drag me there. And one of his men would probably eat my knife in the process.

They knew that. They'd patted me down before I got on the jet. But they let me keep the knife. I just didn't have that air about me, maybe, that I was crazy enough, suicidal enough to take out my father with a knife in the back of a busy restaurant.

Anyway, I didn't want him dead. That kind of thinking, that kind of intent, was a lot of karmic debt to take on. He was my father, after all.

I just wanted him to leave me alone.

I walked right up to his table, the big one in back, in the semi-private room. There was a curtain, not a door, and Vincenzo closed it behind me. Now my father and I were alone, but not completely alone. There were customers out in the restaurant, real customers. It was coming up on the lunch hour.

My father didn't greet me or stop eating, but he looked up at me, his forehead wrinkling. Every year he looked older, exponentially older. He was only fifty-one. Crisp suit, expensive gold watch, diamond rings, plural. Slick dark hair going grey. Broad shoulders in his suit. Square jaw. Cold, dark eyes. The man was formidable.

I might've been impressed if I was still capable of those kinds of feelings for him.

"Daddy," I greeted him.

His eyes twitched. He didn't appreciate the sarcasm or the sentiment. He'd never appreciated my sense of humor. Maybe because it showed itself at such inappropriate times. Honestly, it made people like me. People who weren't my father.

It made them whisper in his ears not to kill me, maybe.

The owner of the restaurant came in, greeted me enthusiastically as I stood staring at my father. I was Joe Montanari's special guest, why didn't I look honored? The guy didn't seem to know what to do with me. I wasn't hungry. I wasn't thirsty.

My father told him to bring more of what he was eating, for me. "And get him one of those, what do you call them, Steam Whistles or whatever," he said with distaste. "My son likes beer." Beer was beneath him. It was a poor man's drink, he would say.

When the man left and we were alone again, he told me, "You're late," though he'd never specified a time. It was a lunch meeting. They were always lunch meetings—my preference. The flight took a few hours, and I wanted to get this over with as soon as possible and get back home. Get back to my life out west.

The owner came back, lightning fast, with my beer and a glass on a tray, smelling vaguely of sweat and fear. He set them down on the table for me and left. My father stared at me.

"Are you here to make amends?" he finally asked me, like he always asked me. "To come back to the family?"

"No."

This was the ritual: he asked, I declined. The tribute was demanded. The penance was paid.

"Sit," he said, "and eat with me."

I sat down at the table across from him.

"Go ahead and ask me," he said gruffly. "It's your birthday."

Yes, it was. How unfortunate for him.

The fact that I was born at all was probably irritation enough. His wife would've made it so. I heard that, from my mom; that his wife knew about me. She'd given him two daughters, but my mom, Laurinda, had given him a son. His only son. So, here I was. I was valuable to him, whether he liked it or not. Or, I could be. I *should* be. I should be an earner.

In his mind, I owed him today, for all the days of the year I refused to work for him. To earn.

But first, he'd give me something. A birthday gift. Maybe to try to convince me that he wasn't unreasonable. It wasn't all *take*. So every year, it was the same. Part of the ritual: I was allowed to ask him for something. One thing.

There was only one thing I wanted from him, though.

Let me go.

But it wasn't something he would give. I'd asked, long ago. He'd made it clear it was never going to happen. So I asked him for the same thing I did every year.

"If I die here, bury me out west. Take me back to my mother."

He eyed me, nodded briefly, then resumed eating.

Would he keep that promise?

I wanted him to have to look her in the eye—a woman who'd loved him, the mother of his son—when he handed her my ashes. It was the one card I could play that might make him rethink whatever plans he had for me. I wanted him to have a memory. I wanted him to have a conscience.

I wanted him to have a heart.

Despite the fact that maybe he'd loved her too, once, I wasn't sure that he did.

I took a sip of the beer I'd been served, maybe as part of the illusion that I wasn't afraid of him. I still was. I always would be. I pretended that I wasn't.

Then he spoke again.

"Natalia De Santis."

Her name crackled through the air. Like a fine line snaking across a windshield—that silent vacuum of terrible pause, an intake of breath, before glass exploded into your face.

I said nothing.

My father looked at me.

"You're friendly," he said.

"We're not friends," I forced out, in a cool, measured voice. You always answered his questions.

Even the terrible ones.

You spoke up. You showed respect. You told him what he wanted to know. You tried not to say shit that would get you killed.

Or get other people killed.

While you tried to figure out what he really wanted.

Why did he just say Talia's name?

In my head, a thousand questions at warp speed. I couldn't fathom the answers to any of them. As far as I knew, my father only knew Talia De Santis as the daughter of a casual associate we saw on summer holidays a few times when I was a kid.

"You work with her."

"I don't."

His mouth set in a hard line.

It was true, I didn't work with Talia right this minute. But technically we could work together at any time. All it would take was a text from Jude telling me to come work security at some band party he needed me at. And there she'd be, in the VIP section or at the bar, or mingling on her semi-fiancé's arm, pretending not to notice me noticing her.

"I barely know her," I said, to fill the silence.

"You know enough."

"What do I know?"

Again, silence.

"I want to know," he said slowly, "what you know."

The owner of the restaurant walked in with a huge oval plate as my father stared me down. He set the enormous cannelloni in front of me, looked at my father, who twitched his fingers like, *Get the fuck out*, and he scurried out.

"She works for one of the bands," I told him. He'd know that already, if he knew enough to know we'd worked together. I didn't say which band, though it would take no more than a Google search to verify that she worked for the Players. I didn't say anyone's name. I didn't like saying their names, the names of people in that part of my life, in this kind of room. "I don't work for them."

"So you do know something."

I held his gaze. I'd told him what I knew. What else could he possibly want to know?

"I want to know about her," he said, and an ice-cold wind that didn't exist whipped me in the face, filled with broken shards of glass. I heard tires crunching, skidding across frozen pavement in my ears where nothing was there. I felt like I was pumping a brake, but the brake line had been severed. There was nothing but air, nothing to stop the frantic slide into oblivion and darkness.

But I said nothing. I did nothing, but listen.

"I want to know where she spends her time. I want to know how she gets there and when."

I want.

My father always got what he wanted.

No. Not always.

If it was always, I wouldn't have been wearing Kings colors.

He'd made it clear what he wanted this time, but the glass-speckled wind was still in my ears. *I want to know where she spends her time.* He wanted intel on Talia and her movements. He wanted her whereabouts and her whens.

And the only reason he could want those things was because he wanted an opening. An approach. He wanted to know where she was vulnerable.

He wanted something from her, something more than he was saying.

"You'll be the one to get me these things," he informed me.

"I will," I said. Because there was nothing else to say.

He went back to eating his cannelloni. And I watched him.

I remembered how his men had held me down when I was eighteen. How they ripped out my teeth. It wasn't even anyone I knew that did it, just some guys on his crew. Some guys who'd picked me up in Vancouver and brought me to my father. He gave the order. It went down the line, and it was done.

If anyone refused to do it, it would happen all the same.

You couldn't stop an order from the boss.

I tried to eat my cannelloni. I could feel phantom shards of glass in my mouth. I could feel the concrete floor beneath me, and the weight of men almost cutting off my breath. I could taste the blood.

I ran my tongue over my smooth, fake teeth, and I could still feel the pulpy, fresh holes, raw and gaping, where my teeth used to be.

Chapter Six

Talia

I practically shoved my roommate out the door. "Bye, babe!" I called after her. "Have fun!"

She gave me a weird, suspicious look over her shoulder as she headed for the elevator. I shut the door behind her and leaned on it. *Thank God.*

It was so hard to get alone time in this place.

My dad owned the condo, it was a three bedroom, and I had two roommates, neither of whom currently had boyfriends—or lives of their own, apparently. They were constantly hanging around the living room in their lululemons, the one who was in college doing homework and the other one "online dating" on her phone but never actually going out to meet men in the flesh.

I'd managed to clear the both of them out for a few hours and it already felt heavenly. I sucked back a deep breath. *That* was the sweet smell of privacy.

My phone dinged and I lunged for it. *Front door.* Yes!

I picked up. "Hey!"

"It's me," came Roni's voice. "Buzz me up, it's cold out."

I buzzed her in before hanging up and racing into the kitchen for staples. Popcorn, pretzels. My favorite candy, Fuzzy Peaches. And a bottle of Chandon with two champagne glasses. Not that we had anything whatsoever to celebrate, but it was all I had on hand. Plus, I needed Roni as relaxed as Roni got—which was very relaxed—for this talk.

She was the only friend I could talk to about this particular problem.

I laid out all the goodies on the coffee table and turned on some music, popped the Chandon open and started to pour when I heard the tap on the door. I went to get it, glass of bubbly in hand, and tossed the door open, feeling breathless. "Welcome!"

Roni's green eyes widened.

I let out a breath in a burst. "Sorry. Should I crank down the intensity?"

"Maybe just a notch." She gave me side-eye as she drifted in, air-kissing my cheek. "I brought guacamole and chips."

"Great. I have bubbly." I shoved the glass at her.

Her dark, finely arched eyebrow went up as she paused in the middle of slipping off her leather boots. "I take it we've already gotten started?"

"Not actually." Instead of handing the glass over, I took a swig. "I'll pour you another."

She followed me into the living room and started unpacking her bag of snacks while I poured another glass of bubbly. "This is exciting," she said tentatively, eyeing me again, obviously trying to gauge my mood. Or rather my strange, chaotic energy. "You got rid of the roommates…"

"Yeah. That's good." I was shifting from one foot to another like I had to pee. Maybe I did. "That's not why I invited you over, though. I mean, it is. But—"

"Why don't you just sit down and have some of that drink?" Roni plucked the second glass, which I was still clutching, from my hand and nodded toward the couch.

"Right." I sank into the cream-colored leather and took another swig of my Chandon. She sat down in the armchair opposite me, still examining me.

"So…"

"So." My knee was bopping up and down. I couldn't sit still.

A slow smile spread across Roni's face. "What's up?"

"Right. That." I took another sip. The bubbly was permeating my system and helping me relax, a little. I was actually more wound up than this earlier. Just before the tears came. Since then, I'd reined in the emotions, somewhat, had a shower, and urged my roommates to leave or I'd have to evict them at the end of the month. They knew I was shitting them, but they got the message.

I felt much more rational now. I was nervous, though, to come out with this.

Would Roni judge me? No. Roni wasn't the judgmental type. Plus, she was in love with a biker. Maybe she'd even understand.

But it still felt hard to say the actual words.

I downed the rest of the bubbly in my glass.

Roni lifted the bottle, never missing a beat. "Refill?"

"Yes, please." She topped me up, then looked me in the eye. "Spill, sweetheart. We don't have all night. What if the yoga pants brigade comes back early?"

"I think we're good for a few hours. They put on jeans."

"Even so."

I took a breath. "Okay. Here's the thing. You know Carl proposed."

"I do."

Whoa. Just hearing those two words, and a shiver ran through me. How could I stand at an altar and say those words to Carl, feeling like this?

But how could I not say them, and hurt him?

I downed more Chandon and forced out, "I haven't said yes yet."

"I know that, too."

"So… the reason I haven't said yes yet is that I'm not totally sure how I feel. I mean, I know I love him and everything. We fell in love. I know how I feel about *him*, I mean, I think I do, and everything was all good—"

"Breathe."

"*Shit*." I took a deep breath in. Then I let it back out in a flurry of words. "But then I'm also not sure how I feel about this other guy, see, there's this other guy who keeps popping up and I can't seem to get rid of him and then he pops up again and then I keep thinking about him and I don't know why and it's not like anything has happened with him except it sort of has, right, because why do I keep thinking about him?" I stopped babbling to take another deep breath and gazed at her imploringly.

Roni blinked at me. "Talia," she said slowly. "Who is this guy?"

"No one."

She cleared her throat, like *Don't make me choke on this bullshit of yours.* "You just said that you can't seem to get rid of him."

"Right."

"You don't want to get rid of him."

"I…" Why did she say that like a statement? Was that a question?

"You clearly don't want to get rid of him. You just said you keep thinking about him."

"I know. But that's bad, right?"

"It's not good or bad. It's a fact. So what do you do with that fact?"

I leapt to my feet, sloshing Chandon. "I don't know! That's why you're here. Okay, look." I put my drink down, took a steadying breath and started pacing around the room. "Don't judge me. You of all people better not judge me."

"Talia. I won't judge you."

I buried my face in my hands. "It's Lex," I muttered into my palms.

Silence. When she said not one thing, I peeked up between my fingers. Yup, she heard me. She was sitting there, sideways in her chair, watching me.

"Lex," she said, when our eyes met.

I dropped my hands and started pacing again. "What do you mean, '*Oh, Lex, whatever*'?"

"I didn't say whatever."

"You infused it with whatever. Like it's no big deal. But it's not whatever. It's *wrong*."

"Why, exactly?"

"Because he's wrong. He's wrong for me. I can't be with a biker." I dropped my voice, like the furniture had ears or something. "His dad's in the Mafia!"

Roni did a quick eye roll, like, yeah, okay, that's a hard fact, *but*. "I know. Jude told me."

"And this doesn't concern you? Roni, his dad isn't just *in* the Mafia," I whispered. "He's *the Mafia*. Like, the boss of one of the most powerful crime families in the country. My dad told me so."

"Why are you whispering?"

"I don't know!"

"Clearly, this is upsetting to you," she said calmly.

"Would this not be upsetting to you?"

"We're not talking about me. This is about you. I don't have a crush on Lex."

"I didn't say it was a crush."

"I was kidding. It's obviously much worse than a crush."

"Ugh." I covered my face with my hands again.

"Lex, huh?"

I peeked at her between my fingers. "What?"

"Nothing."

Obviously, it wasn't nothing. Knowing Roni, she was probably picturing Lex and wondering what he'd be like in bed.

My hands dropped from my face. "*What?*"

"He's cute," she said thoughtfully.

"He's not," I said firmly. "Baby bunnies are cute. He's…"

She watched me squirm, unable to find the right word. Then she decided to inform me, "Devi calls him 'stealth sexy.'"

Devi? Devi Davenport?

Devi married Lex's half-brother, Dane Davenport, last year. Besides that, Devi's best friend, Katie Mayes, was married to Jude's best friend, Jesse Mayes, Dirty's lead guitarist. We were a tight knit bunch that had just gotten more... entangled... over time. I really couldn't have avoided Lex Davenport if I tried. And I *did* try.

Really, I did.

"What does that even mean?" I said, frustrated. Annoyed, too, that the girls had been talking about Lex. And calling him sexy.

"You know," she said casually, "like chill sexy. Laid-back sexy. Sexy that sneaks up on a girl."

"Stop saying sexy."

"Why?" she inquired, not innocently. "Did his sexiness sneak up on you?" There was some not-small part of her that was loving this.

"No."

Yes. Unfortunately, Lex had snuck up on me when I was ten years old, invaded my system, and never really left.

"Look," she said gently, "from what I've heard from Jude, Lex isn't involved with the Mafia. He's patched in with the Kings, which means he *can't* be involved with the Mafia. He doesn't even see his dad. And if that's what Jude says, it's true. He doesn't lie to me."

"Honestly, does he tell you everything, though?"

Roni's eyes narrowed a little, and I worried that I'd offended her.

"I'm sorry—"

"Of course he doesn't tell me everything," she said simply. "He protects me. And he'll protect Lex."

"It's that simple?"

"It's that simple. It doesn't matter who his father is. Lex has *brothers* who will kill and die for him. That's what it means to wear Kings colors. You don't need to worry about his dad. So, moving on," she said crisply, like that was all solved. "Let's assume that the Mafia thing is not a problem. Is it really a problem for you that he's a biker?"

"Not just a biker, Roni. An outlaw biker. I don't have to explain to you what that is. We're not talking about guys who ride motorcycles on the weekend because they like bikes. It's a *gang*."

She rolled her eyes again. "It's not a gang."

"It's a criminal organization, any way you slice it. You can Google that shit. It's not a secret. Ask any cop."

"I know what the Kings are."

"And it doesn't bother you?"

"No. Frankly, it doesn't. I've known bikers all my life. And yes, I mean outlaw bikers. They're not bad people. At least, the Kings aren't. These guys aren't smuggling stolen women in cargo crates for sex slavery. They're not evil. If Lex was evil, believe me, the Kings wouldn't allow him in their midst. They wouldn't accept him as a brother."

Okay. That was calming my nerves a bit.

"So," she went on, "let's also assume that you can get past the fact that Lex is a biker. Now we have Lex, the man. How do you feel about *him*?"

"I don't know. That's the problem."

"Well, you feel something. You dragged my ass in here and put on Emotional Oranges," she pointed out, referring to my music selection, "and cracked a bottle of Chandon, kicked out your roommates, and now you're pacing a hole in the carpet. Over Lex."

"Not just Lex," I protested. "Carl, too."

"Okay. So let's start with Carl. How do you feel about him, really?" She added that *really* with a dose of skepticism. And I could see why she'd be skeptical. Because here I was, sweating over another man.

"I do love him," I insisted. That question was easier to answer.

"Uh-huh." She sounded unconvinced. "But are you *in love* with him?"

"Yes. I mean…" I paused, thinking about that. What did it feel like to be in love anyway? Did I even know? "You know… in general."

"Talia." Roni leveled me with an *Are you fucking serious?* look. "You don't fall in love with a man *in general*. You fall in love with very specific shit. Now tell me some very specific shit that you love about Carl."

"Well. I mean, I care about him, a lot."

"Sure. Let's cut right to it, babe. Does he or does he not make your lady parts scream? And I don't even mean when he's touching you. I mean, from across a crowded room. He catches your eye, and what happens? What do you *feel*?"

I wasn't sure. I couldn't even quite picture that scenario.

For some reason, all my mind conjured was the look of self-doubt and fear on his face when he found me kissing Lex in her bathtub.

"We have a great connection," I insisted, failing to come up with an example of said connection. All I could think about was how quickly he'd forgiven me for kissing Lex—and how I still couldn't decide if that made him a hero or a pussy. "At least, we had. On tour. I don't know. It's been… different since I got home."

"Since you saw Lex again at my house party," she filled in.

I said nothing, just started gnawing on a fingernail.

"If you're gonna do that, at least chew something tastier." She tossed the bag of Fuzzy Peaches at me.

I tore into it and popped one into my mouth.

"Okay. So that's Carl," she said. "Now let's talk about Lex. And not Lex the biker. Lex the man. And don't give me this *I don't know* shit. Dig deep, baby. How do you feel about Lex? Right now."

I sucked in a deep breath through my nose as I chewed on the sweet-sour peach gummy. "Not sure?" I said, but I knew that wasn't gonna fly with Roni, either.

"Close your eyes."

I sighed and closed my eyes, still chewing.

"Picture him in your head."

"Okay." I pictured him at her party, staring at me across the room, and I felt my whole body squirm. Roni probably saw it.

"Remember, he's not a biker. So, take the Kings cut off him."

Yeah, I could do that. All I had to do was picture him at her summer barbecue with his shirt off—

"And while you're at it… take off his pants."

My eyes flew open.

"Ha! I knew it."

"Roni. *Help me.*" I stashed a few more Fuzzy Peaches into my mouth. Chewing furiously, I confessed, "I need to find out what this lingering, annoying, frustrating thing is! Am I really into Lex, despite all my better sense? Am I just trying to avoid my future with Carl? Is this cold feet already? When I haven't even said yes? Should I say yes??" I was now walking in a circle, round and round the living room carpet, the same way my mind had been going in circles ever since I saw Lex at her party. "Am I crazy? Would I just be tossing away a good thing with Carl if I don't say yes? Does Lex have anything to offer me? Could he actually be the man for me? Why do I kind of want him to be the man for me, when I know he's so wrong for me? Should I try to convince Lex to take a chance on us, and see what happens? *Why do I want to do this so bad??*"

"Do what?" Roni said calmly.

I felt so not calm, I was dizzy. Maybe it was the circles. I stopped, and my head was all woozy. The room spun.

"Do *Lex*," I grit out.

Roni plucked the candy bag from my hand. "Okay, clearly, you're at a crossroads. And you're deeply confused. To me, you sound like you're trying to convince yourself to say yes to Carl and not to give Lex a chance, and I don't know why that is. I don't know if that's the right way to go or not. I'm not saying go with Lex. But I am saying… you can't say yes to Carl when you feel this way. It's not fair to either of you."

"But—"

"No buts. Not right now." Roni eyed me as I tried to swallow the chewy wad of peach candy in my mouth. "Honestly babe, you need to get some sleep. You don't seem to be doing so well right now." She got to her feet. Then she smoothed my hair off my forehead, like a big sister or something. "You need to take care of yourself."

"But—"

"Nope. No buts. You come first."

I blinked at her. I did not expect this. Roni was five years older than me, she'd always been strong and independent, but she'd never given off "concerned big sister" vibes. When I met her she was single and, frankly, she was a party animal. She told me Jude's friends called her *wild card.*

She really hadn't changed since then, in most ways, though she was devoted to Jude now. And I could see why. Tall, dark, and the silent alpha type, Jude Grayson was a giant slab of virile, muscular man candy. With dimples. And a great ass.

She was in love with a badass biker. So why wasn't she encouraging me to go wild on this?

"Give it some time, Tal."

"Time," I echoed stupidly.

Time? Like Roni gave her thing with Jude, fucking years of pining for each other from afar, breaking each other's hearts, before they finally got together?

No thanks. This was already torture enough.

At least Roni knew what she wanted all those years. She wanted Jude.

I didn't even know what I wanted, and I kind of hated myself for it right now.

"Should I... Should I go see Lex, though?" I squeaked out. "Like, go talk to him, and—"

"No."

"But maybe we could—"

"No, Talia," she said firmly. "Just no."

So, I agreed with her.

I promised her I wouldn't go see him. I wouldn't even consider talking to him until I sorted myself out and could see more clearly on this. Until I was feeling way more rational and less vulnerable. Until I knew, for sure, what I wanted.

I even promised her I'd go to bed early tonight and get some sleep, take care of myself and see how I felt about things in the morning.

I put aside the Chandon and drank some water. We ate guacamole while we listened to music and chatted about the tour; Roni was an event promoter and had joined Dirty's management team in planning out the last tour. We hadn't really debriefed/dished about it yet, just the two of us.

All the while, she seemed to be making sure I was chilling out, that I was okay.

I wasn't okay.

I was feeling torn between a man I was supposed to love and a man I knew was wrong for me. Very, very torn.

And as soon as Roni went home, I went out.

Within an hour of lying to one of my best friends and sneaking out of my own home like a rebellious teenager, I rolled up to the compound where the Kings had their clubhouse, alone.

Chapter Seven

Talia

I parked along the grassy shoulder of the dark rural road, a little way back from the gate to the Kings' compound. They called themselves Vancouver Kings, but the clubhouse wasn't even in the city; it was on the outskirts of Maple Ridge.

It was quiet out here. Mostly farmland, some industrial lots. No one seemed to be around, and I felt weirdly like a thief stealing through the night.

At least my car was super silent. I drove a brand new Nissan Leaf, paid for by my dad, because Antonio De Santis believed in providing for his daughter. Unfortunately, he didn't believe in providing me with a Porsche. Too much power.

I could've bought my own car, maybe not one this new, but who turned down a free car? It never occurred to me before that maybe it wasn't cool enough.

As I got out, I felt like a daddy's girl—and I wondered what my dad would have to say about this.

Nothing good.

I also wondered, as I looked up at the unwelcoming fence

around the compound, what Lex would think of my ride. He drove a Chevelle from, I wasn't even sure, the sixties or seventies? Black with white racing stripes up the hood, one of those old cars that polluted both the air and your ears. Loud engine, loud exhaust, loud music you could hear thumping a block away when he pulled up to a party.

When he wasn't riding his motorcycle.

Ugh. Just the thought of him straddling his Harley, all laid back as he tore down the road with his club brothers like some gangster god made ridiculous things happen in my groin area.

My knees were bare, wind was blowing up my cooch, and I was already starting to shiver in the cold. Why did I decide to put on this dress? I was really more of a jeans girl. I'd chosen this dress deliberately, though; it was clingy and soft, a light-blue knit, mid-thigh length, and I felt both cute as hell and sexy in it. It was wet out but not raining, and I'd decided to pair it with boots. And because I was pretending it was warm enough, I'd put on my little white leather jacket, the one that came only halfway down my ribs.

What was I trying to be, ready for this? Because I owned a leather jacket?

I so wasn't ready for this.

When I came here the other night with Jude and Roni, I'd been a guest. At a big, raucous party. And even then I wouldn't have gotten in the door without Jude. Roni had told me so; that she didn't get in the door without Jude, and she lived with him.

I dug into my purse and fished out the open bag of Fuzzy Peaches. I stuffed a couple in my mouth, but before I could get the bag back into my purse, I spilled a bunch. They scattered into the mud and mucky grass at my feet.

Shit. And now I'd left a candy trail that I was here. That was creepy, somehow.

But hey, at least if anything bad happened to me, maybe the police could use the DNA in my spit, recovered from a Fuzzy Peach, to identify me.

Very funny.

Chewing furiously, I stuffed the rest of the candy back into my purse, trying not to step on one and get it stuck on my white boots. They were mid-calf height and cute, and glaringly bright in the dark. When I used to work with Roni on nightclub events, I'd drive home late at night, past this one street corner in downtown Vancouver where a whole bunch of prostitutes hung out; they all wore tall white boots. It was like hooker code for *I'm open tonight.*

Why I was remembering that right now and not at the moment I bought these boots, I'd never know. I swallowed my Fuzzy Peaches in a glob.

Yeah, I couldn't do this.

I got back into my practical car that still smelled of new car smell and peach candy. Lex's car probably smelled like weed and car exhaust and sex.

Why did that even sound appealing?

It totally did.

Because it probably also smelled like *him.*

I liked how he smelled. Like fresh laundry and leather and guy hair product and, yeah, weed. And sometimes beer. And sometimes so much lust for me that it oozed from his pores and threatened to drown us both. Like the other night when I licked his neck and sucked on his nipple… and almost gave him a blow job.

You know, if he'd actually *let* me give him a blow job.

Why didn't he let me give him a blow job??

My stomach sucked itself into a tiny black hole just thinking about it.

You can do this, I tried to pep talk myself. *You need answers.*
You need to do this.
No, actually. You don't.
Yes. No.
Yes.
No.
It was like a devil and an angel on my shoulders, except for

some reason I was picturing my boobs arguing with each other. Because obviously, I needed psychiatric help. And maybe because as soon as I started thinking about Lex's smell, my nipples started humming. One of them was in Lex's camp, and the other was firmly in camp Carl. I was split right down the middle.

"No. No, I can't do this," I said. *Out loud, to my fucking boob.*

Like a crazy person.

And I could've sworn my left nipple whispered at me, *Yessssss.*

Then I looked up and saw a biker staring at me.

There was a massive chainlink fence topped with razor wire, all around the Kings' compound, and a wood fence just inside, so you couldn't even see through. Except at the big gate across the drive-way. There was a guy in a biker vest standing there, just inside the gate, smoking and looking right at me.

Well, fuck. *Busted.*

Which would be worse, now? Actually going in there to see Lex, or leaving with my tail between my legs, and Lex hearing about it? I mean, how many blondes in hooker boots who drove a Pearl White Nissan Leaf and ate Fuzzy Peach candies while they argued with themselves could they possibly see around these parts?

I grabbed my purse and hopped back out, pasting a smile on my face for my new friend, the random biker. I tossed my hair back and walked on over to him, almost twisting my heel as my boot sank in the soft, grassy mud.

"Careful," he said mildly, as I approached the chainlink gate and he tossed his cigarette or whatever he was smoking casually aside. Yup. Cigarette. The cloud of smoke he exhaled hit me full in the face. "Slippery out there."

"Thanks," I said brightly, trying not to cough. "Oh, and... hi!"

He said nothing in return, just stared at me, like *What the fuck do you want.*

I searched his vest for a hint at his identity, and maybe his importance?

Important enough, if he's inside the gate and you're not.

He had one of those patches with a rank on it like Jude's brother and some of his friends did—Vice President, Sergeant-at-Arms, etcetera—but this guy's said *Prospect*. Also, some of those guys had their nickname on a patch, too. They called it a "road name." This guy didn't. I didn't know what that meant.

Lex didn't have one of those patches either. He didn't even have a road name, that I knew of.

Wait. Did Lex have a road name? A secret name that I didn't even know?

Holy shit, what was I doing here? I didn't belong here. Did I seriously think I'd just look pretty and say hi and they'd sweep open the locked gate for me? How many girls had tried that one and failed?

"Um." I cleared my throat when he just stared at me, choking on any actual words.

Okay. *Read the room.*

All I knew about this guy was a) he didn't seem thrilled to see me, b) I met him in passing at Lex's birthday party and thought he must've been wasted because he kinda talked funny, and c) I could now see that he had a hearing aid in his ear. His brown hair was clipped short; I couldn't see the other ear because he was sort of side-eying me, even though I was standing right in front of him. But that probably explained why his speech was a little odd. He was deaf, or partly deaf?

"Um," I tried again, "I'm here to see Lex." I leaned closer and mouthed, "Lex-ing-ton," exaggeratedly, in case he needed to lip read.

"I'm not stu-pid," he enunciated back. He raised a finger and pointed it like a gun at his hearing aid. "And I can hear you."

"Oh, right. Sorry. Um, amazing what they can do with medical science these days, huh?"

He just stared at me some more.

"You can ride a motorcycle, pull guard duty at night, imagine what you can hear that you couldn't hear before. Do you have to turn it down, though, when you ride, so it doesn't hurt your ears? My aunt has one and she has to adjust the levels depending on what she's doing, how noisy the environment is…"

You're babbling again. Please stop.

"Hopefully it doesn't rain. Do you have to stand out here, even if it's raining?"

Stop. Talking.

"What do you want, Blondie?"

"Um… Lex." It was humiliating how fast I felt myself blushing. "I mean… is he here?"

"You don't know if he's here," he said, "I've got no reason to tell you."

"Right. Of course. I get that. He's a friend of mine, though. A coworker. He'll want to see me." *I think.* "Look."

I dug out my phone and searched for the photo I knew was on there somewhere. It took a while, and the guy sighed a little. But I finally found it and showed it to him. It was me and Lex, smiling at the camera, a random image that our tour photographer, Amber, had taken on the first night of the Hell & Back tour—while we were making nice and pretending to be friendly when people were looking. And yes, I'd seen it on her website, downloaded it and kept it.

We could examine that later though. Or not.

"See? Friendly. Can you please tell him I'm here? My name is Talia. Or, let me in so I can go find him? If you're busy with guard duty, I don't want to trouble you."

He laughed. I thought that was a very nice offer on my part, but he actually laughed at me.

"Here's what I can do for you, sweetheart. Why don't you go back to your little car and drive your ass home, and I'll let him know you stopped by. Whenever he's finished banging the lineup of hot bitches he's got inside."

Well. That was rude.

I stood back a bit and took a better read of this guy.

He was really trying to scare me away. But I heard bullshit talk like that all the time. Hello, I worked and toured with a rock band. I practically lived with our road crew half the time. This guy didn't even look as rough as a roadie. He looked like the guys I went to high school with. The ones who smoked outside and skipped classes and wanted to be badasses when they grew up. He was probably younger than me, too.

On closer inspection, he didn't scare me much. He was just a baby biker. A biker in training. He probably wasn't even allowed to actually hurt me or anything.

If he so much as blew smoke on me again, I'd make damn sure Jude heard about it. I'd keep that in my back pocket, just in case. No way this guy wasn't afraid of Jude. Roni told me that the "prospects" generally hung around outside to guard the members' bikes and do grunt work and stuff. They wanted into the club, but they weren't even in yet.

I narrowed my eyes at him. "So, what if he is banging a lineup of girls right now?" *Let's hope not. It's counterproductive to our goal here,* my left nipple whispered. "And what if I'm his favorite girl, you know, like his old lady—" that was what they called their girlfriends, right? "—and you talked to me like that?"

He stared me down, cold. But I could see it in his eyes: a little flicker of uncertainty. Yes, he was doing his duty. But. What if Lex was gonna kick his ass for sending me off into the night?

"You're just a prospect, right?"

His eyes narrowed as he took a better read of me. He didn't like that the girlie girl in the electric car understood the lingo.

"That's why you're out here, manning the gate. And I'm sure you get all kinds of people showing up here wanting in, telling you stories, lying to you. But I'm not that person. I just want to see Lex. I know he lives here."

He seemed to be thinking about it, or maybe just considering how to rephrase telling me to fuck off, when a car approached on the road behind me. A loud car. A classic, powerful, panty-dropping kind of car, thumping music into the night.

I turned as it rumbled up, slowing to a stop. The driver revved the engine, like *Get the fuck out of my way.* I squinted into the headlights and saw white stripes leading up the black hood, and my stomach did a ridiculous flip.

Then I heard metal clinking and turned back to find the prospect unlocking the gate.

"You want Lex, sweetheart," he said, "you just found him. Now, I'd suggest you move your ass so he doesn't run you over." He drew open the gate, moving aside with it.

I scrambled to follow him as Lex's car roared past, into the lot. For a split second his eyes met mine through the driver's side window, and *yikes.*

He did not look happy to see me. Like, way less happy than this prospect dude.

"*Tssst,*" the prospect hissed, as he jabbed me in the clavicle with his fingertips—like he was the fucking Dog Whisperer and I was a naughty stray who'd stepped out of line or something. "Back," he snarled. "Didn't say you could come in."

I backed up a few paces as Lex's car jerked to a stop. The engine died and he got out, slamming the door. And stalked right over to us.

"Why you standing out here with her?" he demanded.

Oh, thank Christ. He was yelling at him, not at me.

The prospect's jaw unhinged, then snapped shut.

"You gonna let her just stand there freezing to death?" Lex growled.

The prospect's eyes shot straight to my bare knees, with a guilty look. I was hugging myself in my tiny leather jacket and bouncing from foot to foot to try to keep warm.

"And *you,*" Lex snarled, turning his dark gaze on me. *Ruh-roh.* "The hell are you doing here?"

"Uh... I..."

"Forget it," he snapped. "Get your ass out of the cold." With that, he grabbed my hand and started toward the clubhouse so fast I had to follow or fall on my face. His grip on my hand was like a vise.

A hot, manly vise that was sending all kinds of erratic signals back and forth between my nipples and my vagina. *Yes. No. NO. Oh, but YES!*

And once again, the yeses won.

———

Lex dragged me into the clubhouse bar, which looked and felt completely different than it did two nights ago. Maybe partly because I was so sober.

Angry, bluesy, lust-heavy rock music was playing quietly and the room was dimly lit. Glowing beer signs. Christmas lights that had obviously been there all year, wrapped around the bar. Pendant lights with chips in them over the pool tables.

There were five guys, all bikers, splayed out on the couches, plus one woman sitting in a guy's lap.

They all looked at me when we walked in, and stopped talking. They'd been drinking beer, but now they were doing nothing but staring at me.

The guys were wearing Kings vests, but I only recognized one of them. He did a shot with me at Lex's party. The huge Sergeant-at-Arms guy.

Lex said nothing to them as he dragged me past. But they were still staring, so I lifted my hand in a little wave. "Hello. I'm Talia."

"Nice to meet you, Talia," said the woman, slyly. She gave me a big smile. She looked and sounded drunk.

The guy she was sitting on squeezed her boob right in front of my eyes.

She laughed, and I averted my eyes, focusing instead on the back of Lex's vest. There were four patches on the black leather. One that arched across the top and said WEST COAST KINGS. The one at the bottom said VANCOUVER. There was a little one on the side that said MC. And then there was the big one in the middle, with the skeleton king on it. Just like the tattoo on his back, it was the king of spades, like from a playing card except all black and way less friendly. And more dead.

"You know," I told him, as he pulled me right past the bar where some young guy was stocking booze, and through a door next to it, "you guys might not have such a problem with people assuming you're bad all the time if you changed up your logo."

"Quiet," Lex ground out.

Wow. *Grouchy.*

He pulled me all the way down a long hall, up a flight of narrow stairs, into another hall lined with doors. He produced keys from his jeans and unlocked a door, then basically tossed me into the room as he flicked on a light.

It was a bedroom.

Lex followed me in and slammed the door shut. I noticed he locked it behind us.

I looked around. "Is this your room?" It was fairly neat, with an unmade, queen-sized bed, just a mattress and boxspring on the floor, a cheap dresser, and a bedside table with a bag of weed and lighters and books stacked on it.

At the top of the stack was a well-read paperback of *The Count of Monte Cristo* with like twenty Post-It Notes poking out of it. Underneath that, I glimpsed a translation of *The Iliad.*

"You read... Homer?"

Lex didn't answer me. He just yanked open a deep drawer in the bedside table, swiped the entire stack of books into it and unceremoniously closed it.

I blinked at him, curious. "It's poetry."

"It's not."

"It literally is. It's a love story."

"It's war and destruction," he growled.

"Uh-huh. Because of..." my voice faded at the look on his face, "... a love story," I whispered.

I watched him go into the adjoining bathroom. He closed a door on the far side, then came back into the bedroom, locking the bathroom door behind him with a scowl still affixed on his face.

Okay… *Change the subject.*

"You have a roommate? That's cute. Me, too. Actually, I have two."

Wrong subject, apparently. Lex glared at me as he sat down on the edge of the bed, right in front of me. Not relaxed at all. Elbows on his knees and hands pressed together in the middle.

It was the only place to sit, so I kept standing.

He looked up at me, like *Start talking.*

I looked around again, but there wasn't much to see. There wasn't even a window.

It smelled like him in here. Like clean laundry and his man soap and weed.

When I met his eyes again, he was still glaring at me. "What are you doing, opening your mouth out there?" he demanded. "Telling them your name? You shouldn't even be here, much less talking to those guys."

"I was here the other night."

"Does this look like the other night to you?"

"I thought they were your club brothers."

"You don't belong here." His eyes raked over my body, from top to bottom. They landed on my white boots, then met my eyes again, looking even more… irritable.

Okay, I got it. I showed up here unexpected and unannounced. And maybe he just came back from… a drug deal gone awry? Or who knew what. I had no idea what he did with his time when he wasn't working security for Dirty.

"I know I don't belong here. But… you live here." It was barely more than a whisper. I swallowed when that just seemed to annoy him more. "How else am I supposed to find you?"

"Why do you need to find me?" he said, his voice low and even.

Man, he was really in a worse mood than the last time I saw him, when his dick was hard.

"I just needed to talk to you."

"So, talk."

"That guy outside said you were having sex with a lineup of girls in here," I said, avoiding getting to the point. "To try to scare me away."

"That guy outside is none of your business. Same with everything else that goes on here."

"But you live here," I repeated.

"Yeah. I live here."

I looked around again at his very basic room. In this veritable fortress. And I felt like a jerk nosing my way in. But did he really not want to see me, at all? Was he really trying to protect me from those guys in the bar?

Or was he trying to do the honorable thing, because I told him I was semi-engaged?

Maybe it was the way he'd tried to resist me, even when his dick was hard, but something told me he'd *try* to do the honorable thing. Not for Carl, though. For me.

"You keep trying to act like there's nothing between us," I said softly. "But there is. You can't deny that there is. Maybe there always was, in a weird way."

He said nothing. He didn't deny.

He also didn't agree with me.

"I think you were hot for me on the Hell & Back tour." There. I said it.

His eyes darkened as he studied me, and I tried not to squirm. As kids, we'd been alone together a lot. As adults, I'd never been alone with him in close quarters like this. Except for that one horrible night on my tour bus when he blew me off. And, in that bathtub the other night.

The uncertainty between us charged the air with an electricity that was at once exhilarating and mildly terrifying.

I wasn't even sure how I was going to survive it if he ever actually touched me. Like put his hands on me—and not to push me away.

"I was hot for you," he said, his voice like sex on fire, "long before that."

Whoa. I did not expect him to admit that.

At the same time, I felt the molten rush of victory flood my veins. *I fucking knew it.*

But why did he still seem angry?

"Then why didn't you ever act on it?"

"Because Jude suggested I leave you alone."

"Suggested?"

"Strongly suggested."

"Oh." I considered that. I wasn't even sure if I should be irritated that Jude stepped in like that, or appreciative. "Is that like a rule or something? You can't touch me now?"

"It's not a rule. One of my brothers would never cockblock me like that without a reason. He was just looking out for you. That's what he does. He could see the career path you were on with Brody's team, and he didn't want me to cause a problem for you."

"What do you mean? What kind of problem?"

"The kind of problem where you let me up your skirt one night," he said bluntly, "and then I turn around and tear out your heart and stomp it into the dirt. And now Jude and Brody have a problem where one of their valued employees is refusing to show up to work because she might run into the dirty biker who broke her heart, instead of doing the job they need her to do."

I frowned. "Jude said that?"

"It was implied."

I shook my head. "But… you still want me?"

"I never said that."

"But, this thing between us—"

"There is no thing between us."

I stared at him. He stared right back. He was lying to me. I knew he was.

Why?

"Look, all that time we spent on the road," I tried again, "I sensed you were avoiding me. There has to be a reason and not just because Jude made a suggestion. Maybe you were drawn to me, and that was complicated, I know. We're... different. But that doesn't mean it couldn't work."

He looked unmoved. "That was a long time ago."

"It wasn't that long ago."

"You went on a whole other tour since then. I stayed here."

I studied him. His impenetrable gaze. His rigid, closed body language. His attempt to shut me out.

"Is that why you didn't come on this tour?"

He didn't answer right away, and I knew. That was exactly why.

"Don't tell me you missed me," he said flatly.

"I didn't." *Damn*, I was a terrible liar. "I was busy."

"Right. Carl."

"I meant, I was busy with my job. And yeah... then there was Carl."

"So what the hell are you doing here?"

I dug deep for the right words. What *was* I doing here? "Finding out."

"Finding out what?"

I took a small breath and held his gaze when I said, "If I should marry the man I love, or if that would be a mistake."

Silence.

As we stared each other down, his tongue swiped over his bottom lip. He either wanted to eat my face or kill somebody. And my ovaries twitched with want. *Yes*, they hissed, like witches over a cauldron, *we like this one*. I could practically feel them priming eggs for release.

"Do you love him?" Lex growled, his voice like gravel.

"Yes."

NO! my ovaries chorused. *Tell him you want HIM. Only him. We'll save him the best eggs!*

I shook my head. God, my imagination was annoying at times.

"And he loves you?"

"Yes."

"Then what are you doing here, Talia," he growled again.

"I just… need to know," I said, aggravated. "Because my ovaries are turning into conniving witches who speak to me when you're around, and I'm going crazy."

Now he frowned, like I *was* fucking crazy.

I gathered my thoughts and tried again. "I… I just need to know if whatever this is that's drawing me to you is *something*. If it has substance. If it's worth throwing away a marriage and a life with a perfectly good man over. If you could give me any of the things that he could. If any of the time I've spent thinking about you and asking myself these questions *means* anything. If it's all been a waste. If I'm a fucking fool. If I'm just confused and hopeless. If you want me like I want you or not. If I can be that girl who breaks a good man's heart for no damn reason just because she's chasing a fantasy with someone who's not even worth her time. If you're as wrong for me as I think you are—" I ran out of breath, then words. My voice broke.

Lex said nothing while I stood panting in front of him, laying everything out for him.

"Are you really just gonna sit there and let me do this all myself, like some one-sided conversation, while you stare at me?"

"Yup."

"That's not very nice."

"I'm not the one who just showed up where you live, unannounced, looking to bare my soul."

I sighed in frustration. "It's not my soul I want to bare."

His eyes flared.

But it was too late. He couldn't have stopped me. My leather jacket was on the floor, and my dress up over my head in seconds.

And here's the really twisted part: I wasn't wearing anything underneath.

I tossed the dress aside. I stood naked in front of Lex and I could see the shock on his face. Probably the only reason he didn't try to stop me. It happened too fast and too unexpectedly, and now I was panting in front of him, completely starkers.

His Adam's apple bobbed when he swallowed. His jaw flexed, then hardened, as his dark eyes drank me in. His entire body hardened.

"You keep hiding from me," I gushed in desperation, "from *us*, vanishing into the night like some cold ghost, pretending I've got nothing you want. But now maybe you can't ignore me. Not if you want me like I think you do."

His eyes were lost somewhere near my pussy. Actually, they were laser locked on my pussy.

Then he blinked and dragged his gaze back up my curves, to my breasts. My nipples thrummed as his eyes raked over them.

I squirmed, trying not to cover myself. It was instinctual. Instead, I clasped my hands behind my back.

His eyes met mine, and the look in them solidified. And not into devout lust or appreciation or even resistance—but into a thousand shades of mean.

I took a step back, bumping into the wall behind me, as he got to his feet. All six-feet-tall of him. Lex wasn't a huge guy compared to some of his biker friends, but he was huge enough. Like way bigger than me.

And I'd never seen him look like *that*.

Was this him turned on? Because it looked kinda… murdery.

"Lex, I—"

He took the few steps to get in my face—and my words choked off as he wrapped his hand around my throat.

Chapter Eight

Lex

I held Talia against the wall, by the throat, which was literally the only place I trusted myself to touch her because she was *fucking naked.* So much blood was slamming to my dick, my jeans felt two sizes too small and I was lightheaded. I could barely focus on her face.

Her mouth was open. She smelled sweet, like peaches and candy and the most wholesome thing I'd ever been this close to.

I could feel her tremble, her breaths coming hard and fast. She was definitely at least half as turned on as she was scared. Her eyes had glazed over with lust and trepidation. With that fucking sex look girls got when they were so turned on they'd probably let you do anything.

What did she think I was gonna do?

"Listen to me," I told her, my voice low and tight. I looked her dead in the eyes at close range and told her, "You're a good girl, Talia. Go marry your good boy. And don't come back here."

I released her and was out the door, slamming it shut behind myself, before she could blink. I strode down the hall with a fucking hard-on and down the stairs so fast I barely remembered taking them, and slammed through the door to the bar.

"Prospect!" I snapped, and Toad, who was working the bar, looked up.

He hustled straight over to me. "Yeah, Lex."

I grabbed him by the shirt, yanked him into the hallway, put him up against the wall.

"Listen closely," I growled, right in his face. He smelled like beer, pickles, and dude, so at least that was helping kill the hard-on. "Three things."

"Yeah, Lex."

"First. There's a girl in my room. You make sure she gets out of here, fast and safe. You put her in her car and send her on her way. It's parked out on the road."

"Yeah, Lex."

"Second, give me your keys."

"What?"

"Keys. To your truck." I put out my open hand.

He started to protest but thought better of it, dug the keys out of his jeans and put them in my hand.

"Third," I told him, "after you walk her out of here—" I slammed him against the wall again to make sure I had his full attention on this "—you *fix my fucking car*."

His face went red as he realized he'd fucked up. He was supposed to take care of that, fucking yesterday while I was in Ontario.

"I—"

"It just about died on me again. And you know what happens the next time that happens?"

I released him and he smiled a bit, nervously, waiting for the punch line. Usually, I was the guy cracking jokes around here. I wasn't in a real humorous mood today, though. I'd rather let him hang and wonder what his punishment would be if he didn't get this right.

His smile evaporated. "Sorry, Lex. I'll get it fixed. Take it over to my brother's shop, right now—"

"You do that."

I stalked back into the bar. Left him there, probably wondering what the hell was up my ass. I never went off on guys like that. I didn't toss people around to get what I wanted, and I usually went pretty easy on the prospects.

I ignored my brothers who were still hanging out, listening in, amusing themselves with the entertainment I'd just provided.

"Have a nice time with your little blonde guest, Lex?" Blazer smiled at me from a couch, smug as shit. Obviously, I wasn't acting like a guy who'd just gotten good and laid.

"Yeah, Lex," Axel put in with a lazy grin. "She waitin' for us back there?"

Assholes. Axel, though, was like an actual brother to me. Maddox's big brother had basically adopted my bastard ass years ago. I gave him the finger.

"No one touches her," I informed them.

I pushed out through the front door and gestured at Finn to open the fucking gate, as he materialized from the shadows. I stalked over to Toad's truck. He had an old F-150 that he loved, and as far as I was concerned it was mine until he fixed my car like he was supposed to.

Fucking prospects.

I got in and slammed the door. Stashed a blunt between my lips and lit up. An entire goddamn year I wore that prospect patch, working my ass off to prove myself to the club, and look at these fucking kids we let in here these days.

I waited, smoking in the dark and fucking fuming. That *No one touches her* shit would only go so far. They wouldn't go out of their way to touch her now. But if they thought, for any reason, that she *wanted* to be touched, different story, maybe. Depending on the guy.

Like maybe if one of them walked into my room and found her buck naked?

Shit, why didn't I lock the door?

I just had to fly out of there so fucking fast, put space between me and her naked flesh and that look in her eyes. The one that said *I want you inside me.*

I gripped the steering wheel, white-knuckling it, resisting the urge to go back in there. Couldn't believe Talia De Santis just took off her fucking clothes in my room, showed me her pretty pussy and her perfect, perky tits, practically begged me to put it in. And I walked away.

Fuck my life.

And fuck my fucking father.

I watched, my eyes locked on the clubhouse door. What was taking so damn long? Ten more seconds and I was going back in there and dragging her out myself.

I pulled out my phone to call Toad, when the clubhouse door opened and Talia stepped out. Fully dressed, hugging herself, her purse clutched to her ribs. She looked embarrassed. And like she wanted to be anywhere but here.

Good.

Toad followed her out. She walked quickly across the parking lot and through the open gate. She stumbled on the way to her car, on the soft shoulder, and I wasn't sure what pissed me off more— the fact that Toad touched her when he caught her arm to try to save her from falling, or the fact that he was too slow about it. He caught her after she'd already steadied herself.

She shook off his hand, turned to say something to him. Knowing her, it was a thank you.

He stood there and watched her get into her car.

I waited while she started up. Headlights went on and she rolled out, slow, doing a tight U-turn on the road, then heading back to Vancouver. I gave her a generous head start, then followed at a distance.

Since meeting with my father yesterday, I'd barely slept. I'd barely eaten.

I'd tailed her everywhere.

Only lost sight of her today, briefly, on the way to the clubhouse, when my fucking car died and it took me a few minutes to get it going again. But by that point, it was obvious where she was headed.

Why, though?

I thought maybe she was upset about the other night, how I'd turned her down at the party, sent her home. Maybe she was coming to give me a piece of her mind. Tell me she was marrying fucking Carl, and she never wanted to see me again. Make a scene.

But, no. What she wanted, apparently, was to ask me if she was making a mistake marrying her semi-fiancé.

And to get naked in front of me.

What the fuck was she thinking?

I'd rolled out that excuse about Jude warning me to stay away from her because it was both convenient and true; didn't seem to faze her, though.

Neither did the fact that I was no good for her, and clearly, she knew it.

Jude made that suggestion on pretty much day one of the Hell & Back tour, when maybe he'd picked up on the vibe between her and me. It was a powerful vibe, and obviously, it wasn't going anywhere.

But Jude, her career, her semi-engagement, none of this was the reason I needed her to stay the fuck away from me.

The girl was innocent to a fault.

She had no idea the heat of the fire she was playing with.

———

I followed Talia all the way home from the clubhouse.

That night, I slept in Toad's truck, parked up the block from her modern steel-and-colored-glass condo building in Mount Pleasant. Same as I did the night before.

Now that she wasn't on tour, and the Players were on a little break before they started writing their next album, she had a pretty casual schedule. I knew that, because I followed her the next day and the next.

I tailed her all fucking week.

I followed her from her place to the stores where she went shopping, and waited outside. I tailed her to a hair salon, to a home decor store where she bought a lamp, to the fucking bakery. I tailed her to Brody's house a few times, where she obviously had meetings. And at night, I tailed her to various restaurants and bars, to meet her girlfriends for drinks.

And yeah, it occurred to me how fucked-up it was that I could stalk her like this, and she never even knew I was there.

But the fact was, I was born a criminal. Theft was in my blood. And right now, I was stealing Talia's privacy, one moment at a time. For my father.

Because I really didn't have another choice.

Chapter Nine

Lex

T he first time my father made me pay penance for the sin of abandoning him was on my eighteenth birthday.

I'd lived in Toronto growing up, not with him but with my mom. When I was thirteen, she'd brought me out to Vancouver to visit friends and we ended up staying. She didn't tell me beforehand that was the plan, but I wasn't exactly mad about it.

By that point I'd already heard enough, seen enough, to be scared of my own father.

I knew she was scared of him, too, at least sometimes. Like the times when he was back with his wife, according to her.

Truth was, he was always with his wife. He never left her for us.

I thought my mom had finally had enough and was running away from him. Apparently, she was running around with her sister's ex-husband—Dane's father. I didn't know that then. I only found out last year, same time Dane did, that my mom was his mom; that she'd had an affair with his dad that had lingered, on and off, for years.

Just like the affair she had with my dad.

When I graduated high school at seventeen, I didn't immediately heed my father's order to come see him. I didn't hop on the family jet—it was his father's jet, back then—to fly back to him, join him in the family business like I was supposed to when I became a man.

That was the understanding, and he'd made it clear to my mom: she could keep me in Vancouver to finish school, but after that, I was his. I belonged to him, and that would never change.

He didn't have to belong to us. It didn't go both ways.

In the Mafia, the money and the power flowed up. And so did the loyalty in my family, according to my father.

By then, I already had deeply mixed feelings about him, about the Mafia, about so many things in my life. And I'd already been hanging around an outlaw MC, the Sinners, in Vancouver. I'd become friends with a guy who was prospecting for the club. I wouldn't admit it yet to myself—I was too scared of my father—but I was looking for a way out.

I didn't really know if there could be a way out for me. For most people, there wasn't. Except death, or maybe witness protection. I knew that much, at seventeen years old, but I wasn't interested in either.

I went so far as to earn myself prospect status with the Sinners, by proving to them that I could be bad. Just bad enough to join their ranks. I didn't tell them who my father was. I'd never had his last name. I was a Davenport, like my mom.

And maybe I was trying to be just bad enough, in my father's eyes, to get him to disown me—the way the Davenport side of my family had disowned me for my mother's sins.

But not bad enough to end me.

In my father's eyes, being a Davenport instead of a Montanari was bad enough. If I also became a Sinner? He'd hate it. I knew that.

When I was a kid, he'd often disparaged bikers in front of me.

He called them "trash." And unlike some of the other Mafia families we knew, he refused to be friendly with the Dead Kings MC, the most powerful club in Ontario. *See those patches?* he'd say to me whenever we saw those guys out riding. *Never trust a man whose allegiance lies elsewhere.*

A few months after I'd graduated high school, when I still hadn't flown out to see my father, he sent three of his guys to collect me. On my eighteenth birthday.

They brought me to him.

I stood before him, not in that Italian restaurant but in a house somewhere, a basement. How stupid the fuck was I to let them get me into a basement?

I was scared of my father in that moment, yes.

But I also felt strangely secure, armored in a way I never had before in his presence—in my new biker vest.

My father's eyes moved slowly down, over the telltale leather cut. Black leather, with a small patch on the chest that read *Prospect* and a larger one on the lower back that said the same. When I got patched in to the Sinners, I'd earn my colors: three patches with the name of the club, my chapter and the club's insignia.

Fuck, my father would hate those colors on my back.

I smiled at him. I couldn't help it.

In that moment, I'd thought my prospect cut would set me free. I'd lived with that delusion out in Vancouver, drunk on the first taste of freedom in my veins.

But I'd never really be free of being my father's son.

Instead of disowning me, he reprimanded me. For failing to come see him on my own. And for wearing the leather cut with the *Prospect* patch.

His men removed it from my body, before they removed my teeth. They yanked out six upper front teeth, using pliers, while they held me at my father's feet. Until I begged him to stop.

You think you've got teeth, he said to me as I bled. *You try to take a bite out of me, and what's owed to me, again, you'll see what happens. You show respect, if you can't show your face around here for anything else. And we'll see what you have to keep smiling about.*

That was his favorite thing to harp on when I'd pissed him off. My smile.

As a kid, I smiled a lot. My father would point it out, all the time, and I could never tell if it was because he was actually proud of me, in his way, or he was mocking me. *Look at him, smiling again*, he'd say, and whoever was around would look at me, because he told them to.

My father was really the only thing in my life that made me unhappy.

He changed my smile that day, permanently, because I disrespected him. So we'd never stand face to face again and forget that moment. The moment he put me on my knees and reminded me he'd always be boss.

Then they set fire to my leather prospect cut. I watched it melt as I bled.

Then they dragged me back onto the jet. Not my father. Never my father. He let his guys drop me off in a farmer's field somewhere east of Vancouver with a bloody rag stuffed in my mouth. And my birthday gift.

It was a fat roll of cash, wrapped in a rubber band. They shoved it into the pocket of my jeans before they left me.

He took my teeth and he gave me money.

The message was clear: *I can take away but I can also give. Come back to me and be rewarded.*

I'd pulled it out and stared at it, peeled the corners of the bills back. My maternal grandparents, the ones who'd disowned me, were billionaires. My paternal grandfather was a Mafia boss, and my father was his underboss by then. But I'd never had that kind of cash in my hand.

I took that money and went straight to the Sinners' clubhouse. I told them what happened to my teeth. At that point, I had to. No way I could hide it, and if I didn't talk, they'd stop trusting me and cut me loose.

I paid with cash, my father's cash and pretty much everything else I had, for my new teeth and the platinum canines. If my father wanted to be reminded of the power he had over me every time I showed my face, to pay him his respect, he'd be reminded—that I was not, and never would be, what he wanted me to be.

I had top notch work done. The Sinners were connected, but at the time I had no idea who they were connected to. I was a kid. An outsider. I'd been a prospect for mere months.

And I was no longer a prospect.

The Mafia took my cut, my prospect patch. It was a degradation. You didn't let anyone touch much less take the cut off your back. I wasn't even sure if the Sinners would want me anymore. Or what I'd have to do to earn my place back.

But a few weeks after my new teeth were in, I was called back into their clubhouse. It was more house than club. A rambling old dive house in East Vancouver. I sat in the living room drinking a beer with my buddy who was still a prospect. Then the door to the back room, the President's office, opened, and this big blond dude strode out.

He wore a West Coast Kings cut. It was Piper Grayson, but I didn't know who Piper was.

I got to my feet. He just commanded attention, respect, like that. In a different way than my father did.

He told me to come with him and I did.

He took me to the Kings' clubhouse. And I learned.

I learned that the Sinners were operating on the Kings' turf, with the Kings' permission. That they kicked money up to the Kings. That they were a support club, what Piper called a "puppet club." No one had told me that before. The Sinners I'd met seemed to hate the Kings. When you were a hangaround, even a prospect, they didn't tell you much. They didn't yet know if they could trust you. You might be a narc, or anything at all.

But now that they knew who I was, who my father was, they didn't worry that I was a narc. The Kings thought I had value, maybe, just like my father did. Or maybe they assumed I'd be capable of great and terrible things, like my father was.

They never told me what was said about me in that clubhouse office that day, or why they decided to patch me over. The Kings didn't even patch me in, for a whole year. They were way more regimented than the Sinners. And way more thorough.

First thing they did was interview me, for hours on end; Piper and Axel in a concrete room. Then they put me on a polygraph, did an extensive background check.

They ran surveillance on me, for months. They made sure everything about me checked out before they trusted me enough to make me a brother.

Because once you'd earned that status, the club relied on you to have every other brother's back.

While I was prospecting, I barely had contact with club members, especially the officers—except for Piper. He was my sponsor. Ultimately, it was up to him if I passed or failed their extensive tests.

But that very first day I met him, after he and Axel interviewed me, Piper invited me to prospect for the Kings. He gave me a new cut with a prospect patch. I put it on, and I never looked back.

I thought I was safe now. Safer than I was with the Sinners.

And I was. Relatively.

———

When I turned nineteen, I didn't expect to hear from my father. I hadn't heard from him since he took my teeth, a year ago. But he didn't summon me on my nineteenth birthday or send anyone to come collect me.

Instead, he killed my dog. My Lola.

He didn't kill her himself, of course. That wasn't his style. He had someone else do it. Flew all the way across the country to put down my dog.

I couldn't prove who did it. I didn't see it happen, just found the body. But I knew.

It was my birthday.

And whoever stopped by my apartment also left me a roll of cash. The cash gift that year was smaller, the message from my father, again, clear: *I can give, but I can also take away.*

As if the promise of money could ever make up for the things he'd done, could ever entice me back.

I'd never been that hungry for money. I was starving for something else my father had failed to provide.

Family.

He expected me to come crawling back to him, someday. I knew that. I was young, but a lot less stupid than he took me for.

I took my dog out to the Kings' clubhouse and we buried her. And I put down all my childish illusions with that dog. I was never getting free of my father without paying the price. Now, I knew.

I got a room in the clubhouse that night. Prospects weren't allowed to have a room, but when I told Piper what happened to my dog, he took it to King, and they gave me a room. I still had my apartment, but I could crash at the clubhouse anytime.

Soon after, they patched me in anyway. I was now a King.

When they gave me my colors, Piper asked me what I wanted to see happen. And I knew what he was asking. I could see it in his eyes: if I gave him a reason to go after Joey Montanari, the reputed Mafia Devil, for a club brother, he just might.

But I didn't want that.

The Kings, my new brothers, weren't going to war with a Mafia boss out east because of me and my dog. So I told him: I wanted nothing. My father was officially dead to me.

Piper respected my choice. But if my father wanted to kill me next, he could come through a wall of Kings to do it. That much was clear.

I had brothers now. Family.

But I'd made a great mistake. The mistake of having something my father could get to, something I loved, something he could take from me.

Lola.

That was my payment that year.

———

So, why was he having me follow Talia now?

Was it about her, or was it about me?

Did he think I wanted her? That I loved her?

That it would hurt me if she got hurt?

Because her showing up at the clubhouse, twice in one week, was doing nothing to dispel that idea, if he was having me watched.

I had no doubt that my father had me watched. Not tailed. But watched, from a distance. Checked in on, now and then.

He knew that I knew that if I refused to follow Talia for him or failed to get this job done, someone else would do it.

And he'd find a way to collect from me anyway, what was owed. Some other form of payment.

Mom, maybe. Just maybe, he would go there. If it meant hurting me.

You just never knew.

My mom liked to pretend she was free of him. But she wasn't free. Like me, she probably never would be.

And the question burned a dark hole in my brain: if my father could do what he did to his own son, his flesh and blood, his only son, the boy he'd held in his arms as a baby and taught to ride a bike… what would he do to that boy's mother in order to hurt him, if he was angry enough?

Or worse, to a girl like Talia, a girl he barely knew?

———

The year after Lola died was the worst year.

At least Lola went quick. They didn't make her suffer.

There were worse things than a quick bullet to the head at close range. Much worse things. Lives destroyed slowly, collateral damage. An accident, with ramifications that spread far and wide.

Accidents that weren't really accidents; those were common in my father's world.

It was all orchestrated so well. But it was a week after my twentieth birthday. I almost thought nothing would happen that year. They were taking their time, that was all. Getting it done right.

From the top of a mountain, there was nowhere to go but down.

Faster, if your brake line was cut.

I never knew if he thought I'd be in the car; if he got that part wrong, or exactly right.

But the more I thought about it, I realized the hard truth: that whoever cut that brake line knew exactly who was in the car. Or more specifically, who wasn't. My father still wanted me alive, earning for him. If he didn't, there would be no need for this ongoing cat-and-mouse.

This time, there was no cash gift. The threat was amplified. The message, again, clear: *I'm through being generous. Continue to defy me and it will only cost you more.*

The next year, when I turned twenty-one, my father summoned me for the first time in three years, and I went to see him. I met him in that Italian restaurant for the first time.

By then, he knew there was nothing he could take from me anymore, unless he wanted to start severing limbs. I'd learned not to keep a pet. I didn't keep girlfriends. I'd even distanced myself from my mom. I didn't let anyone get so close that they could be used to hurt me, that they could be hurt because of me. Not anymore.

How far would he go? I couldn't stand to know.

So, I distanced myself.

There were my club brothers, the Kings, but the Kings had more power than any crime family in the country. They had alliances my father didn't have. My father didn't want a war with the club. I told myself that he'd never risk going after a King—unless provoked.

And I'd promised myself when I was patched in: I'd never spark that flame and risk getting my club brothers killed for me.

My father wouldn't touch a Davenport for the same reason. They had too much power, financially, and too much public exposure. I was pretty sure of that.

Joey Montanari preferred opponents he could squash, overcome. He preferred doing business by his own set of rules. I'd failed to follow his rules, so he'd made me pay. But I'd learned to keep my attachments clean; I no longer had any. Not any that would appear vulnerable to him.

So, he made me pay in other ways, starting with that year.

He made me earn for him.

Most often, he had me collect payment from someone who owed him a large amount of money—by whatever means necessary. And I did, without question. I never killed anyone's dog, though, or ripped out anyone's teeth.

There were other ways to get what you wanted out of people. Especially people with loose morals to begin with. And anyone owing money to a man like my father was morally loose.

Every year, I knew I was getting off easy. Thug work, once a year, and lunch with my father, though brutal, was a small price to pay compared to what he could take.

———

The thought of someone else, some guy on my father's crew, doing what I was doing right now...

Watching her.

Her blonde waves tumbling down her back. Her pink fleece jacket, her tight ass in her jeans, her little white sneakers. Hugging a brown paper bag from the liquor store with a bottle of wine poking out the top, laughing into her phone as she chatted with a friend.

Walking down the sidewalk to her car like no one was paying attention, like she had the freedom to do that without some creep following her around.

No. I couldn't let some asshole on my father's crew tail her.

So I tailed her.

She looked happy. Not like she was destroyed over what went down between us at the clubhouse, or losing any sleep over it. But then again, I only saw her in public.

I went almost everywhere she went, unless the club needed me for something and I had to break away.

Then I'd be back, parked outside her condo in the middle of the night. In Toad's truck. He'd gotten my car fixed, but his truck was better cover anyway.

I'd set an alarm on my phone to wake me up. Then I'd sleep, and I'd dream about Talia in my room. Not naked. Not good dreams like that. I'd dream of her spewing all that shit she'd said, over and over again, all of it spinning around in my head in fragments. Like shards of glass in the wind. All those words she'd hurled at me.

Marriage. Good man. Fucking fool.

Confused. Chasing a fantasy.

Wrong.

She'd been thinking about me. About *us*.

A lot.

Knowing it didn't make any of this any fucking easier.

In the morning, I'd wait for her to come outside while I drank cold coffee I'd bought the night before, while she slept.

Sometimes she'd drag herself to the gym, early, and I'd watch her on the treadmill through the big front window. Her tits bouncing in her sports bra, her chest glistening with sweat, ponytail bobbing and earbuds in. She looked angry, like she was running away from something. Or towards something she wanted to kill.

While I sat outside in the truck, hands buried in my armpits, cold, in the rain. Wondering what she'd done to catch my father's attention.

Or what I'd done to put her on his radar.

I tailed her for twelve straight days before he summoned me again.

Chapter Ten

Lex

This time, he didn't give me any notice.

My father's jet was already waiting for me when Vincenzo called. It was Saturday morning. I'd just tailed Talia to the mall when I got the call and pulled over.

When I got off the phone, I texted Maddox to let him know I was gone, up to my brother's cabin for most of the day.

He sent me back a drunk face emoji and a bottle. Meaning he assumed I was getting wasted in Dane's hot tub. Which would've been a really decent way to spend my Saturday, come to think of it.

Instead, this shit.

Then I texted Dane to tell him if anyone asked, I was up at his cabin, until I told him otherwise. My brother texted back: *Are you actually heading up there?* And I replied: *Don't ask.* He sent me back a frowny face, but I knew he'd come through.

So far, none of the Kings had ever reached out to him to ask him where the fuck I was or anything. It wasn't likely. Unless I was MIA for days on end or something. But when you were sneaking around doing dirty deeds for the fucking Mafia, you had to cover all your bases.

Then I burned it straight out to the airport.

When I got there, Vincenzo greeted me, same as last time.

On the plane, he was less chatty. It was a shorter flight, though. Much shorter. We touched down outside Regina, at some airport I'd never been to.

The Kings had a couple of chapters here in Saskatchewan, but I really hadn't had much cause to spend time in the province before, and I had no idea why my father would have me brought here. It must've been convenient for him in some way. Maybe he was in the province.

Not a good feeling.

I liked to think of him staying put in Ontario, with thousands of miles between us. This was still many miles, but too close for my liking.

We got in a car, me, Vincenzo and the other two tight-lipped mafiosi who'd come along for the ride, and we drove to a farmhouse in the middle of nowhere.

Not great.

There were several cars parked outside when we pulled up, but not the kind driven by rural farm folk. I considered making a run for it, but where the fuck would I go? We were in the middle of the prairies, surrounded by wide-open farmers' fields. There was literally nowhere to hide.

When we walked in the front door, I could hear men talking somewhere in back, voices low. Vincenzo led me through the living room, where a couple of guys, my father's bodyguards, hovered ominously.

"Hey, boys," I said casually. "Looking good."

No one else said anything.

Most of the Italians I'd met in my life were friendly people. Including the gangsters. Boisterous and expressive. Not these guys.

If they had a sense of humor, or a personality, they didn't show it around me.

I followed Vincenzo into the bright kitchen. Normally, my father would send one of his guys to follow up with me, to collect whatever I'd acquired for him. Money. It was always money.

This time it was information. A schedule. The day-to-day moments of a regular life.

Talia's life.

But it wasn't one of his men who waited for me in that bright country kitchen. It was my father himself.

He was sitting at the small table, one of those old ones with the formica top you'd see in retro diners, with chrome around it. The whole place looked like an old lady lived in it. Or some sweet old couple.

Probably did.

I wondered where they were right now.

There was takeout food spread across the table, greasy paper bags and foil containers. And my father's lunch, laid out on someone's best china. It had a pattern of blue flowers on it. So often, he was eating when he ruined my life. The man's appetite was endless, in all ways.

The other guys in the room slipped out, leaving us alone.

I didn't love that we were in this non-public place. This was the first time, in all the years since my teeth were ripped out, that I'd met my father anywhere but that Italian restaurant he loved.

I didn't have to come. I could've resisted.

But what would that mean for Talia?

And really, what good would it do?

Fucking none.

Anyway, I didn't think I'd done anything to cross my father this time. I'd watched her, like he asked.

"You can't get a decent fucking risotto in southern Saskatchewan, I tell you that," he muttered. Like I came here to hear his thoughts on the local cuisine, or gave a damn what he ate for lunch.

"I think it's more of a meat and potatoes province. Decent pierogies, maybe."

My father looked at me. I wore my Kings cut. The usual. That hadn't changed since the last time he saw me.

As always, it was a disappointment.

"You did what I asked." It was a question, even though he didn't say it like it was one.

Maybe he already knew the answer.

"I did."

"Good boy."

I said nothing.

He continued eating, and that's when I noticed it. Sitting there on the table, tucked under one of the greasy brown bags... and all the air went out of my lungs. I felt my father look at me sharply, and I wondered if I'd made a noise.

It was a notebook. With a worn black leather cover, the cover and the pages curled from the whole thing being folded in half and tucked into my back pocket. *My* notebook. It was a gift from my mom; I'd carried it around with me when I was twelve, thirteen.

It was one of the many things I'd left behind when I left Toronto with my mom. Not knowing, at the time, that I'd never be going back to our apartment there.

My father was watching me as he ate. He washed his food down with wine. Then he said, "You know what that is?"

"What?" I said neutrally.

"The fucking notebook."

My eyes went to it again. I couldn't stop them. "I don't know. A notebook?"

My father's eyes pinched at the corners. He probably always assumed I was lying to him about something. But he could probably smell that lie across the room.

"It's the ramblings of a romantic fool." He wiped his face with a napkin and tossed it on the table. "It does get interesting, though." He reached for my notebook. "I always knew you had potential. A little earner in the making." He flipped it open and sifted through the pages, which I knew were covered, every one of them, with my handwriting, until he got to the one he'd bookmarked. He took the bookmark out, then slipped a pair of reading glasses from his jacket pocket and put them on. "*I, Keri Kerrington*," he read aloud, "*agree to marry Lexington when he turns twenty-nine.*" He looked at me. "Sound familiar?"

"No."

"What's even more interesting is this one." He broke the spine of the notebook to make it lay flat, and tossed it, open, at my feet.

I glanced down at it.

"You know why I find that one so interesting? It's in blood."

It wasn't in blood. The words were written in my own hand, in pen.

I, Natalia De Santis, agree to marry Lexington when he turns 29.

And there was her signature, and mine.

But the fingerprints below those were in blood.

"Look at those sweet little fingerprints. Is that your blood," my father asked me, "and hers?"

I met his eyes and lied again. "I don't remember."

"You said you barely know her."

"I don't."

My father stared at me for a long moment.

Then he took off his glasses, slipped them back into his pocket, and resumed eating. "Antonio De Santis owes me money."

He let those words explode in my face like napalm.

I blinked. And everything shifted, gradually clicking into place.

It was happening again.

I saw ice on the road. Snowflakes hitting the windshield and melting. Trees sliding by, round and round, as the world spun out.

I blinked the illusion away and swiped my hand over my face.

"How much money?"

"A lot of money," my father said.

I took a deep breath. My heart was hammering. It'd started hammering as soon as I saw Talia's name on the page of the notebook at my feet.

I tried to think.

As far as I knew, Talia's father was a casual associate of the family. Our neighbor on summer holidays a few times when I was a kid. I knew he was Italian. I knew he'd come around often on those summer days, paying my father respect like so many men did. I didn't know there was money involved. I didn't know he'd ever been into anything this deep with my father.

Like deep enough to put his daughter in danger.

Every word I said now would have to be chosen carefully. To minimize the risk to her. The potential damage. I couldn't afford another severed brake line in my life. If Talia died because of me, or even got a scratch on her, I couldn't live with that. I'd murder my father. Or die trying.

"I didn't know you did business with him," I said carefully.

My father was sizing me up with his dark eyes. Reading me like that old notebook. "I do business with anyone who makes me money."

The implication was obvious. I needed to keep making him money, even in this small way. My yearly tribute. Otherwise, I was dead to him.

Maybe he thought there was some greater value here that I wasn't telling him. Maybe he thought he had more potential leverage with the notebook, that childish marriage pact, than I was letting on. But the threat of it was clear, laid out at my feet: *Don't try anything stupid. I know you care about her.*

And I can hurt her.

But if he thought I loved her, he was wrong.

I'd figured out, long ago, that the very worst thing my father could do to me wasn't to kill me. It would be to kill someone I loved.

So I didn't allow myself to love.

He watched as I bent to pick up the notebook. "We were just kids." I folded it and tucked it into my back pocket. "I really don't know her."

I really couldn't say if he believed me or not.

"I followed her, like you asked."

"And?"

"She's clean. Her job is legit. I know her boss. He pays me when I work security. The band she works for isn't touring right now. They're on a break, so she's got a pretty casual work schedule. Meetings, working from home. She goes to the gym, restaurants, shopping. She has friends. She has… a fiancé." Fuck me. Why did I have to hesitate on that part?

Because she told you they're only semi-engaged.

My father didn't miss it. His eyes twitched slightly, taking it all in.

"She's just a regular girl, with a regular life."

"Good," he said. "Then it will be easy to do what I need you to do."

Do.

Meaning what he needed me to do, where she was concerned, was not yet *done*.

Cold dread burned down my spine. The leather notebook was making me sweat. I could feel the warm, damp spot where it pressed against my back.

Did I bring this down on her?

Because of a stupid blood pact we made when we were kids?

"De Santis has been unwilling to pay what he owes. So, you take her. And you keep her until her father pays up."

Take.

He wanted me to take Talia. Like, *abduct* her.

And hold her for fucking ransom.

"I can go talk to him," I said evenly. "You know I always collect."

Damn right, I'd collect. I'd saw off her father's fingers, one by one, until he unclenched his fucking purse strings and paid what he owed to the Mafia, before his daughter got killed for his stupidity. The man was a model dad when we were kids; nothing like mine. He wore Chinos and hosted barbecues. He'd treated his daughter like a princess.

What the hell went wrong with him since then?

My father stared at me for a long moment. Then he said, "The time for talking is done."

"I can get the money."

Now he just looked disappointed again. Like I'd spilled my milk on his newspaper. "You think it's all about money. That's the trouble with you, Lex. You always failed to see the bigger picture."

What bigger picture? *More* money?

Or that he wanted Talia's dad to not just pay, but to suffer?

Or that he was a fucking lunatic? A psychopath? Yeah, I knew that. I knew that fucking years ago.

"Two million," he said, "by the end of the week. You get me what he owes. Then you do with her what you like."

I stared at him as he calmly resumed eating his risotto.

It was moments like this that I couldn't even believe I was related to the man. And yet, I was. I could see it in his eyes. He looked too much like me to be anyone other than my father.

But the man was Satan. Just like everyone said he was.

He wanted me to abduct Talia, and he didn't even care what happened to her afterward. Which implied that he didn't even care if I turned her back over to her father after he paid the ransom to get her back.

Two million dollars; it was a lot of money to owe a man like my father. Hell, five dollars was too much to owe a man like my father.

But like he said, this wasn't just about money.

Like every move my father made, this was a power play, calculated, to play into some larger scheme, to be revealed however he saw fit, possibly over time. This kidnapping wasn't his end game. It was just the beginning.

Maybe it was even some sick test.

Maybe, on top of getting his money, he wanted to find out what I'd choose to do with her *after* I'd abducted her. Which would tell him how much potential leverage she might prove to be against me.

As always, with my father, the possibilities were horrifying and potentially endless.

"I have to get back," I forced out. "Only so long I can disappear to fucking Saskatchewan without a good reason, before my brothers get curious."

My father's dark eyes went black. I never mentioned the Kings in meetings with him. It was a disrespect.

But clearly, my father wasn't afraid of the Kings. At least, not afraid enough to stop fucking with me.

"If you fail, I'll have someone else do it," he told me as I turned to leave, but I already knew that part. "And who knows what happens to her then."

Chapter Eleven

Lex

That night, back in Vancouver, I headed downtown, into Gastown, and walked into the Back Door. It was dank and loud in the bar, the room crowded with bodies. I slipped off my lumber jacket and tossed it to the coat check girl. I didn't bother waiting for a ticket. She knew who I was.

Or at least, she should.

I left my Kings cut on, which got the message across. There were certain places Kings colors were welcome within the city, and the Back Door was one of those places. No name on the guest list required.

Like any event where members of Dirty took the stage, the show was sold out tonight. The band onstage was a supergroup, one that put on occasional shows for the hell of it and usually for charity, under the name Wet Blanket. Dirty's frontman, Zane Traynor, was up there now, along with a few other musicians—including my buddy, Johnny O'Reilly, on guitar; they were rocking out a lust-heavy cover of Måneskin, "For Your Love."

I'd promised Johnny I wouldn't miss this show. It was a small show, but Dirty was the biggest band on the block, so to speak, and since Johnny and Zane had never really seen eye to eye, it was a pretty big deal to get invited to join Zane onstage, here at home in Vancouver.

No surprise, the show seemed to be going over shit-hot with the crowd—a mix of Kings and Kings associates, industry VIPs, friends, family, and superfans—and it would raise a ton of money for whatever cause the band had chosen to support tonight. I didn't stop to read whatever it was on the marquee outside. I just placed a wad of folded bills in the palm of the owner, Snake, when he greeted me. He knew what to do with it.

If anyone ever tried to say the Kings did nothing good for the community, they were fucking clueless. We pulled together for a night of fundraising and debauchery as often as the next legit organization.

"Jude's in back," Snake said in my ear. He nodded toward the area at the back of the bar, the closest thing to a VIP section that existed at the Back Door. Slightly above the rest of the crowd, with a great view of the stage.

But I wasn't looking for Jude. I locked onto one person in the crowd.

Talia.

She was right there at Jude's hightop table, standing next to Roni. Her hips swiveled to the music as she watched the show, drinking a beer.

Promise to Johnny aside, she was now the entire reason I was here. Thanks to my fucking father.

I moved through the room—toward my friends, my club brothers, my coworkers, *Talia*, feeling like a wolf in their midst. Still looked the same, still acted the same, but that dark thing in my gut, the fetid place where my father's hook still dug in was rotting me from the inside out. I could feel it. It was always going to destroy me, one way or another.

No matter how I tried to pretend like it wasn't there three-hundred-and-sixty-four days a year.

I was still reeling from his orders in that farmhouse.

Two million, by the end of the week.

You get me what he owes. Then you do with her what you like.

When I reached their table, I greeted Jude and Roni and some others. I kept away from Talia, but our eyes met. Her eyes flashed with a wounded look before she looked away, actively ignoring me.

This was the girl who'd peeled off her clothes in my room and pretty much begged me to fuck her, just over a week ago. While she had a man waiting to make her a bride.

She basically told me that she knew I was no good for her.

She had to know that she could do better. That she'd been offered better. And still, she'd offered herself to me.

I'd seen drop-dead gorgeous women throw themselves at the ugliest dude you could imagine, just because he was wearing Kings colors.

Still, the fact that Talia De Santis wanted me like she did was majorly fucking with my head. I wasn't sure I would've known what to do with it on a good day. I didn't exactly have a track record as Prince Charming. But on the worst of days—like today—I wished I'd never met her.

Because the day she met me, and my father, was basically the day her life was destroyed.

She just didn't know it yet.

There was no other way to look at it anymore.

We were both fucked.

I pretended to ignore her right back. There were like seven tables of VIPs up here, all the band's family and management team. I said my hellos as I made my way past.

I found Dane and our friend Shane sitting at a nearby table, with Dane's wife, Devi, her best friend, Katie, and Katie's husband, Jesse Mayes, who was Dirty's lead guitarist. I greeted them all and pulled up a tall stool next to Shane, from where I had a decent view of the stage—and a better view of Talia. Her bare right shoulder, where her pink shirt had slipped halfway down her arm, exposing her tanned skin. And her black bra strap.

She tried to look my way a few times like she wasn't looking. I watched her toss back a shot with one hand, lift her beer bottle and take a swig with the other. She was drinking heavily again. That didn't seem to be normal for her. Never was on the Hell & Back tour. I wondered when that changed.

When I came back into her life?

She was wearing the engagement ring. I saw it as she gripped her beer.

Was it official, then?

And why did that bother me?

Because yeah, it fucking did. That dick compensation diamond was becoming a real thorn in my side. Felt like a giant *fuck you*, glittering on her finger.

Even though I told her to marry him.

I didn't fucking want her to marry him, obviously.

But that wasn't my call.

What I didn't see anywhere was her fiancé. I hadn't seen him once while I tailed her, either. Assumed he was in Toronto, or maybe traveling for work.

I wondered if he was faithful to her when they were apart.

I wondered if he really deserved her. Or if he'd only cause her pain, like I would.

I looked around the room, feeling unusually paranoid. Searching every dark corner for signs of my father's men. Spies in the shadows, watching me.

They weren't there. But somehow, the whole world looked different than it did this morning.

Maybe because I now knew Talia was in danger—and exactly what that danger entailed.

Two million dollars.

Then you do with her what you like.

Onstage, the song came to an end. The lights went down on the band. The audience gave up their appreciation, long and loud. And once the applause died down, the crowd started breaking up in front of the stage.

I must've arrived at the end of the encore; looked like the show was over.

Shane headed up to the bar. Dane and Jesse got talking as I scoped the room. People started flooding the bar and the washrooms. The lighting shifted.

Then the house DJ dropped The Killers, "All the Pretty Faces," and most of the girls in our vicinity jumped up and headed for the dance floor; Devi and Katie included. Jude had a thing about not letting the girls go onto the floor when the band was onstage and the crowd was too tight, so they were off like a shot. Devi even poked me and invited me to go with them; maybe she figured I was the only guy at the table who might actually dance with them.

She was wrong.

Jude sent one of his on-duty security guys after them, to keep an eye on them from the edge of the dance floor. Then he came over to talk to Jesse and Dane, and I watched Talia.

She didn't go dance. She was still talking to Roni and some other girls, leaning against the table two over from ours, her back to me. Now that the crowd had thinned out, I could see her from head to toe. Her shirt was tucked into her black jeans, which were high-waisted, skin-tight, and showcased her ass to perfection. All those hours on the treadmill had paid off.

My head went straight to peeling down those jeans and fucking her in those little booties… while I closed my hand on the back of her neck and pinned her against that table.

It had been several hours since my father ordered me to abduct her for ransom, and it already felt unreal.

But it was fucking real.

I'd spent the better part of those hours trying not to lose my shit. While my father's men had delivered me back to Vancouver, I'd tried to figure out how I could somehow avert this kidnapping gig, not piss off my father, not betray my colors by committing a serious offense on behalf of the Mafia, not betray Jude by fucking over a girl who was essentially under his protection, oh, and somehow save Talia from this shitstorm that was swirling around her in the shadows.

And maybe even end up with her thanking me? Yeah, that would be nice. With her legs spread and her beautiful brown eyes begging me, again, to put it in.

However, I highly doubted I'd ever be seeing Talia De Santis naked again.

"Who dat?" Shane had reappeared, fresh beers in hand, and put one in front of me.

When I glanced at him, he was eyeing Talia with zero subtlety. The faded bruises on his face from his last fight gave him a menacing look, but Shane had that thing going on—dark hair, light eyes and big, pretty lips like a chick—and no matter how beat-up his face got, the girls never seemed to mind.

I wanted to smack his eyeballs right off Talia's ass, but he'd probably just laugh.

Shane liked fighting, fast cars and fast women, and since he wasn't fighting tonight he'd be looking for a party. He probably expected me to be the one guy at the table who'd get drunk with him and join him on that quest.

Also wrong.

He eyed me, waiting for a response. One of my best friends, I'd known Shane since high school, and since he'd almost died one dark night because of me, I definitely owed him something I'd never be able to repay. So instead of telling him to shut the fuck up and stop looking at her, I said distractedly, "No one."

"No? Then you weren't just contemplating her ass like it's a fine-art masterpiece you're about to heist?"

I gave him a deadeye look, the one I'd picked up from Piper and

Jude. Obviously, I'd never quite nailed it like they did, because Shane grinned at me.

"Don't know who you're talking about. I'm seeing someone."

"No, you aren't."

"Uh-huh. Tall Amazonian chick with massive tits." His eyebrow rose. "Can we move on?"

I felt him exchange a glance with my brother, as Dane tuned into the conversation. Jude and Jesse had wandered over to another table, but Dane had stayed put. He met my eyes. Tall, dark-blond and clean-cut, Dane had the look of a star football player, though it was his dad who'd played football; Dane was the billionaire president and part owner of the Davenport family's media conglomerate. I was halfway surprised he wasn't wearing a suit tonight. My half-brother and I were pretty different, but we'd always been tight, like brothers, even when we thought we were just cousins.

If I had a girlfriend, Dane would definitely know.

"Well," Shane chuckled, "you ever need someplace to hole away with your Amazonian for a while, feel free to use the shack." He slapped me on the back, ribbing me. "I'm sure she'd appreciate it. You don't get any privacy at that clubhouse."

I grunted. "The shack" was Shane's secret house, the one his family didn't know about but Dane and I did. Part doomsday hide-out, part shag palace, it was Shane's bachelor pad away from home, in the woods, and I shuddered to think of the kinky shit that had gone down there.

"Hard pass," I told him, taking a swig of my beer, "but thanks."

"No worries. Hear she's getting married anyway."

I swallowed my beer. "You heard what?"

"The blonde in the tight black jeans you weren't noticing." He flicked his chin at Talia. "She was just over here talking to the girls about the wedding. I guess they threw her a stagette party last night?"

I heard his words, but my brain struggled to compute.

I glanced at Dane. My brother raised an eyebrow at me. Like, *What is it to you?*

I'd never mentioned Talia to him, much less that I wanted her to sit on my dick or be my girl. But his wife and Talia were friends. He knew who she was.

Last night.

Last night, I'd tailed Talia to a nightclub downtown where I saw her go in with some of her girlfriends. Hours later, she'd come back out with a couple of them, gotten into a cab alone. I'd tailed her home. I had no idea it was a stagette party.

"Wedding?" I finally choked out.

"Huh?" Shane had checked out, scoping out some women at a table below ours. I swore the guy just got more ADD the more he got hit in the head.

"What wedding?"

"Dunno. Guess there's gonna be one?" He gave me a strange, slightly concerned look, like, *That's usually what a dick compensation diamond on a chick's finger means, buddy.*

"You didn't hear about it?" Dane was still eying me with curiosity.

"Hear about what," I said flatly.

"Talia's getting married on Tuesday. I'm going to the wedding with Devi. You weren't invited?"

"Nope." I sipped my beer again, trying to look disinterested as my mind raced. Tuesday? Fucking *Tuesday.*

That was three fucking days away.

"I thought you worked with her," my brother probed.

"Not really. Hate weddings anyway." I didn't, particularly. Usually they were a decent excuse to get drunk and laid. But this wedding?

Hated it already.

"Heh. We should crash," Shane said.

"Please don't," Dane said seriously. "My wife's already disappointed enough in me for being BFFs with you."

Shane grinned. "I bet the bride will look real nice in her dress, though." He was still poking at me, like the shit disturber he was. "Wonder if she'll wear one of those little garter things…"

I was saved from the conversation when Johnny showed up, looking flushed, like a warrior after a victory, doling out hugs. His blonde hair was wet. He'd changed out of his sweaty stage clothes, but he felt hot and damp when I hugged him.

"Got a table downstairs," he informed us.

Downstairs meant Misty's, the strip club beneath the Back Door. And no doubt Johnny's first order of business would be securing himself some after-show pussy.

Shane was already on his feet and nudged my shoulder. My gaze had drifted over to Talia again. "You coming?"

"I'll catch up in a bit."

I watched Shane and Johnny head down to the door to backstage; it led to a back staircase, where VIPs moved between the two bars.

Then I watched as Roni and Talia headed in the same direction, one of Jude's guys on their heels. They, too, disappeared through the door to backstage.

I glanced at Jude, who was still talking to Jesse. He didn't often leave Jesse's side when they were in public together. Roni's either. But no doubt Jude knew where his woman was headed, or she wouldn't be headed there.

I was about to slide into Shane's vacated seat to talk to Dane when my brother got to his feet. "You heading down?" I asked him.

He gave me a look that said fuck no, he wasn't heading down. "I'm hitting the men's room," he said, "then finding my wife."

I got up and followed him. The men's room was probably a better place to have this conversation anyway.

When we got to the back hall that led to the small, crowded washrooms, I squeezed my brother's shoulder. "Trust me. A man of your class, you do not wanna piss in there."

Dane kinda chuckled and followed me deeper along the hall, where we passed one of the bouncers, who shook my hand.

"They just let you wander back here?" Dane inquired as I pushed through a door.

"I could have an orgy with donkeys back here for all they care." I led him past the office and a locked storage room, then pushed open the door to a staff washroom. "Kings own more in this town than you want to know, brother."

"I don't doubt it." Dane gave me a slightly disapproving look but headed into the washroom. The door swung shut and I paced out in the hall, waiting.

Since we'd met as teenagers—even when we'd thought we were cousins by our estranged mothers, and even when he was instructed by his family not to talk to me—Dane and I had become instant friends. He was one of the best friends I'd ever had. And now he was the wealthiest man I knew.

His life was the life I was supposed to have, according to my mom.

If only she hadn't hooked up with a gangster. But then, of course, I wouldn't have been born.

Catch-22.

I'd never begrudged Dane that life. By the time I was a teenager, I understood that my part in it was just a fairytale. A myth. I wasn't destined for a happily-ever-after. Dane was the prince of the Davenport family and the heir to their fortune.

I wasn't even a monster or a dragon or a token troll in this fairytale.

I was the son of the beast.

I'd inherit nothing but the mantle of shadow bestowed upon me by my father. A legacy of darkness and shit, betrayal and murder.

There was no magic kiss from a princess to make me clean, to reverse the curse.

But maybe I could still dip into the family treasure chest if I needed it badly enough.

I gave my brother a few minutes to piss, then walked in. I shut the door behind me and turned the lock.

Dane was still at the urinal but he glanced over his shoulder at me and cracked a small smile, his eyebrow cocking. I was staring at him.

"Can I help you with something?"

"Maybe."

He zipped up and crossed to the sink.

"If I needed money, cash, would you give it to me?"

Dane looked at me in the mirror as he started washing his hands. He knew I'd never been motivated by money. Not like he was. I'd never asked him for a dollar before.

He straightened, shaking his hands off over the sink. "Are you asking?"

"I'm not asking. If the need were to arise. No questions asked, could you get me cash?"

The question wasn't so much *could* as *would*. And we both knew it.

"How much?"

"Two million."

Dane ripped a towel off the dispenser and stared me down as he dried his hands. "I don't keep that kind of cash just lying around," he said evenly. "My businesses are all completely legit—"

"I'd never ask you for anything unless I needed—"

"I know."

"I know it would have to be untraceable to you. I wouldn't want it coming back on you. But if I asked, it would be because I needed the money."

He considered that for a long moment. "I'd need a few days." His eyes flickered over my Kings cut. "And assurance from you that wherever that money was going, I could sleep at night. You know, next to my wife. And I'd know we were safe."

"Of course."

"And I wasn't going to hell."

"It's not like that."

He tossed the paper towel into the trash and faced me. "I'm not naïve, Lex. Two million sounds like murder money to me. As in, it would be more than enough for someone to get murdered over if it went in the wrong direction. For the wrong reason. Or even… for the right reason."

Yeah. *Fuck.*

He was right about that.

I couldn't tell him it was ransom money, though. Fake ransom money. Money demanded by my father.

The money would be for Talia, to very possibly save her life. But… it was also to fund my father. That's where it would be going.

I couldn't ask him for this.

Could I? Even for Talia?

Yes. It's just money.

But I knew it wasn't just money. It was power. And the last thing the Devil needed was more power.

Especially at the potential cost of more innocent lives.

"I'd never want you to lose sleep," I told him. "Especially over me."

"If you'd take the money, Lex," he said, his gaze on me steady, "I'd give it."

Yeah. Because my brother had always trusted me. I'd never given him a reason not to.

Yet.

"You'd just need to give me a few days," he repeated, "to get it together for you."

A few days.

Christ. I might not have a few days.

"I take it from the look on your face," he said dryly, "you're more accustomed to the kind of cash transactions that happen instantaneously. And possibly on demand."

True enough.

We never talked about what I did for work. For the Kings. My rule, not his. To protect us both.

But my brother was incredibly far from stupid.

"It's fine," I said vaguely. "I get it."

"That's just not how it works in my world, Lex. I don't launder dirty money. This is *my* money we're talking about. My family's money. Money that needs to be accounted for."

"I know."

"Tell me when you need it," he said. "If you do."

"Sure."

I opened the door for my brother, following him out. But I didn't actually ask him for the money. I wasn't yet sure if I would.

I wasn't yet sure if it would solve any of my problems, or just create more problems.

Dane paused in the hallway, eyeing me. Trying to read me, even as I tried not to be read. Not possible, with him, probably.

"You know," he mused, "they all said you'd be a bad apple."

"Uh-huh. Like my father."

This was one thing my brother and I had in common; both of us, living in the shadows of our fathers, the tainted legacies they'd left for us. Swimming against the currents of those blackened whirlpools as hard as we could, trying not to get sucked in.

"Yeah. Like your father." Dane's expression grew serious. "But you've never been rotten to the core. Not like they wanted you to be."

"Guess I'm a disappointment all around."

"Don't start now." He gave me a meaningful look, tapped me lightly on the chest, then headed back out into the bar.

I followed, but broke off and headed backstage. Downstairs, to Misty's.

I had no idea what the fuck I was gonna do, or who I could risk drawing into this. I'd sworn to myself, long ago, after what happened to Shane, that I'd never let anyone in my life get hurt by my father again.

But he was expecting me to abduct Talia.

When I reported back to him—or worse, if he sent someone to check up on things… he'd expect to hear that she'd disappeared.

And that the ransom was on its way.

He'd demanded his payment, and he'd named the price. There would be no way around paying it, one way or another.

Chapter Twelve

Lex

Whn I reached the bottom of the stairs, I stopped in the hallway, right at the back entrance to Misty's. Shinedown's "DEVIL" was playing, loud and heavy. There were a few girls onstage, the one at center stage wearing a twisted pair of devil horns and not much else.

My gaze swept the room. I saw Roni at a table with some people over on the far side. I didn't see Talia.

Then she stepped out of the women's washroom in the hallway. When she saw me, she came to a dead stop.

"What are you doing?"

"Uh, using the ladies' room."

"Down here?"

She balked at my tone. "What, should I use the one upstairs that's overcrowded and disgusting?" She crossed her arms. "Smart girls know the ladies' room down here is pristine, because hardly any ladies use it."

"That's not what I was asking."

She rolled her eyes a little. "What, you mean a nice girl like me, in a place like this, etcetera?"

I took her by the arm and pulled her with me, deeper into the hall. She made a peep of protest but came right along with me.

As we approached, the bouncer standing in the shadows greeted me with a nod.

"Need a room," I growled.

He led us to one of the closed doors at the far end of the hall, close to the EXIT sign, and opened it. The music was as loud inside as it was out on the bar floor. "Turn it down," I told him, as I led Talia into the room. "And turn the cameras off."

"Sure, Lex." He shut the door behind us, passing that order along by way of his earpiece. By the time Talia tugged her arm from my grasp and paced to the other side of the small room, the music had lowered several notches.

"Where are we?" She turned in a circle, taking in the dark walls, the pink lights, and the single, vinyl-upholstered chair in the center of the room, not chosen for comfort but because it was easy to wipe clean.

"We're in a back room at a strip club," I told her as I started digging for my Zippo and my weed. This conversation definitely needed a tension breaker. For both of us, totally different reasons.

Well, somewhat different.

She finished her perusal then looked at me. "What happens in here?"

"Exactly what you think happens."

She wrinkled her nose and looked into the corners. "There are cameras in here?"

"Yes."

She gave me a creeped out look, like I had the feed from said cameras beamed straight into my phone or something.

"They're video only. No audio. It's security. For the girls."

"I take it you come here often."

"No pun intended." She bristled as I lit up a joint. "It may surprise you to know, Talia De Santis," I said, taking a pull off the joint, then offering it to her, "that I've never put my dick in a girl who stripped for a living. Nor do I have any particular interest in doing so."

She looked at the joint in my hand. "Why not?" she said dubiously. Then she gave a small sigh of annoyance or resignation, took the joint and took a little puff.

"Not my type."

"You're lying," she said, smoke swirling between us as she exhaled.

"Why would I lie about that?"

"I don't know." She handed the joint off to me. "But it really might've been nice to know stripping wasn't your thing. You know, before I got naked in front of you, thinking you might appreciate it."

I stared her down, heat rising through me at the memory. Her pupils grew big and dark as she held my gaze. "Never said I didn't appreciate it."

"Then why did you kick me out like that? It was humiliating."

"I'm sorry about that."

"Are you?"

"Yes."

"So…" She glanced at the chair between us. "If I did it again, right here…"

"You'd get the same result," I told her, a little growl in my voice. "So don't even try."

She swallowed. "You don't want me to. Because you're afraid of what will happen…" Her voice lowered. "You know, if you *don't* kick me out."

I said nothing, just smoked.

"Why is that?" she asked me.

Because if you keep taking off your clothes in front of me, I'm gonna have to touch you, and if I touch you, I'm gonna have to fuck you, and if I fuck you, I probably fall for you and then bad things happen.

Worse things than whatever's about to happen.

"You're wearing the ring," I observed.

She rubbed her engagement ring with her thumb.

I still couldn't believe she'd been planning a wedding and I didn't even know, when I'd been following her around for almost two weeks. How was that possible?

How was it possible she'd said yes to him? Since she'd walked into the clubhouse, what, like twelve days ago and stripped naked in front of me?

I mean, I told her to marry him.

But did she really care that much whatever I had to say?

I offered her the joint again. She took it, and as she smoked I studied her eyes, the way she watched me. With care. Not affection, but... caution. And yeah, interest. Desire.

Unsatisfied, frustrated desire.

I knew the feeling.

And yeah, for some reason, she cared. She cared what I wanted from her.

Was that why she was rushing to get married now? Because she thought it was the quickest way to kill whatever she felt for me?

Or convince me that it was killed?

"Where's the wedding?"

She handed the joint back to me, but didn't answer.

"All I have to do is ask one of our many mutual friends," I reminded her.

"Yet you're cornering me," she said softly, "and asking *me*."

I stepped aside, clearing her path to the door. "Door's right there."

She didn't budge.

"I hear it's happening in three days."

"So?"

"So, what's the rush?"

She shrugged. "No reason to put it off. And Carl was so thrilled when I said yes, he thought we should do it right away. What can I say." She held my eyes meaningfully. "I guess some men just like having me around."

Right. More like he wanted to lock that down before she had second thoughts. Any guy was pushing that hard to get to the altar, he was afraid the bride was gonna jet.

"And you're getting married on a Tuesday?" Wasn't sure why I found that odd. I was no wedding expert, but it seemed anticlimactic somehow.

She hugged herself, defensive. "Why not? It's cheaper. And much easier on short notice."

I took a slow step toward her and her arms tightened around herself. "And that's your main criteria for planning the most special day of your life? It's cheap and convenient?"

"Why do you care?"

"You seem like more of a romantic than that."

"I guess you don't really know me."

I studied her, trying to gauge how drunk she was tonight. How confused she might still be despite that ring on her finger. And how twisted up over what happened between us.

Somewhat, very, and astronomically, as far as I could tell.

"I know a lot of things about you." Stalking her the last two weeks aside, I'd always known a lot of things about her.

I'd always wanted her, even though I knew I couldn't have her.

So, I'd paid attention.

And now I knew how much she wanted me. Enough to risk showing up at the Kings' clubhouse, twice now, and basically throw herself at me and take whatever came. Rejection included. The girl had courage. I'd give her that.

So why was she marrying this other guy?

Could I get her to call off the wedding and stall?

Get the money to pay my father what her father owed, somehow? Make it look like ransom when it wasn't?

But if my father ever found out the money didn't come from her dad... it would not be pretty. And knowing my father, he'd make her suffer for it, just to teach me a lesson.

Nope. Still no idea how to save this shit show from the fire.

It had to be ransom. It was the only price my father would accept.

Which meant I had to make her disappear. With me.

Before the wedding?

Make it look like she ran out on her groom? Something like that.

I was thinking this shit up on the fly, but fuck, that sounded like the best idea I'd had in years.

Maybe she *would* end up thanking me for it.

Ha. Fat fucking chance.

She'd never choose me if she knew why I was standing here right now.

And even if she did... would she ever be safe? From my life? From my father?

No. Fuck, no.

"You're really marrying him?" I asked her, when she said nothing.

"Are you here to stop me?" she said softly.

"I haven't decided yet."

Not true, exactly. I had pretty much decided. Just wasn't sure *when* I was going to stop her yet.

Or how.

"Well," she said slowly, looking kinda shaken, "if you have something to say, say it now or forever hold your peace, right?" She laughed softly, though she wasn't joking.

Neither of us was.

"Don't marry him."

Clearly, she did not expect me to say it.

Her jaw dropped. Then she threw up her hands, distraught. "I bought a cake today, for fuck's sake!"

"Huh?"

"A wedding cake. I put in the order today. They're doing a

special rush custom order for me at my favorite bakery…" She watched me drop the remains of the joint on the floor and crush it under my boot as she babbled on. "… and Brody and Maggie and Roni have called in about a thousand favors to everyone they know in town to make this happen, and Carl is flying out, and three days from now we're getting married in front of everyone at dusk, and —" Her words choked off as I grabbed her by the back of her neck, my hands sliding into her hair.

I leaned in and kissed her softly. She sucked in a breath.

I held mine.

My head swam with the warm, fuzzy feeling of the pot and her lips, her taste, her breath fanning against my face as she exhaled.

When I drew back, she stared up, wide-eyed, into my eyes. She whispered, "Oh, shit."

"Don't marry him," I said again.

"Why?" she cried, gripping the chest of my shirt in fistfuls. "You have to give me a reason, Lex. You can't just say *Don't marry him* and expect me to change my entire life! Just give me *one good reason.*"

She was begging me. And I wanted to give her a reason, but I really didn't fucking have one. I'd never had shit-all to offer her.

So I kissed her again.

But this time, she jerked away.

"You're so very hot, Lex Davenport," she said, breathless and shaking, her gaze raking over me. "And so damn cold. You're going to make some unlucky woman very crazy one day." Then she pushed past me and walked out.

After the door shut behind her, I just stood there, hissing out a breath between my teeth.

Well. Really fucked that up nicely.

Then I kicked the wall and flopped into the chair I probably shouldn't have been sitting in but just didn't care.

Seconds later, there was a knock at the door. Then it cracked open and one of the waitresses appeared. In a "skirt" so microscopic two inches of red panties showed below the hemline. I stared at her blankly. "Uh, hi," she said. "There's a guy outside who wants to talk to you. He says his name is Nico?"

At first, the name didn't even ring a bell. Then recognition zapped up my spine. An electric shock, ice-cold.

Fucking Christ. Exactly what the fuck I needed right now.

"Send him in," I muttered as I got to my feet.

She stood aside, holding the door open for him as he strolled in.

"Thanks, babe," he rasped at her. The waitress shut the door behind him, leaving us alone.

Nico leaned a shoulder against the wall as he sized me up. I did the same to him. His feet crossed casually in white Adidas, his midnight-blue jeans still crisp, probably freshly stolen. His tight wife-beater a hint at one of his future pastimes, should he ever find a woman stupid enough to marry him. Scar from an old bullet wound on his shoulder. Dark hair cut short, the tips bleached blond. Shitty jailhouse tats, one on his face. Permanent shadows under his eyes really rounded out the dirtbag look.

My cousin, Nico, had always reminded me of a sinister cartoon weasel in a bad acid trip.

"Well, well, if it isn't the Prince of Darkness himself," he greeted me. That's what he'd always called me: *Prince of Darkness. Son of Satan. Heir to the Bloody Throne.* All that shit.

Because he was jealous.

Nico would've loved it if his dad was Satan. Or at least a captain in Satan's mob. But Nico's dad had never climbed that high before mysteriously disappearing and resurfacing as a corpse in a lake, so many years ago.

The result? My cousin had serious daddy issues, and unfortunately he worshipped mine.

"It's been a while, Nico," I greeted him neutrally. It had been, a long, long while. Like a decade. The timing on this was totally fucked.

Too fucked to be a coincidence.

He eyed my cut. "And he's wearing his Kings colors." He bristled dramatically, then snickered. "Last time I saw you, you were a lowly prospect."

"Things change."

"Daddy ever see you in that?"

I said nothing. I was surprised he'd have the balls to walk into this place, but then again, no one knew him around here. The guys on my father's crew didn't exactly walk around with MAFIA stamped on their jackets. They didn't advertise who they were. They didn't wear colors. They got off on the fact that they were a secret society. That no one really knew who was in and who was out.

But I knew enough.

"You just walked into a bar filled with Kings," I informed him.

He lifted a shoulder, like he didn't give a fuck. "I counted six Kings." His eyes drifted down my cut again. "Plus you."

"Your math's way off on that." There were closer to a dozen Kings in the bar upstairs, and I didn't even get a good look at the crowd in Misty's. "And I *am* a King."

"You're a Montanari," he corrected me.

"Actually, I'm a Davenport."

He feigned boredom. "You've been given a job to do. So have I. You wanna split hairs, do it with your dad."

"And what job is that?"

A small, weaselly smile flickered over his lips, and his fake-diamond grill flashed at me. "Joey thought you might need an accomplice."

A sick feeling crept slowly through my gut. But I told him neutrally, "I don't need anything."

He shrugged. "Just the same. I like doing jobs. Especially blonde jobs. Those perky tits... That ass you could bounce a coin off of..." I moved toward him and his eyes sparked at whatever he saw on my face. "You really don't wanna drag her off somewhere, keep her warm 'til Daddy pays up? I'll do it myself—"

His words cut off as I smacked him so hard his head hit the wall. So hard, my hand stung.

It was the first time I'd ever bitch slapped a man across the face in my life.

I braced for him to hit me back, or to try, but instead he laughed.

"Say that again," I told him, "and I skull fuck you with the business end of my Glock."

Nico rubbed his jaw, his expression darkening, but still halfway amused. "Maybe Joey's on to something. Maybe you're not just a waste of skin, like we keep trying to tell him you are." He spat on the floor, then licked the side of his mouth where I could see blood. He held my gaze for a long moment while I breathed slow and deep, trying to keep calm. I didn't lose my temper much.

But there wasn't much that could piss me off like my weasel of a cousin coming in here and talking shit about Talia.

"Maybe Joey's right about something else, too," he said, eying me. "But if I were you, I'd think twice about going Romeo for that girl. There's a price on her head. And no one, not even you, can stop it."

He shoved me back, out of his space, and walked out the door.

I raked my hands through my hair and exhaled violently. Thought about putting my fist through the wall. Thought better of it.

By the time I'd followed him out to the bar, Nico was long gone. Like the tricky, slimy bastard he'd always been.

Obviously, he was here to watch me for my father. As much to spy on me as to be my "accomplice." To make sure I carried out my father's orders.

Which meant he didn't trust me.

Or maybe he just wanted intel; a set of eyes on me. A play-by-play on how I was handling this.

My gaze landed on Talia across the room. She was at Roni's table now. She wasn't looking my way. She was smiling, but I could see the conflict in her, the tension in her shoulders, even across the bar.

One week.

I had one week left to know Talia De Santis before I burned whatever fucked-up relationship we'd ever had to the ground. She'd never forgive me for what I was about to do.

I wouldn't want her to.

When I was twelve years old, I made her press her bloody fingerprint into my notebook because I wanted her to be mine. I wanted to impress her, so much, that I was willing to press my bloody fingerprint next to hers, to promise my future fortune to her.

At the time, I had no idea what it would end up costing her.

Chapter Thirteen

Talia

I t was my wedding day.

I'd be marrying Carl in less than an hour, just after dusk. It was going to be a candlelit service, simple and beautiful, in the private back room of an upscale restaurant.

But right now, I was alone for the first time all day, and as it turned out, that wasn't a good thing.

After the hair and makeup team left, my mom and bridesmaids helped me polish off the bottle of Dom that Carl had sent to the hotel room for us, in a little pre-ceremonial toast to the bride. Now that the girls had just cleared out to do last minute prep in their own hotel rooms—I'd insisted I needed a moment alone to chill before I walked up the aisle—I dumped the remnants of my glass into my mouth. Sadly, there was no more than a drop. I almost licked the champagne flute in desperation.

Then I dove into the bar fridge and rifled through the bottles on offer. Half-bottles of local wine, miniature vodka. Champagne. Holy God, there was peach schnapps!

There was a ribbon on the bottle and a tag with a recipe for a

"Blushing Bride" cocktail. The other side of the tag said: *Talia, enjoy a toast with your favorite drink on your wedding night. Love, Maggie.*

Oh, sweet Maggie May. That woman was a giver. One of my bridesmaids and my coworker/former boss, Maggie knew my favorite drink was peach schnapps plus anything. She probably expected me to share a toast with my new husband tonight. You know, just before we got naked together.

My stomach turned over in a weird way.

Carl and I had never been totally naked together. His call. Part of his whole courting-me-old-school thing. Though I had given him a blow job. He'd acquiesced to that. A few times.

Unlike Lex, who'd refused to let me blow him on his birthday.

Nope. You are not thinking about that man on your wedding day.

Okay, I definitely needed a drink to stave off these pre-wedding jitters. Apparently, cold feet were a thing, and I was having them.

Speaking of feet, maybe I needed to go for a walk. Get some air. After I had a little drink. I checked the recipe on the tag and popped open the Champagne.

As I was pouring bubbly into my flute, someone knocked on the door. I went to open it, peach schnapps in hand, and found Roni in her cute peach bridesmaid's dress.

"Only for you would I wear this color," she informed me, adjusting the ruched fabric over her stomach. I hadn't seen her in it yet, not since it was altered to fit her like a sexy, silky glove. Earlier, she'd been barfing while the rest of us drank Dom. But she looked fine now, if a little underwhelmed about the color scheme I'd chosen.

"You look so beautiful, though!" She did. The pale peach totally complimented her pale skin and black hair, to say nothing of her green eyes. I waved her in, urgently, and shut the door behind her. "Are you okay?"

"I was about to ask you the same." She raised an eyebrow at the bottle in my hand. "Far be it for me to suggest you put the bottle down, but. You are walking up the aisle in approximately twenty-five minutes."

"It's just to take the edge off."

"Uh-huh. What edge is that?"

I tossed her a look as I finished fixing my Blushing Bride on the bar. "I love him."

She didn't respond to that. "Where's your mom?"

"I got rid of her." I flapped my hand toward the door and took a deep swig of the cocktail. It was strong, but I tried not to shiver so Roni wouldn't worry that I was losing it. "Sent her ahead in the first limo with Carl's mom. She was making me nervous."

"I see that. You're a little frizzy right now."

"What?" I turned to the big mirror on the wall, checking my hair. It was wound up in a beautiful updo, with some loose waves around my face.

"Your hair is perfect," she said, appearing in the reflection behind me. "It's your general aura that's fucked."

I turned to blink at her. "It's wedding day jitters, Roni. I'm jittering all over the place."

She took me by the shoulders, steadying me with her sure grip, and looked me straight in the eyes. "You've got this, Tal. This is your special day. If it's anything other than perfect for you, just tell me and we'll fix it, okay?"

"Okay."

"I'm here for you."

"I know. Thank you."

"And he is one lucky man to have you. Never forget that."

I sighed and it went through me in a long, chilling shudder. In that shudder I felt echoes of all the tears I'd cried last night, as I resolved to forget about that other man who didn't seem to find himself lucky to have a chance with me at all. Nope, he acted more like every time he ran into me he was being punished by the universe or something. Like just talking to me was torture.

Even when he kissed me in the private room of a strip club three nights ago. Then vanished into my nightmares again.

I sipped my drink, feeling shaky. But Roni's steady grip on my shoulders and her support, her strength, were incredibly stabilizing.

"Okay?" she asked me.

"Okay."

She squeezed, then released me.

I did feel calmer. "Damn. You're good at that. How are you so good at that when you've never been married?"

She shrugged. "I've fallen in love. It all amounts to the same damn thing. At some point, it's terrifying."

I laughed, a weird, high laugh, because when she mentioned falling in love, Lex flashed in my mind. Then I kept laughing.

Roni actually recoiled ever-so-slightly, as if she feared the hysteria might be catching. And Roni was not the type to recoil from much.

"Okay, look, Talia…" She watched me as I started to pace. "We have like twenty minutes to meet your fiancé at the altar."

"Uh-huh." The "altar" that had been set up for us in the private party room in the restaurant where we were getting married. He was probably on his way there, right now, while I was pacing, sweating heavily in my dress. Thank God it was sleeveless or it would probably stink of my fear right now.

"I'm only gonna say this once, okay? But… is this what you want?"

"What?" I turned to my maid of honor. "Of course. *Of course.* This—" I indicated my sweating self "—is just cold feet. My mom said she had the same thing happen on her wedding day. And my parents have been married for decades."

Roni eyed me like she was unconvinced, but she'd still do whatever I wanted.

"I want this," I insisted.

"Okay," she said gently.

"I mean, how could I not want this? Everyone's waiting for me right now." I swallowed, hard. "Carl is waiting."

Roni softened. "Oh, Talia. Don't worry about *everyone*. This is about you and—"

"You know who's not waiting?" I grabbed the bottle of peach schnapps and dumped another shot of it into my flute. "Lex." I put the bottle down loudly on the bar. "Lexington Miller Davenport Montanari whatever his name is. Mr. Mysterious. Mr. Doesn't Want Me But Doesn't Not Want Me. *Not waiting.* Never was waiting for me. So you know what? I've taken my heart off the wait list. I mean, I thought he might—"

I stopped dead just as my rant was spiraling up, when I registered the look in Roni's eyes. She looked on the verge of crying for me or something. And Roni Webber was no crier.

"Roni…"

"Talia," she said softly. "What are you doing?"

"What I'm saying is," I tried again, more forcefully, "I know what love *isn't* and I know what I'm doing. I'm marrying a man who loves me. Today."

Roni just stared at me.

"I'm okay, really," I promised us both. "I'm just nervous. It's the rest of my life. It's a big deal."

Now she looked uncertain. Maybe she was wondering if this really was normal.

"Plus…" I hesitated, wondering what she'd say to this one. "We haven't fucked yet. I guess I'm nervous about that. It's kinda making me *extra* frizzy right now."

"You… *what?*"

"I know. Weird, right?" I fiddled with my engagement ring. "But super romantic if you think about it. I mean, we've done like, all the other things. Well, most of the other things. He just hasn't, you know, put it in."

Roni kinda gaped at me. Then her mouth shut. She cleared her throat. "Uh…"

Holy shit. Was she speechless?

"I don't think I've ever seen you speechless. It's freaking me out."

We stared at each other.

There was a knock on the door and I jumped.

"Drink that," she advised me, snapping into maid-of-honor mode as she went for the door. "That'll be Maggie. She's rallying the girls to the lobby."

I put back the rest of my drink. "I'm not ready," I coughed, as the liquor burned my throat, and Roni came to a dead stop. "I need a minute. Just… to catch my breath. You know, powder my nose and shit." I was already scurrying to the bathroom to hide.

"I really hope that wasn't a cocaine reference!" she called after me. "You are *not* getting married high as fuck!"

I popped my head back out of the bathroom. "It wasn't!"

"Good." She stared me down. "I'll load everyone into the limo with the bouquets, make sure everything's ready to go. Then I'll come back to collect you, okay? Just make sure everything you need for the party after dinner is in your bag. Dancing shoes, etcetera." She pointed at the tote bag that sat on a chair.

"Will do!" I disappeared back into the bathroom.

"And don't drink any more!"

"Okay!"

As she left, I heard the voices of my girlfriends and my cousin out in the hallway; my bridal party. They sounded happy. They were all done up in their pretty dresses, hair and makeup. Their dates, husbands and boyfriends, were waiting for them at the restaurant. This would be a fun party for them.

For them.

I looked at myself in the mirror now, right into my own eyes, and I saw what Roni saw, maybe.

Doubt.

Confusion.

Stone cold fear.

Admittedly, this whole thing had seemed like a way better idea a couple of weeks ago. After Lex rejected me so brutally in his room at the clubhouse.

And you know, before he kissed me out of fucking nowhere in a strip club.

Yup, I needed air.

Maybe I should go for a quick walk around the hotel floor, or get some air at that Juliet balcony up the hall? Or smoke a joint. If I had any weed. Why didn't I bring any weed?

You know who'd have weed for you right now?

Lex.

Yeah. If he was here. Maybe I should've invited him to the wedding.

So we could run out the back door together.

Ha. I glared at that stubborn bitch in the mirror who refused to let thoughts of him go.

She scowled back at me. *You brought him up.*

I rushed out of the bathroom, trying not to trip on my dress, suddenly singleminded about it. I had to get out of here. Just for a sec. It was this room. It was stifling me.

Where were my comfy shoes?

I found them in the tote bag I'd been packing. Or someone had. I couldn't even remember packing it. As my hands closed around them, I wondered if I was actually considering running away, and I stopped before putting them on.

You're not running away.

You're not crazy.

"You are not talking to yourself."

I said that last part out loud. To myself.

Air. I needed air.

I slipped the shoes on, ballet flats, and opened the door. My assigned bodyguard was standing in the hall, right outside the door. Jude had insisted, probably because of Roni more than anything, that the bridal party had coverage today. And my personal safety had been assigned to none other than the lowly Kings prospect with the hearing aids.

I'd learned his name was Finn, though we weren't exactly on a first name basis.

"Don't suppose you have any weed?" I asked him when his eyes met mine.

He said nothing. He still hadn't warmed to me. The monosyllabic grunts and deadeye looks were getting old. Jude's guys were tough, but they weren't always so stony.

Thugs, my dad called them, but at least they had personality.

Not this guy.

"Look, I know you probably get prospect points for making sure I stay put, but I'm just getting some air." I brushed past him. "I won't go far." I gathered up the long, full skirt of my dress and headed straight for the Juliet balcony up the hall, not bothering to look if he followed me. If I ignored him, it was pretty much the same as him not being there, right?

A set of French doors stood open at the Juliet balcony. The narrow, false balcony didn't actually have much of anything to step out onto, just a thick window ledge. I stepped onto it and pushed right up against the iron railing, leaning out as far as I could into the cool autumn air.

I took a deep breath. The balcony faced the back alley. Not much to see but the old brick building across the way in the dusk, some distant street lights, a few cars parked down below.

Hopefully no one would wander by and look up, see a bride hanging over the railing and think I was about to jump. I wasn't that desperate.

But maybe I did want out.

I tried to take some deep, slow breaths. Ask myself what I was really freaking out about.

Was I *that* hurt that Lex rejected me, yet again? Did it bother me that much that he told me to marry Carl, then *not* to marry Carl— but wouldn't give me a reason why? Like, *Because I want you?*

Why was I thinking about him so much? On my goddamn wedding day? After I'd pushed, pulled and begged my family, my boss and my friends to help me make this happen? And rallied everyone I knew—except Lex—to get onboard this train with me.

After I'd told Carl *yes*, and he'd been so happy he'd said to me, *Then let's do it. This week.*

And again, I said *yes*.

Was this natural? To have your whole life and all the other possibilities, different roads you could've taken—different men you could've ended up with—all flash through your mind just moments before you walked up the aisle? Was this just wedding day jitters?

And if so, why was Lex the only man coming to mind?

I didn't think I could even conjure the memory of another man's face right now if there was a gun to my head.

I *felt* the dull thud in the hallway behind me, and the answering thump in my gut. Tingles moved up my spine. I knew someone was approaching me, in silence, even as I started to turn and the goose-bumps spread across my skin.

And somehow I knew, before I'd even turned, who it was.

But I didn't believe it until I stood face to face with him.

"*Lex*," I gushed.

He stood a few feet from me. Me in my wedding dress and him in his typical informal attire, a dark hoodie over his Kings cut, faded black jeans, biker boots. My heart slammed like a sledgehammer in my chest. Dread and euphoria crashing together in a terrible, sickening rush.

What are you doing here? would've been a stupid question. I glanced past him, at the rumpled form of my bodyguard, in a heap on the floor.

"He's just having a little nap. Don't worry, he'll be fine."

I gawked at Lex. "Won't he get in trouble for that?" His hands were in the pockets of his jeans. He looked relaxed, as always, and like there was so much more going on in his head than he ever let on.

"Do you really care?" He gazed at me from under lowered eyelids, his chin tipped up a little.

I wasn't worried about the prospect. I highly doubted Lex would hurt his club brother, even a prospective brother. But I was floored. My hands were shaking.

When I couldn't find any words to speak, Lex reached to take my hand in his. And when I felt his hand squeeze mine—I lost it.

I started crying.

My insides went molten, and I knew I'd leave Carl in a heartbeat for this man. If he ever actually told me he wanted me.

Standing here in my wedding gown, I felt like a fraud. I couldn't believe I'd agreed to marry another man. How could I have agreed to that?

Lex looked deep into my eyes. "Come with me," he said, in a low, lulling tone.

"Why couldn't you have said that years ago? *Days* ago?"

"I'm saying it now."

"What if that's not enough for me?" He shifted closer to me. "You can't just show up here out of the blue and steal me away…"

He leaned in close to my face. Then his fingers touched my chin, holding me captive as his gaze entangled with mine. "Talia, you can't marry that guy. You know it and I know it."

Oh, God. He was really here. I could feel him, his heartbeat, slow and steady in the tips of his fingers as he dragged them gently down my throat, and a warm shiver ran down my body.

He'd come for me. He was here to stop me from marrying Carl.

He was, finally, claiming me for himself.

And holy fucking hell was I relieved.

I sighed with relief, long and shaking. "Then get me out of here."

"You need to change."

"What?"

The corner of his mouth tipped up in the slightest smile. "You're slightly conspicuous right now. Do you have other clothes?"

"Yes." I hurried back to my room, stepping carefully over my unconscious bodyguard. I grabbed my tote bag and on impulse, I shoved the bottle of peach schnapps inside.

When I turned, Lex was dragging Finn into the room by his ankles. He left him laid out on the floor.

"Safe and sound," he said, when our eyes locked again. It felt like we were committing some crime, together, and that thought just made my heart slam harder. And not in a bad way.

Holy Christ, I was fucked for this man.

I watched as he pulled an iPhone from Finn's jacket and pressed Finn's limp thumb to the home button. He scrolled around, then tucked the phone in his back pocket.

"What're you doing?"

"Turning off his hearing aids."

"Oh. That seems… wrong."

"Might slow him down when he comes to," he said simply, coming over to me. "Anyway, he wants to be a King, he's really gonna need to update his phone to that newfangled Face ID lock, so no one can break into it when he's passed the fuck out." He offered me his hand again. "Trust me, it'll come in handy at the clubhouse after a night of drinking."

"I guess…"

I took his hand, watching Finn's chest rise and fall as he led me out into the hallway.

He led me past the elevator bank and around the corner, to another elevator at the far end of the hall. A service elevator. The door stood open, like it was waiting for us.

I followed him inside. He swiped a card over the reader, the door slid shut and we started to descend.

"How did you do that?" I asked in wonder.

Did he know someone at the hotel? Did he steal that key card from a staff member? Did he make his own?

I realized, in that moment, that I really had no idea the reach of his criminal powers.

"You need to get changed," he said calmly. "Right now."

"Uh… I'll need help with the zipper." I turned my back to him, my heart still thudding.

Lex unzipped the back of my dress, from the nape of my neck to the base of my spine, setting off a long, delicious shiver. Then he turned his back to me like a gentleman, as I pushed the dress down. I fished my skirt out of the tote, the fluffy little white grenadine one I was going to wear to dance tonight, and stepped into it.

Then I discovered that I'd forgotten to pack the shirt that went with the skirt. All I had on top was my white satin bridal bustier, but the elevator was already slowing to a stop.

"I don't have a shirt!"

Without hesitation, Lex slipped off his hoodie and handed it to me. I pulled it on, then looked up into his eyes. He was gazing at me, his eyelids lowered slightly.

"I knew it," I said in a daze.

"You'll have to leave the dress," he said in that same calm, lulling tone, as he took my hand again.

I grabbed my bag and he pulled me from the elevator into a quiet service hallway. I smelled food cooking and industrial cleaner as I hurried along behind him.

I looked back, once, at my beautiful white bridal dress abandoned on the elevator floor, like a confection ripped open to get at the sweetest stuff inside. And I remembered those chocolates we'd coveted as kids; how we'd licked the creamy filling out, then let them melt in our mouths until nothing was left.

Then the elevator door slid shut, and my wedding was officially done.

I only realized later that I hadn't thought about Carl in that moment. From the moment Lex had taken my hand in his, he'd been the only man in my pounding heart.

Chapter Fourteen

Lex

I led Talia along the staff hallway, quickly, and through the exit door to the alley out back. The alley was clear. No bodies. Just a few parked cars in the designated spots. And the one I'd left parked illegally, next to the dumpster at the far end.

I tugged Talia toward it.

Then I saw Nico, leaning on the hotel wall at the other end of the alley. He brought a cigarette to his smirking lips. His eyes flashed in the shadows as he took a drag, smoke coiling up into the air and away.

I hadn't seen him since the other night in that back room at Misty's, but I had zero doubt he'd be here tonight, lurking. In case I fucked up or failed to pull through, he'd be lying in wait to devour the debris, like the scavenger he was.

Fuck that.

He flicked his cigarette into the shadows, watching as I tugged Talia in the other direction, gripping her hand. For sure, I did not look like a guy who was kidnapping anyone right now. I looked like a guy who was running away with the bride.

Which I was.

I let her hand go, wrapping my hand around her upper arm instead. I steered her over to Shane's car a little more forcefully; she hurried along with me. It was last year's Mustang Shelby, black on black, and at the moment Shane had no idea it was in my possession. The Shelby was only one of his cars, though, and we had a pretty long history of jacking each other's rides whenever we felt like it; I'd fill him in eventually. Meantime, he'd probably figure it out.

I opened the passenger door and Talia slid right in. She didn't even seem to notice when I held on to her bag. By the time I looked up again, Nico had vanished.

I doubted Talia even noticed him. She seemed distracted. Upset.

Tormented, enough to let me walk her right out of her own wedding.

I tried not to think about that part and what it said about me as a human—that everyone she loved was now waiting on her and would soon notice she was missing, and start to worry—as I slipped on a glove. With my gloved hand, I dug her phone out of her bag, switched off the ringer and tossed it into the dumpster. Then I wiped my prints from Finn's phone and tossed it in, too.

I knew I was harming Talia right now, whether she wanted this to happen or not.

I wondered if I'd be doing this anyway—stopping her wedding —even without my father's orders.

Or if I'd leave her in peace, to marry a guy who loved her enough to propose and do whatever it took to lock her down, like she deserved.

But all I needed to keep me moving forward was that Devil breathing over my shoulder.

I stashed the glove in my back pocket so she wouldn't see it, got into the driver's seat and dropped her bag by her feet. We pulled out of the back alley and onto the street.

In my rearview mirror, I could see the waiting limo in front of the hotel as we slipped away.

We blended into traffic and slid through the streets of Gastown, away from the hotel. Away from the restaurant where the wedding was supposed to happen. The streetlights glowed overhead and the sky was growing dark.

We passed the steam clock and I noticed the time. Six-twenty-one.

Dusk was passing into night.

Talia was due at the altar any moment. To be followed by dinner and dancing. Her new life as a married woman.

But instead… chaos.

Roni would be looking for her by now. Someone would be finding Finn. At some point, Finn would wake up.

But Finn didn't see me. He didn't see anything. My image wasn't captured on any cameras in the hotel. I touched nothing.

I'd left no trace, except Talia's dress and her absence.

We turned south, then east, heading out of downtown. As we were crossing Main Street, she finally spoke. "We did it," she said softly, her voice hollow. "I ran away from my wedding." She sounded like she was in shock, but aware enough to feel guilty. She also sounded relieved.

I said nothing.

She didn't ask whose car we were in. She didn't ask where we were going as she played with the hem of her fluffy little white skirt, and fiddled with her engagement ring.

"Roni will take care of things," she said softly, almost to herself. "She'll take care of everything."

She was staring straight forward, at the road ahead, like she wasn't really seeing it. Her eyes were wide and glassy.

"She'll know," she whispered.

"Know what?"

"That I took off. As soon as they realize I'm gone…"

I considered that. "How will she know?"

Silence. Talia looked out the passenger window, her face turned away from me.

"You were having cold feet?"

"Something like that." It was barely a whisper.

Damn. I didn't want to be so glad about it.

I'd seen Roni leave Talia's room, moments before Finn went down. And I'd wondered what kind of girl talk they were having in there.

Hopefully not the kind that included my name.

As soon as Finn realized he'd been drugged—or possibly sooner, if Talia said anything to Roni about *me*—Jude might assume that Talia hadn't acted alone. And it wouldn't take long to run down a list of people Talia might've run away with.

Like maybe the only guy other than her fiancé who'd been alone with her lately—in a bathtub, outside the clubhouse, in his fucking room at the clubhouse—and who wasn't invited to the wedding.

But I could only hope that when they found that dress in the elevator, and Roni shared whatever Talia had told her, maybe they'd assume she cut and ran. Alone.

And that there was no reason to suspect I was involved.

I wasn't even in the city.

According to Toad, who'd dropped me off at Pitt Meadows airport again this afternoon, I was in Ontario with my mom.

"Maybe she'll even guess that you came for me," Talia added.

"Why?" I glanced over at her, cold trickling through my veins. "Why would she guess that?"

Her eyes met mine, wide. Still glassy, but determined. Softening. "Because she knows how I feel about you."

I looked away. My hands tightened on the wheel. I felt her looking at me, but I kept my eyes on the road.

Yeah; how she felt about me was getting clearer all the time.

The way she'd gripped my hand in the hotel and basically pleaded with me to get her out of there… pretty much said it all.

"Anyway…" she said softly, "they'll find out soon enough, I guess."

Right. Because in her mind, we'd just run off into the sunset together.

It hadn't even occurred to the girl that she might be getting kidnapped.

But then again, why would it?

I wasn't fucking kidnapping her. Or so I kept telling myself. What I was doing was taking her to a safe place where I could debrief her on the situation. Or at least, some of the situation.

And keep her safe while I figured out how to defuse this ticking bomb that had become her life.

I told myself that she'd walked out on her wedding herself. But I really had no answer to the question: if I didn't show up, would she be marrying him right now?

And the more uncomfortable elephant in the getaway car: now that she was here, how far would she go, for me?

And how far would I go, for her?

———

By the time we were clear of Vancouver, heading east on the Barnett Highway, Talia had fallen really quiet. Once we got through Port Moody and into Coquitlam, I pulled off the Number 7 into the lot of a landscaping service. The office was shut down for the night. I pulled up next to my car, parked, and killed the engine.

Talia looked at me.

I got out, went around to her side and opened the door for her. Then I ushered her from Shane's car into mine.

Once we'd hit the highway again and maybe it really sank in for her how calculated that was—switching cars, in a parking lot after hours, where no one was around to see us—she finally started asking questions.

"Whose car was that?"

"A friend's."

"Were you planning this?"

"No."

Truth. Ish. Before three days ago, when my father ordered me to do this, I was definitely not planning this. I didn't even know she was definitely getting married until that night, so how could I be planning this?

But, yeah. I'd definitely planned out the last hour or so of our lives in detail. And the next few, too.

Beyond that, it was still looking a little murky.

I glanced at her. She was staring at me, wide-eyed. The little hollows beneath her eyes shone with sweat. She'd started breathing more erratically. Louder.

"Do you have a paper bag?" she asked me.

"No. Just breathe, okay?"

"I... I can't believe I did this to everyone," she wheezed.

"You didn't do anything to anyone."

"I ran away. I abandoned everyone I love. I..."

I met her eyes again.

That just made her breathe harder.

I focused on the road ahead.

"You didn't so much run as I took you," I added quietly.

"That's not making me feel any better."

As we pulled off the highway, she looked around into the night. We were headed north, along a road lined with cheap houses and dull street lights.

"It's dark out here," she whispered.

It wasn't all that dark, but it was darker than downtown. I could tell she didn't know where we were. That she hadn't been paying attention, and now it was making her uneasy. Maybe she really was in shock.

I didn't think she was afraid of me.

"Don't worry," I said, because there really wasn't much else I could say. "You're safe."

She pulled a bottle of peach schnapps from her bag and started drinking.

"Easy on that," I said, halfheartedly. Maybe it was a better idea if she got wrecked tonight and we had our little talk tomorrow anyway.

But that was just the coward in me talking.

———

By the time we pulled up to Shane's house in the woods, Talia seemed calmer. And oddly happier.

Alcohol could do that.

We parked in the gravel driveway. The house was a long, low rancher, dark stained wood, nothing special. But it was well-kept. Chopped firewood was stacked neatly against the front. The yard disappeared into the woods on all sides, the property extending into the dark among the trees.

When I shut down the car and the headlights went off, we were pitched into blackness. The sparse street lights on the road were blocked by the towering trees.

"Wait here. I'll get a light on."

I got out, took the spare key Shane had given me forever ago, unlocked the front door and flipped on lights, including the exterior ones. Then I collected Talia from the car. I carried her bag while she carried her booze, gripping the bottle by the neck.

She weaved a little, probably more from emotional exhaustion than intoxication, sinking against me when I put my arm around her. I steered her into the house, where we took off our shoes and she wandered into the sparse living room/kitchen area, looking around.

She didn't ask if the place was mine.

She didn't ask anything.

There was a wood-burning fireplace, an original brick hearth. The kitchen was newer, but nothing special. The only real indulgence was the new flatscreen TV on the wall.

There wasn't much else to speak of. Other than Shane's stuff scattered here and there. Some coats and shoes at the front entrance. His magazines across the coffee table. Dirty dishes, even, though it didn't look like he'd been here in a while.

Shane had another place where he lived; this was where he came to do other shit.

Talia completed her brief perusal and stood looking at me. She didn't say *nice place* or anything like that. It wasn't all that nice. It wasn't terrible, but there was a reason Shane kept it pretty low on the frills. This was where he came to get away from family bullshit. Or brought women he didn't particularly want to tell about his family or how much money they had.

A place where he could just be a regular guy with a regular life, which he was not.

I understood the appeal.

I'd never really been that guy either.

"So," Talia said softly. "I guess this is the honeymoon suite."

When she put it like that, I actually felt like a bigger dick than I already did.

I wondered if her and Carl had a honeymoon planned, and felt a stab of jealousy in my ribs.

Either way, I told myself that I'd done the right thing. If she took off on some honeymoon after the wedding, just made it harder for my father to get what he wanted. And put her in more danger.

"I'm sorry," I told her.

And now she looked like she felt bad for me. For implying that she didn't love the place I'd swept her off to.

This was getting sicker by the minute.

"I didn't mean…"

"It's fine."

"*I'm* sorry," she said.

"Don't be."

We stared at each other. I swallowed thickly.

She's mine.

That was the main thought in my head, overriding everything else. Talia was now *mine*.

I had her, right here, and she didn't even know where she was. No one did. She wasn't marrying that other guy.

She'd chosen me, on a moment's notice.

She'd chosen whatever I offered her, which as of now, was not much. An escape. And... this place.

She was upset about walking out on her wedding, yet she'd done it. She felt guilty about it.

But mostly she felt guilty because she wanted me.

She wanted me to want her.

More than she wanted to marry Carl, apparently.

Clearly, she also thought this whole thing was an admission of feelings for her on my part. But I didn't exactly have the luxury of having feelings. We were kind of in the middle of a giant shit show, and I had more pressing issues to deal with than getting distracted by her soft, glassy eyes, begging me to take her in my arms and make everything alright.

The only way I was pulling this off was by shutting a door on all that shit. So that was what I did.

"Come on. Let's get you settled." I avoided her eyes, took her hand and led her to the back of the house. Down the hall, past a washroom, a pantry and a laundry room, there were two bedrooms, one on either side of the hall. I led her into the larger one. Shane's bedroom.

I flicked on a lamp by the bed and took her straight into the en suite bathroom. It was small, but there was a bath where she could soak for as long as she wanted to and have some privacy. I'd give her the big bed tonight and I'd sleep in the smaller guest room. That was the plan, and I was sticking to it.

"What are we doing?" she asked me as I turned on the water and got the bath running.

"Giving you a bath."

"What?" She looked at me blankly, still clutching her peach

schnapps bottle by the neck. She was still wearing my hoodie over her satiny white bridal corset thing. I tried not to look.

"Drink up," I said, and she took another sip from the bottle without hesitation. "Now put the bottle down."

She set it on the counter.

"You wanna get undressed?" I suggested, when she just stood there, looking to me for direction.

She blinked at me with such a loaded, hopeful look, it sucked out all my breath.

Quit looking at her.

"But... I don't want you to go," she said softly, from somewhere behind me as I made myself busy checking the water temperature and making sure there was a fresh towel for her.

When I realized she was still just standing there, waiting for me to say or do something, I moved behind her and slid my hoodie off her shoulders.

She let me.

It landed on the floor, and I started unhooking the back of her lingerie. Quickly. It had little hooks like a bra but like ten of them. I peeled it off and dropped it on the floor, trying not to think about what I was doing.

Then my hands went to her waist, settling on the waistband of her skirt for a moment. Hesitating.

She sucked in a little breath.

I needed her in that bath. And away from me. So I took a breath, found the zipper on the back of the skirt and slid it down.

Her panties were white and lacy.

And meant for her new husband.

My cock throbbed. It was already so hard, crammed in my jeans, it fucking ached.

I pushed her skirt down and it fell to the floor. My eyes dropped to the flare of her hips and her fantastic, treadmill-toned ass.

Then I hooked a couple of fingers into her lacy panties—not

thinking about it—and slid them down to her knees. When I let go, she wiggled a little until they fell to her ankles.

I stared at her naked, golden skin. The pale triangle of less-tanned skin on her beautiful, peach-shaped ass.

Entranced, I let my fingertips drift back up her spine. She shivered.

I decided right then and there that no, this would not be fucking happening if it weren't for my father.

I wouldn't have been stopping her wedding today, because it never would've gotten that far. If it weren't for my father, Talia never would've been marrying another man—because she'd already be mine.

I would've fucked her four years ago on that Dirty tour and made her mine.

I took my hand back.

"Get in the bath, Talia." My voice sounded rough and strange. I could barely get the words out.

She looked at me over her shoulder. "Come with me."

"You're drunk."

"You told me to drink," she protested.

"Just get in."

She got into the bath while I looked everywhere else. I didn't look at her nakedness. I mean, I did. But I didn't. And I did.

Christ, it was hot in here. The mirror was all steamed up already. I flipped on the fan.

"You're really not coming in?"

I met her eyes, trying to ignore the rest of her in my peripheral vision.

"I'd love to." I swallowed. My voice was all gravelly. "But I can't. I, uh, have some things to take care of first." I did. Like making sure I'd covered our tracks.

I handed her the bottle of peach schnapps.

"Okay," she said, softly, trusting.

"I'll be back."

I walked out, shut the bathroom door and took a giant breath, willing my brain cells to snap out of it and do their job. They'd gone mysteriously unconscious in that bathroom.

Focus.

I pulled out my phone and texted Shane. *Using the Shelby and the shack. Need privacy. Tell no one.*

I had zero worries about Shane telling anyone anything. He'd probably probe me for dirty details the next time he saw me, but meanwhile, he'd keep his mouth shut. Shane Madrigal didn't generally play well with others, and he could hold his own. Anyone, including a King, came around asking questions about me? They'd get a fat load of nothing in response.

Or maybe a fist in the face, depending on his mood.

Then I went straight to Talia's bag. I'd left it on the floor in the bedroom when we came in. I dug through it, found her wallet and stashed it in the waist of my jeans, in back, right next to my Glock. I left the bag on the bed for her.

Then I looked through the bedroom to make sure there wouldn't be any surprises. I didn't find any hidden weapons, though I did find an array of kinky sex shit that was kind of astonishing, even for a sick fuck like Shane. I left most of it alone.

But I pulled the cuffs out of the dresser drawer I found them in.

They were wide, supple brown leather with sturdy metal buckles, attached by a short metal chain. I stared at them in my hand for a moment.

Seemed like someone could work those buckles open if they really wanted to, bound or not.

In the same drawer, I found a pair of actual handcuffs with a set of keys. I dropped the leather cuffs and picked up the metal ones. I shoved the keys in my pocket and stashed the handcuffs where they were more easily accessible, in the drawer of one of the bedside tables.

Just in case. That was what I told myself.

Just in case Talia refused to stay put until I could make sure she was safe to show her face in public again. And desperate times called for desperate measures.

When I headed back out front, to the living room/kitchen, I stashed Shane's razor, which I'd swiped from the bathroom, in a drawer, along with Talia's wallet. That's when I heard the gravel crunching in the driveway.

Car tires.

Headlights slashed through the living room, shining briefly through the curtains. Then I heard a car engine shut off.

I stole over to the window by the front door, nudged back the little curtain, but couldn't get a clear view of the driveway. My hand had already gone to my gun and now gripped it, ready to pull it on whoever tried to come through that door—if it was anyone but Shane or some hapless chick who'd come around looking for him.

Whoever it was, they knocked on the door. Three times, slow, with a heavy fist.

Then I heard his voice; muffled through the door, but unmistakable.

"Open the fuck up."

Shit.

My car was in the driveway. The lights were on in the house. I could hardly pretend I wasn't fucking here.

I unlocked the door and opened it.

Nico walked in—shoving Roni, bound and blindfolded, in front of him.

Chapter Fifteen

Lex

"Sorry we're late." Nico kicked the door shut behind him. "We were pretty tight on your tail, but then someone decided to kick me in the back of the head while I was driving. Had to take a little detour."

He gave Roni another little push forward.

I stared at her, as all the blood in my body seemed to drain into my feet. I couldn't move. It was like I had concrete in my bones.

There was a dark bandana tied over her eyes. She'd been gagged with another one.

She was wearing her bridesmaid's dress, with a little black motorcycle jacket overtop.

She growled against the gag.

"What's that, sweetheart? You have something to say?" Nico yanked at the back of her gag, untying it. She spit it out of her mouth as it came loose.

Then she turned and spit on him.

I grabbed her by the arm and yanked her back, away from him.

Really didn't care if she spit all over the fucker. And kicked his head in. But I did not want him retaliating.

My cousin wiped the spit off his neck. "Girl's got an attitude," he noted, though he didn't seem too broken up about it.

Roni tried to yank away from me, but I held tight. He'd handcuffed her wrists behind her back.

The weasel had come prepared.

The fact that those handcuffs might have been meant for Talia made my nerves light on fire. I sucked a deep breath in through my nose, grinding my teeth together to keep from saying a word.

Stay calm.

You need to stay fucking calm.

In my grip, Roni didn't put up much of a fight. She was panting. Knowing her, she'd probably exhausted herself already doing her damnedest to kick the shit out of him. There was a bloody scratch on his neck, and I wouldn't doubt there were bruises all over him.

I pointed at her cuffs, then put out my hand, palm up, like *Give it the fuck here.*

Nico dug in his pocket and slapped the key to the cuffs into my palm.

I took Roni by the arms and steered her down the hall. Past the door to Shane's bedroom, where Talia was hopefully deep in her bath and her bottle of schnapps.

I nudged Roni into the guest room, where I sat her down on the bed. She didn't say a thing. I unclasped a cuff, threaded it around the old metal bed frame, and locked it around her wrist again. The whole thing was done in less than a minute.

"You're really messing with the wrong girl," she said quietly. I could hear the simmering outrage and the fear in her voice.

She had no idea how much I understood that statement.

But then again, she probably had no idea who she was talking to. She still had the blindfold on. I hadn't said a single thing since Nico brought her in. If I did, she might recognize my voice.

I walked out of the room, shutting the door behind me. Opened the door to Shane's bedroom, quietly. The bathroom door was still closed.

I shut the door and stalked into the living room, where Nico was poking around.

"What the fuck have you done," I hissed, as quietly as I could.

"Whose dump is this?" He glanced at the flatscreen on the wall. "You think they've got Netflix or Prime? Or porn?"

"You just elevated this, you dumbass piece of shit."

Nico looked at me, unfazed, and dropped onto the couch.

"Do you even realize what you've done?" I raked my fingers through my hair, pacing in front of him. "What this means? It means *death*, Nico. We're fucking dead."

My cousin lounged back on the couch and put his feet up on the coffee table. "So fucking dramatic. Why don't you just sit down and shut the fuck up. We've got a call to make."

"They'll kill us." I paced, my skull squeezing as the depth of the shit we were in really took hold. "You just *took* a King's old lady." I pointed down the hall, keeping my voice low. "Do you know who that is in there? She's basically my VP's sister-in-law."

Nico looked unimpressed. "I had to take her. She saw you leaving with your blonde bitch, you dumb, lovestruck fuck. Wandered right up the sidewalk and into the alley, talking on her phone, and you didn't even see her. I grabbed her and put her in my car to save your dumb ass."

"Save me? Are you fucking kidding me?"

"She *saw* you. Would've taken all of seconds for her to report back to her man that you took off with the bride, and what car you were driving, your fucking license plate. Then what? The neighborhood would've been crawling with Kings. You wouldn't get ten blocks. I was covering your tracks."

"You didn't tell her who you are, did you?"

He looked at me like I was the dumbest creature ever born. "I didn't tell her anything. She barely even saw me."

"Did you tell her I was involved? Does she know I'm here?"

Nico almost rolled his eyes. He reached for a magazine on the table, like he was just gonna flip through 'til I calmed down. "She doesn't know shit. I shoved a gun in her back and threw her in my car. Then I sat on her and put her in cuffs. End of story."

Jesus.

We were dead.

We were both fucking dead.

And Roni was probably fucking terrified. I should've gone in to talk to her. But the last thing I wanted to do was implicate myself in her kidnapping.

Because I did not fucking kidnap her.

You just handcuffed her to a bed.

"Just stay cool and we'll work it all out," Nico said blandly, like the fucking sociopath he was, as I kept pacing in front of him.

"This is very, very bad, Nico."

"Yeah. It is. Because you're blinded by that blonde dick warmer. You got sloppy. This is your fault."

"Like fuck it is."

He flipped through his magazine at a leisurely pace. "The black-haired bitch is gonna be useful to us. You'll see."

"How? By getting us killed faster?"

His eyes rolled up to me. "She's a King's old lady, right? Jude Grayson, right?" The fact that he knew who Jude was did not put me at ease. "So, we use her as collateral. Hold her until De Santis pays up. It'll keep the Kings in line." He studied me with cold, dead eyes. "De Santis is in bed with the Kings, right?"

"Not that I know of."

He slapped the magazine down on the table. "That's bullshit. I've seen guys in Kings shit all over his properties."

I considered that.

I'd spent some time checking out Talia's father and his properties, the last couple of days. Didn't have much time to do it, and I couldn't exactly ask anyone to do it for me without raising flags. Yeah, I'd seen some brothers from one of the local chapters working security on one of his construction sites, but that was it. And the man definitely had security of his own. But this wasn't exactly unusual. Property developers were often wealthy, and they were often targets for extortion by organized crime—the Mafia especially.

But there could also be another reason for the guys in the dark track suits following Antonio De Santis around. It crossed my mind that they could be Mafia; that maybe Talia's dad was a made man.

That maybe he was actually some sort of legitimate threat to my father.

But he was just as likely a simple associate. A man who owed my father money, like he said.

There was no way of knowing, and no time to find out.

"The Kings have a lot of security contracts," I said, still thinking it over.

"Naw. It's more than that. You're fucking blind about more than that girl if you don't see it."

"What if it isn't anything more?"

"Either way. De Santis gets a call that his daughter is being held for ransom, who do you think he's gonna call for help? The cops?"

"The man's not dirty just because the Kings work security for him."

"Keep telling yourself that. Look, De Santis and the Kings won't even know who took the girls. De Santis pays the ransom. It goes up to Joey. He takes credit for it, if and when he wants to. And you know he'll want to. When it suits him. Meanwhile, you get yourself an alibi, keep your little blonde's mouth occupied with your dick or whatever you've gotta do to shut her up, and we'll all be just fine."

Right. Everything was just fucking fine.

"Now, you finished with your hissy fit yet?" He watched me pacing as he pulled out a cheap burner.

"Who're you calling?"

"I'm calling De Santis."

Fuck.

It didn't escape me that he had Talia's dad's phone number, at the ready.

This was all going down way too fast.

"Yo. Daddy De Santis," Nico said into the phone. "That you?" He paused and listened to whoever was on the other end as I paced. *Holy Christ, was this happening?* "Got your daughter here. Not giving her back 'til I see cash. Two million. Paid in twenty-four hours."

I looked over at him. He met my eyes and made a jacking off gesture with his hand.

"Yeah, yeah. I'm sure you'll find a way, you ever want to see her again. Now, let's coordinate our clocks. Mine says you've got 'til eight o'clock tomorrow night. You pay, you get her back." Another pause. "Yeah. We'll get to that. Right now, I'm making the demands. And you can tell the Kings that we have Jude Grayson's old lady, too. We'll be keeping her until you pay up. Actually…" He looked up at me.

I stopped pacing, meeting his eyes.

"The Kings can cough up payment of their own if they want Grayson's girl back. I'd say she's worth… let's say a hundred grand." I lunged across the room, but I wasn't nearly fast enough. Nico tried to dodge, squeezing out some more damage before I cut him off. "Consider it a tip for treating her well while she's in our care—"

I ripped the phone from his hand, hung up and flung it across the room.

Nico watched the phone slide under the shelving unit in the corner.

His eyes met mine. "Just like I said. Fucking dramatic." He got up and strolled over to collect the phone.

"What the *fuck* did you just do."

"Upped the ante. You can thank me later when you're spending your half of that money on blondes and blow, or whatever the fuck you're into."

Jesus fucking Christ. He was off the fucking rails.

My father would never have sanctioned that move. Nico, piggy-backing off this abduction to make some extra pocket money of his own.

Plus, he'd just given up a valuable piece of information: *we have Jude Grayson's old lady...* He'd just revealed to the Kings that he wasn't working alone.

"What did he say?" I demanded.

"He said he wants to speak to his daughter. Which means you're gonna need to get her on the phone and say whatever we need her to say."

This could not be happening.

And yet. It totally was.

Because my father was fucking evil. And his nephew had fallen straight out of that tree and hit his head on the way down.

I tried to scrape my head together. There had to be some way out of this. And whatever it was, I did not need Nico fucking with it. "Okay. Whatever. You've done your part. Now you can go."

A slow, feral smirk spread across Nico's weasel face. He flopped onto the couch again, sprawling out. "Not going anywhere, cuz. You need my ass."

"No. I really fucking don't. At this rate, your ass is getting us both killed."

"So, you're telling me that *you're* gonna roll up to the drop, collect that money, face down whichever of your club brothers they send to hand it over, and hand over the girls to him?"

I stared at him, with no fucking idea how I'd unweave this web he'd just ensnared us in.

He shook his head. "You're such a fuck-up. Heir to the fucking throne, and you don't even want it? What a fucktard. I'd kill for that position."

I knew he meant that literally.

"I'd do anything Uncle Joey, the *boss*, asked of me, because that's how it fucking works. You earn your place."

"So, you're pissed off that my dad hasn't given up on me yet, and this is how you get back at me? What are we, twelve?"

"It pisses me off," he growled, "that he insists on playing this game, giving you chance after chance, year after year. That he doesn't see you don't deserve to be made, much less become boss. That you're a waste of blood, and good fucking riddance. Let the bikers have you."

"Uh-huh. Because you're the one who should be following in Joey's footsteps, running the family when he's too old to do it anymore?"

"Fucking right. I'd honor what he built. I'd do him proud. And I'll tell ya something else. I'd make sure we *crushed* that fucking MC. Joey is too tolerant of your bullshit. Too forgiving. And we're way too tolerant of the fucking Kings."

The guy was insane. Or fucking stupid.

Both?

My dad had no love for the MC, but even he knew he couldn't just crush the Kings.

"Yeah," I muttered, "good luck with that, and I'll see you in hell."

"Don't need luck," he bit back. "When Joey called me in, to help you pull off this kidnapping, I was *all the fuck in.* You know why? Because the more I earn, the higher I rise."

Yeah. And he'd probably step on anyone necessary along the way. Including me, and either of those girls.

"Good for you. You keep blindly following his orders. See where it gets you. Hope you can swim." I held his gaze.

He didn't fucking like that. Being reminded what happened to his father.

Not because it wounded him. Because it was a reminder that his father had been a failure.

But he didn't let it ruffle him. Sociopaths were pretty hard to ruffle.

"If it's what the boss wants," he said, devoid of emotion, stretching his legs out on the coffee table, "it's what the boss gets. I'll expect the same kind of loyalty when I'm boss."

The threat—and his intentions—weren't lost on me.

If I couldn't collect the ransom, he sure as fuck would. Either way, he probably planned to deliver it to my father himself. And maybe his dream would come true—that Joey Montanari would finally see that his nephew was the one deserving of his favor, not his wayward son.

And no one, including me, was gonna stand in his way.

I pulled my gun out of the back of my jeans while he just sat there on the couch, watching me. I slipped the magazine out of a pocket in my cut, loaded the gun and held him at gunpoint. His eyes were wary on me, but creepily undaunted.

"Where's the gun?" I demanded in a low voice.

He lifted his shirt, showing me the Beretta shoved in the low-slung waistband of his crisp new jeans, right in front of his Calvin Kleins.

"Empty it. Slow."

He sighed with annoyance, pulled the gun slowly from his jeans and unloaded the magazine.

"Now put the gun down."

He tossed it on the coffee table.

"Gimme the magazine."

He held it out to me and I took it, tucked it into my pocket.

"How did you follow me here?"

"GPS."

"Where?"

"On your car, fucknut."

"So, go get it." I flicked the gun toward the door, telling him to get his ass up. He did, slowly, looking bored.

I followed him outside, where he crouched down next to my Chevelle, reached deep under the car, behind the front passenger tire, and yanked. He tossed me a small black device. A GPS tracker inside a waterproof case, that he'd secured to the underside of the car with a magnet.

I followed him back into the house. He sat down on the couch—and I smashed the GPS device with a wrench I found in a toolbox under the kitchen sink.

Then I unloaded my gun, put the magazine on the kitchen counter in a semi-offering of peace.

Nico watched me the whole time, assessing with his weasel eyes.

"You'll sleep on the fucking couch," I informed him. "And stay away from the girls."

"You always were a tempestuous prick," he said mildly. "Moody and emotional, like a chick on her rag."

"Congrats. You just used a four-syllable word for the first time. You sure you know what it means?"

He gave me the finger lazily.

"I'll take care of the girls," I told him. "You don't go fucking near them."

He blinked at me. "Now why would I?"

I headed down the hall, and out the back door to get air. As soon as I stepped outside, I took a deep, shaking breath.

I was so fucked.

So.

Fucked.

The Kings would never let this lie.

Didn't even matter if I was one of them.

Actually, it just made it worse that I was one of them. Betrayal; disloyalty; these things didn't go over well when you wore club colors.

Couple days ago, I'd decided that the only sensible move I could make was to fake Talia's abduction, for my father's benefit—by making it look like she ran out on her wedding. I figured I could keep her in hiding long enough to collect the ransom money and pay my father, then take her home. No real harm done, except I'd conveniently stopped her from marrying Carl, which let's face it, was a fucking bonus.

I'd planned to tell Talia what was going on, at least the short of it, have her ask her father to pay the money to my father.

If her father didn't pay up, I figured my emergency backup would be getting the money from Dane and telling my father it was from De Santis, then going to the Kings for help.

That was my last resort option, because it would mean getting Dane involved, plus having to come clean with the Kings that I'd been working for my father behind their backs—and I'd have to take whatever consequences came with that.

Probably losing my club.

That was the whole plan. What there was of it.

But then Nico showed up and pulled a classic Nico move—fucking everything to hell.

Now, I'd have to make it look, to Nico, like I'd actually abducted Talia. In order for Nico to think I'd done what I was supposed to do, I'd need her to behave like she hated me for abducting her on her wedding day.

Which meant she probably actually needed to hate me.

And I definitely had to get Roni back to the Kings, somehow. I had to get her out of this.

Her and Talia both.

In that moment, it really hit me: I'd officially kidnapped Talia.

No one would believe otherwise now. Even Talia herself would start rewriting the whole event in her head.

As soon as she found out her friend was handcuffed to a bed in the next room.

And too bad for me, that was just how it had to be.

Let her believe that I was to blame here. That I was as bad as she probably always feared that I was.

Maybe that was the only way to truly protect her from me.

"*Fuck.*"

I clawed my hand through my hair. Shoved my gun into my pants, under my T-shirt—at the front this time. I didn't trust my cousin at my back, or to have my back. But one thing was true: we were now in this mess together.

I would never trust that fucking weasel.

But I needed him to trust me, if I was going to get the girls out of this disaster, unharmed.

Chapter Sixteen

Talia

I soaked in the bath, alone, until the water started getting cold. Sipping peach schnapps straight from the bottle. I kept thinking about my parents, how much my mom loved my wedding dress.

And the shit show I'd just left my maid of honor to deal with.

Roni, of all people, would understand that I just couldn't go through with the wedding, though. That I'd made a mistake. And she'd take care of everything for me. I'd owe her the world and possibly spend the rest of my life paying her back, but that was what friends—best friends—were for, right?

Roni had definitely become my best friend over the last few years, and I'd just have to make sure she knew it. And that I loved her for it.

Could I ever pay her back for this?

And *this* was telling, wasn't it? That I was more worried about how what happened today might affect my relationship with Roni and how it was coming down on her right now, than I was about Carl.

I couldn't even think about Carl right now.

Obviously, that relationship was over.

Because how could he ever forgive me for this, even to stay friendly?

I was supposed to love him. I thought I loved him. But how could that be true if I did what I just did, running off with another man?

The thought of betraying a friend like Roni the way I'd just betrayed Carl was unconscionable. So how could I do it to him?

I should've given the ring back the moment I choked on it.

On that thought, I slipped it off and set it on the side of the tub. Lex was right. I was never going to marry Carl. The universe had been screaming at me that he wasn't the man for me. I should've heard it. I should've heard my own inner voice, my own doubts, instead of letting my dad's voice drown them out.

He's good for you, Dad told me. *He's the best you'll ever do.* He didn't mean it as an insult. He'd meant it as a great compliment to Carl.

Because Carl Caldwell was everything my dad ever wanted for me.

I thought he was all *I* ever wanted for me.

Until the moment I saw Lex again at that party and I'd felt ripped in two. So torn, I'd climbed into his lap in that bathtub.

And I still ran after Carl, begging him to forgive me.

He did forgive me, but even that wasn't what I wanted. I could admit that to myself now. Even when Carl forgave me, I just kept thinking: Lex wouldn't forgive me. If I was his, he'd never get over me touching another man.

I wouldn't want him to.

And I wouldn't want to touch another man.

I sank some more schnapps, trying to drown my guilt, wondering vaguely if I was gonna be sick later. And wondering if I cared either way. I wasn't sure I'd ever felt this shitty about myself or my life choices.

Eventually, I got out of the tub. It was so quiet.

Where was Lex?

I dried off with the towel he'd left for me and started getting dressed. Put my bridal lingerie back on, and my skirt. I still needed a shirt, though. *What a mess.*

I looked at my hazy reflection in the fogged-up mirror. The bustier was sexy. It was supposed to be for Carl. But I was glad it would be for Lex instead.

How awful was that?

Yup. I'm going to hell.

I headed through the bedroom to look for Lex, but stopped before reaching the door. Was this *his* bedroom? I didn't know he had one, besides at the clubhouse.

There was no bag of weed on the bedside table, no stack of well-worn books. No pictures on the walls. No personality whatsoever. Just mismatched old furniture in various wood finishes that didn't match. And a big bed with an old farmhouse headboard, wrought iron with chipping paint.

It maybe could've been considered some form of shabby-country-chic, if it was done intentionally. But it felt more like an afterthought, putting furniture in the room at all. It barely even felt like anyone lived here.

The bedroom door was closed and there was no sound from beyond.

I started looking around the room, just a little. When I peeked into the bedside table, I found condoms. And a pair of handcuffs.

I knelt down, picked them up and studied them carefully. They were the real deal. I didn't see any keys to go with them, though.

I laid them carefully back in the drawer and looked at the condoms. Several strips of them, spilling out of a box.

Okay. No big deal. Maybe Lex was into some bondage stuff? Nothing too hardcore. I mean, they were just handcuffs.

Really wasn't my business whatever went on in this room before I got here, right?

I'd be lying to myself if I pretended my pulse didn't race, in a good way, when I touched those cuffs, though. Was that the alcohol? Or was I, Natalia De Santis, kinkier than I ever realized?

What the fuck was happening to me?

I slid the drawer shut, my heart racing. Lex had *handcuffs*. I'd never touched an actual pair of handcuffs before. But it wasn't like he had a full rubber straitjacket and zipper-mouthed leather hood in there, with floggers and nipple clamps and duct tape.

What if he did?

I glanced at the closet, wondering what he kept in there.

I was just getting up when I glimpsed something lacy on the floor, just under the edge of the bed. I picked it up, carefully, by the edge of the lace. It was a woman's turquoise thong.

When the door opened and Lex suddenly stepped into the room, it was dangling from my fingers. His eyes met mine.

"What is this?" I asked him.

He shut the door behind himself.

"What is this place?" I flicked the lacy thong into the corner of the room. Handcuffs were one thing. If they belonged to him, fine. But that lacy thong was definitely not his, and it was incredibly sobering.

He glanced at the lingerie in the corner but said nothing.

"You bring other girls here?"

He looked at me, eyelids low. "What if I do?"

Right. Nice.

I was getting the picture, slowly. Kinky cuffs. Some other girl's lingerie. This was his bachelor shack. His fuck pad.

"I can't believe I ran out on my wedding for you." It just fell out of my mouth. But I was jealous. Jealous of some invisible girl who'd left her panties here to haunt me on the worst day of my life.

"Really?" His cold eyes held mine, flat and empty. "I can."

Holy shit. Untouchable, cold-ass biker Lex was back. And I was not feeling him today.

Not at all.

"I know what you are," I said, all of it hitting me, hard. What I'd done... "I *should* know. My dad told me, all those years ago..." I spun around, suddenly feeling trapped, my head swimming with booze and guilt and this whole terrible day. "I can't believe... I broke his heart."

"Your dad's?"

"Both of them!" I spun to face him. "I broke Carl's heart today, and I broke my dad's. For this!" I threw my hands out at his shag palace, the old metal bed frame I'd thought might be rustic-cool, but I now knew was probably just cheap at some yard sale and easy to cuff a girl to. "I walked out on my wedding for this! Oh, God. Everyone will be looking for me. I need to call someone..." I started pacing, distraught. "I need to talk to Roni, explain to her what happened—"

"Talia," he cut me off. "You didn't run out on your wedding. I stole you."

"No, you didn't."

"I took you."

"No. You didn't. Shit, I need to talk to my mom."

I was still pacing when he got in my way, forcing me to stop. "Talia, you've been kidnapped."

"What are you talking about?" I was starting to get creeped out, the way he was staring me down. Why was he saying that? It was twisted, even for him.

"I kidnapped you," he said evenly. "This is in no way your fault. You didn't have a choice."

But I knew, as I stared into his eyes, I did.

I did have a choice.

I just made the wrong one.

"But... I got into the car..." My voice faded as his words really sank in.

Was it true? The dark, dead look in his eyes said it totally fucking was.

A cold chill ran through me.

"But... I didn't even fight..." My voice didn't sound like my own. It sounded like some poor, pathetic drunk version of Talia at the end of a long, terrible tunnel that was closing in so fast, I'd never be able to rescue her back through it.

Lex said nothing.

"You kidnapped me on my wedding day?" I whispered. I shook my head slowly, unable to process. "What the fuck is wrong with you?"

"Yes, all that. We can get into that later. Right now, I need you to focus. Things are progressing a lot faster than I expected, and they've taken a turn for the worse."

I backed away, slowly. Who was this man?

What the fuck had I done?

"Worse," I hissed at him, "than ruining the best day of my life?!"

He rolled his eyes. "May I remind you, you got in the car."

"*Shut up.*"

"Listen. I need you to calm down."

"I'm calm."

"And sober up a bit."

"I'm sober!"

"You aren't, but we'll just have to work with what we've got. I need you to make a phone call."

"Yeah. Great idea. I'm gonna call my dad, right now." I went for my bag, which sat on the bed, and dug for my phone. It was in there, somewhere.

"Talia," he said behind me. "Which part of *I kidnapped you* are you not getting? Your phone is gone."

Gone.

Like I now was.

He said it just as I realized: my phone was no longer in my bag.

I turned to him. "Who are you?"

"Don't get hysterical. You know who I am."

"Jesus. Oh my God. I should never have—"

"Let's save the introspection for later."

"Why? Why shouldn't I tell you that you're a fucking asshole and walk out of here, right now?"

"Because maybe you don't want to."

"Fuck you," I spat. All I could think of right now was Carl. And my parents. The people I should've been thinking about all along.

But I stood, rooted to the spot.

"There's the door," he drawled.

I went for it and he caught me with an arm around my waist. I slapped him across the face, hard. He grabbed my wrists so I couldn't do that again, or leave. So I did the next best thing. I rammed my knee up into his groin, hard.

But as always, Lex was faster, stronger, and taller than me. He blocked my knee with his iron leg, yanked my body against his, and locked his arms around my back. I was plastered against him, my arms locked down at my sides. He even shoved a knee between my legs so I couldn't ram my knee up between his again.

All in like two-point-five seconds.

"It doesn't have to be like this," he said. "Just calm down and we can talk."

"Talk. Right! You showed up two seconds before I walked down the aisle so we could *talk*. Just admit it. You ruined my wedding on purpose!"

"Yeah. I admit it. But you're the one who jumped into a car with me."

"You drove off! You could've told me to get out! You didn't have to kidnap me!"

"If I kidnapped you, it's halfway your fault."

What the fuck! What a *prick*.

I struggled, but I couldn't get loose. His arms were like steel.

"And whose fault is it that I'm here right now," I demanded, struggling, "and I don't even know where I am?"

"Mine," he admitted. "And I'm gonna make it right. You just have to trust me."

"Trust you? I don't even know who or what the fuck you are right now."

"I'm the guy you walked out on your groom for."

We stared at each other. Our faces were way too close. I was panting, he was panting, and we were still fused together. It was a hundred degrees in here. My boobs were flattened against him, I could barely breathe in my bustier… and this was the most of him I'd ever had. His body wrapped possessively around mine…

I loved it, and I hated it that I loved it.

"Fuck you, Lex Davenport," I said, my voice shaky.

"You can't walk out of here," he said calmly, "because you can't. You said it yourself. You don't even know where you are. It's dark out, and you don't have a shirt, a wallet or a phone."

"You took my wallet, too?!"

"I just told you, you've been kidnapped, babe."

I struggled again, trying to squirm out of his arms. Impossible.

He sighed. He got tired of struggling with me, maybe, because suddenly he was walking me backwards and putting me up against the wall. He pinned me with his weight, his hands gripping my arms to hold them in place, his thigh still wedged firmly between mine. A little too firmly.

Every time I moved, the pressure of his thigh against my crotch set off sparks.

"What fresh hell is this?" I almost moaned, squirming.

"Don't fight," he said in a low, gruff voice, his caramel eyes holding mine. "It's probably better if you don't fight."

"What the hell does that mean?" I stopped squirming, but I was still panting. So fucking angry.

Aroused.

Yup. This was turning me on. Lex, plastered against me, was just way too hot. No matter what the circumstances.

"It means, we don't have time for that," he informed me, his eyes drifting down to my squished boobs, heaving against him, "so don't get carried away."

"Time for what?"

"Talia. I know what you want."

I spat in his face. "You are the most disgusting, egotistical villain I've ever met."

He wiped his face on the shoulder of his shirt. Then his eyes hit mine again, ablaze.

Okay, Tal. Maybe don't totally piss off the very strong man who's holding you captive.

"Yes," he said slowly. "I am. You're finally getting the picture."

I growled in frustration, struggling again. Bad idea. The thigh-to-pussy pressure was way too much. Much more of that, and I'd very possibly suffer the most embarrassing orgasm there ever was.

"*Why?*" I demanded. "Why my wedding? Could you not have pulled me aside somewhere else and said, 'Hey, I need to talk to you'?"

"You didn't exactly leave me another opening. You were with your wedding party, twenty-four-seven, for the last three days. And you ignored my calls." His hips shifted against me, snuggling into place against my pelvis as I squirmed again.

Fuck. *No.*

His *dick.* Where the hell did that come from? Long and unmistakably erect, jammed up against me.

Oh God, that felt good.

He was *hard.*

"You… didn't…" I gasped. "I didn't know you wanted to… to…" My words tripped up and faded off. I was sweating. Overheating. Starting to shake as my heart hammered inside my ribcage.

Yeah, I'd ignored his calls. Of course I'd ignored his calls. I was marrying another man.

He'd given me no reason not to.

I hardly needed him calling me to fuck with my head any more than he already had.

"What do you think I was calling you for," he growled, "to wish you a happy marriage?"

"Well, I didn't think you were calling to tell me you were going to kidnap me!"

"I was going to talk to you."

"About?"

"About ditching your wedding."

Oh. *Shit.*

I yanked against his hold and went nowhere. All that did was make his hands tighten on my arms and his body press harder against mine, so I had to tilt my face up at a more severe angle. I wouldn't have broken eye contact with him right now if someone ordered me to with a loaded gun to my heart.

"Lex..." I breathed. And my hips did a thing of their own, pushing back against him. My heartbeat throbbed in my chest. In my head. In my clit, jammed against his cock.

His cock flexed in his jeans and a terrible, desperate noise escaped my throat.

His eyes darkened as he studied my eyes, holding me pinned by his gaze and his weight. His breathing was low and ragged, his lips parted as he stared at me. And he truly must've had the Devil's blood pumping through his veins, because holy God I wanted him to kiss me.

He shifted his hips again.

"Ohh, please..." My words were involuntarily. My voice sounded far away. My pulse raged like a river, drowning my senses in *him*. "Lex..."

"Talia." He shifted his hips again, his eyes hazing over, and I hissed in a slow breath.

He did it again, and my clit hummed under the friction of his hard length grinding against me. The tears dribbled from the corners of my eyes. My core ached with an emptiness so acute, I thought I might die if he never touched me inside.

He did it again, grinding against me, slow, and I bit my bottom lip. I swallowed a sob.

He looked as entranced as I felt.

I pushed against him with everything I had, but I could barely move. He felt me straining against him, though. His pupils enlarged, drowning out the color in his eyes.

He did it again, a slow flex of his hips, that hard, hot ridge scraping against my clit, and I shuddered in his grasp. "I just…" Tears streamed out the corners of my eyes. "I can't. *Please.*"

He searched my eyes, carefully. "No?"

I shook my head, biting my lip, begging for mercy and relief.

He moved his hips—at once merciful and cruel, as the pressure of his dick digging into me shifted away. But then something else bumped up against my pussy.

"Uhh…" I looked down, but I couldn't see whatever was under his vest. I could feel it, though. "Is that…" I squeaked; abject panic as my muscles strained toward some terrible end that I didn't even want to see coming. There was a monster around the corner—and I was about to throw myself in its path. "Is that a gun in your pants? Or… are you just happy to s-see me?" My voice trembled as my hips shifted. I felt the hard thing in his jeans, unyielding. Different than his cock. Hard as that was… this was much harder. *Cold.*

I met his eyes. The look in his was entirely savage as he watched me like a hungry animal, his tongue sweeping over his lip. His silver teeth peaked out, those fucking fangs.

"Yes," he said.

My heart leapt into my throat and my clit lit on fire. He moved infinitesimally, and I wriggled, dragging myself against it. Against the metal barrel of a gun through his jeans.

Oh. My. God. I was making out with a gun.

"Is it… l-loaded?" Holy Jesus, I'd never heard my voice like that before. Fucking terrified. Needy. Terrified because I felt so damn needy as I clung to him.

"No." His eyelids dropped, dangerously low. "Why? You wanna touch it?"

I was hanging on by a hairpin trigger—and that set it off. I came with a scream. While rocking my clit against the gun in his pants.

But before the scream clawed its way up my throat and out of my mouth, Lex covered my mouth with his, burying his tongue deep inside. He devoured my scream while I blew apart.

Chapter Seventeen

Lex

Talia screamed into our kiss as her body bucked against mine. Her thighs clamped around mine as I rocked my hips a little, pulsing the shaft of my straining cock against her hip. Did nothing for her, no doubt, since her clit was busy elsewhere.

She was deep in the throes of a throbbing orgasm, courtesy of the Glock in my jeans.

As she clung to me, the scream broke and she made soft little whimpering, sobbing sounds against my tongue. Through the soft layers of her flimsy skirt, I could feel her warmth. I could feel the shudders of her orgasm run through her body as I lapped my tongue against hers, forcing her mouth open wide with mine.

I couldn't stop.

I couldn't even remember what I was doing anymore.

Making her hate me?

Trying to make her happy?

Soon as she'd started rubbing her clit against my dick, everything just kinda went... sideways.

She kissed me back, sucking desperately as I smothered her

cries with my mouth. As she took my deep kisses and her body softened, I could imagine, too easily, sliding into her wet heat, shoving myself up between her legs.

Heaven.

I finally ripped my mouth from hers because I was so drunk on kissing her, on the sensations of her orgasm shaking her apart, that I almost forgot where the fuck we were and what the fuck I was *supposed* to be doing—turning her against me—and I almost slackened my hold on her.

Instead, I crushed her against the wall with my weight as she shivered in the aftermath of the orgasm she'd just had against my gun.

That was the hottest fucking thing I'd ever experienced while not actually coming myself.

Nope. Correction.

That was the hottest thing I'd ever experienced, anytime, anywhere, under any fucking circumstances.

Talia wouldn't meet my eyes, though. She was panting softly and looking anywhere but at my face.

"Talia," I murmured.

She swore under her breath.

She looked embarrassed and like she wanted to vanish into the wall. And angry, but not enough to want to knee me in the balls again or anything. She looked wilted. Drained. She tried to tug out of my grasp again but I just tightened my hold.

I wasn't letting her go anywhere right now. All I wanted to do was hold her and make it okay. But I just pressed her against the wall, trying to catch my breath.

"Babe," I muttered.

Her eyes flicked to mine. She looked like she was gonna start crying again. The tears had smeared on her cheeks while we kissed and run dry. She blinked at me.

"Roni's here."

It was the only thing I could think to say right now to get her focus off what just happened. And anyway, I had to tell her.

As much as I'd rather not.

As much as I'd rather just ram my thigh up between her legs a little tighter, dig my gun into her again and see if that magical thing might happen a second time.

My cock was throbbing so hard, trapped between us, everything was kind of a blur.

I swallowed thickly as she blinked up at me.

"Wh-what?"

"Remember when I told you to focus?" My voice was low and hoarse and I cleared my throat, as I told *myself*, again, to focus. I held her gaze, willing her to understand that what I was telling her was life-or-death important. "Your friend is in the next room, in her bridesmaid dress. Handcuffed to a bed."

I could see it in her eyes when that image hit home, hard. "You *fucker*!" She tried to push me off, to go find Roni, but I held her tight.

"She got caught up in this," I grit out. "I didn't want her to."

"Caught up? What do you mean caught up? You kidnapped Roni??" She was livid. Way more pissed off about Roni in this situation than she was about herself.

Interesting.

"I didn't take her. I have… an accomplice."

"Oh! That's so much better!"

"You need to stay calm," I repeated, calmly. "I'm not gonna hurt her. But the other guy out there, I can't say the same about him."

She stopped squirming. "What do you mean?"

"I mean, I won't be able to keep Roni safe if you don't stop fighting with me. I kinda need my energy for other shit right now."

That got through. She went totally still.

I let her catch her breath. Then I eased my weight off of her. When she stayed calm, I released my grip on her arms, slowly. I let her go. I eased back a foot, keeping a wary eye on her.

"There," I said. "Now maybe we can talk—"

She slugged me in the gut.

I caught her fist, kind of, absorbing the impact.

"You brought a friend? What fucking great news," she spat out, as I pinned her arms to the wall again. "*Two* assholes Jude can castrate when we get out of here!"

"Yes. And you can get out of here as soon as we collect the ransom."

She went kinda pale, suddenly, like I'd just slapped her or something. "Ransom...?" It slipped out in a whisper.

The sick feeling, low in my gut, where she slugged me, probably felt a lot like what she was feeling right now.

She lost her fight, softening in my hold. She sounded wounded when she said, "You kidnapped me... for ransom?"

"Yes."

I could see it plainly on her face: this shit just got real for her.

"We're going to call your dad, and I need you to speak to him."

She shook her head, like she was trying to make all of this disappear. "Why would you want me to speak to him right now?"

"Proof of life."

"Proof of..."

"It means proof that we have you, and that you're alive."

"I know what it means. *My God...*" Her eyes widened, and she seemed to look right through me as her head went somewhere else. Or all over the place. "Does my family know I've been kidnapped?" She gasped. "My poor *mom*! Is Jude already looking for Roni? Yes. Yes, of course he is. Has anyone called the police? Are the Kings searching for us? Are we on the news? Has someone found my dress? My phone...?" She drifted off.

"Can you stay calm?"

Her eyes met mine again and snapped to focus. "*Yes.* I want to talk to my dad." Her eyes were tearing up again, and I hated it.

I didn't want to see her like this. To see how this was hurting her.

But I could tell she was trying to stay calm now, for real.

Or maybe she'd finally just broken.

I let her go, and she didn't move. This time, she didn't strike out.

She just stood there.

"Okay." I eased back. "Good girl. You're doing good, Tal."

She blinked at me, struggling not to let the tears show. "Did you really just say that to me? Call me a *good girl*? Because I'm doing what you want me to do, in the middle of this horrid mess?"

I said nothing.

"Yes. You fucking did. Because that's all I ever was to you. The good girl." She blinked the tears back, faster. "The good girl you were never going to touch. Except to use me for a little while. And not even in the fun way. For *money*. For fucking ransom."

"Talia…"

"I want to see Roni," she said, standing up straighter. "I need to know she's okay."

"I'm not gonna hurt either of you," I promised her. "You can trust me on that." As much as I needed her to hate me right now, I didn't want her to think that.

"What about your *accomplice*?"

I shifted closer again, but I didn't touch her when I growled, "He's not getting near you."

She stared up at me, her eyes wide. "What about Roni?"

"Roni's fine. We're gonna get this over with as fast as possible. No one needs to get hurt."

But that wasn't true, and maybe she knew it; that one of us stood to get hurt.

Me. Definitely me.

She stared at me in silence.

"Just do what I need you to do, okay? Talk to your dad, we get the ransom, and then you can go back to your life."

We stared at each other for a long, tense minute.

"And what about you?" she said quietly.

"Don't worry about me."

Her voice was soft and it shook a little when she said, "I won't."

But we both knew that was a lie.

I led Talia into the bedroom across the hall, gripping her by the arm. I couldn't risk her trying to make a run for it—and running straight into Nico.

Roni was just as I'd left her. Handcuffed to the bed, blindfold on. She lifted her head, tensing as we walked in. Talia gasped when she saw her. She tugged away from me and I let her go.

"Can't you take that shit off her?" she demanded.

Roni sat up straighter. "Talia?"

I really didn't want Roni to know I was here, but Talia already knew. She could blurt it out at any second. And really, my days were numbered anyway. Probably in the single digits.

So I removed Roni's blindfold.

She pulled back, staring up at me in disbelief. "What the fuck, Lex," she grit out.

She watched me as I moved back to stand by the door. She looked from me to Talia and back, a few times, as Talia moved in, slowly, and sat down next to her.

"Are you okay?" Talia asked her. She ran her hands up Roni's arms carefully, over the sleeves of her leather jacket, like she was looking for damage. Like she was afraid of breaking her.

"I'm just fabulous," Roni said sarcastically. "Are *you* okay?" Her eyes raked over Talia in her bridal lingerie and fluffy little white skirt, then landed on me again. If looks could kill, I'd be strung up from the roof by my toenails right now. "What the fuck is wrong with you?" she growled at me. "She chose another man, Lex. Be a man and walk away. Don't kidnap her on her fucking wedding day!"

"Uh," Talia said, "I kind of went with him."

Roni looked at her. "What?"

"I ran out on my wedding."

"Because he made you," Roni corrected her.

"No, he didn't."

"Yes," I said, "I did."

Talia glared at me. "It was *my* choice."

"Then why am I handcuffed to a bed?" Roni said.

"Because you've been abducted," I told her.

"No shit," she fired back.

"Just like she was," I added.

"I wasn't!" Talia protested.

"Stop defending me," I growled. Then I told Roni, "Listen, Talia has nothing to do with this."

"Then let her go," Roni bit out.

"I can't."

Roni studied me for a long, cold minute. "Jude is going to end you," she informed me.

"I know."

She looked at me strangely, like *Why are you doing this, then?*

"I'm gonna get you both out of here as soon as I can," I told her. "Just chill and I'll be back to check on you." I met Talia's eyes. "Come on, Tal. We need to call your dad."

I waited for a moment while the girls whispered to each other a bit, reassuring each other that they were okay. I couldn't hear it all. Talia gave Roni a long hug, which she tried to return, except, handcuffs.

The promise of vengeance in Roni's eyes when she looked at me, as Talia got up and came over to me, spoke bloody volumes. That I had to get her the fuck out of here was not a question. I just had to find a way. But trying to convince Nico to let her go would make him suspicious, make him wonder where my loyalties lay.

I had to do it, somehow, without him stopping me.

Then I'd deal with Talia.

When this is all over, I swore to whatever god or devil might be listening as I led Talia out to the living room, *if I can just get them both out of here safe, I'll stay the hell away from her. I promise.*

Of course, if I was dead, that would be taken care of.

————

In the living room, Nico was waiting. He got to his feet. When he looked Talia over, I regretted not finding her a shirt yet. But things were moving along at a fast pace. Priorities.

"She ready?" Nico grunted at me.

"I'm right here," Talia said, before I could answer. She jerked her arm out of my grasp. "I can speak for myself."

"Yeah," he said, "and you'll shut your mouth unless I speak directly to you."

Talia's mouth fell open. Her eyes met mine.

I rubbed my jaw, choking that one back. I would've happily bitch slapped him again for that, or worse. But it definitely served her better to let her fear him a little.

"Whatever you do," I told her, as Nico started dialing, "don't tell him who has you."

"What if I do?" she said defiantly, and Nico stabbed her with a look.

"Then I die a lot faster," I said.

Her eyes held mine. She swallowed.

Nico got her dad on the phone. Then he handed the phone to her. "Behave," he told her.

Talia took the phone and brought it to her ear, her hands shaking a little. "Hi, Daddy." She sniffled, squeezed her eyes shut and took a big breath. "Yes. I'm okay. Just do what they say, okay? Give them the money and we can go." There was a pause. Then her eyes met mine.

Her voice was even softer when she said, "Jude?"

I took a step toward her, the hairs on the back of my neck standing on end.

"Yes," she said gently, "Roni's fine. I promise."

She was talking to Jude? He was right there, with Talia's dad?

"I just talked to her," Talia said into the phone. "She's in the other room, resting—"

Nico snatched the phone from her and hung up.

Before he could say a word, I shot him a murderous look. He was way too close to her right now. He put his hands up and backed off, rolling his eyes.

I took Talia by the arm and led her straight back to her room. The less time she spent in Nico's presence, the better.

I shut the bedroom door behind us, releasing her.

She turned to me, pushing her hands into her hair. "Why can't Roni talk to Jude? He's worried about her."

"I know."

"Don't you want her to give proof of life?"

"You gave it for her. That's enough for now."

"Please," she begged me. "Jude is my friend. You should've heard his voice. He needs to hear hers."

I looked away. I was pretty sure there was a special place in hell for men who betrayed their sworn brothers and I was headed straight there. "I can't trust her not to give up my name, Talia."

She took a step toward me and I met her eyes. "They're going to find out who did this. I mean, where do they think you are right now?"

"Out of the province. Visiting family."

"And how long will that lie hold?"

"I don't know. They're used to me disappearing. It's kinda what I do."

She stared at me. "So, after you collect the ransom... you're gonna disappear?"

"I don't know."

She hugged herself, looking away, like she was trying to pretend that didn't bother her. "I don't like that guy out there."

"Neither do I."

"Then why is he here?"

I didn't answer that.

She started pacing. "So, you don't trust Roni enough to put her on the phone, but you trusted me? Why? Am I so easy to manipulate?" We locked eyes. "I am, right? At least... I am for you." She kept pacing. "I always have been. When we were kids, you could get me to do anything."

"Not anything."

"You got me to agree to marry you and I didn't even like you."

"You wouldn't kiss me," I pointed out, and she stopped pacing.

She looked confused. "You wanted me to kiss you?"

"You didn't like me?"

She said coldly, "I liked you about as much as I do right now."

Good. She was still pissed at me.

That anger would protect her, make her keep her distance.

Maybe.

"You're safe here. I promise you that. You can just try to get some sleep. I'll leave you alone."

"Sleep? How the fuck can I sleep?"

"I told you, nothing will happen to you."

"Right. Because this night has been totally uneventful so far."

"You haven't been hurt."

"And that's how you justify this?"

"I can't justify this at all. Except to tell you that if it didn't go down this way, it would be worse."

She stared at me.

My fingers were twitching. I wanted a hit of nicotine in a way I hadn't in a long fucking time. I dug in my jeans for my cigarette case, lit up a blunt and offered it to her.

"You mean... I'd be here anyway... with..." She glanced in the direction of the living room, fear flashing over her face. "Some other guy?"

I didn't answer. I didn't want to think about that scenario any more than she did.

She took the blunt from my hand and went to sit down on the edge of the bed. She took a small drag, studying me, then held it back out to me. "Why are you doing this, Lex?"

I came to take it and sat down next to her, smoking as she kept staring at me.

"Money?" she said doubtfully. "Really? You'd betray your motorcycle club for money?"

"Looks that way."

"How much money?"

"Two million."

She made a choked, disturbed noise. I couldn't even tell if she was astonished that the amount was so high, or offended that it was so low. "Who is that guy out there?"

"I can't tell you that."

"Well, what do you think Jude and your club brothers are doing right now? Going to sleep?"

"No."

"No, they're not. They're hunting down whoever abducted Roni, right? How do you know they're not on their way here right now?"

"I don't. But I don't think they know who took you or where we are."

"Why?"

I looked her in the eye. "Because if they knew, we'd probably already be dead."

I could see the fear washing over her, cold and scalp-tingling.

"Me and him, I mean. You're not getting hurt here."

She shook her head a little. "You keep saying that. It's almost like… you care."

"Talia." I raked a hand through my hair. Took another drag and exhaled, looking at her.

Trying to make her hate me, scare her away, didn't exactly work as well as I'd hoped. I mean, she *came* for fuck's sake. I was way out of my depth here. And I was wavering again, between my empathy for her, how vulnerable she must feel after what just happened between me, her and my gun… and what I was supposed to be doing, which was keeping her safe. From me.

But I was not gonna let her sit here feeling shitty, thinking I never gave a fuck about her. She didn't deserve that shit.

"Let's get one thing straight," I told her. "There is no universe that has ever existed where I didn't always care about you."

Tears pooled in her brown eyes.

She took the blunt when I offered it back to her, took a drag, and handed it back to me. Her fingers trembled a bit as I took it. Her lips trembled. She looked away.

"You," I told her gently, with gravel in my throat, "are the most beautiful, funny, determined, gentle—"

"And when did you decide all these things about me?" she interrupted me, blinking back tears.

It was a fair question. More than fair.

Because I sure as fuck never let her know I thought all those pretty things about her. And so many more.

When I was watching you seemed like a fucked-up stalker thing to say. But it was true.

I'd been watching her for years.

"I notice things," I said vaguely.

She sat with that as we shared the rest of the blunt. Then we just sat in silence. I leaned forward on my knees and stared at the carpet.

"How long will it take them to figure it out?" she asked me.

"That's impossible to know."

"But they *will* figure it out, right?"

Yeah. Unfortunately, she had that right.

"The Kings are powerful, Talia. Connected. Like you have no idea. And they'll be on this until they get answers."

"And that's it?"

"No. That's not it. They'll want retribution, too. And they'll get it."

"How can you be so sure?"

I almost laughed. "You don't fuck with the Kings. The club has money, probably way more than you think, but money isn't the only currency we deal in. Respect, power, dominance... You don't threaten the dominance of the Kings and get away with it. You get taught a lesson. You get put in your place."

"Even if you're a member?"

"Especially if you're a member. You don't betray your club brothers, and you don't betray the patch."

"What patch?" I felt her light touch, skimming over the patch on the back of my cut. "The Kings thing on your back?"

"That 'Kings thing' is a code of honor, and it's sacrosanct." I looked at her, hard. "And you do not repeat anything I just said. As far as you know, the West Coast Kings are a social club for motorcycle enthusiasts who throw great parties. End of story. I don't talk about the Kings to you."

She seemed to consider that. And the fact that I had just talked about the Kings to her.

"Do you think they'll find us? I mean, before they pay the ransom?"

Us.

She was thinking about this in terms of *us* now, and I could tell: she didn't just mean her and Roni.

"Maybe."

"How?"

"You did not just ask me to explain to you how the Kings do what they do. After what I just told you."

She held my gaze in challenge. Like she already knew: I'd tell her anything I could, if I thought it would help her understand. If I thought it might keep her any safer, in the long run.

Or keep her away from me.

"You're a smart girl, Talia. How do you think they'll find us? They'll get their hands on every bit of surveillance they can find in the area you were last seen, looking for evidence, doing everything investigators would do, but they'll do it better. And they'll do it dirtier. They'll be on it around the clock, and they'll do shit the police wouldn't do. They'll get answers any way they can. The thing you should understand about the Kings, and you will never repeat to anyone, is that the law doesn't apply to us."

She blinked at me. "How can you say that? Of course the law applies to your club. It applies to everyone."

"Then why aren't we in prison?"

She stared at me for a long, silent moment.

Of course, there were a few Kings in prison, but she probably didn't know that. Anyway, there weren't nearly as many Kings in prison as there should've been, if the law really did its job.

"You're more scared of them than you are of the law," she said slowly, "of going to jail. Aren't you."

I considered that. "I've never had a reason to be afraid of them before."

"And now you do?"

"Yeah. Now I do." I dug into my pocket. "You want another one?"

She eyed me as I lit up again. "Aren't you afraid of getting stoned? Letting your guard down?"

"What, with you?"

She held my gaze. "Yeah. With me."

I took a long, heady drag, looking into her gorgeous eyes. "The ship sailed on that one, Natalia De Santis. Long-ass time ago."

Her eyes got all soft as she gazed at me. "I love it when you call me Natalia. It reminds me that we're just kids."

"We're not kids anymore."

"Yes, we are. We're just two kids sitting on a dock on a sunny summer day, eating chocolates." Her eyes traced my face. "I never wanted you to leave at the end of summer."

"I think *you're* stoned."

"Will they really hurt you?"

I sighed, exhaling smoke. "Feel like I've answered that one

already. Is there some other version of the truth that you're hoping to hear?"

"I'm hoping to hear that you're not going to die in the next twenty-four hours."

Well, that was sweet. But misguided.

Probably the very best thing for her would be if I vanished off the Earth.

"Maybe I'll make it to forty-eight," I mused.

"So, you're telling me, either they hunt you down and kill you, or you get your ransom first, if you're lucky, then they hunt you down and kill you?"

"Pretty much."

"There's no other way?"

"Well, there's a slight chance that I manage to return Roni to them, ransom free, then collect your dad's ransom, let you go, then beg the Kings for mercy."

"Are they merciful?"

"I guess we'll see."

"Why would they be?" She narrowed her eyes. She seemed to be searching for cracks in my facade. "Because someone put you up to this?"

I sighed again.

"There's a reason you're doing this. *Tell me.* You didn't want to do this, did you? It's that guy out there... Is he forcing you to do this?"

"Don't try to make me the hero here."

"But you're not really the villain if someone is forcing you to do bad things, Lex."

"Just because you don't want me to be the villain, doesn't make it not true."

"Why are you pretending to be rotten? You said you won't hurt me. You're not evil, Lex. You care—"

"I told you," I growled, rubbing my eyes and suddenly feeling exhausted, "we don't have time for this, okay?"

"Well, when is there ever time in your schedule to admit how you really feel about me? What you really want with me? Because, I don't know about you, but ever since you interrupted my wedding and kidnapped me and brought me to some creepy house in the woods, my schedule is pretty clear!"

I frowned. "The house is creepy?"

"Any house where you detain a girl against her will is creepy, Lex."

"That may be true. But you never really asked me to let you go."

"Really. So I can just walk out that door, if I ask you?"

"No," I said honestly. "Not now."

"Why not?"

"Because he won't let you go." I let that truth sink in, for both of us.

Tears filled her eyes again, just like that.

"Talia…" My voice softened. "You need to stay calm."

"Why? Because it's too much for you to deal with my emotions in the middle of trying to plot how to get out of this alive?"

"Yes."

"Well, too bad! You've never wanted to deal with my emotions. But guess what? I'm emotional right now! I'm drunk and high, it's my wedding night, I got kidnapped—wait, no. I got *lured* by a man I have stupid, mixed-up feelings for, who I *thought* might have feelings for me, and now I'm being held for ransom and my family is probably worried sick that I'm going to get killed. I can't believe you fucked me over like this, and I'm so fucking angry at you for fucking me over like this, and the stupidest part is I'm fucking *crushed* that you fucked me over like this when I thought you wanted—"

I kissed her suddenly, wrapping my hand around the back of her head and crushing my lips to hers, and she froze.

"I'm sorry," I muttered against her lips.

I tried to pour all the sorry I was into that kiss, and slowly, she kissed me back. We melted together as I poured more sorry into the next kiss, and the next, because she was right about all of it. And I knew what she was really saying.

She liked me.

She'd always liked me, even when she tried to pretend that she didn't.

She'd trusted me, in the middle of what was probably the most vulnerable, scary, heartbreaking moment of her life, standing on that hotel balcony in her wedding dress, and yeah, I'd fucked her over.

And now I was probably gonna die for it.

I had nothing to offer her. Not even my lowlife self.

I was nothing but the rebel heir to a Mafia family, an outlaw, disloyal to my brothers, and I was about to lose everything I had.

Talia De Santis deserved far better than me.

As we kissed, I pushed against her and she lay back on the bed, taking my weight. Her hands went to my neck, gripping me as her mouth opened wider, letting me sink my tongue deep. As she moaned softly, her body undulating beneath mine in a slow roll, so fucking responsive... my dick hardened against her hip.

I pulled the handcuffs out of the drawer.

I broke the kiss, grabbing one of her wrists and forcing it into a cuff. I clicked it shut.

She didn't even fight. Her movements were languid, the pot making her sluggish and docile. Or maybe it was the desire. It burned up the air between us, making me sluggish, too. Making me want to melt into her and forget everything else.

If only I could.

Her mouth fell open, her lips flushed from kissing me.

She tried to wrench away as I got up. But I flipped her over, twisting her arms behind her back, where I clicked the other cuff onto her other wrist. When I released her and stood back, she twisted around, sitting up to face me. She stared up at me, her wrists cuffed behind her back, in shock. Shaking her head slowly as the tears flashed in her eyes again. Angry tears.

"Try to get some sleep," I told her. "And don't leave this room. You do not want to run into that guy out there."

"You're… you're leaving me here like this?"

I wasn't even sure which part she was more upset about. The fact that I'd just put her in handcuffs, or that I'd stopped kissing her.

But if I didn't stop, that kiss was gonna put us on a runaway train, bound for a place she wouldn't look on too fondly after she sobered up. Basically, she was my captive right now, and I was not fucking a woman while I held her captive.

Even criminals had limits.

"I need to go check on Roni."

"And what the fuck is this?" She tugged at the cuffs, rattling them behind her back.

"Insurance."

"Insurance?" She laughed, a wild, bitter laugh. "What, like the insurance you turned me into when you had me sign my name in your little notebook and seal it with my blood?" Her angry smile died and she gazed up at me sadly. "That's what I was to you, right? I wasn't even the good girl you'd never have. I was just insurance, in case you needed me, when all your other luck ran out."

"I've never had any luck."

She just stared at me, like she was waiting for me to turn this into something else. Something it wasn't and could never be.

"*This* is insurance," I explained, "that you won't do something stupid like try to run away. You won't get far without a phone, a wallet, a shirt, a weapon, or your hands. And even if you did… how would you explain the cuffs to whoever found you? You're gonna give up the name of the guy in the living room? A guy whose name you don't even know?" I let that sink in as her eyes blazed at me. "Or are you gonna give up my name?"

We stared at each other as my heart slammed blood through my veins; adrenaline and arousal. It was taking everything I had to stay cool, to force myself to step away from her. To walk away when she so obviously wanted me to stay.

But I knew she wouldn't give me up.

And she knew that I knew it.

"You gonna leave Roni here alone?" I pressed.

Her chin trembled, outrage and fury at war in her eyes. "I hate you," she whispered. "I should've run the other way the moment I met you, Lex Davenport."

"Yes." I reached to trace the tear off her cheek with my thumb. "You should have."

I stood looking down at her, wanting to touch her again. And because sometimes I had a stupidly big mouth that just didn't know when to shut the fuck up, I said, "You weren't insurance, Talia. You were always the one I wanted."

"That is not true," she hissed behind me as I went for the door.

"You know," I told her, "this would've been a lot easier if it wasn't."

Then I left the room.

Chapter Eighteen

Talia

After Lex left, I got up off the bed and paced the room, my hands bound behind my back. I listened at the door but heard nothing.

I took a look at the window. It looked out into the dark of the woods behind the house. It looked like it had been sealed shut by layers of paint, years ago, and couldn't be opened.

I looked through the whole room and bathroom for something I could use as a weapon, but found nothing. There were some clothes in the closet, some men's shirts hanging, but with my hands bound behind my back I couldn't exactly put one on.

Oh, and there were a whole bunch of sex toys and bondage stuff in the dresser, which I found a lot less exciting than when I'd found the handcuffs.

The handcuffs that were now holding me prisoner. And not in the sexy way.

Idiot. When had I become such a fucking idiot?

The place was otherwise pretty empty, not even a razor in the bathroom or a pointy hair brush. Unless I wanted to try to smash the mirror and stab Lex with a shard of glass next time he came in here.

Nope. Too hardcore.

As much as I hated him right now, I really didn't want him to die.

Not to mention it would've been impossible to pull off, what with my hands cuffed behind my back.

Which is exactly why he cuffed them.

God, this was maddening. I couldn't even decide if I was more frustrated by the fact that he'd handcuffed me—without my permission—or that he'd fucking *left*.

Eventually, I listened at the door again. I couldn't hear anything. I turned the knob behind my back so slowly it took like a full minute to make it release; it clicked loudly and I froze. It was still quiet out there. I eased the door open an inch and listened, and now I heard them. Male voices, whisper-growling at each other in the distant living room.

I eased the door shut and slowly let the knob rotate back.

Fuck.

He was right. I couldn't escape.

Even if I could escape, which was pretty fucking doubtful with that sinister-looking Machine Gun Kelly wannabe prowling around out there, I wasn't leaving Roni behind.

And in the meantime, I really didn't need to push my luck.

I was pretty sure Lex's *accomplice* would be far less gentle in his handling of me than Lex had been. I shuddered to think of that guy pushing me up against a wall. And I highly doubted having an involuntary orgasm on the weapon in his pants would be the result.

I could not fucking believe that even happened.

Actually, I couldn't believe the last few hours of my life had happened.

But oh, they fucking did.

Too bad. *Get over it.*

I decided on the spot that I was hellbent on surviving this night, with or without Lex Davenport's help. I could die of shame later, for letting him gun-job me and kiss me into handcuffs like the idiot I apparently was.

Right now, I had more important things to deal with.

Like getting out of this whole strange abduction situation.

Lex was hiding something, I could tell. He didn't want to do this. I was sure of it.

I looked around the room again. And again. I wasn't even sure what I was looking for.

A solution?

A magical portal to yesterday?

Eventually, finding nothing, I lay down on the bed. Exhausted, on my side with my hands cuffed behind me. It was not comfortable. I was sobering up and I felt like shit. It had to be the middle of the night.

Or maybe it was nine o'clock and I'd totally lost track of time?

There was no sound from the direction of Roni's room, and I prayed she was getting some sleep. I had to pee but I couldn't with my hands bound, and I wondered if Lex had taken Roni to use a bathroom. Getting ready for the wedding today, she had to pee like a dozen times.

I tried not to think about it.

For a while, I thought I could hear those whisper-growling voices from the living room, but that was just my imagination filling the empty void. It was so silent in here.

I lay thinking about Roni in that silence, and Jude, and Carl and my parents, and Lex, and I cried.

For a bit.

Then I decided to get my shit together. I couldn't just take this lying down and sobbing like a baby.

And suddenly, the solution came to me.

I just had to escape—and take Roni *with* me.

If we escaped, then there was nothing to be held for ransom anymore. I could go to Jude myself, appeal to him for help. Tell him that the guy in the living room forced Lex to do this. I didn't know his name, but I knew what he looked like. I knew the ugly tattoo on his face.

I had to get us out of here.

I just had no idea how to do it.

But I did know I needed a weapon, in case someone caught me on the way out. My eyes landed on the only thing in the room that might work, if I could get my hands on it.

The lamp by the bed.

I got up, backed up to it, and lifted it, feeling the weight in my hand. It was tall, brass, and solid. I switched it off and, with difficulty, unplugged it so it was free of the wall. I unscrewed the lightbulb and put it in the bedside drawer. That way, the bulb wouldn't shatter on impact; it would just be a quiet thump on the head.

Plus, if I had to use the lamp on Lex, I wouldn't want the glass to cut him.

Oh my God.

You're in love with a man who kidnapped you. Just admit it.

You're fucked.

You want to escape so you can save him, not Roni or yourself.
You're the poster child for Stockholm syndrome.

Except... you loved him before all of this.

You can't even blame it on the trauma.

The click of the doorknob startled me and I melted onto the bed. Whoever walked in found me lying quietly on top of the covers, in the near-dark. The curtain on the window was still open from my foraging about, and the moonlight streamed in through the trees.

I heard him shut the door and move quietly to the bed. Something about the care of his movements told me who it was.

"Lex?" I said sleepily.

"I thought you were asleep," he muttered. He was rustling around a bit and I realized he was taking off his leather vest. I saw him lay his gun on the bedside table. "It's not loaded," he said. "So don't get any ideas."

"What's going on?"

"Can I please just lie down," he said, lying down.

"What are you doing?"

"I'm sleeping here with you. So I know you're safe. There's nowhere else to lie down anyway. Unless you want me to try to sleep on the floor and basically get no sleep. I'm a bitch when I don't sleep."

"What about Roni?"

"Roni's safe."

"Did you let her pee? Did you get her some water? Did you let her lie down?"

"Yes. All of the above. I told her to sleep if she can."

I made a grumbly, *fat chance* sort of noise. "You really know how to treat a girl."

He ignored that. "Nico's passed out in the living room. I told her to scream if anyone comes in her room except me. I think she believes me that I don't want to hurt her. I told her I'll get her back to Jude as soon as I can."

"Jude is going to peel your skin from your body if you don't," I informed him. But he probably already knew that.

We lay in silence.

"Nico?" I whispered.

Lex groaned softly. "Shit. I didn't mean to say his name. I'm tired."

"You're traumatized."

"Jesus Christ. Are you on this again? I'm not the victim here. Don't pity me."

"I'm not a victim," I informed him. "I chose this."

"No, you didn't."

"I chose you," I said quietly. But he knew that was true, too.

Silence.

I wasn't sure what I was doing. But… if I could get him to come over here, take off the cuffs, and maybe distract him enough… I could reach the lamp. One swift crack over the head, it would knock him out.

Or, maybe it would knock him down just long enough that I could get out of the room? And if Nico was asleep and we were quiet about it, and fast enough, maybe I could free Roni and we could get out of the house...

If I could get her cuffs off her somehow. Maybe I'd find the key in Lex's pocket? In his vest? After I knocked him out cold with the lamp?

I mean, if this was the movie of my life, I'd pull it off for sure. Jennifer Lawrence could play me, and she'd defo pull it off. Come to think of it, Emma Roberts probably looked more like me, but Margot Robbie would totally kick ass in the role—

I realized as I listened to Lex's breathing that he hadn't said anything. Not one damn thing since I said *I chose you.*

"Did you really not choose me?" I demanded. "At all?"

"What?"

"When you showed up at the hotel..." My voice faded. Was I really this much of an idiot? "I thought, for a second... I thought you really chose me."

"Yeah. I chose you."

Right.

"How is that possible if you're about to turn me over for ransom?"

"Maybe I won't turn you over," he said darkly.

Oh, God.

What did that even mean?

I was sweating again. And so tired of being hooked into this stupid bustier. And hungry.

Fuck, I never even got to eat the chicken Florentine. Or my wedding cake.

And I had to fucking pee.

"Lex, can you take off these handcuffs? It's hard to rest like this."

"No."

"Why? I'm not strong enough to fight you."

He scoffed. "Pretty sure you could do some damage if you had a chance and you really wanted to. Especially if I was asleep."

That made me weirdly proud.

"Who do you think would play me in a movie?"

"Huh?"

"Nothing."

"Diane Kruger," he said after a moment. "But twenty years ago."

I tried not to smile. Diane Kruger was gorgeous. She was Helen of Troy, for fuck's sake. "Look, I've had to pee forever. Can you please just uncuff me and let me go to the bathroom?"

That was met with silence. Then a small sigh.

"Unless you really want me to pee this bed…"

He got up, helped me up, dug a key from his pocket, and uncuffed me. "Don't try anything," he said sternly.

"I'm just a girl," I said mildly, and he grunted.

I went to pee. When I opened the bathroom door afterwards, Lex was sitting on the side of the bed, waiting for me. He looked up at me and I flicked off the bathroom light.

I moved to stand in front of him, slowly. "Could you leave my hands uncuffed?" I asked softly. "Please? Just so I can actually rest a bit?"

"Lie down." He got up so I could slide into the bed, under the covers. Then he lay down next to me, covers pushed aside.

Unfortunately, he was between me and the unplugged lamp.

I sighed, stretching out on my back. My muscles ached. I wondered what time it really was. "This is so much better."

"It's just for a bit. Then I have to cuff you again."

I looked over at his profile. The moonlight on his face was epic. "So you can sleep?"

"Yeah."

"But how can I touch you if my hands are bound…?"

"Talia..." He exhaled in a quiet groan. "When I kissed you before..."

"You liked it," I whispered, because we both knew he did. I'd felt his cock pressed against my hip like a steel pipe. Again.

"You're my captive," he said gruffly, "if you didn't notice. Anything happened between us, it would be fucked-up."

I swallowed and forced out, "More fucked-up than me coming on your gun?"

He answered with a low growl, deep in his chest.

I reached to touch him anyway.

He moved, and I realized with horror that he was reaching to turn on the lamp beside him. It clicked but didn't turn on.

He clicked it a few more times, then swore.

Then he reached over me and turned on the lamp on the other side of the bed. Light spilled over us. He was now right above me and looking down at my face.

I wriggled a bit, trying to push my boobs into his chest as my cleavage spilled out of the bustier, hoping to distract him from investigating why the other lamp didn't turn on.

It seemed to work. His eyes moved down, away from my face.

"Please," I said breathlessly.

He seemed to be at war with himself as his eyes slid back up, then burned into mine. "You really want that...?"

"Yes. Why don't you?"

"I fucking do," he said tightly, almost like he was in pain. Of course, he didn't exactly get to come when I did, so... maybe he was in a kind of pain.

"Then why don't you just do it?"

His eyes darkened, as maybe he considered it. "Because... even if you weren't my captive—"

"I'm not." I wiggled my free hands in the air to prove it.

He ignored that. "I know I'm wrong for you. I'm *bad* for you. I'm—"

"Dangerous?"

"Yes."

"How much more dangerous can it get? I'm already in max danger here. I've been kidnapped from my wedding by a biker and some stranger who looks at me like a starving rat, and I'm being held for ransom in some house in the woods while other bikers may or may not be hunting us down." His eyes on me seemed to be softening, a little, so I went on. "Whether you were kidnapping me or not, I didn't know it. I walked out on my wedding for you." I held his gaze, trying to make him really absorb that.

Maybe in his mind, he really kidnapped me. But I went with him willingly. Neither one of us could deny that.

"I know," he breathed.

I went ahead and said it. "I'd rather be here with you than marrying him." *Holy shit.* It was painful how fucking true that was, even now.

He swallowed. "Talia…"

"I'd rather do anything with you."

He hissed out a breath through his teeth. "That's fucked-up, Talia."

I slid my hand down between us and grasped his cock. It was stiff, and flexed in my hand when I squeezed, hard. "Then why are you so hard?" I whispered.

"Because I'm fucked-up, too," he said, his voice rough.

I started rubbing my palm against him, slowly, and his eyelids flickered lower. But he shifted away, removing my hand. "I can't give you that." He reached and shut off the lamp, but I grabbed his arm before he could slide away. He stayed where he was, half on top of me.

I held his gaze in challenge. "Then give me what you can."

His eyes held mine for a long, breathless moment. I realized I was holding my breath, hard. My heart beat steadily in my chest, an adrenaline-charged thumping, as he studied me.

Then he dipped his head and pressed his face to my neck.

"Natalia," he breathed quietly against my skin, a restrained sigh, and I exhaled in a rush.

I could feel his exhaustion in that sigh. How hard he'd been fighting... whatever this was between us.

He hovered there for a moment. Then he pressed his lips to my throat... as my heart thumped pure lust and hope and crackling need through my veins.

Holy Christ, I wanted him.

I *still* wanted him.

I knew I couldn't have him like this, though. He was right—it was wrong. In every single way you looked at it, it was wrong.

But then he dragged his lips down, over my collarbone, and down my chest... and lightning streaked through me. My back arched in the wake of his touch, my body undulating under his like a cat's.

Yesssss...

Noooo...

Shit, it was everything I dreamed it would be having his lips on my skin.

Christ, this was working.

Wait.

I was supposed to be distracting him. So I could smash a lamp over his head.

But how could I do that... when he was...

I looked down at him. He was kissing his way down between my breasts, making hot, hungry sounds of surrender in his throat as his mouth and his breath warmed my skin.

My boobs were shoved up by the bustier and when he flickered his tongue between them, I let out an involuntary moan.

He reached behind his head, gathering his shirt to his neck—like he was suddenly burning up and had no need of clothes. He tore the shirt off over his head, flinging it away. I could see the tattoo on his skin, the king's broken crown that ran up the back of his neck.

And the muscles in his shoulders working as he spread his arms wide, over me, bracing himself on either side of my body—as he lowered his mouth to my skin again.

He kissed my breast, his stubble scratching lightly against my skin.

I wriggled beneath him, sob-sighing, desperate for more, as my hands delved into his hair. Then he ran his tongue under the edge of my silky bustier. He found my barely contained nipple. He made a growly *mmmmm* noise that rumbled through me… waking up every nerve and setting it on fire. He tongued my nipple until it popped free of the satin.

Then he latched on with his soft lips and sucked, and I forgot what planet I was on.

What was I doing? There was a plan.

Wasn't there?

Oh, *fuck*.

Chapter Nineteen

Lex

Talia dug her fingers into my hair, her fingernails scratching my scalp, sending shivers down my back while I sucked on her sweet nipple. Then I tongued the other one free of the satin and went to town on it, too.

"This what you want?" I mumbled, my voice rough, and she mewled a soft, pleading sound. Her nipples swelled as I teased with my lips and tongue.

"*Yesss.*"

"Right now?"

"Yesterday. And the day before. And all the days before that…"

Holy fuck. My head was spinning.

Lying here, Talia's body beneath me, her skin against my lips… her heart beating fast and her little moans as I sucked on her… felt about as close to heaven as I'd ever been. I knew I shouldn't have been touching her like this. It was fucking twisted. It was dead wrong, even if she was pleading for it.

And she was.

But I'd frayed my last nerve out there, arguing with Nico about letting Roni go after we got off the phone. Another call to Talia's father, to give him a location for the ransom drop.

I'd come in here exhausted and mentally strung-out, wanting nothing more than to just pass out next to Talia and maybe dream of waking up in a life where I wasn't so totally fucked.

I'd shown up at the hotel today wanting nothing but to stop her from getting married, take her away so we could talk, she'd be safe, and somehow I'd keep her out of harm's way. I didn't intend to kidnap her.

But then fucking Nico happened. And he was right; I was blinded by her.

I didn't see Roni see me taking her.

I'd spent the rest of the night trying to figure out how to get out of this alive. How to get Roni back to the Kings, when Nico was bent on holding onto her until we got the money. I *had* to get Roni back to Jude before that ransom deadline hit tomorrow night.

I could *not* hold my club brother's woman for fucking ransom.

But Talia…

Fuck if I ever wanted to give her back.

If I was being honest with myself, I knew I had to give her back, but no way I fucking wanted to.

Did *she* really want me to?

I figured she was up to something when she seemed so bent on getting her handcuffs off, getting me to touch her, but she definitely wasn't faking her responses. She was moaning and panting as I kissed her chest, her neck… and before I could stop myself I was fucking consumed with the need to fill every soft, wet part of her body with mine and fuck her until this all went away.

But I was not gonna do that.

As she arched her back, thrusting her tits towards me, I reached under her and unhooked her corset thing. I ripped it off and tossed it on the floor. She was topless, her chest heaving beneath me, her hair all over the pillow, her eyes shining up at me.

Most beautiful thing I'd ever fucking seen.

I tried to memorize it perfectly, store it away in a box in my mind where it would remain untouched, untainted.

Because I wanted to remember this shit for the rest of my life. No matter how short it was.

Because I knew there was no way I was ever gonna see anything this good—*feel* anything this good—ever again.

"We need to find you a shirt…" I muttered, before sucking a nipple into my mouth again.

"Uh-huh," she breathed.

I sucked on the other nipple as she squirmed and sighed. Then I kissed and nibbled the softness of her breasts before kissing my way down. I lifted the soft layers of her skirt, slowly, and when she made no move to stop me, I yanked her panties down her thighs.

Her pussy was right in my face, and she was doing nothing to slow this down. She panted softly, stirring with impatience.

I took a heady breath. I felt so high, like I was gonna pass out, and I wasn't even stoned anymore.

I kissed her clit, and she made the most gorgeous, ecstatic, soft cry, I almost came in my pants. My dick flexed and I shifted my hips. I was practically fucking the bed, she had me so turned on.

My tongue snaked out to lick her pussy and she made a happy, sobbing sound. I wrapped my lips around her clit and sucked, and she gasped, her hands digging into my hair and holding on tight.

I glanced up at her.

Her mouth was open. She looked like an angel in the dark. The moonlight fell softly over her curves, and that's exactly what this was, right? She was an angel, and I was the demon feasting between her legs.

"I'm dying," she whispered, her voice shaky.

My mouth was too full to say anything. I just kept doing what I was doing, trying to kill her with the pleasure. Lapping my tongue all over her pussy, dipping inside, sucking on her clit as her hips bucked.

Her legs shook. Her breaths came in short, sharp little pants.

I slid my hands up her body and grabbed her nipples with my fingers, squeezing them gently, then not gently, as I ate her out.

"Is this wrong?" she gasped out, but not like she was scared. More like… curious.

"Yes." I suckled on her clit, then shoved my tongue inside her. Then swiped it all the way up to her clit again, slowly. My heart was drumming, hard and fast, but I tried not to rush what I was doing. "Tell me to stop. Now." I swept my tongue over her clit, then sealed my lips over her again and sucked. Hard.

Because I did not want her to tell me to stop.

"But it feels so… *right*," she gasped out, her voice getting scratchy now. Ethereal. A broken whisper in the dark.

"Tell me to stop, Talia."

"*Augh*… I don't want you to stop," she groaned, as I lapped the flat of my tongue over her clit. Maybe I just wanted her to say it. To beg me to keep going. Her legs were shaking something fierce now, her fingernails digging into my scalp. "I want you to… *oh fuck*."

Her hips snapped up and I felt the spasm under my tongue. I stopped trying to hold back and went full throttle at her pussy with my tongue, lashing her flesh, fast and hot, as the shudder moved through her body. Then another one. And another…

Yes.

Her breaths came in sharp, choked-off gasps and soft cries. She swore and sobbed, this tearless, desperate sound.

Pleasure.

I didn't stop.

I wanted to drown Talia De Santis in more pleasure than she'd ever felt in her life, all at once.

I wanted to fuck her.

I fucking wouldn't.

I released her nipples and trailed my hands down her body. I moved my mouth to her soft inner thigh. I kissed her there, licked, nibbled a little as she came down, my hands settling on her hips and squeezing, restless.

My cock was so hard I wasn't sure I'd ever recover. My balls ached, hot and swollen in my jeans.

Why didn't I jerk off in the bathroom yet or something? Was I truly this much of a masochist?

I tried not to think about it.

Her panting gradually slowed. She went totally limp.

Then I went at her again.

I buried my face between her legs. I ravaged her pussy with my mouth as she whimpered and choked back soft screams and stuttered out my name.

L-Lex...

I wrapped her thighs around my head and kneaded my fingers into her soft flesh, to stop myself from snaking my hand between her ass cheeks and shoving several fingers all up inside her.

I swore up and down to myself as I licked and sucked and smothered her in pleasure that I wouldn't fuck her, wouldn't enter her body in any way.

Except... my tongue. It slipped inside again and again. I couldn't stop myself. I ate up her little moans and cries as my tongue wriggled inside her.

Then I suckled on her clit like a delicious, forbidden candy until she went off again.

She whispered something in tongues, something about *fireworks* and *holy God* and wrapped her hands around my neck. She squeezed, her fingernails digging in as she made a beautiful choked sound of total rapture—and the second orgasm kept pulsing through her body, deep and brutal.

She squeezed her hands around my neck and her thighs around my head and fucked my mouth, totally lost in it.

I sucked gratefully, grinding my hips against the bed.

Fireworks was right. I was seeing stars and fucking glitter. I was so close to coming... I probably could've rubbed one out just humping the mattress while I ate her pussy. But I held back. I tried to lie still and calm the fuck down.

She let go all at once and went limp again.

I kissed her inner thighs as she shuddered. I'd never felt anything so fucking soft.

I never wanted to stop kissing her.

But she stirred and moaned a little, like she couldn't take any more, and I stopped.

I looked up at her in a daze.

"Did you like that?" fell out of my mouth. It was literally the stupidest thing I'd ever said to anyone in my life.

But I just needed to hear her say it.

She laughed, a soft huff of breath. "I think I died and went to hell. I definitely caught fire. And then the angels lifted me up and shoved me back into my body. Through my pussy. While your mouth sucked my heart out through my clit."

I blinked at her. "That sounds... painful."

"It wasn't," she breathed. She gazed at me with a kind of devotion and wonder that I did not deserve. And a hint of shyness that almost killed me on the spot. "And... it was."

Fuck, this girl. She was the perfect girl.

I just wanted to tuck her in my pocket and bust out the back window, run off into the night.

But the Devil cast a long, relentless shadow, and I'd always be in it.

And I could never forget it.

I kissed her thigh again and she sighed softly.

Then I kissed my way back up her body, slowly, and sealed my mouth to hers. She didn't seem to care if I was dripping with her pussy juice, so I didn't care, either. She licked and sucked at me eagerly, her hands straying tentatively across my back.

It took every last drop of my will not to shove her thighs wide, let the throbbing sledgehammer loose from my jeans and drive into her, pound her against the bed for a nice, long hour or so. Felt like my dick was three times the usual size.

It was a long, hot kiss that I never wanted to end. But it had to.

When I broke away, we were both panting. It felt like my pupils were spinning, like I was on the world's strongest sex drug. I could barely feel my hands anymore. They were gripping her arms, shoved above her head. I couldn't even remember doing it, and I couldn't remember her fighting it, either.

She didn't fight. She didn't resist anything I just did to her, at all.

I was pinning her down, my hips flexing restlessly against her thigh as I fought the urge to fuck us both into oblivion.

She blinked up at me. "Aren't you going to...?" she said softly, shifting her hips under me a little. "I mean," her eyes flicked down, "we could—"

"No."

I barely heard my own voice. All I could feel was the pounding need. And the ache in my chest. It was so tight in there, I could barely breathe.

I couldn't decide which hurt worse, my balls or my chest.

And as I looked into Talia's eyes, I could feel all her feels, washing through me. They radiated out from her core, from her kisses, from her shuddering breaths.

They were in her eyes. Like they always were when she looked at me.

"You and your poker face," I muttered affectionately, with a broken sigh.

"What?"

"Nothing."

I swallowed thickly, willing my heart to slow the fuck down. Somewhere along the way it had taken off like a speeding train. I could feel it chugging endorphins and adrenaline through my veins. Blowing steam up into my brain and fogging out my better sense.

Making me high on her.

I'd probably already done too much. I wasn't thinking straight.

How could I, with the hard-on from hell?

I shifted off of her. I sat up, turning my back to her.

Right now, I probably would've given anything to be able to sweep her away somewhere no one would find us and keep her there, safe. And strung out on orgasm after orgasm until maybe she forgot what a terrible bastard I was. For even just a little while.

But I'd already tried to sweep her away somewhere no one would find us, and it didn't work out so well.

I didn't get to have her. Not even for a little while.

And forever? Fuck forever.

Forever would be way too much to ask for.

I'd never been destined for forever with a girl like her.

I probably already knew it, deep down, when I was a kid and I made her write her name in that notebook. As if sealing it in blood would make any difference.

"I'm sorry I can't be good to you," I told her, my voice rough and broken. "You deserve better." Then I turned back to her and clicked a handcuff shut on her right wrist.

This time, she struggled a bit.

"Fuck!" she panted, as I fed the other cuff around the bed frame at the head of the bed. "Are you serious?"

I clicked the cuff shut around her left wrist.

She was now handcuffed again. To the bed.

"You can't be serious," she gasped, gazing up at me with wide, sex-hazed, but weary eyes.

Betrayed eyes.

I took a deep breath, willing the equipment in my jeans to calm the fuck down. And trying to reason with my dick that no, she was *not* any sexier now that she was handcuffed to a bed, topless.

And we were not fucking her.

My dick did not get that message.

I tried to focus on her eyes. "What did you do to the lamp, Talia?"

She watched as I went to investigate, her jaw dropping open. Girl seriously had zero poker face. "Nothing!" she cried, tugging at her cuffs to no avail.

I found the lamp cord unplugged, the bulb in the drawer of the bedside table.

I left it as it was.

When my eyes met hers again, she bit her lip.

"I'm sorry," she said, like she was afraid I'd be mad.

"Don't be."

"Fine," she said hotly. "I'm not."

I sighed heavily, and laid down on my side of the bed again, trying not to smile. I tossed a blanket over her. Obviously I was a very twisted individual, because I was actually proud of her for trying to betray me.

I'd just settled in when she spoke again, quietly. "Diane Kruger is beautiful and talented, but I want to be an action hero. I want Margot Robbie to play me."

"Okay," I said, like I could make that happen. Like I could make anything happen that she wanted me to right now.

I would, if I could.

She was silent for a bit, but I knew she wasn't sleeping.

"Who would play me in this movie?" I asked her.

"No one," she said. And when I didn't say anything else, she added, "You know why?"

"Because I don't belong in your movie."

"Because he doesn't exist yet. He'd be pretty and badass and so slick, no one would ever know he was the bad guy until we stole off into the night together at the end, with all the diamonds."

"You have terrible instincts with men."

"I was going to hit you over the head with that lamp."

"Good. Nice to know you have some survival instincts." I sighed again and tried to relax, hopeful that I might actually get some sleep tonight. But I couldn't really leave that one alone. "You might want to rethink your lamp idea, though. Choose something sharper. You'll only get one chance, and you'd better do serious damage. Otherwise all you do is stoke a guy's lizard brain and make him fight back."

"Why do you hate me?" she asked into the dark.

"I don't hate you."

"I wasn't talking to you. I was talking to God. Or my guardian angel, or whoever the fuck is supposed to be looking out for me."

"Hate to tell you this, but the only one looking out for you right now is me."

"Oh, that's rich."

But she really had no idea.

When we'd called her father again to put pressure on, I was fifty-fifty on believing he was actually gonna cough up the money. Sounded a lot more like he'd prefer to slowly murder the idiots who had his daughter by hacking us into tiny pieces and flushing us down a toilet.

I was starting to suspect that Talia's dad was more of a badass than I'd taken him for. And that it wasn't just the Kings we should be afraid of.

Figured.

There was a part of me that knew this was exactly where I'd end up one day—in way over my head.

I mean, this story always went the same, right?

If the Devil wanted your soul, he'd get it. And if you proved unwilling to sell it to him, he'd just take it from you, piece by piece. Get you to cross lines you would never have crossed on your own, one at a time and so far apart, you'd soon forget where the last line was. Until one day, you were in so deep there was no way out.

Except, maybe, to run for your life with whatever meager piece of your soul you had left.

I wondered how far I'd get before the Devil caught up with me this time.

"You should really take a self defense class," I mused aloud. "And get a gun. You seem to like them."

"Bite me."

"I will, next time, if you want me to."

She muttered, "And he thinks there'll be a next time."

I laughed. I was so fucking broke right now, I just laughed.

"Oh, you like that?" she said, all fake coy. "Why don't you bring your dick over here and I'll give you that blow job I offered you on your birthday?"

My dick, which had finally chilled out a bit, throbbed enthusiastically at the thought. I adjusted myself in my jeans. "Babe, you think I don't know I get my dick anywhere near you, you're gonna bite it off?"

"Good. You have survival instincts, too." She added quietly, "Maybe we'll get through this okay after all."

I wished I could tell her that we would. But I knew that wasn't true.

Just like I knew there would never be any *we*.

Chapter Twenty

Lex

In the hazy light of dawn, I lay next to Talia with a thudding erection. She was asleep. She'd fallen asleep pretty quick last night, actually.

I might've enjoyed the fact that she trusted me enough to fall asleep next to me, but she was probably just fucking exhausted, and the multiple orgasms didn't hurt.

I hadn't slept much all night. Too much on my mind.

I'd crept out to the living room like five different times to see if Nico was sleeping deeply enough, maybe I could sneak Roni out of here. But he'd woken up every fucking time.

And what was I really gonna do, leave Talia here with him while I snuck Roni back to the Kings? Or take Talia with me, on the run?

Fucking nope, on either count.

So instead, I got a shit sleep.

Plus, as dawn crept in and I lay here restless, I knew Talia was wearing nothing but a skirt under the blanket, with her hands cuffed to the bed next to me. That was poorly planned.

I finally got up, and found one of Shane's T-shirts for her in the closet. Talia looked like an angel sleeping, even sweeter than usual. It hit me with a pang of guilt. I lay the shirt next to her on the bed, like a peace offering. Proof that I was capable of doing one nice, selfless thing for her.

As I slipped out of the room, my phone started vibrating in the pocket of my jeans. When I checked the screen it said: *Jude*.

A cold, sick feeling spiked in my gut, but I tamped it down. I'd had a few calls, texts, from the club. Maddox, mostly. I'd called him back last night, before going to bed, pretending to be in Ontario—and both shocked and appalled when he told me the news: that Jude's woman had been abducted.

He'd talked mostly in code, Maddox-style, and kept it brief.

I hadn't heard from Jude yet, though.

I headed to the far end of the hall and stepped quietly out the back door, into the dawn light. Birds were singing in the trees. The forest surrounding the yard was thick, the air green and crisp. I took a deep breath and picked up.

"Jude," I said, my mind rapidly calculating as I woke up. I was in Ontario. Three hours ahead of him. Outside somewhere; he'd hear those birds.

"Where are you?" Jude demanded. He sounded rough. Way worse than last time I spoke to him; before someone stole his woman and his life went to hell.

I cleared my throat. "Toronto."

"With who?"

"My mom's out. What's going on? You get a lead on Roni?"

He didn't answer that. "You know, just now, as the sun's comin' up and I'm pacing up and down the damn road in front of the club-house for the millionth time since last night, not able to fuckin' sleep or do any fuckin' thing except worry about my girl, I find something in the grass at the side of the road. You wanna know what the fuck I found?"

"Uh, yeah?"

"Peach candies. The kind Talia's always eating like they're going outta fuckin' style and it's the last bag she'll ever have. She fuckin' loves those things. You connecting any dots here, Lex, or is it just me?"

I didn't say anything, while I scrambled to think of what I should say. But he was already talking again anyway.

"Because I sure as fuck am. I'm thinking, why the fuck are Talia's favorite candies sprinkled at the side of the road where Talia's never been, except if she has been, you know?"

"Right." I cleared my throat again. "That's weird."

"Yeah. Less weird after you take into account that it takes me all of seconds asking around to find out Talia came by here, night after your birthday party. To see *you*."

I breathed out, long and silent. No use trying to deny it. "Yeah. She did."

"And why would she do that?"

Fuck.

Go with the truth.

That's what my father always said about covering your tracks. The closer to the truth it is, the easier it is to uphold the lie.

"She said she wasn't sure about marrying Carl."

There was a long silence as Jude took that in. Then he said darkly: "And what did you do with that information?"

"Nothing. She wasn't in my room five minutes."

Silence.

"Axel and Blazer and Bane were all there. You can ask them."

"And what the fuck did you say to her?"

"I told her to marry Carl and not to come back. Toad saw her get in her car and leave."

Silence again.

Then he took a deep, growly breath. "You didn't think you should tell anyone this," he asked me slowly, "when Maddox calls you to tell you she's been abducted, along with Roni?"

"I didn't realize it was relevant."

Silence again.

"I mean, you guys said she was abducted, right? Not like she ran away from her wedding or something. I don't know. It never occurred to me to mention it."

"You know, you don't sound real bothered about it."

"What?"

"The girl comes to you, to your room at the clubhouse, to tell you she's thinkin' about breaking off her engagement to another man, and then you find out she's been abducted. And you do not sound that broken up about it."

Shit. I struggled to figure out what to say.

I couldn't exactly flip and start crying about it now. I wasn't that good an actor.

"I... I'm in shock. Talia and me... we had a weird relationship. I like her. But we weren't going anywhere together. I told her to marry her fiancé. I knew it was what was best for her. But..." Fuck... *Think.* "What do you need me to do? How can I help?"

Jude sighed, and in that sigh, I heard everything he was going through.

Roni. *Taken.*

He was basically living out his worst nightmare, and I was off, what, having lunch with my mom?

Where I should've been was at the clubhouse right now, offering any help I could. Like every other brother probably was. That was what you did. When a brother needed you, you dropped everything to be there.

What was the point of wearing colors otherwise, if you couldn't count on your brothers?

"Should I come home," I offered, like I probably should've already, "help search for Roni?"

"No. We've got enough guys on it. We need you, I'll let you know."

"Do you have any idea who took them?"

There was a long silence again that I really didn't know how to read.

"You know," he said slowly, "we really don't know who to suspect. Anyone who fucks with the Kings knows that's a bad idea. Who would take that risk? King says it's gotta be about power. A lot more money than that ransom. Or, it's personal." He paused and I waited, tense. "The more I think about it, it feels personal. You don't abduct a bride and her maid of honor on her wedding day unless it's personal."

"Yeah... That makes sense."

"Whoever it is, we'll find them. We'll make them pay."

"Of course we will. Just... look, I'm sorry about Roni—"

"Yeah," he said. "I know, brother." Then he hung up on me.

———

The next twelve hours or so were pure misery.

I mostly hung with Nico, who was wearing a deep dent in the living room couch. I wanted to keep an eye on him—and keep him the fuck away from the girls.

He mostly scrolled around on his phone and complained that there was nothing to do, in between disappearing outside for smokes. He seemed grumpy but energetic, like he'd slept like a baby. Probably had. The guy had no conscience that I'd ever met. And for all I knew, he was on something. Or several somethings.

He'd been watching a *Breaking Bad* marathon all morning, but when he tried to find porn on the big screen I cut the cord out of the back of the TV so he couldn't. No way was he sitting here bored and watching porn and getting any ideas about creeping on either of the girls.

I also told him if I found him watching porn on his phone, I was smashing it with the wrench and flushing it down the toilet.

He just rolled his eyes.

I took breakfast and lunch into Talia and Roni from the meagre offerings of the cupboards. Beef jerky, dried mangos, some rice I cooked up. I uncuffed Talia long enough to let her put on Shane's giant Vancouver Northmen hockey T-shirt. I let each of them use the bathroom a few times.

Roni threw up in the bathroom, after breakfast, and asked me for a bowl she could keep by the bed in case she needed to do it again while she was cuffed there. I gave it to her, trying to reassure her she was safe.

The fact that she was sick about the situation was making *me* feel kinda ill.

Whenever I was with Roni, I was careful not to take my eyes off her. I didn't ask her how she was doing or if she'd slept. Was pretty sure I already knew the answer. She still looked at me like she intended to personally murder me if her man didn't do it fast enough for her liking.

I spent as little time as possible in Shane's bedroom with Talia.

Every time I went in to check on her, she stared at me from the bed, where she sat with one hand cuffed to the bed frame, the other free, the way I'd left her. She didn't say much. Neither did I. Both of us had been kind of quiet around each other since last night.

Maybe she didn't want to push her luck and get the other hand cuffed again, so she didn't ask to be let free. But when I brought her lunch, she said, "If Nico ever comes through that door, I'll be using my free hand to punch him in the balls, just so you know."

"Good," I said, noting that she hadn't punched me in the balls. Yet.

It was a risk, but I'd left the lamp as it was. I really didn't think she could take me with that thing anyway.

Mainly because I was pretty sure she didn't really want to.

Nico had one more conversation with her dad that I didn't tell her about. During which De Santis still hadn't confirmed that he'd cough up ransom money, but he did describe how he planned to disembowel Nico, in colorful detail, before Nico hung up on him.

The man had come a long way from those family barbecues. I

wondered idly what Antonio De Santis would be like as a father-in-law.

Irrelevant. If the Kings didn't end me (doubtful), I was pretty sure by now that Talia's father would.

Then Nico had a conversation with Jude that went pretty much the same way. The Kings had given us their terms: as long as we had Roni, they weren't handing over a cent. We were to hand her back over, unharmed, and in exchange our pathetic lives would be spared.

But that was bullshit. I knew how the club worked, and abducting a patched member's woman was an unacceptable crime. A declaration of war.

As soon as they found out who'd abducted her, we were dead men.

———

By five p.m., with three hours left to go until the so-called exchange, Nico was getting edgy. "Why isn't this asshole coming around?" he kept griping.

"He will," I kept telling him. Antonio De Santis might talk a tough game, but at the end of the day, he was a father and we had his daughter. And he hadn't gone to the police. If he had, they would've made contact by now.

Which meant he was planning to play our game, eventually.

Or, the Kings' game.

He either planned to pay up or hunt us down. Or both.

"Why aren't they afraid of what we could do to those girls if they don't pay up?"

I looked over at Nico, sprawled on the couch and glaring at his phone. His thumb jabbed at the screen, probably playing yet another sniper game, but there was no sound. I'd told him to mute it hours ago because it was fucking annoying me.

"We're not doing anything to those girls," I said evenly.

"We're not giving them back. Not without the money."

"What the fuck are we eating for dinner?" I tried to sound as hungry and irritated as I was. But he didn't take the bait when I changed the subject.

Instead, his eyes lifted from his phone. "What the fuck are you doing in that room with her all the time?"

I glared back, trying to project boredom. "Nothing."

"You fucking her?"

"No. I'm working her for information. Stuff we can use against her father."

He lowered his phone. "And?"

"All she tells me is that Roni is tight with the Kings, but she isn't."

He sighed, like that was useless.

"We need to give Roni back," I told him, "then deal with De Santis. Forget your hundred grand. The Kings won't negotiate until we give Roni back. We don't need her. Let's just give her back."

"No. We give her back, we give up all our leverage with the Kings. You said so yourself. Your little blonde isn't tight with them. We're not giving up our leverage. We may need it to get out of here." He went back to his phone.

I got to my feet. "I'm gonna check on them again. Then we make one last call, and get this shit over with. I want to sleep in my own bed tonight."

Nico grunted.

When I walked into Shane's bedroom, Talia looked up from the bed. She was still sitting against the headboard.

As I shut the door behind me, she said, "I want to see Roni."

"That's probably not a good idea," I told her. Mainly because Roni loathed me right now and I didn't need Talia seeing that. "She'll be fine. I'm gonna get her out of here."

"How?"

"I'm working on it."

"How much time do you have left?"

"A few hours."

She watched me walk over and sit on the edge of the bed, an arm's length away from her. "What if my dad doesn't pay?"

"Then we renegotiate, I guess."

Her eyes held mine. "What if he does?"

"Then I guess I have to give you over."

Shit, there was not a hell of a lot of conviction in that statement.

I wondered if it made her hate me more or less.

"I'm not a side of beef, you know. You can't just take me or give me. I'm a person."

"Yeah, well, if he gives me two million dollars and I don't give you back in return, pretty sure if we try to run off into the sunset together, we don't get far."

She shook her head, looking guarded. She didn't want me to know she'd been considering that possibility, just like I had. That she'd been fantasizing in any way about the two of us making it out of here alive—together. "You really think my dad has that kind of money just lying around?"

"If he doesn't, my brother will."

She frowned. "Dane?"

"Yeah. I'll get it from him if I have to."

"Why? Why do you have to? What is the money for, Lex? Are you in trouble? Do you owe money to someone? Someone bad?"

I considered that. "Kind of. But more than money… my soul."

"What are you talking about?"

I sighed. There was really no point not telling her, was there? It didn't put her in any more danger.

In fact, it would probably go a long way to keeping her safer if she understood why the hell she should stay away from me. If she was as scared of my father as I was.

"My father made me abduct you."

Her jaw dropped.

"Look, Talia, I don't know what kind of business your father's really in, or what you might know about it or don't, and trust me, you probably don't want to know. But my father says he owes him money. And what my father wants, he gets."

"My dad owes your dad money?"

"Lots of it, apparently."

"Your dad is in the Mafia, though."

"Yup."

"My dad's in construction."

"Yeah. You know who else is in construction in this country, and in deep? The Mafia."

"But… construction is a legitimate business. My father builds buildings. I've walked through them."

"And how do you think criminal organizations launder their dirty money? Through legit business activities."

"So… my dad is laundering money for the Mafia?"

"I don't know. All I know is my father demands payment and this is how he's getting it."

"He told you to take me to make my dad pay?"

"Yes."

"But then where does it end?"

Truly, a great question.

"I don't know," I told her honestly.

She looked confused, like, *You seriously have no plan here, do you?* "Well, will this clear the slate?"

"I don't know. But I fucking hope so."

"That's all you're going on? You kidnapped me on an 'I fucking hope so'?"

"I didn't mean to kidnap you, Talia."

She sighed in frustration. "You kidnapped me. You didn't kidnap me. Which is it?"

"I thought I could make you disappear," I explained, carefully, "to satisfy my father. Take you somewhere safe and get the money, maybe from my brother if I had to, worst case. Pay up to make the problem go away."

"And then what?"

"I don't know. I didn't get that far."

She just shook her head at me in disbelief. "How was that going to work?"

"It probably wasn't. But it was worth a shot."

"But… then Nico took Roni and fucked everything to hell?" she filled in the blank.

"Pretty much."

She huffed. "On principle alone I don't even want my dad to pay that creep."

"Then you're fucking brave. And naïve. My father and his orders aren't just gonna go away."

She studied me carefully. "You say that like you know."

"I know he won't stop until he gets what he wants."

"But maybe there's a way we can give him what he wants *and* get out of here," she said. "Some way to negotiate—"

"He almost killed one of my best friends."

Talia looked horrified, as she should.

I dragged my hands through my hair. I didn't want to terrify her. But it was time she got it through her head that this wasn't some game. That she was in danger—and not just from me.

Real danger.

"He… did *what*?"

I took a breath and prepared to tell her something I'd never told anyone before.

"I'd just turned twenty and I had this old Mustang I'd been driving. It needed to be restored, but I was gonna fix it up over time. My friend Shane was crashing with me, at my apartment. He had a falling out with his family and his girlfriend kicked him out. It was always like that with him. Anyway, he loved that Mustang. Was always taking it out, cruising around."

I went silent, lost in the past for a moment, and she waited for me to go on.

"One night while I was out, at the clubhouse, he drove my car up Cypress Mountain to meet some friends. His buddies were snowboarding, but he just met them afterwards, at the bar for a beer." I looked at Talia. She was watching me with trepidation in her eyes. Bracing for what was coming.

I could already feel the cold wind in my face. The shards of glass.

But I'd never actually felt them on my face for real.

I wasn't even there.

"They cut the brake line while my car was parked in the lot. They probably followed him up there."

"They?"

"My father's men. Whoever he sent to do it."

I let that sink in, let the images take form in her mind. I could see her thinking it through, the ramifications of everything I said.

"By the time Shane was heading down the mountain in the snow, on that winding road, it was too late. He was picking up speed and the brakes lost power. He couldn't slow down. He lost control on the icy road at a turn and went right off the road into the trees, flipped the car and crashed."

"My God," she breathed.

"The doctors said he was lucky he wasn't paralyzed. They had to lift the car out of the trees, use the jaws of life to get him out. He was hurt pretty bad. Years of rehab." I nodded at the team T-shirt she was wearing. "He'd just been drafted that year, but he never played hockey again."

"Lex," Talia breathed. "That's…"

"Horrifying," I finished for her. "The thing you've gotta understand is that my father had no beef with Shane. Wouldn't have had anything to do with him, known anything about him, if it wasn't for me. He could've killed him. To hurt me. Maybe he meant to kill him. I'll never know."

"I don't understand. How could he get away with that? Wasn't there an investigation?"

"Yeah. Of course there was. The brake line was pretty obvious foul play, but without a suspect, a motive... The cops looked at me for a while, since in their eyes, anyone with Kings colors on their back is a criminal. But what motive did I have to cut the brake line of my own car and put one of my best friends in the hospital? Eventually, the investigation went cold."

"And what about the Kings? Didn't you tell them what happened?"

"They knew what happened. They knew about the accident and what happened to my friend, more or less. They didn't know it was because of me. I told them Shane had a lot of enemies. It wasn't untrue."

"You didn't tell them it was your dad?"

"What was I supposed to say to them? 'My dad cut my brake line and put my buddy in the hospital, can you please go after him for me?' I can't go to my club, my brothers, my President with that."

"Why? Because they wouldn't do that for you?"

"Because they absolutely fucking would," I told her. "And when the West Coast Kings make a move on a member of the Italian Mafia on the other side of the country, that means our MC brothers out east, the Dead Kings, get involved. The Nine Families of the Canadian Mafia and their Commission get involved. The godfather gets involved. The entire fucking underground gets involved, because there is no organized crime in Canada that isn't somehow affiliated with the Kings or the Mafia."

Talia's eyes darkened, widening as she took on the weight of what I was telling her. What I was admitting to her.

Stuff she knew she couldn't repeat, to anyone.

"It means war, Talia. War in the underground. I can't bring that shit down on my club because of some ancient grudge between me and my father." I couldn't. I would've done anything to protect my club, my brothers—even die. That was what it meant to wear Kings' colors.

Besides that, they'd been the best family I'd ever had.

"But your dad… almost killed your friend," she said softly.

"Yeah. Because I fucked up. I tried to walk away from him, and I paid for it. I learned my lesson. As long as I keep the peace between us…" I looked at her, sitting there in handcuffs, and the words tasted like bitter acid in my throat. "No one gets hurt anymore."

"How can you say that to me right now?"

"You're safe."

"For how long?"

"As long as I'm alive."

"And how long is that?"

"My father doesn't want me dead as long as I'm following his orders, Talia. And as hard as this may be to swallow, this probably isn't about you. It might not even be about your father or the money. It's just as likely a test. And if I fail, I pay anyway. And pay harder."

"So… when he told you to abduct me, you didn't go to the Kings for help because you didn't want to start a war? You thought you could just handle it yourself?"

I didn't answer. She got the picture.

But the rest of the picture was that I'd been going behind my club brothers' backs dealing with my father for years, thinking I could handle it myself. And right about now, I knew that was a terrible fucking mistake, with a certainty that was hitting me like a sledgehammer to the heart.

But too fucking late.

I almost wanted to laugh at how fucking happy this would make my father.

He was smarter than me. He always had been.

He'd fucking love it if this abduction gig blew up in my face, got me thrown out of the MC. After that happened, he knew I'd have nothing.

And maybe he figured if the Kings cut me loose, I'd finally need him.

Maybe he'd be right.

But hey, the joke was on him. Thanks to Nico, I probably wasn't gonna live long enough to get kicked out of the club. Or to go crawling back to him.

"My father wants power over me," I told her, trying to make her understand, "but that's not about money. Not exactly. He might say it is, but it's not. He also wants power over your dad, and maybe that is about money. For all I know, he wants to keep extorting money out of your dad, or using your dad to do his bidding, whatever. Whatever it is he really wants, he thinks he can keep using me to get it."

"Why?"

I held her eyes, knowing I was about to tell her the worst fucking part of it, because she deserved to know. "Because he found that notebook. The one with our marriage pact in it."

"Oh. *Shit.*"

"So... he seems to have decided that he can use you... this abduction... to manipulate me. And he's probably right."

"Lex." For the first time, Talia looked truly and deeply scared. And not of me, or even Nico. "What are we gonna do?"

Because she deserved the whole truth, I told her, "I don't know. But I won't let him use you. I won't let this happen again. I can get more money. There has to be a price. My father probably won't negotiate, but he will take more money in exchange for you, if he thinks I'm cooperating with him. And when I get him his two million and find out how much more it'll take, I'll get it."

She gazed at me like I'd just told her I'd give her my castle and the golden stable filled with unicorns out back. "But what if the price is too high?"

"My brother is a billionaire," I reminded her.

"What if the price is *you?*" she said softly. "What if the only thing he'll accept is you, doing his bidding?"

I didn't want to answer that. I'd never considered going back to him. Ever.

But if it meant buying Talia's life? Her freedom? If it meant he'd forget about her, never bother her again?

I'd do anything to make that happen. Even sell my soul to the Devil.

For her. Only for her.

"I'll handle it," I said.

"What if it means turning your back on the Kings?" she asked me quietly. "Even if they'd forgive you for this... they won't just let you go back to the Mafia, will they?"

"Talia. They'll never forgive me for this."

I reached to touch her face, running my knuckle lightly down her cheek. How many more chances would I have to touch her?

"The only chance I have that they'll leave me breathing after this is if I get Roni back to them alive and unharmed, and if they believe that I didn't take her in the first place. And..." My hand dropped from her face. "If I give you back to your dad, unharmed, too."

Something changed in her eyes then, a ripple of worry across her brow. "You mean... there's really a chance? If you get Roni back to them?"

"Sure. There's a chance," I told her. But that chance was pretty fucking slim.

Slimmer, if you took into account the fact that Roni seemed to think I was guilty as sin of abducting Talia, if not her. Not great odds she'd be singing my praises to Jude anytime soon.

"Then there's something you should know," she said seriously, sitting up. "If she's the only hope you have... you need to let her go. The sooner Jude has her back in his arms, safe, the better for you."

"I know."

"I don't think you do." She reached and took my hand with her free one, and ran her thumb lightly over my wrist. My eyes dropped to our joined hands, my fingers curling automatically around hers. "Nico didn't just take Jude's girlfriend, Lex. He took his baby, too."

I met her eyes, and I could've sworn to God my heart stopped beating.

Then she whispered two little words, piercing and final, like the sound of nails slammed into a coffin: "Roni's pregnant."

Chapter Twenty-One

Lex

I 'd abducted *Jude Grayson's woman... and his unborn child.*

I stood in the hallway between the bedrooms, trying to absorb this. I'd made Talia repeat herself, like four times before I even wanted to believe it.

She said Roni told her she was pregnant at the hotel while they were getting ready for the wedding—to explain why she wouldn't be drinking at the party. And, apparently, to explain all the vomiting from the morning sickness.

No one else knew about the pregnancy yet. Except Jude. And now Talia.

And me.

Talia said she didn't tell me before because Roni asked her not to; when they were whispering to each other yesterday, Talia had promised her she wouldn't.

But now that it meant possibly saving *me*, she'd broken that promise.

That part alone was killing me slowly. If I didn't save these girls, both of them, and that baby, I really didn't deserve any more than a one-way ticket straight to hell.

I'd handcuffed my club brother's pregnant woman to a bed. While she sat there nauseous and hormonal, and probably fantasizing about all the different ways her man could kill me.

Jude and Piper were already second generation Kings. That baby was their legacy. There was very possibly a future King in Roni's belly, and I was so dead, they were gonna bury me alive, then dig me up and kill me again.

No. You didn't kidnap her.

Nico did.

But fuck of a lot of difference that would make if I didn't get Roni back to Jude. Fucking now.

"I'm fucking starving," I announced as I paced out to the living room. I knew Nico was starving too, 'cause he wouldn't shut up about it. "Let's order up some Uber Eats or something. There's nothing left in the kitchen."

His eyes rolled up to me. "You are an absolute fucktard."

I glared at him.

"You're not going on some fucking app, putting in all your personal shit and getting some delivery dude rolling out here." He shook his head, going back to his magazine. "How fucking stupid are you."

Yeah, he took that bait.

"You telling me you're not hungry?"

"I'm hungry."

I kept pacing, like I was trying to come up with something. Then I stopped and looked at him. "There's a pizza place on the highway, next to the turn off, right by the gas station."

His eyes rolled up to me again. "So?"

"So, just roll in and put in an order. They're fast." They totally weren't. "Pay cash, bring it back here so we can all fucking eat a decent meal."

He dropped the magazine. He was listening. "Why don't you go?"

"Because I'm watching the girls. We've only got a few hours 'til the exchange. You wanna go in there fucking tired and hungry?"

His weasel eyes narrowed at me. "You can leave me in charge of the girls."

"Never happening."

We had a staring contest that stretched on so long, my stomach actually rumbled.

"Fine." He got up. "Fuck, you're a pussy. I'll go. Put my number in your phone, in case you need to call me."

I did, then stood right where I was, watching as he left. I went to the window, watched his car peel out. A Honda Civic Type R with a custom neon-green paint job.

Seriously. When the Kings found out that a dude in a car that obnoxious snatched Roni right out from under their noses, they were gonna shit.

I watched his taillights disappear through the trees, checked the time, and set an alarm on my phone. I had a good fifty minutes, at least, before he rolled back in with the pizza. Plenty of time to get Roni the fuck out of here.

I'd deal with Nico's tantrum about it when it happened. And hopefully, with a belly full of pizza.

One thing at a time.

I picked up the magazine I'd left on the kitchen counter, the one for my gun, and shoved it in my pocket. Went back to Shane's bedroom and walked in. Talia was still cuffed to the bed. I went straight to the bathroom to grab my hoodie off the floor; she watched me pull it on over my cut, trepidation on her face. Our eyes met.

"I'm taking Roni," I told her, so she'd know I wasn't just running out on her, "getting her out of here."

She perked up. "Thank God. How?"

I stood there, looking at her, and made a spur of the moment decision.

"I'll take you, too." I strode over to her.

"What?"

I uncuffed her, tugged her gently to her feet. "Come on. I'm giving you both back to the Kings."

She rubbed her wrists, gazing at me. "But what happens to you?"

"For fuck's sake, Talia. Stop worrying about me. I'm the asshole who dragged you into this."

"So?"

"So? Are you kidding me?"

She wasn't kidding. I could see it in her face.

"I fucking told you. I'm not your hero." Even as I said the words, we both just stood there, tangled up in each other's eyes. It was ridiculously intimate, every time she looked at me like that, with her goddamn non-existent poker face all out.

Just like when she'd peeled off her clothes in front of me that night at the clubhouse.

She was always getting naked for me.

"I *stole* you on your wedding day," I reminded her.

She said nothing, like, *We're done with kicking that dead horse, what else have you got?*

"Look where you are." I tossed out my arms. "This isn't your honeymoon, okay? I'm not here to marry you. I'm not Carl."

She studied me carefully. "You're trying to hurt me. Make me mad so I'll go back." She sat down on the bed. "I'm not going back."

"Do I have to force you into the car?"

"Don't you dare."

"Then get up."

"I'm not going."

"*Why?*"

She gazed up at me with big brown eyes. "Because as soon as they have me back, they'll kill you."

Very good point.

And touching, that she cared. But I didn't exactly have time to properly enjoy it.

I rubbed my hand over my face, thinking. "Look, Piper's place isn't far from here. I'll take you back there and drop you off at the back end of his property. You can take your sweet time crossing the field to his house. He might not even be home. He's probably at the clubhouse overseeing operation Hunt Down the Fuckers Who Took Jude's Girl. By the time you talk to him, I'll be long gone."

"Gone? Where?"

"There's no time for this, Talia. I've got about fifty—" I checked my phone "—forty-seven minutes before Nico potentially gets back here. Just get in the car while I go get Roni, okay?"

"Nope." She picked at the bedspread. "I'm not coming."

I stared at her, my jaw unhinged.

Was she fucking *pouting* now?

Was this some chick shit about me proving my feelings for her before she'd bother listening to me anymore? *Right now?*

"Then what the fuck do you want me to do, Tal? I've gotta take Roni back."

"Of course." She softened, sliding to the edge of the bed and gazing up at me with such trust, it made my limbs feel weak. She wasn't pouting at all. She was digging her heels in. "Take her to Piper's where she'll be safe. Then come back for me."

Fuck. This girl.

I swiped my hand through my hair. Took a deep, ragged breath.

Fuck, but I wanted her to stay. Right here. Waiting for me.

Because I was a terrible fucking person.

"Why don't you just come with us, then?"

"Because you need me right here. For the ransom. I need to be here to show Nico that you didn't betray him or your father. We need to collect the ransom money, pay your father, like you said, then figure out our next step."

"There is no *we*."

"There is now."

We stared each other down for one painfully long-ass minute as I breathed long and deep and weirdly raspy. *Shit.* I did not want to give her up.

It was the right thing to do.

"Talia. I can't drag you any deeper into this."

"Lex. I'm not going. I won't get you into trouble with your father. You're already in trouble with the Kings."

"You're insane."

"You're running out of time."

"*Fuck.*" She wasn't wrong. I glanced at the timer on my phone.

I took her hand and pushed the key to her handcuffs into her palm.

She blinked up at me, so trusting, it cracked my heart wide open. "You're not cuffing me to the bed?"

On the odd chance Nico got back before I did? Fuck, no.

I slipped my knife out of my boot and handed it to her, too.

"What's this for?"

"Just in case."

Her eyes met mine, and I could see the flash of fear.

I took her face in my hands. "Look, if Nico gets back before me, just pretend you're cuffed to the bed. If he realizes Roni's gone, he'll come check on you. Just play dumb like you had no idea we left."

"I can do that."

"He won't get back here before I do, though," I promised her, our eyes still locked.

"He'd better not," she said lightly.

We stared at each other. Felt like if I looked away, I wouldn't be able to breathe. But somehow I knew if any woman could handle Nico for a few minutes until I got here, it was her.

"He's my cousin," I told her. I wasn't sure why. Maybe to give her some reassurance that he was human? And therefore, vulnerable?

"You're kidding me."

"Wish I was. I just want you to know… he tries to touch you, I know where he lives."

"Forty-seven minutes?" she said softly.

I shifted closer to her. "Probably much longer, I'm just playing it safe. I sent him for pizza. At the slowest dive in the country. I think they milk the cows out back *after* you put in your order, to make the cheese."

A grin spread slowly across her face. She whispered, "You're such a badass, Lex Davenport."

"You say that like it's a good thing."

"It is." Her smile faded, her eyes still locked on mine. She swallowed. "And, I—"

I kissed her, long and deep, before she could say anything else. My heart was pounding.

I don't want you to leave.

I want you to come back.

I love you.

Whatever the fuck she was gonna say, I did not need to hear it right now.

"I'm gonna kick you in the balls so hard if you leave me waiting for you," she finished, when the kiss ended.

I almost laughed, but I didn't. Because nothing about this was funny.

"I'm holding you to that," I told her.

Chapter Twenty-Two

Lex

I t was dark out, night creeping in, as I drove down through Burke Mountain and into the outskirts of Coquitlam, a mix of suburbs, industrial lots and farmland.

Roni was in my backseat, handcuffed to the headrest on the passenger seat, her ankles duct taped together and tied to the seat base with rope so she couldn't pull what she'd pulled on Nico—and try to kick me in the head.

She was also blindfolded.

If I ran across a cop car out here, I was in some deep shit.

I'd hardly thought about that part.

Right now, the Kings were a bigger threat.

"You know, I really considered telling Talia to leave Carl for you." She broke the strained silence, her tone light and conversational, with a nasty sharp edge beneath. "So glad I didn't, since you turned out to be a rotten filthy pile of steaming dog shit."

Unfortunately, I hadn't gagged her. Figured there was no point.

"Why did you consider it?"

"Hmm. She seemed to like you. A lot. I suppose you must have some kind of magic twelve-inch silver dick to go with those fangs," she said fake-pleasantly, "because you sure have the girl dicknotized."

"Talia's never been near my dick." *Other than when she rubbed up on it through my jeans, then came on my gun.* "Guess I must've hypnotized her some other way."

"Maybe it was your charming penchant for dragging women around while handcuffed."

Yeah. Real charming.

I turned off the gravel road onto the long dirt road that ran along the back end of Piper's property, farther down. I knew Roni was just doing what she could to try to protect Talia from me, which wasn't much, considering the circumstances. That must've been hard for her to swallow.

When I told her I was taking her back to the Kings, pretty sure she didn't even believe me. But Talia had tried to convince her to go with me, even as she explained that she was staying put. I assured Roni that my accomplice was gone, but she still didn't want to leave Talia alone in that house.

Talia insisted she was fine, that she wanted to stay. To wait for me to come back.

At that point, Roni probably assumed Talia had gone straight off the deep end or something. For me. And that she needed some serious therapy over her choice in men. But it was hardly the time to get into it.

Talia urged her to think of the baby, swore to her that she'd be safe with me, and I managed to get her out to my car. She even sat still while I secured her in the backseat, then carefully searched the car—and found a fresh GPS device that Nico had planted.

Obviously, I removed it and left it in the driveway. Fucking knew he'd "trusted" me a little too easily when he'd agreed to take off for pizza. The guy was hungry but he wasn't stupid.

He could smell how much I hated him. How much I hated my father. How loyal to him and the Mafia cause I was not.

How slippery I might be about sneaking one or both girls out of there.

And he thought he had that covered with his dumbass GPS.

Obviously, he thought I was a lot stupider than he was.

"You won't have to put up with me or the handcuffs much longer," I told her, when the silence grew heavy. "We're almost there."

"Where?"

"Piper's."

I glanced at Roni in the rearview mirror as she stirred. "You're taking me to Piper's?"

The note of hope and relief in her voice, which she tried to hide, killed me a little. Maybe she really thought I wasn't taking her anywhere better than she'd already been.

"You didn't seriously think I was gonna hurt you, Roni."

"When do we get to Piper's?" Her head was turned to the window, listening, though I knew she couldn't see through the blindfold.

"Soon. When I drop you off, give me some time to clear out before you tell him everything, okay?"

"And why would I do that?"

"Because I'm all Talia's got. If I don't get straight back to her, fast, guess what, she's all alone. With that guy who kidnapped you. I know you don't want that. I'm the only one who knows where she is. I'm the only one who can protect her."

"Yeah, you've done a really fucking bang-up job so far."

Other than that one note of softness when she found out she was getting dropped off at Jude's brother's house, she'd given me nothing but heat and snark. Even bound and blindfolded—pregnant —the woman was brave, strong. I could see why Jude fell for her.

Fuck, Jude was gonna personally destroy me.

"Do me a favor. Just tell them everything."

"Oh, I will."

"I didn't hurt you. And I let you go."

"That remains to be *seen*," she said, referring to the blindfold.

But I didn't have time to try to convince her to go easy on me anymore. We'd pulled up to the old fence that ran along the back of the field, and I parked. I killed the engine, got out and looked around. Silence.

There was no one around, no street lights on this dirt back road. Just the moonlight and a bright spotlight on a farm building on the other side of the road, way across a field.

I checked the countdown on my phone. *Twenty-four minutes.*

I went around to the passenger side, freed Roni from the backseat and helped her out. I took the blindfold off for her and she looked around, blinking into the night.

I left her cuffs on as I took her wrist and led her over to Piper's fence. It was an old estate fence, up to my thigh. Two-rail, the upper rail topped with barbed wire, meant to keep animals out. I climbed easily over it and helped Roni over in her bridesmaid's dress.

Roni kept looking around, trying to get her bearings. She'd probably never approached Piper's house from this direction, because why would she? We were at the ass end of the acreage, an untended field with random stands of trees and bush. Couldn't even see the house from here.

I stopped her with a hand on her arm. "Here." I unlocked the cuffs and let her go. Then I handed her the flashlight I'd brought.

"Thank you," she said grudgingly. Then she shone it in my face. "You're a royal dick, Lex Davenport."

"The house is that way, through those stands of trees." I pulled my gun out of the back of my jeans. "I really can't risk you getting hurt out here, so." I held the Glock handle-out to her. "Can you handle this?"

"No," she said with sarcastic venom. "I'm just a girl."

Right. Last time a girl said that to me, she had a lamp on standby to knock me out.

Of course, Jude would've made sure his woman could handle a gun. Probably took her to the range once a week.

To be sure she wouldn't shoot me in the ass the second I turned to walk away, I didn't load it. I took the magazine from my pocket, reached toward her slowly; aware that she had more than enough reason to clock me right now. She didn't. She just stared me down like she was thinking about clocking me, as I slid the ammo into the pocket of her leather jacket. Then I handed her the gun.

She took it.

I scratched the back of my neck. "Well. Tell Jude I say hey."

She glowered at me.

I turned and sped-walked back to my car. As I opened the door, I looked back and saw her slam the magazine into the Glock. *Shit.*

I jumped into my car and started up—as Roni aimed the gun right at me. Both arms straight out in front of her, legs spread in a solid shooting stance. The engine coughed a little as I turned the key, stuttered.

Jesus Christ—did Toad not get this fixed?

I turned the key again and the Chevelle roared to life. I took off up the road, but I heard no gun shot.

When I looked back in the rearview mirror, Roni was gone.

————

The car officially died at the first stop sign I hit. As I eased to an almost-stop while already turning the corner, it shuddered and went dead.

This time, it didn't start up again.

Since it died *while* I was driving, yet again, I was gonna go ahead and assume the starter was no longer the issue. Alternator? Battery? Both?

"*Motherfucking shit.*" I pounded on the steering wheel, tried to start it up again.

Nothing.

Goddamn Toad and his goddamn brother's useless auto shop. Did they *not* go over this thing with a fine toothed fucking comb, make sure it wasn't gonna die on me in the middle of the worst fucking shit show of my life?

I got out and slammed the door. "Fuck!" I kicked the tire, feeling like my heart was exploding out of my chest. I checked my phone.

Nineteen minutes.

Shane's house in the woods was like a fifteen minute drive away.

The pizza was probably in the oven by now.

I threw open the car door and put it in neutral. Thank fuck I was on a slight decline. I rolled it the rest of the way around the corner, sort of, and into an old drive that used to lead into a property, but clearly wasn't used anymore. It was overgrown with weeds and there was a chain draped across, a few meters ahead.

I eased the car to a crooked stop and left it there, parked. Nothing else I could do. I tried starting it again, just in case, but it was fucking dead. So I found my gloves, locked up and left it.

After Jude murdered me, I was gonna come back as a ghost and haunt that little fucknut Toad, for sure.

I pulled on my gloves, threw up my hood and started running.

The first actual house I came across was on the big acreage next to Piper's, on the corner. I slipped up the driveway, along the side, in the shadows. No motion activated lights went on, but there was a light on over the front door. It was a rambling old farmhouse with kids' artwork taped up inside the front window, a late model Toyota Forerunner in the driveway. No way I could hot wire it. Too new.

I went up to the side of the house and looked in the window. A dark front room. I followed the wall to the back, looked in. A family room. There was a dude in a recliner watching TV.

Okay. Think.

You're a forty-something dude with a wife and kids and a mortgage and you spend your evenings in front of the TV. Where do you put your car keys when you get home?

Hopefully not in your pants pocket.

I went around back and tried the back door. Unlocked. I eased it open, slipped into the kitchen. It was dark, but light spilled in from the family room.

There were coats hanging on pegs in the hallway off the back door. I quietly searched through pockets. No keys.

Then I saw them: a set of keys, lying on the kitchen counter. There was a breakfast bar that stuck out between the kitchen and the family room, keys lying on top. As I was eying them, footsteps came down a set of stairs I couldn't see.

I faded back into the hall as a woman appeared and grabbed the keys.

"Going to pick up Jamie from soccer," she said. "You want smokes? I'll probably stop."

I didn't quite hear her husband's reply.

The woman disappeared for a moment, kissing her husband goodbye or grabbing her purse or whatever, and I melted out the back door.

An exterior light flicked on and I fell back against the wall of the house. The woman stepped outside and headed for the Forerunner. As she unlocked the car with a blip of the remote, I slipped up behind her, wrapped a solid hand over her mouth. She stiffened.

"I'm not gonna hurt you."

A scream crawled up, but died in her throat when I tightened my hand.

"I just need the car. Don't scream. Nod if you understand."

She nodded.

"Toss the keys towards the car."

She did.

"I'm gonna let you go. Get down on the ground and don't look at me."

She did as I said. She was crying softly.

Christ, I was going to hell.

I'd never robbed a woman before. Or held one, much less two, captive. Seemed like a particular low to hit in the same day.

"Count to twenty," I told her, "then go inside."

I grabbed the keys and sprinted into the car. As I was burning it out of the driveway, she was already up and running into the house.

Shit. She'd be calling the cops in seconds.

I needed to ditch this vehicle. But I had to get back to the house before Nico did. I did not trust him for a second alone with Talia.

What the fuck was I thinking?

Twelve minutes.

I floored it back down the road I'd come in on, past the back end of Piper's property where all was silent and dark. I wondered if he was home. If Roni was sitting on his couch right now pouring out the whole story.

Or if she was sitting on his doorstep in the dark, crying, holding my gun, waiting for him to come home.

Don't think about it. She's safe.

Talia's not.

Focus.

But thinking about Talia was even worse. My head went straight to the worst scenario: I failed to get back to her fast enough. I left her wide open. Nico found her alone. He was pissed that Roni was gone; that I was gone.

And he took Talia straight to my father, to punish me.

I could not let that happen.

Why the fuck did I leave her there?

So the fuck what if I set a goddamn timer? Had I lost my mind? I nudged the brake, taking a corner too fast and fishtailing on the loose gravel.

I gripped the wheel and pressed on the accelerator, my heart pounding in time with the ticking time bomb in my head.

I saw her in my head, ten years old, signing her name in my notebook. Her soft hair falling over her face. Letting me prick her finger with a pin; a bead of scarlet blood on her soft skin. And pressing her finger to the page… the way she'd looked at me. Shy and defiant all tangled together.

I'd let the blood dry carefully in the sun when she went home, not wanting it to smudge. I wanted proof. I wanted her, in my book.

She made me a promise that day that was way too big for either of us.

I'd never earned it. I'd never made good on it.

I wasn't about to let her down now.

I ripped along the rural roads until I saw what I needed. I pulled into a driveway, parking the Forerunner out of sight, next to a barn. Then I ran back down the road to the next driveway over. To the 80's pickup truck parked there. As long as it had gas in the tank and it ran, I was golden.

I hot wired it, fast and easy, adrenaline flooding my veins. Then I backed it out of the driveway and took off, speeding all the way back to Shane's house, taking different roads than I did on the way out. And a different road than Nico would be traveling, when he came back with the pizza.

Four fucking minutes.

Let this not be the fucking day they decide to make a pizza in a reasonable amount of time.

I did everything I was ever taught to do. Driving one car then ditching it, switching vehicles. Altering my route. My father taught me young. When I grew up, the Kings taught me better. The Mafia was vicious, but the Kings were diligent, sophisticated. So sophisticated, they rarely got caught.

I never took it so seriously before.

Even living under my father's threat, I realized that it was all just a game to me. You played it well, you stayed ahead of the game.

But now it was about *her*.

I had to get back to her.

Once I did, once I made sure she was safe, I swore to myself I'd let her go. I could try to get the money from her dad myself. I could try to get it from Dane. I could try to negotiate with my father.

There had to be another way. One that got her the hell out of the line of fire.

Right now, she was in it.

Because of me.

Maybe I *was* just like my father. Making decisions—like the decision to keep her—based on my own greed.

Selfish. I was fucking selfish.

I didn't even have a gun anymore.

What if Nico flipped out on her when I wasn't there? Or flipped out on me, soon as I got back?

She had nothing but my knife to protect her.

Did I really expect her to use it?

Unless she stabbed him dead, it would only put her in more danger.

My foot pressed down on the accelerator.

Talia and Nico, *alone*.

While I drove, I pulled out my phone, tried calling Nico to stall him, add another pizza to the order, whatever it took, but I got no answer.

"Shit!"

I was losing it, slowly, the wall around whatever I'd always felt for her toppling down around me, one brick at a time.

I, Natalia De Santis, agree to marry Lexington when he turns 29.

I should never have written it down. I should never have asked her to sign her name in that book.

I used to write in that notebook all the time. I had a lot of notebooks, filled with my thoughts. Observations. Fucking poetry. When I grew up, I thought I was gonna be a poet. For real. I had no idea that was barely a thing.

If Homer could do it, why couldn't I?

I had some serious delusions of grandeur back then, probably thanks to my father.

But that changed when I grew up and realized how the world

worked. At least, my father's world. And I learned: you never write things down, least of all your deepest thoughts. Or the things you loved.

You didn't even say them out loud.

I couldn't afford words, the aftermath of words left in my wake, the damage they could cause. It was best to say nothing to no one, even when you were saying something. It was better to use empty words.

The ones that meant something, you kept those to yourself. You didn't let them come back to haunt you. Or to destroy people's lives.

That was child's play.

But even as a child, I should've known better.

I should've known, when I was eighteen and he had my teeth ripped out, and he asked me *What is it you want?* and I told him, *Freedom.* And he laughed at me.

You'll never be free of what you are, boy, he told me.

I should've known that he was right.

Chapter Twenty-Three

Talia

As soon as Lex took Roni out the front door, leaving me alone in the house, I went exploring.

I wasn't sure what I was looking for. But I took some time picking through the living room—for clues about this Nico dude who'd kidnapped Roni, in case I needed them later. For the Kings.

Because I sure as fuck was gonna throw him to the wolves if it meant saving Lex.

Hell, even if it didn't mean saving Lex.

Unfortunately, I didn't find anything. But I did know Nico's first name and the fact that he was Lex's cousin. And even if that wasn't his real name, I knew what he looked like. I knew he was taller than Lex, maybe a few inches over six feet. I knew he had a grill and a face tattoo. Those details would surely help the Kings hunt him down.

I've got you, Roni. He's not getting away with it.

Then I explored Shane's house out of pure curiosity, wondering if I could find any clues about Lex. Did he hang out here a lot, with his friend? The former hockey player, about to go pro, before Lex's dad fucked him over? That seemed like a pretty deep friendship. I could tell, when Lex told me about what happened, he was pretty broken up about it.

I shuddered just thinking of that car skidding off the icy road.

All I knew about Shane before was that he was Dane Davenport's best friend. I'd met him a few times at parties and stuff. He was an underground fighter; that's what Devi said. That was how he got all the bruises on his face.

The only time I really talked to him, briefly, he'd flirted with me. He was gorgeous, but I'd just slotted him into the "bad boy" category in my head and brushed him off as not my kind.

Now, I wished I'd paid more attention to him. But I didn't know he was so close to Lex.

If I knew, I would've paid more attention.

The cord on the back of his TV was cut. That was weird.

He had a couple of porn mags, which was funny, because who bought porn mags anymore when the internet was pornapalooza, all day every day, for free. But then I realized the date on the magazines was from the 1990s and they probably came with the house. I stuffed them back into the magazine rack.

The other magazines were all about cars.

There were some books, but again, probably came with the house. They were dusty.

I sat on the couch and wondered how long it would take Lex to get back here. Not long. He said Piper lived pretty close.

Unfortunately, I had no idea where Piper lived.

I realized I'd been snooping through the house as a distraction. I didn't want to think about why I was here. Or the fact that I had no idea where I was. I just wanted to get out of here.

As soon as Lex got back.

Maybe I could convince him to let me tell my dad the truth. Help him get the money. Figure out how we could deal with his dad, together.

I startled when I heard a car coming up the driveway. I got up, but I was afraid to peek out the window. I backed down the hall to the bedroom and shut myself inside, just in case.

Then I realized I'd left Lex's knife on the coffee table in the living room while I was looking through the magazines.

Fucking brilliant.

Some action hero you are.

I heard someone come into the house; the front door slammed and my heart started slamming in my chest. The walls were surprisingly soundproof, but I thought I could hear what sounded like a man's heavy bootsteps on the floor.

I hoped it was Lex, so I could kill him for putting me through this. Or maybe throw myself into his arms and beg him to run away with me?

God, what was wrong with me?

Stockholm syndrome. *It's perfectly natural. You'll work it out in therapy.*

Someone was moving around out there, I was sure of it, maybe in the kitchen. It was taking too long. It wasn't Lex.

If it was Lex, he'd come straight to me, make sure I was okay, right?

I hurried back to the bed and sat by the headboard, pretending to be cuffed to it. Now what? I had no weapon. Just the damn lamp. It was still unplugged and at the ready. But like Lex said, it probably wouldn't be enough.

Shit.

My heart was racing. I couldn't think. Panic was starting to set in.

What the fuck was I supposed to do here? If Nico tried to hurt me?

Karate chop my way out? I didn't even know karate.

When I hit Lex, did I actually want to hurt him? No.

But that Nico guy?

Fuck that guy.

Think.

I tried, hard, to remember what I'd learned in that single self-defense class I went to a few years ago. This wasn't some girl power, make-you-feel-tough fitness class. This thing was hosted by several badass lady cops, and it was all about one objective if you were attacked: getting the fuck out of there.

Surviving.

How did you do that?

You needed to hurt the guy in a way that got his focus off of you —so you could get away. Which meant hitting his most vulnerable areas. There were like four of them. Or five or six. Eyes and throat. What were the others? Kneecaps? Nose? Fuck, I couldn't remember.

What I did remember was that aiming for his balls wasn't effective enough. It would hurt, probably piss him off, but it wouldn't break his focus off of *me*. I needed to do damage, enough that his focus snapped away from me, and I could get away.

There was something about the legs, the arms; how to break out of his hold if he grabbed you? But fuck me, I could not remember.

I thought I heard footsteps out in the hall, and my breath got sharp and shallow. A door. I was pretty sure whoever was out there just went into Roni's room.

Okay. *You can do this. Don't panic.*

I took a deep breath.

For all you know, it's Jude.

And if it's not…

Eyes, nose and throat. Eyes, nose and throat.

I repeated it to myself like a mantra.

I will be okay.

I'm an action hero.

I'm Margot Fucking Robbie.

Eyes nose throat.

The door opened and Nico appeared.

I scrambled farther up the bed on instinct, perching on the

pillows, my heart slamming with fear. I kept my hands tucked behind me so it would look like I was handcuffed there.

He looked around the room. Then his eyes slammed into mine. "Where are they?"

"I'm handcuffed in here," I snapped. "How should I know?"

He stepped into the room and slammed the door shut behind him. Then he locked it.

Oh, fuck.

I'd hoped we could be decent about this and he could just wait out in the living room for Lex to come back like a civilized kidnapper. But considering he'd just locked us in here together, that ship had sailed and sunk.

This dude was the enemy. He'd abducted my pregnant best friend, in her pretty peach bridesmaid's dress, like a fucking brute.

Eyes nose throat.

He looked around the room with sharp eyes, like he didn't trust the air just because I was in it. "I'm supposed to believe he just left you here?"

"Why wouldn't he?"

"Because he's in love with you."

I laughed, but it came out strangled. "Right."

"He stole you from your wedding." He came closer, slowly. "And he doesn't give a fuck about the ransom. He tell you that?"

"Well, maybe you're right about that. Because apparently, he abandoned me here with *you*."

He looked into the bathroom, making sure we were really alone.

I sighed. "Are you really that dumb?"

His cold eyes cut to mine.

"What do you think he's doing in here with me all the time?"

His gaze raked down my body. "If I had to guess? Fucking you."

"I wish."

His eyes leapt to mine again.

"I tried, believe me. But Lex is a prude. Has some kind of moral objection to fucking a girl he's got handcuffed to a bed. You believe that?"

He snorted. "Actually, I do." He'd reached the side of the bed and stood there, eyeing me.

I shored up every last drop of courage my dad had ever instilled in me. He was the one who'd sent me to that self-defense class. He'd taken me to the shooting range, several times. When I was eleven, he took me out for ice cream and told me that it was okay to kill a man who touched me wrong.

Fuck, I loved my dad.

He was strict and old school, but he adored me and I was not gonna let this thug hurt his daughter.

"Well," I forced out, "we don't all have to be prudes."

"Meaning?"

"Meaning, I'm sick of being handcuffed to a bed. I'm fucking bored. If you be nice to me, I'll be nice to you."

His eyes flashed. But clearly he didn't trust me.

Not as stupid as I'd hoped.

Still. The way he looked at me... he wasn't gay. And I highly doubted he had any moral objections about doing just about anything with me right now.

He was ripe for the taking. If I could just lure him in.

Men were dumb like that.

At least, most men were. Maybe not Lex.

I rolled my eyes a little. "I'm hungry, okay? You smell like pizza. Just bring me some food and we can see."

His eyelids lowered, but he didn't budge. This guy was a class A asshole. He had a girl handcuffed to a bed, basically offering to fuck him, and he didn't even want to share his damn pizza?

How was this guy even related to Lex?

Oh, right. Lex's dad was the Devil. Genes didn't have to make sense.

"I meant to say please," I added.

He considered for another moment, then ran his tongue over his ugly-ass fake diamond grill. Unlike Lex's silver teeth, it was gag worthy.

Then he left and I exhaled. I heard his footsteps fade down the hall, and with my eyes on the open door, I quickly snuck the lightbulb out of the bedside drawer. I scrambled back into place just in time, lightbulb behind my back. Nico was back, with a box of pizza.

He sat it on the foot of the bed, open. The smell wafted up to me and my guts cramped. Fuck, I was hungry. I gazed at it longingly, then found him staring at me.

He licked his lip. "First, you give me a taste."

Asshole.

He walked up to the head of the bed and looked down at me.

It annoyed me that up close he was actually good-looking. If you could see past all the filth that had encrusted his soul and oozed out his pores. And his rodent eyes and ugly face tattoo. It was a cheesy spider web, clinging to one temple. He had amazing cheekbones and even with the grill, he probably got plenty of pussy.

But then again, Lex's genes. Maybe I shouldn't have been all that surprised.

He reached out and grabbed my throat, lightly, just under my jaw, holding me in place. Then he bent down and kissed me.

His stupid grill scraped my lip. He forced my mouth open and his tongue entangled with mine. It was slimy. Why were some guys slimy, while other guys were fucking perfect? It felt like being kissed by a giant, drooling rat.

I almost gagged, but choked it back. I made a yummy, moaning noise like I was into it—and promised myself a scalding hot shower and a bottle of peach schnapps to scour this memory from my mind and body, after I got out of here.

Then his other hand landed on my breast and squeezed. I stiffened.

He discovered I had no bra on under the thin hockey T-shirt and groaned into my mouth, his grill scraping my gums. I was forgetting to breathe and tried to suck in a deep breath through my nose. He stank of stranger and yesterday's cologne. But he was getting into this, his tongue plundering my mouth like he was searching for cavities. I'd had more arousing dental work done.

I realized he was probably getting hard and almost gagged again.

Eyes nose throat.

Eyes nose throat.

Gripping the lightbulb around the metal base, I slipped it out from behind my back. I counted to three in my head. *Eyes. Nose. Throat. This one's for you, Daddy.* And in one quick movement, I smashed the lightbulb with all my strength against the edge of the bedside table. Thank God it broke.

As Nico jerked away from me in surprise, I smashed it into his face. *Eyes.* I went straight for his left eye.

There was a delayed moment of horror as I let go, the broken stub of lightbulb stuck in his flesh.

Then he screamed.

I scrambled the fuck out of there and ran. But not before grabbing my tote bag off the floor—and a slice of pizza from the box. Which either made me queen of the badasses, or fucking insane.

"You fucking bitch!" he roared behind me.

I didn't stop to hear whatever else he thought of me as he tried to extract a broken lightbulb from his face. I snatched Lex's knife from the coffee table and a flip phone from the kitchen counter where it lay next to another box of pizza. Then I heard Nico smashing around and didn't bother stopping for my shoes. I didn't see them, anyway, and I had no time to go looking.

I snatched a men's lumber jacket off a hook by the front door. I fumbled and dropped the pizza as I ran out the door, slamming it behind me, and ran for the woods.

I didn't even get a single fucking bite of that goddamn pizza.

If I ever saw Lex Davenport alive again, I was gonna kill him.

Chapter Twenty-Four

Talia

I ran through the dark, as fast as I could with no shoes on. The floor of the woods was matted down, a carpet of leaves and mud, soft pine needles, but it was scraggly brush and twigs and rocks too. Lots of little trails, deer trails, maybe, snaked all over the place.

I had no idea where I was, or where was safe to go.

Anywhere but the road.

For all I knew, Nico was already in his car and searching for me.

I hurried through the woods for a while, then hit a wide path. It was a gravel path, fairly well-groomed, and my best guess was I'd stumbled into some kind of public park. I followed the path, weaving on and off of it, afraid of running into some late-night jogger and scaring the shit out of them.

And even more scared of Piper or Jude finding me, and Lex losing his chance at mercy.

I could see the moon through the wispy clouds above but no stars, no mountains in the distance to tell me which way was north. I sorta guessed from the position of the moon, but I couldn't be sure.

I was pretty sure that I was north of the highway, at the foot of the mountains. But how far north, I had no idea.

Eventually, I got freaked out following the path and hit the woods again, but kept to the edge where I could still see the path. Then I caught sight of a road with houses in the distance and followed it.

Not a single car drifted past in the sleepy neighborhood.

How late was it?

Now that the adrenaline of fight and flight was subsiding, I was fucking terrified. The Mafia wanted me for ransom—but I could be free, totally free of this bullshit. I could run to the road, knock on a door, call the police.

Call my dad.

But if I called my dad, the Kings would find out. They'd know I was free. With me and Roni safe, they'd have no reason not to hunt down Lex and take their revenge.

I was able to keep going for a while, even though I had no fucking shoes. All those miles on the treadmill at the gym. I'd for sure cut my feet, and I once clubbed my head on a tree branch and had to slow down.

Eventually, I ran out of breath and had to stop for a minute.

Then I followed the woods along the edge of the road until I reached a small, silent intersection. The road had turned to dirt, no more pavement. There was a single street light over the road that I could see, no houses. And the moonlight.

Where the fuck was I?

I sat down against a tree at the side of the road and opened the flip phone. It was a burner, I was pretty damn sure. Otherwise I wouldn't have grabbed it. GPS and all that shit.

Then I called Lex.

Yes, I had his phone number memorized. I'd never called him. But I'd committed his number to heart. As if one day I just knew I'd be calling it in some really low, desperate moment.

Well, that low moment had been reached.

I sniffled when he picked up and I heard his voice. "Yeah." There was bite in it that wasn't meant for me. He didn't know I had a phone.

I didn't know if I could trust him. After everything, I didn't know.

He stole me from my wedding. He handcuffed me to a bed.

He held me for ransom, whether or not he wanted to.

And I still didn't want him to get hurt.

Nico said he's in love with you.

But even if that wasn't true, I was more worried for Lex right now than I was for myself.

How fucked-up was that?

I almost hung up.

"Lex."

"Talia?" I could hear the worry in his voice. "Tal, are you at the house?"

"No. Nico is."

"Where are you?" It sounded like he was driving.

"I'll tell you where I am, but only if you come alone. No Mafia creeps."

"I promise. Just me. Tell me where you are."

"I'm at a crossroads. Between one shitty dirt road and another, about a fifteen minute stagger through the woods in bare feet from the house."

"Are you safe?"

I laughed and sniffled again. I was crying. "Yeah. So safe."

"It's okay," he said firmly. "You're gonna be okay, Tal. Just stay where you are. Don't move. I'll find you."

"Lex?"

"Yeah?"

"Don't be a shitty dirt road." I hung up on him.

Then I cried, as all the events of the last twenty-four hours hit me and I actually felt the effects of them all. Including the last hour or so, which was the fucking worst.

Eventually, I heard a car coming.

I'd curled up into a little ball around my tote bag for warmth, but I'd grown kind of numb to the cold. I unraveled myself, getting up slowly. I saw the headlights.

Whoever was coming, if it happened to be some random person, they were probably gonna think they were seeing a ghost—this girl in a giant lumber jacket and fluffy white skirt poking out and bare legs, just hovering at the side of the road in the night, a wreck of blonde hair swirling in the breeze.

The car slowed down.

Nico's car.

I'd seen it parked in the driveway when I ran from the house. It was neon-green and as ugly as his stupid grill.

I turned to run.

I heard the car abruptly stop and the door open as the engine cut off. "Talia, it's me!"

Lex.

I whipped around.

He stood there in the open driver's side door. There didn't seem to be anyone else in the car. He shut the door and stepped away from it, moving slowly like he was trying not to scare me.

Too late. My heart was slamming so hard I was almost choking on it.

I backed up a bit. There was a ditch flooded with rain water between us, and he came around, walking along the edge of the road at the little intersection.

"Why are you driving his car?"

"Because I stole it." He was panting like he'd sprinted all the way here.

I inched closer, looking him over. He did the same to me, then looked around.

He didn't break my trust. He'd come alone.

I didn't break his. This wasn't a trap. There were no Kings waiting to ambush him from the woods.

"Where's Roni?" I demanded. "Is she okay?"

"Yes. I took her to Piper's place. I gave her a gun. She's fine."

I shuddered. A long, exhausted sigh. Thank God. She was safe. Her baby was safe.

But there was that other little problem...

"Then they know you're involved."

Lex took a step closer. We were still a good distance apart. That distance was filled with all the pain and distrust and uncertainty that this night, and every day since we'd met, had caused.

"They'll know whatever she tells them," he said.

"They'll be coming for you."

"No one knows where we are. It's just the two of us." He inched closer. "But we can't stay here. We need to keep moving."

Moving.

Because if we were running away together, that's what we'd have to do.

I stared at him. I'd never said I'd run away with him.

And he'd never asked me to run away with him.

I'd stayed because he needed me for the ransom. For his father.

If that was the plan, there was nowhere to go but to hand me over in exchange for the money.

I didn't even want to get my hopes up that the plan had changed.

"Where's Nico?" I didn't want to know. But I needed to know. "Is he... dead?"

"No. I found him picking glass out of his eye socket."

I exhaled. *Shit.* I hated that I felt relieved. I didn't want his death on my hands, though. At the same time the anger rose in me so fast, it made me feel sick. I could feel his grill in my mouth, his hand on my chest. I could taste him.

"You took too long coming back. He tried to fuck me."

Lex's face dropped a mile. "Talia... I'm sorry." He took a step closer. "Why's your head bleeding?"

I touched the sleeve of the lumber jacket to my forehead, trying to absorb any blood. I thought it stopped bleeding already. It was tender as shit, though. "I'm fine."

"He did that?"

"No. I ran into a tree. I had to stab him with a lightbulb, though."

"Fuck." Lex scraped his hand over this face. "I'm sorry you had to do that to escape. I should've been back in time. I tried to get back—"

"Yeah. You should've. How long 'til he calls in the Mafia cavalry? Or he comes after us himself?"

"Well, I got his car and his phone, which I destroyed. You've got his burner. And I cuffed him to the bed."

My jaw dropped. "You didn't."

"How do you think I got his car keys?"

Holy shit. He'd fucked over Nico.

"We're like... accomplices now," I said, kinda floored.

He frowned and held out his hand. "Give me the phone, okay?"

I stepped forward to put it in his hand. I had no desire to keep it. It served its purpose. It brought Lex back to me.

He tossed it into the dark water of the ditch.

"Now let's go." He held out his hand to me.

I didn't take it. Instead, I reached into my bag and carefully found the handle of his knife.

He didn't seem to notice. He was too busy puzzling over why I didn't run into his arms.

His hand dropped. "I know you're angry, Talia. You have a right to be. You can punish me later. For now, let's get you safe."

Right. Safe, unharmed and ready to fork over for ransom.

"No."

He took a step closer in the shadows. "No?"

I shook my head and backed up, dropping my bag on the ground as he advanced. But I had the knife in my hand.

He still didn't notice. He was too close. I looked up at him in the moonlight as he got closer, until I had nowhere left to go. Somehow, he had me backed against a tree.

"What are you gonna do, kidnap me again?"

He sighed a little. "I never wanted to kidnap you, Tal."

"Right. So why do you have me pinned against a tree in the woods, half-naked?"

"You're not half-naked."

"I have no shoes. It's cold out here."

His eyes flickered down. I had the giant lumber jacket wrapped around me, but the October night was breezing right up my skirt. And yeah, I was fucking mad. If it wasn't for him, I wouldn't be here right now, in this mess.

So what if I went with him willingly?

Still his fault.

He shrugged off his hoodie and offered it to me. I took it, then dropped it in the dirt.

"Also, my bra's gone. Thanks to you. That bustier was expensive."

"I've got it for you. It's in the car."

"How noble. Thank you for collecting my lingerie from the scene of the crime for me."

He held my gaze. I saw frustration in his eyes, for sure. But also... desire. His tongue swiped over his lip and his canines flashed. They gave him a wild, menacing look whenever he smiled. It was a wolfish smile. But right now, he wasn't smiling.

"My, what big teeth you have," I said mildly, but a shiver ran down my spine.

I wanted those teeth all over me.

"All the better to bite you with," he said softly.

"Bite me?" I tried to laugh, but his words turned me to molten goo inside. "I wish you would have in the first place. Then maybe all this mess could've been avoided."

Because you'd already be mine.

And I'd be yours.

I didn't say it, but we both knew what I meant.

"Just get in the car, Talia."

"No."

Seriously, he thought I was just gonna get in a car with him again, that easily?

How fucking pathetic did he think I was?

"Is this about me luring you away from your wedding, and you feeling bad about it? Guilty? Pissed off?"

"No."

"Then let's go."

"No."

"Why?"

"I don't want to."

He sighed a little. "Where're you gonna go, Tal?"

I didn't answer that.

"You just called me begging for my help."

"I didn't beg."

"You need me."

"You're a dick."

He just stood there. Like he was waiting for me to give in at any second, do what he said. But I didn't. So he called my bluff. "If you have somewhere to go, just go."

"I will."

"Don't worry about me and the Kings, and my father and the ransom."

"I won't."

"Just run away and pretend none of this ever happened."

"Don't tempt me."

Neither of us moved. But I was spitting mad. I felt like a bull in a cartoon, nostrils flaring and steam huffing out.

He studied me for a long moment, like he was reading my mood. And how best he could get me to do what he wanted.

Just like when we were kids.

"You know, I can run faster than you," he informed me.

"So?"

"So it's no use trying to run away from me."

"Is that so?"

"You don't trust me," he said. It was a question, and he seemed to be waiting for an answer.

"Do you really expect me to answer that?"

Instead of answering, he reached out and slipped his finger down the front of the lumber jacket, slowly… splitting it open, as he studied my eyes.

I let him.

Then he ran his finger up my side, beneath the hockey T-shirt, pulling it up. His gaze fell to my chest. I drew a tight breath as his fingernail scraped up and over my naked breast, taking the hem of the shirt with it, baring my breast to the night air.

My nipple peaked in the cold. I shivered.

I should've smacked his hand away and put on that hoodie.

But I just stood there, desperate for his hot mouth on my skin. Kissing, taking… *biting*.

Forget being a good girl. I wanted to get fucked in the woods by the bad boy while no one else on Earth knew where we were.

I could've died during this whole ordeal. Things could've gone horribly sideways. And he'd basically told me that the Kings were gonna kill him. I didn't want to think about any of that right now.

I was alive and so was he.

I wanted him inside me, our bodies entwined, feral and unfettered, in the dirt, pumping with life.

His eyes met mine for a lingering moment. A silent challenge. A question. Was I gonna punch him if he tried to kiss me?

Find out, fucker.

Slowly, he dipped his head and his hot breath warmed my breast. I felt the flicker of his tongue, warm and wet against the tender peak of my nipple. My skin prickled with pleasure at the caress. My body flooded with a pang of heat and I squirmed against the tree, gripping the knife at my side.

Before I could recover, he'd lowered himself to his knees in front of me.

I froze as he pushed the soft layers of my skirt up, then tugged my panties down. My pussy was right in his face, and his attention made me throb—as I remembered the incredible ecstasy I'd already experienced down there, courtesy of his mouth.

He leaned in and I felt his warm breath on my flesh. He ran the tip of his nose through my little strip of hair, making the flesh below tingle, and I almost died from the intensity of the anticipation that hit me. I was barely breathing.

He nuzzled me and inhaled deeply. For one long heartbeat he looked up at me, his caramel eyes taking on a decidedly animal quality.

Or maybe that was just the effect of the dark, creepy woods and the moonlight.

Then he returned his attention to my pussy and nuzzled me again. I melted. My heart thumped with impatience. And he murmured, "You're so sweet. You taste like sex and candy. I want to eat you. Fuck, I wanted you in my mouth for so long…"

"Say please," I forced out, interrupting him when he was a breath away from putting his mouth on my pussy.

His eyes entangled with mine, and I realized he was panting a little. "Please."

It broke me, how fast he said it. How he held my eyes until I nodded, just a little.

Then his gaze drifted down my body. His tongue snaked out and licked me tentatively between my legs. My entire body shuddered with desire. All my anger ebbed away.

Well, most of my anger.

"Do not call me a good girl again," I managed, breathless. "I hate it."

His eyes met mine again. "Do you?"

He lapped me slowly with his amazing tongue, and he knew exactly what he was doing. I shuddered helplessly in response. I needed to stop him and give him crap for kidnapping me, then leaving me to Nico, and you know, torturing me for four long years, but I couldn't find the will. I twitched and stirred against the tree but I let him trap me there.

Then I realized that he wasn't holding me at all.

"You're a villain, Lex Davenport," I complained, though my voice had no substance, and my words did nothing to stop him. He just delved deeper with his tongue. He caressed my opening, but he didn't force my thighs apart. He was being all gentlemanly, doing very nice things to me while he was down on his knees, like he was asking me to forgive him—to trust him—and I both loved and hated it right now. "I'm really, really mad at you."

His warm breath plumed between my thighs. I couldn't see it, but I was sure I felt him smile. He licked my lips apart, then licked me delicately in-between. The raw sensation sent tingles through me, shivers upon shivers, and my nipples throbbed almost painfully with need.

As if he sensed that need, he pushed the shirt up again, exposing my breasts to the cold night. I shuddered gratefully as goosebumps rose all over my body. He kept licking me as his fingers sought the stiff points of my breasts. He pinched and tugged in time with his gentle licks, and I burned with frustration even as the pleasure tumbled through me.

His licks turned into sweet little sucks. Then his tongue played with my clit. Between licks, he suckled softly again.

He was taking his time.

He was fucking teasing me.

I jerked my hips back a bit, but I couldn't get far. I was pressed up against the tree. He made a hungry sound, a deep growl that was way too hot, and nudged his way deeper between my thighs, taking more of my flesh into his mouth—and sucking insistently. At the same time, his fingers tugged on my nipples even harder, pulling in rhythm to his suckling pulls between my legs.

I stirred again, but not to get away. The growling and pulling between my legs was setting me on fire.

Then I gasped in pleasured surprise as the suckling suddenly changed—into a tentative nip of his teeth.

I shuddered and bit my lip to keep from screaming out. I couldn't afford to scream. What if someone heard us?

Lex snaked the tip of his tongue over my clit. A splash of pleasure erupted at the gentle caress, so different from the nip of his teeth—and my body jerked. My breasts bounced, and he redoubled his grip on my nipples.

The sharp but achingly sweet sensation burned through me as his teeth nipped me again and my back arched, breasts pulling against his hold. I was halfway to crying again, but blinked back the tears.

I should've been stopping him.

But I didn't stop him.

He nibbled gently around my clit with his teeth, growling softly as he did. His teeth sent jolts of pleasure and the sweetest pain through me, all the way to my twitching toes, my clawed fingertips against the tree. My other hand was still wrapped around the handle of his knife. I sobbed with agony, my lips pressed shut. I was helpless to him.

No. *Fuck that.*

I would not be helpless to him.

I was not gonna come like this, shuddering and out of control, with his teeth teasing my clit. I just knew it would feel too incredible—a shot of pure liquid ecstasy through my veins, to trust him like that… I'd immediately need it again and again, and if he flipped back into ignoring-me mode, I'd have to fucking murder him for real.

"Please, Lex. *Please.*" I didn't even know what I was begging him for. For mercy maybe, for him to stop. For him to keep going and suck harder, faster, and relieve the torture.

I was tripping toward the edge of sanity as he brought down his teeth on my clit again, gently, and pleasure scorched through me—and I bucked and shoved him away before I came.

Lex blinked up at me, panting roughly, his eyes wide and dark. He dragged his tongue along his glistening lip.

I lifted the knife between us, pointed at him. My hand shook a little. The other hand fumbled with my panties, pulling them back up. Blood was slamming through my body. I felt lightheaded and out of breath, and my whole core was throbbing.

My nipples ached and I wanted him so bad I could taste it in my mouth. I was salivating.

Pure lust and agonizing longing.

But fuck him. He didn't get to run this show anymore.

"Don't come closer," I warned him at the end of the knife. He looked at it, then his eyes met mine again.

And whatever was in them… it was not what I expected. Suddenly, he looked like that murdery Lex I'd glimpsed in his room at the clubhouse when I got naked in front of him—and he wrapped his hand around my throat.

Except this time, the lust in his eyes was unmistakable. It was dripping off of him, like it was off of me. I could practically smell it as he got slowly to his feet, his tongue sliding over his teeth.

He wanted me in his mouth again, between his teeth. He wanted me like I wanted him.

I raised the knife a little higher.

"You like that, huh?" My voice shook a little. I swallowed; the lust was making it hard to speak. "Well, get used to it. Because I am not your good girl. You want it, you fucking come and get it."

And with that, I turned and ran.

Chapter Twenty-Five

Talia

I didn't get far.

Lex tackled me so fast it took my breath away, and once he had me on the ground, my back to his front, he pressed my knife hand to the ground by the wrist.

Then he snaked his other hand around my throat and pulled me tight against him—so I felt his arousal, jammed against my ass, hard and hot. We were on all fours, my body trapped beneath his.

"Don't run," he whispered brokenly against my neck as he forced my head back. "It excites me."

Holy fuck.

I'd awoken the beast.

"You... you have a thing for chasing women down, before you...?"

"Don't know," he rasped, his voice thick with lust. I could feel his heartbeat in his chest, in his hand, *everywhere*, slamming against me. "Never had to chase one down before." But his hips shifted, and his swollen cock nuzzled between my ass cheeks made it pretty clear. He sounded like he was barely in control of his own voice. "Just stay still a minute."

It was a warning. A gentle-ish warning, and it turned me the fuck on. The thought of exciting him beyond anything he could handle, the thought of him losing control of himself over me, made my whole core shiver with arousal.

If there really was a villain inside Lex Davenport, I'd just broken him out of his cage.

My breasts ached beneath the T-shirt, the fabric rubbing my peaked nipples like a tease as I panted. I spread my knees wider and arched my back into him, pressing my ass against his erection. He kept one hand at my throat but the other one shoved roughly up my shirt to fondle my breast, to pinch and tug at my tight nipple and torment me as I gasped—and he sucked on my neck.

When his hand moved down toward my pussy, I reached behind my back to work his jeans open. I peeled his underwear down to free his cock. It jutted out, smooth and hard. The tip was leaking and wet. He shuddered as I ran the palm of my hand against it.

Oh, Christ. He had a good cock. Long and thick and veiny, and hard as rock. Touching that velvet-coated steel made me lightheaded with arousal.

But I wasn't giving in that easily.

Distracted, he loosened his grip on my throat. I yanked myself forward and scrambled away, and he let me go.

I staggered to my feet and started running again, wondering how far I'd get, my heart thumping wildly. I felt like an animal. We were both animals, torn down to our basest impulses in the dark of the woods, and I didn't want it any other way. I didn't want to get away.

I wanted him to give chase, to lose control of himself, to bare his fucking soul to me.

Whatever was inside of Lex, I wanted him to let it all come pouring out. Literally.

I wasn't a good girl any more than he was the guy who was

going to do the right thing. He was right—he wasn't the hero. He was my villain and I'd always love him for it.

It stunned me how fast he had me again. How soon he had me down in the leaves, this time on my back, with my shirt pushed up over my chest. He drove his knee between my legs, pressed up into my crotch. He got one of my wrists pinned to the ground above my head, but I was quick to get the knife between us with the other.

Lex was quicker. He had me disarmed and drove the knife blade into the dirt just beyond my reach before pinning both arms and crushing his mouth against mine.

I yielded to him as he shoved his tongue inside me, softening beneath him in hope of distracting him again… but all the while I was hungry to know how far *he'd* get this time.

I returned his sucking kisses until we were both panting to the point of near suffocation. Then he pulled his mouth free to kiss my neck. He growled softly, the way he did when he'd sucked on my pussy, and nipped at my skin with his teeth.

My eyes rolled back in my head. *That.* Fuck, I loved that. His teeth on my body. Who knew I had such a teeth fetish?

Not me.

Oh, wait. *You're in love with a guy with silver fangs. Get a clue.*

He lowered himself against me, and I felt the smooth heat of his naked cock pressed against my bare thigh. My skirt was up around my hips and his jeans were undone, his dick free and ready.

He released one wrist, to slide his hand down between us. He grabbed my lace panties—and ripped them.

Hunger gripped me as he bit my neck, lightly, digging his teeth in. My arousal flashed through me in a dizzying wave. Had I ever felt anything like this?

No. Fuck, no.

No wonder I'd wanted him so bad for so long. Because there was nothing like *this*.

This pure, agonizing, animal want.

This wasn't making love. This was base instinct, and it was intoxicating. I was drowning in pheromones.

He could've taken me, right now. My panties were destroyed. I didn't have a condom either, and I didn't give a fuck. He could've sheathed himself inside me and I wouldn't have stopped him.

I wanted to see how far he *would* go; if he had any control at all.

As I arched against him, moaning as he sucked on my neck, he loosened his grip on my wrist. I pulled my hand free, drifting both hands up his muscled back through his soft shirt, under his leather vest, then snaking my fingers up into his hair. He shuddered a little, seemed to soften as I scraped my fingernails against the back of his neck.

I scraped one hand lightly down his back.

Then with a violent twist I reached to the side, almost bucking him off, and grabbed the knife. I had the blade to his throat before he could anticipate it.

Maybe he didn't expect *me* to have any bite.

His caramel eyes were a haze of lust and animal heat as they bore into mine.

He pressed down against me despite the blade, lowering his weight on me again, slowly—and I lowered the blade at the same time, keeping it pressed to his throat but not wanting to cut his flesh. He lowered himself until he could kiss me again. His lips brushed mine, hovering. Teasing, soft kisses, a little nip of his teeth on my bottom lip.

He pretended to be unaffected by the blade against his skin but I felt the tension in him, different than it was before. Wary, attentive. I stroked the back of his neck, my fingers twisting in his hair, tugging. I kissed him back as he shifted himself on top of me.

He cocked his hips back so his heavy erection dropped between my thighs.

My heart beat like a drum. There was nothing to stop him from taking me now, unless I slit his throat, which I wasn't gonna do.

I would've slit Nico's throat in a heartbeat, if I'd had a knife in my hand and he really tried to fuck me.

I didn't want to cut Lex. I just wanted him to know that I had bite, too.

Now, he knew it.

And it was turning him on.

I felt the warm tip of his hard cock press at my flesh as he flexed his hips. I kept the knife pressed to his throat, my arm trembling with the effort as my blood rushed elsewhere. I felt it pulsing madly in my tight nipples, in my clit. I was so wet, he could've slid right inside.

He stopped kissing me and drew back just enough to look at my face. He reached down and used one hand to guide himself, stroking me gently with his engorged head, nudging me open.

I trembled beneath him with desire. But I kept the knife at his throat, forcing his chin up just a little as I pushed it against him in warning.

Lex watched me with intent eyes, inflamed with lust, yet his face was calm. He shifted again, settling his other knee between my legs and suddenly forcing my thighs wider apart—making me feel helpless again. But this time, I wanted it. Badly.

He nudged the head of his cock into me, gently stretching me open, and left it there. He trailed his hand up my body to one swollen breast, and I knew he could feel my frantic heartbeat. He could probably feel it everywhere.

I arched into his touch as he pinched my nipple. I moaned. His eyes flashed at me and I warned him again with the knife, even as he sank into me slightly, burying the head of his cock in my flesh.

He watched me as he worked his way smoothly deeper, until he'd driven me open and he was deep inside me. Until I was impaled on the floor of the woods on his swollen cock, and I wriggled beneath him in pleasure. I let out a garbled cry of pure lust.

I could feel his heartbeat slamming against mine.

It felt like this was the first real moment between us, like everything before this was just some hazy dream. A memory, which it now was.

Suddenly, we were *us*. Open to each other, naked, when we still had our clothes on… and everything before this only happened so we'd end up right here, like this.

Then he withdrew, leaving me aching for more. He planted his hands on either side of me in the dirt. Then he thrust into me again, giving me no time to prepare for it, pushing his way deeper than he had before. He withdrew and did it again, and it took my breath away as he buried himself inside me with all his weight. He fell forward onto his elbows and I let the knife move with him, my grip loosening.

He snatched the knife from me and threw it away, and I clutched at his muscled ass as he shoved into me again and again.

He rode me without mercy, driving into me more forcefully than I'd expected he would. And still, it was never quite enough. For the first time during sex, ever, I distinctly wanted pain, but Lex had a different punishment in mind.

He planted his knees into the ground and drove deep into me, more slowly this time. He pushed up on his arms again so he could watch himself fuck me. He watched my pussy take his thrusts. He claimed me, so slowly and deliberately that I felt each possessive thrust and then the slow drag as he withdrew.

My pussy clamped down on him as he drove my ecstasy higher. I was beyond words now, beyond fighting him, beyond goading him, and Lex just watched me, feeding off my helplessness to him. He was in control of himself again and took his time, pausing to feel how my pussy contracted helplessly around him.

He leaned down and kissed me as I moaned.

"Say my name, Natalia," he whispered roughly, in a daze, as he buried himself in me again and I shuddered toward climax. He felt so big inside me, so big and unstoppable. And it took me a long moment to realize he'd told me to speak.

"Lex," I gasped. "*Lex.*" I wrapped my legs up around his back as high as I could as he shoved into me again and again. When he made me say his name like that, it made me feel raw and naked, and it made everything feel even better. He was so hard and relentless as he stretched me wide, and I never wanted it to stop. I loved the feel of him inside me.

I'd wanted it for so damn long.

My whole body shuddered out of control now, so close to coming. I took a breath and let my thighs go limp, opening to him. He was controlling me completely, and I wasn't even sure exactly how it happened. I was the one with the knife, right?

But it just turned him on.

It drove him crazy. The look in his eyes. His cock, so hard, as he drove into me…

He wasn't worried about me hurting him. He wasn't worried about hurting me. He was fucking me in the dirt, and for once he wasn't worried about getting me dirty, about being real with me.

The thought of it, of breaking through Lex's restraint as I took him on the ground, drove me suddenly to the edge. "*Lex*," I cried out, almost frightened, and he slowed his thrusts again as he watched me. The contraction started deep in my belly, and when he shoved into me again my body convulsed in a slow, deep wave.

At the absolute pinnacle I screamed inside my mouth, pressing my lips together so I wouldn't make too much noise as I smashed apart. Where were we? Were we even safe here? I was drowning in sensation. My core fluttered wildly around his stiff cock. His rough hand grabbed my breast and squeezed, and his warm mouth closed on my other nipple, sucking. Then his teeth sank into the soft flesh around it. It was heaven and hell as I split apart, darkness and light, sweetness and bitter.

Then Lex pinned my hips to the ground and kissed me as he drove into me, harder and faster, and I screamed into our kiss until my throat was raw, still coming in jagged waves as his hips slammed against me. He lapped his tongue into my mouth until I was breathless and clinging to him, to his kiss.

Then he bucked against me, growling into my mouth. Our kiss broke.

I sucked on his bottom lip, biting into it while he came. He groaned my name. He rocked into me, grabbing a fistful of my hair and holding on tight... shuddering as he released inside me, his cock convulsing, buried in my flesh. And in that moment he felt very human, very vulnerable in my arms. Flesh and blood.

I held him close, possessively, protectively. He bucked one last time and buried himself deep inside me, then lay still, panting against my throat.

I relaxed beneath him and dragged my fingers through his hair. I kissed his temple, feeling his strong, rapid pulse against my lips. As the cool breeze rustled the leaves and the woods made its soft sounds, the world came back to me.

I listened, carefully, to the sounds of the woods. I didn't hear anyone coming. I didn't hear any cars.

But people would be looking for us. I knew we were in danger.

I had no idea what was going to happen, to either of us.

So I just held onto him.

Plus, it was fucking cold. His body was hot and heavy, and I never wanted to let go.

I played with the hair at the nape of his neck. And I found myself saying, "For the record, you're still a dick."

"For the record, you're a badass." His voice was rough and soft at the same time, and he kissed my throat. Then his eyes met mine. "I thought you were gonna cut me."

"I told you. I'm an action hero."

"Well, hate to tell you, but the villain just fucked you senseless."

"Do not get cocky about it. I hate cocky."

He laughed. With his soft, swollen cock still inside me, he laughed at me.

I pushed at him, struggling to remove myself from beneath his big body. He smiled at me, a slow, wolfish smile, the points of his canines gleaming. But he shifted to let me get up.

"What if I did cut you?"

His eyes seemed to darken in the moonlight. "Still would've fucked you."

I looked away as I covered myself with my clothes. Well, Shane's clothes, mostly. And my ripped underwear.

"Natalia—"

"Don't call me that."

When I looked at him again, he was tucking his dick away. He gazed up at me as I stood over him.

"And don't look at me like that. You are not that boy I promised to marry."

"I know I'm not." He got slowly to his feet. "I'm a man you like much better than that boy. And let's both just admit, you loved that boy."

Tears stung in my eyes faster than I could stop them. I turned away and started walking back in the direction I thought the car was parked. "Don't forget your knife. It looks expensive."

"Talia."

I stopped after a few more paces, realizing I had no idea where I was going. I glanced back at him.

Lex sheathed the knife into his boot and swiped his hand through his gorgeous hair. "Car's that way."

I pivoted and headed in that direction, not waiting for him.

I was sure he could keep up.

"I loved you too, you know," he said somewhere behind me, but I didn't stop.

Chapter Twenty-Six

Lex

We ditched Nico's eyesore of a car in the parking lot of the landscaping service, climbed into Shane's car and headed west on Highway 7. Eventually, once we'd hit the Number 1 and we were headed north, towards North Vancouver, Talia asked me where we were going.

I took a deep breath and started singing, "Follow the Only Road," the song the Canadians on that old *South Park* episode sang.

She tried to resist laughing, but gave in. "Why is there only one road?"

I kept singing. She smacked my arm, laughing as I finished. It was a short song. There were only a few lines that I could remember.

I smiled as she laughed.

"Since when do you burst into song out of nowhere?" she demanded. "And not well, I might add."

"Since I quit smoking, few years ago. I also chew gum, pace, read, practice excellent oral hygiene and smoke a lot of weed."

"Yeah. I might've noticed that." She was smiling at me.

"When I feel stressed, I sometimes still want a cigarette. So I do one of the above instead. Spontaneous singing works in the car or the shower, mostly. Otherwise people think you're nuts."

"I was thinking that anyway," she teased. "What made you quit smoking?"

"My grandfather died. He was a smoker all his life and got lung cancer."

"Oh." Her smile died. "I'm sorry."

"I'm not. He was a dirtbag," I told her, honestly. "No one liked him. I don't even think my dad liked him. He was a gangster all his life, did three stints in prison, one for aggravated assault on one of his girlfriends. He got shot five times over the years, and he ended up killing himself at seventy-four. Shot himself when he got diagnosed with cancer, so he wouldn't have to suffer. I heard about it from my mom. She went to the funeral, probably because she felt like she had to or my dad would give her grief. I didn't go. Giving up smoking was... I don't know, just another way to distance myself from him."

Talia was silent. I would've liked to have been able to sugar coat that story a little better for her, but honestly, that was the nicest version of it that I could come up with and still be honest.

"Well," she said after a moment, "I'm sorry anyway. I'm sorry you didn't have a nice grandpa who took you to hockey games and stuff."

"Is that what you had?"

"No. Mine were both gone when I was pretty young. I never met my paternal grandfather. My mom's dad was nice but I barely remember him."

"Sorry. I guess that sucks, too."

"So, why is there only one road?" she asked again. I appreciated the subject change.

"I mean, it's not wrong."

"There's more than one road in Canada!"

"Uh-huh. But we're literally on the Trans-Canada Highway

right now. Stretches from the Pacific to the Atlantic across the second-largest country on the planet, almost five thousand miles long, and like, everything that matters in the whole country is on it."

"Tell that to Edmonton."

I snickered. She was smiling again. I just wanted to keep her smiling.

After driving through North Van, on through West Van, and heading north up the coast, we did split off Highway 1 onto the 99 to Whistler. We weren't going to Whistler, though.

Talia seemed content. She'd fallen asleep somewhere on the edge of West Van, before we even left the city behind.

I realized, as I looked at her sleeping next to me, that I had no intention of letting her go.

If I did, I wouldn't be taking her on the run with me right now.

She was snuggled up to her window, curled around her tote bag and my hoodie, in a worn old lumber jacket that Shane probably used while chopping firewood. She must've been fucking exhausted. Guilt streaked through me as I wondered how much decent sleep she'd actually gotten since waking up on the morning of her wedding day, yesterday.

Very fucking little.

I didn't even put music on while I drove, not wanting to wake her.

It was about an hour and a half total drive to reach Squamish, a little farther past the golf and country club. To the private road that snaked up the mountain off a residential street lined with towering evergreens, tiered rock gardens and cedar shingled homes.

I punched in the code to open the private gate at the end of the public road. Once it closed behind the car, I drove slowly up the winding drive in the dark, keeping an eye out for animals. There were solar powered lights twinkling along the drive, nothing else in the dark but towering trees on both sides.

After a few bends in the road, the drive opened up and looped in front of the house. Two stories of cedar and stone with towering windows, modern version of a big rose window beneath the highest peak of the roof, plants cascading from boxes beneath every window. In winter, dusted with snow, it was probably like something out of a gingerbread fantasy, except without the candy. There was no snow yet, though.

There were a couple of motion activated lights that went on as I parked in front of the house. The three car garage was closed, a single light on in the front foyer of the house through the windows, but I knew no one was home. It was a weekday. Dane didn't generally leave the city on weekdays.

Too much work to do.

For a billionaire several times over, my brother worked too hard. I'd never been more thankful for it.

I opened the front door with the key Dane had given me with a frown and a pointed look at my Kings cut a few months back, "For emergency use." Maybe he knew better than I did that someday I'd be on the run from someone or something, and I'd need it.

I punched in the alarm code, then went back to the car to get Talia. I eased the passenger door open carefully from the outside, reaching in to support her so she didn't fall out. Was hoping I could scoop her up in my arms and put her to bed, let her wake up in comfort, well-rested. But she woke up as I slipped my arms around her.

"Huh? Where are we?" She jolted alert, looking up with wide eyes at the imposing dreamscape of the house.

"Safe," I told her. She relaxed, letting me lift her up.

I carried her into the house as she blinked, waking up.

"I'm not feeble," she muttered, "I can walk." But it was a half-assed protest. She clung to me like she didn't really want me to let go.

I kicked the door shut behind us, then walked her back to the open kitchen. The heart of the house, where Dane and I had drank a lot of whiskey, had a lot of brotherly talks these past six months since he'd bought the place. While his wife, Devi, laughed out in the hot tub with her girlfriends and I wondered if I'd ever have this kind of life, billions aside.

Kinda sad I was bringing Talia here now, under the fucked-up circumstances. Would've been nice to bring her here like a proper guest, have a drink, get her in the hot tub in a bikini and show her off to my brother.

Fuck it. Wasn't happening.

Much more fitting, somehow, I'd just held her captive and brought her here in bare feet and half-dressed without telling her where we were going. I was a real fucking Romeo that way.

I set her on her feet, then turned on more lights.

When I went to the fridge, she immediately zeroed in on the photos stuck to the front. And the ones displayed in frames along the built-in shelving between the kitchen and living room. There were pictures of Dane and Devi. And some with Katie and Jesse, and other people she knew. One or two with me in them, too.

"Is this Dane and Devi's place?"

"Yeah. One of their places. You want pizza?" I'd found one in the freezer. Wasn't sure if that would be a shitty reminder of Nico, but seemed like the quickest, easiest way to get us fed.

"Fuck, yes. I'm starving," she said distractedly, examining a wedding photo of Dane and Devi. "Your brother's very... *hot*," she concluded. "First time I met him, before I even knew who he was, was at that masquerade party last year. He was wearing angel wings and no shirt. I almost melted."

I turned on the oven. "I'll pretend you didn't say that."

She looked over at me. "You were there, too."

Yeah. I remembered. My brother was wasted, thinking he'd lost Devi and trying to get her back. It was a whole pathetic scene.

"Pretending not to notice me..." she said, wandering closer as I pulled a couple of bottles of Whistler glacial water from the fridge.

My gaze swept down her body and back up. "You're hard not to notice."

She studied me thoughtfully. "He looks like you. I don't know how I didn't see it right then. That you were brothers."

I handed a bottle of water to her. "We don't look that much alike."

"You do," she said. "It's in the eyes. And the cheekbones. And... the cock."

Water spilled out of my mouth as I started drinking; I wiped it away with the back of my hand. "The... *what?*" She better not have seen my brother's cock, under any circumstances.

"I meant... the attitude. The confidence. Not the appendage."

I eyed her and she smiled.

Then we both drank like we'd just staggered here across a desert. I drained my bottle without stopping. She got about three-quarters through hers, then we both burped.

"That was gross," she said. But we both grinned, panting. "I didn't realize I was so thirsty."

My smile faded. Add that to the list of shit she'd just been through. She was exhausted, dehydrated, underfed, had a gash on her forehead and probably cuts on her feet from running through the woods. I could tell; she was limping a little but trying to hide it.

And who knew what other damage had been done.

"I'm getting you naked and examining every inch of you."

She almost choked on her water. "Oh. Okay." She read the serious-as-shit look on my face. "You meant that way less sexual than I heard it."

I took her hand, tugging her up the stairs to the second floor. "Let's go clean you up."

"Word of advice," she said, hurrying to keep up. "Never say that to a girl. Makes her feel dirty, and not in the good way."

I flicked on lights as we went, leading her into the largest guest bedroom, the one I always stayed in. It had its own en suite. The lights had a motion detection system, same as the heating, the TVs, and pretty much everything else, but I had no idea how to turn it on. I'd never been here without Dane before.

Talia sputtered all along the way, making impressed noises. "Uh… wait… you're not even giving me a chance to check out this place? It's like a five star resort."

I tugged her straight into the bathroom. "Later. Clothes off." I got the bath water running, then started undressing her as she kept looking around.

She gasped. "They have like five types of guest soap on that three-tiered thing you serve cupcakes on!"

"You just about drooled when you said that."

"Look at the marble counter! It's beautiful! I bet it's Calacatta."

Noted. Talia De Santis liked pretty, fancy, expensive shit.

Probably gonna have to move out of my shitty little room at the clubhouse if I was thinking about keeping her.

If.

You are a dick.

At this point, if I wasn't prepared to fight and die to keep her, I didn't deserve another second with her.

She was now naked but hardly seemed to notice, her tits jiggling as she clapped her hands. "Ooh, I love jetted tubs. And look at the beautiful bamboo bath tray for all your stuff!"

I looked at it. "What stuff?"

"You know, when you have a bath and you want some wine and a trashy magazine and candles…"

I stared at her.

"What?"

"Get in the bath, Tal."

She got in the bath and I went rummaging through the guest soaps, lotions, gels and whatever the fuck, which I'd never actually noticed before. Every other time I'd been here, my eyes sort of glazed over it all like, *Chick stuff, not relevant.*

I found something called bath foam—was that the same as bubble bath?—in a peach mango scent.

"You like mango?" I already knew she loved peach.

"Yes!"

Clearly, this place was impressing her way the hell more than Shane's sex shack did.

Made me feel good, seeing her happy. Even under the shit circumstances.

I dumped some of the fruity foam stuff in the bath for her as it filled up. She sighed, relaxing back into the water. Her hair was still half-in and half-out of her fancy wedding hairdo. I found some shampoo and put it on the bamboo tray she'd ogled, in case she wanted to wash it.

Then I gathered some of the candles from the countertop and lined them up on the tray, too. I lit them with the long wooden matches I found in a box near the candles.

Talia watched me with stars in her eyes. Or maybe it was just the candlelight.

Then I sat down on the side of the tub and grabbed her foot, lifting it out of the water. I went to work examining her skin, and carefully cleaning the small abrasions with a wash cloth. Same with the other foot, while she stared at me like I'd just risked my life to save her crippled puppy from a burning building or something.

"You don't have to do that," she said after I was already done.

"I'll let you deal with the one on your face. It looks tender and I don't want to hurt you."

I turned off the water. The giant tub was finally full.

"Are you coming in with me?" she asked in the silence.

"I'll shower in a bit. I need some air and a minute to think."

We looked at each other, and I could see it all really hitting her; she wasn't doing nearly as well as she pretended. The tender shadows beneath her eyes gave it away. The remnants of her wedding hairdo hung limp and tired around her face. The nasty scrape on her forehead had dried up, and it looked so wrong on her pretty face.

I hated that it was there because of me.

I wanted it gone from her memory, like every other shitty thing I'd put her through.

It was all hitting me, too. I was so fucking tired, could've slept for a week. At the same time, I wasn't sure how I'd ever sleep again. Devil on my back and all.

"You are in so much trouble," she said softly, and if I wasn't wrong, there was affection in it.

"Yeah. Tomorrow. Tonight, let's just get some rest."

"Okay."

"Enjoy your bath. Don't forget to take a look at that cut on your forehead, clean it up, see if you think it needs stitches. I'll find the first aid stuff. When you're done soaking, I'll disinfect the cuts on your feet, wrap them up for you."

Her eyes said *Thank you*, but she just said, "I'm scared, Lex."

Shit. The note of fear in her voice. The shine in her eyes. I couldn't handle it.

I looked away. "I know."

"What happens to my dad now?"

I had no answer for that.

No matter if she knew how long she'd been asleep in the car or not, it was obvious we'd passed the ransom deadline. Whether her dad or one of the Kings or whoever showed up to make the drop or not, I didn't show up to collect it. To hand her over.

I still had to the end of the week to make good on my father's order, but I had no doubt Nico had been keeping him apprised of the situation. At least, until I handcuffed him to Shane's bed.

"Can I call him?"

I met her eyes. "That's not a good idea, Tal."

"I need my parents to know I'm okay, though. Who knows what they're thinking right now."

Yeah, I understood that. I mean, I could imagine what it would be like to have parents who'd go out of their minds if you got kidnapped for ransom. But her parents weren't exactly my first concern right now.

"Do you want me dead?" I asked her sincerely.

"Of course not," she said in a small voice. "And as soon as I catch up on my sleep, I'm gonna punch you in the balls for asking."

I sighed. "Well, that's what happens if you call anyone tonight. Just give me tonight. So we can sleep and I can figure out a way out."

I tried to keep my voice level. Cool. I didn't want her to know how scared I was.

But I was scared.

Because the damage was fucking done.

Nico taking Roni. Lying to my club. Running with Talia instead of collecting the ransom for my father.

Trying to keep Talia safe while there was a target on my back.

I was fucked on so many levels, I wasn't even sure which one to start unpacking first.

"I'll come check on you in a bit. I won't be far. Just downstairs, having a smoke out on the patio, okay?"

"Okay. Watch out for bears."

I smirked a bit. "Think they're probably hibernating right now."

"Really? This early?"

"Talia. No bears are gonna eat me. I'll see you in a few."

"Okay," she said softly. She watched me close the door as I left her there, safe in her bath.

Honestly though, I'd much rather take on a bear, any day, than Joey Montanari.

———

I put the pizza in the oven, then went out on the back patio off the living room. It was strung with soft white patio lights. Insects chirped in the woods. I sat down on one of the patio chairs and took a deep breath.

Like I told Talia, we were safe. For a few hours, at least. Maybe a few days.

But the Kings wouldn't stop until they found us.

Now that we were officially on the run, my most pressing concerns were figuring out how to a) keep Talia safe, and b) keep breathing. For as long as I could, on both counts.

I used my burner to call Vincenzo. Minutes later, I got a call back.

"You're early," my father said when I picked up. I didn't consider it a good sign that he'd called me himself. We never spoke on the phone. "I admire the enthusiasm."

Did he? Or was he just curious why the hell Nico wasn't calling him to report in?

"There was a problem. With Nico. I took care of it, for now. But I'm still working on the rest."

That was met with silence.

Then: "He told me you decided to crash a certain wedding."

"I did."

He chuckled appreciatively. "I imagine that went over rather poorly with the bride's father."

"Yeah. I imagine."

"Where are you?"

"Somewhere safe."

There was a long pause, then my father said, "Sometimes even the best laid plans need to be... flexible. Get me what I asked for by the end of the week, or, you can marry her yourself."

"Marry?" The word fell out of my mouth.

"De Santis has an unmarried daughter. And you know what I like even better than revenge? Amends."

I said nothing as my heart thudded in my chest.

Revenge? Amends?

What the fuck was really going on between him and Talia's father?

"I want an alliance," he said, when I didn't speak.

I want.

There were those words again.

He wanted me to marry Talia, why, so he could control her

father? By keeping her close, squeezing more money out of him, threatening her life anytime it suited him?

No.

"You had a pact, did you not?" he said simply. "She was promised to you first."

"We were *kids*."

"Even so. Your twenty-ninth birthday just passed. I'm sure she won't be surprised that you've come to collect."

And he probably didn't give one fuck if I came to collect with a gun to her head.

"I doubt she remembers the pact." I tried to keep my voice cool and detached. I didn't want my father to know a thing about my attachment to Talia. Or hers to me. Not one fucking thing.

But the fact that I'd taken off with her somewhere, taken her away from Nico? Spoke volumes.

He didn't have to hear it in my voice to know I was trying to protect her.

Or trying to keep her to myself.

"Then you'll remind her," he said. "It won't be hard."

"To convince her to marry a man she barely knows?"

"I hear she didn't know the last one she agreed to marry for very long," he pointed out. "You've always been a romantic. All that poetry... that head full of dreams."

I said nothing.

"She's a beautiful girl, isn't she? I'm sure you can make it work. You've got three days left. You won't need more than that to get it done."

I answered him with silence.

There was really nothing to fucking say to the man.

"And, boy?" he added darkly. "Get it done. I show her photo around... other men won't need so much convincing."

Then the line went dead.

Chapter Twenty-Seven

Lex

After my father hung up on me, I tried calling back. But no one answered Vincenzo's phone. And I didn't even have a direct number for my father.

I lit up a fat blunt and smoked the entire thing.

By then, the pizza was ready. I found a bottle of white wine in my brother's wine room, opened it, and poured Talia a glass. I found a first aid kit in the pantry and took it with the wine and pizza upstairs.

I found Talia in the bath. She smiled brightly at me and the glass of wine. And the pizza.

"I'm melting," she apologized, sounding drunk from her soak. "I'm getting out now, I swear."

"It's no rush." I set the first aid kit on the counter and passed her the glass. I put the plate with two slices of pizza on her bath tray for her.

"Where's yours?"

"I'm not all that hungry." I wasn't, weirdly.

She frowned at me.

"I'll eat, later," I told her, and that seemed to appease her. More or less.

She took a bite, looked like she'd died and gone to heaven as she chewed, then looked at me and frowned again.

She took a sip of the wine, tentatively, but her mind seemed elsewhere as she studied me. "I keep thinking about tomorrow." I could see the worry in her eyes. "Where we go from here…"

"You don't need to think about it."

"Why? Because you're worrying enough for both of us?"

"Something like that."

She set the wine glass on her tray. "I think we should run."

Yeah. I fucking wished it would be that easy.

But all it took were a few words from my father to remind me: there was nowhere to run that I could keep her safe from him.

"Talia. I can't run away with you."

There was a long, terrible silence that stretched between us as she stared at me. "Why not?"

"Because it puts you in danger. Bad guys come after me, they come after you, too, if you didn't figure that out yet."

"Do not mansplain it to me," she said irritably. "I know all that shit. I'm already in danger."

"That's a fucking terrible argument."

"It's my choice."

"This is not the time to go feminist on me. You get a choice in whatever the fuck you want. Except this."

She stared me down. "And being handcuffed to a bed."

"You're just proving my point. This whole situation is dangerous for you. Which is why we need you out of it."

"*We* need? Now you're telling me what I need?"

I looked at the ceiling, taking a breath. "You're not running anywhere with me, Talia."

"Again. My choice."

"You can stay right here, in luxury. Where you're safe."

"And then what? You think Dane's never gonna find me squatting?"

"I can call him to come get you, give me time to get away. He can take you to Jude. The Kings will keep you safe. And I can talk to your dad. Try to figure out how to fix whatever problem he has with my father. If it takes money, or—"

"And you just leave?" Her voice was rising. "Vanish into the night, without me?"

"It's the safest thing."

"For you."

"For both of us. But mainly, for you."

She stared at me. "Fine," she said. "If that's what you really want." But I read her eyes clearly. There was no fucking way she was staying if I was going.

She'd rather hunt me down herself, barefoot and alone, than sit here waiting for Dane or Jude or Shane or whoever I called to come pick her up.

She stood up, water and bubbles sliding off her naked body. She stepped out of the bath, holding my gaze as she paced over to me.

I tried to keep my eyes on hers as I asked her, "You're gonna follow me if I try to leave?"

"No."

"That was a fucking lie."

"Believe what you will." She took a too-small towel off the counter, started drying herself off. Caressing her tits the way men wanted to think women dried off after a bath. Running the plush towel over her skin like it was foreplay, slow. Dragging the fabric across her hard pink nipples. "You want to leave me," she said, dropping the towel on the floor before she was halfway dry, "leave."

"I still have the handcuffs," I reminded her.

"You do?"

"The ones Roni was wearing."

"If you even *think* about putting those things anywhere near me without my permission, ever again, you'll be sorry."

"We're not leaving this house together."

"Yes, we are."

Her fingers drifted over my hip and down, then back up again, tracing the line of my rapidly hardening dick through my jeans. Then she popped open the button.

"I need a shower..." I muttered the fucking weakest of protests as she peeled my jeans open and down. I stepped out of them, then out of my underwear as she stripped them down. I pulled off my shirt myself.

"So?" she said, grabbing me by the dick and pulling me with her toward the shower. "Take a shower."

I groaned as she led me into the glassed-in shower by my hard-on. She turned on the water, got it running warm, her hand squeezing my dick. Then she tugged me with her under the shower head that was so big it was like a rain cloud over us.

My eyelids felt heavy as I gazed down at her. I was all bark and no bite right now. Sex. Restless sleep. More sex? That was about all I was equipped to handle for the rest of the night.

"Think you can just lead a guy around by the dick, huh?"

"Only you," she said smartly. Then she kissed me, deep, while she started jacking me off, wet and slow, and warm water poured over us. I fell into her, slapping my hands on the wall behind her to keep myself upright as she went to town.

"Talia..." I breathed, working my way out of that kiss and sucking my way down her neck. "There might be condoms in here... somewhere. Do you want me to go look?" I met her eyes and stopped devouring her neck as she looked up at me. Her hand slowed way down, but didn't stop.

"Is there something you need to tell me?" she asked softly.

"No."

We stared at each other.

"Good," she whispered. "Then I'm trusting you."

"Me, too."

She started pulling again, long, tight, rolling pulls as she alternated hands, swirling her palms around my cockhead. My groans filled the shower as steam rose around us. I was so jacked up, I barely laid any groundwork with the foreplay. Just nibbled at her neck with my teeth, made out with her with some deep tongue, and forced one hand off the wall to slide my fingers over her little clit, around and around.

She moaned into my mouth and I slid two fingers deep inside her. She was so slippery, drenched, I didn't bother trying to be patient.

I ripped my dick out of her hands, hiked her legs up around my hips and slammed her back against the wall. As gently as I could, which wasn't very gently.

She squealed in surprise/lust. Then I shoved into her, thrusting deep, and she inhaled a ragged breath. Her arms tightened around my back, fingernails digging into my shoulders.

"Too much?" I murmured against her skin, burying my face in her neck again. I liked the way her eyes rolled back and her mouth fell open and all the sweet, hungry sounds fell out when I bit her throat softly. And not softly.

"No. Keep..."

And that was the end of the conversation.

What followed was a slow, deep, wet, up-against-the-wall fuck that ended in her coming twice on my dick, screaming with abandon, before I blew in her so hard I made this soul-deep growl of ecstasy I'd never made in my life.

And almost dropped her when my feet slipped on the tile, I was driving into her so fucking hard.

I got my footing and we clung to each other, panting. I was lightheaded and my dick was still throbbing. Gradually I pulled out and looked into her dazed, dark eyes.

"Welp," she whispered. "That was... dangerous."

I laughed and set her carefully on her feet. My head was spinning. I blew out a breath. "Yeah. That almost ended terribly. Pretty sure I almost took us both down, cracking open both our heads."

"Good thing it didn't end terribly." She wrapped her arms around my neck, pulling me to her as she kissed me, her soft body pressed to mine. I held her like that for a long moment, just kissing her.

Then we showered off. I helped her pull the thousand-and-one little pins from her hair and shampoo it. When she was all clean and conditioned, I washed my hair quick and followed her out of the shower. We both drank some more water. Then I staggered off to another bathroom to piss, to give her some privacy.

When I came back to our bedroom, she was just coming out of the bathroom, holding what was left of her clothes. Guilt swept through me again at the sight of her. I realized I'd forgotten her tote bag in the car. Though there really wasn't much in it anyway.

I still had her wallet, too. It was in my cut, downstairs. I'd have to remember to give it back to her.

I dipped back into the bathroom myself, pulling on my jeans. I got the first aid kit and Talia's wine and pizza. When I came back out she was wearing Shane's hockey T-shirt again, sitting on the bed against the upholstered headboard, bedside lamp turned on.

"I can probably find you something else to wear," I told her, "if you want something clean. I'm sure Dane's got some designer guest robes around here somewhere."

I thought she'd take me up on that in a heartbeat. But she shook her head. "I like Shane's shirt."

Yeah, Shane would love her wearing it, too.

"Let's never mention that to him."

She grinned.

Then she ate pizza, drank wine and tried not to wince while I went to work, dabbing antiseptic-soaked cotton to the small abrasions on her feet. None of them seemed deep, and after her bath soak they looked clean. I wrapped some soft gauze around her feet to keep them protected while she rested.

Talia watched me the whole time, saying nothing.

When I was done with her feet, I asked her if she wanted more pizza. She just held up her wine glass with a sated look. "Please?" she said sweetly, looking tired.

So I took her wine glass down to the kitchen, where I'd left the open bottle of white in the fridge. I refilled her glass, then came back up, put it in her hand, and took a look at her forehead. She hadn't cleaned it yet, so I did it for her, using a soft, damp cloth. Then antiseptic. She winced a few times and only punched me in the leg once.

"Ow!" she complained.

"Drink," I told her, and she took a sip.

"You should have some." She offered me the glass but I ignored it, concentrating on her wound. "It's fantastic. I hope the bottle didn't cost fifty-grand or something."

"My brother can afford it."

"You should have some pizza, too."

"I will," I said vaguely, and she gave me another slight frown. But my appetite had evaporated talking to my father.

I bandaged her up with some gauze and little strips of medical tape. The cut had started bleeding again when I cleaned off the dried blood, but only a bit.

"We'll change the bandage in the morning, check the bleeding. It's not deep. You should be fine."

"Thank you, Dr. Davenport."

I gave her a look.

"You're very competent," she noted.

"Field medic in the war."

She eyed me skeptically. "What war?"

"Kidding." I packed up the first aid stuff.

"And you're likable," she pointed out. "People like having you around."

I took the wine from her and took a sip, giving her a look like *How strong is this shit?*

"I noticed that," she mused. "On the Hell & Back tour. And everywhere else. You make friends easily. And you make people laugh. I mean, not so much lately. But usually you're more… jokey." The ghost of an old hurt flickered across her face. "Except around me."

I set the glass on the bedside table and turned off the lamp. "Slide down. You need sleep."

She didn't budge until she realized I was sliding in with her. Then she slid down to lie next to me. I pulled the covers over us and slid my arm around her. She curled herself against my bare chest.

"Did you really mean what you said about talking to my dad?" she said in the dark. "Trying to work something out between him and your dad?"

"Maybe. It's an option." Probably not a high chance of success, though, given my father's track record as a reasonable human being.

"Maybe you should just call the Kings," she reasoned. "Call Jude. Or one of the brothers you're really close to. Who's your best friend in the club?"

I sighed. "Maddox."

"Then call him, and explain everything. Give them a chance to understand. You didn't hurt me or Roni."

"It doesn't work like that." I could feel her worry for me in her silence and amended, "I can try. Whenever I actually talk to them." That seemed to make her feel a little better, like there was actually a conversation to be had. "But it's not just about you and Roni."

"Then what's it about?"

"Brotherhood."

I could practically feel her eyes roll.

"I don't expect you to understand. It's a club thing. There are ways things are done. And not done."

"So, in the biker handbook, after you abduct a girl and she gets all attached to you, you always have to desert her? You earn a special patch for that or something?"

I looked at her, her pretty face in anguished silhouette. "Talia…"

"I can see it now. It's a broken heart patch, right?"

"I didn't mean for any of this to happen. Including you getting attached to me."

"Well, that doesn't make it unhappen." There were tears in her eyes when she looked at me. "Throughout all of this, including those frantic minutes when you showed up at the hotel and asked me to come with you, you're the only thing that's made me feel safe. After everything that's happened, you'd really leave me?"

I swallowed. "That's how it should've been from the beginning, Tal. I should've left you alone." Couldn't she see that?

"Should've. But didn't. So what do you do about it now?"

Easy; that would've been so fucking easy to answer if she wasn't who she was—strong, a fighter, so determined—and if I wasn't already so fucking wrapped up in her. I'd handcuff her in this house, call my brother, tell him to come get her and be gone before dawn.

Who knew how far I'd get or how long I'd last, but at least she'd be out of it.

But I couldn't do that. If she'd shown even a glimmer of relief at that idea, I'd have done it.

But now, I couldn't do that.

I believed her when she said she wanted us to run. Together. She didn't want to lose me any more than I wanted to lose her.

I knew, even if we stayed together, we'd probably be torn apart before this was over.

And I knew if we stayed together, even if my father got what he said he wanted... she'd never be safe.

But I still couldn't leave. Even after she fell asleep.

I just lay there, watching her, listening to her breathe.

Her head lay on my chest and her arm tightened around me in sleep. She felt so right in my arms, like she was always meant to be there. Like she was destined to end up wrapped around me, and me wrapped around her.

And I knew it right then: we were doomed to fall in love.

And it was all our fathers' faults.

They should never have let us meet if they were gonna be fucking enemies. Maybe they'd always been enemies? And I didn't even know *why*.

But that story always went the same too, didn't it?

War. Over money, power.

Bloodlines and pissing matches.

A winner and a loser.

But no matter who won and who lost, there was always one constant about war, too.

Generals died in bed; soldiers died in the trenches, broken and alone.

———

When I was a boy, my mom told me all about her parents; my wealthy and powerful grandparents. The grandparents I never even got to meet until a few years ago.

She told me all about how rich we were, how rich I was going to be. She told me how, when I turned thirty, I'd inherit billions.

What she never told me was that I'd already been disowned because of her. Because she'd been disowned for running off with my father.

Because he was married.

But mainly because he was a criminal.

I had to find out the truth from my father. Just before Mom left him and we moved to Vancouver, he told me that it was all a lie. That I'd never inherit a thing. That I'd never met my mom's parents because I was dead to them.

That my mom had told me lies so I'd love her.

Maybe he thought it would turn me against her. But all I said to him was, "At least she always loved me."

My mom had faults. She'd fucked up. A lot.

But she'd never hurt me on purpose.

She'd told me those things, not to hurt me, but because she

wanted them to be true.

She'd wanted me to be accepted into her family. She'd wanted to be accepted herself. She'd wanted me to be recognized by my grandparents.

She wanted to be forgiven.

And she wanted me to get the inheritance she believed I was due.

She did a lot of shitty things to try to make that happen.

In the end, she failed.

Last year, when I met with her mother, my grandmother Helena, for only the second time in my life, she offered me an inheritance— if I left the Kings. She said the Davenports couldn't be connected to a criminal organization, financially or otherwise.

I got that.

But I was never walking away from the Kings. They'd have to throw me out, cut the colors off my back. Or put me in the ground.

Kings Forever, Forever Kings.

It was patched onto our cuts. It was inked into my flesh. And it was in my bones.

Brotherhood.

I knew Talia didn't understand it. She didn't have to. It was between me and my club brothers, and there was nothing she could do about it. As much as she'd probably try to throw herself in the line of fire for me, if I let her. I knew that about her now.

She'd make an incredible old lady.

An incredible wife.

I left her in bed and went downstairs, out to the patio again. This time I brought my phone with me; my own phone, not the burner. But I didn't make any calls. Not right away.

Instead, I considered my options one last time. But there weren't many. And none of them were any fucking good.

If I kept running... I'd still be betraying the Kings, I'd be betraying my father, and undoubtedly I'd end up dead for it—or worse, causing more harm to Talia. And of course, I'd have to live with the fact that I really was just like my father, and his father before him.

Selfish, evil, and a danger to everyone who knew me.

Maybe that was my worst fear all along.

I never told my club brothers about the work I did for my father because it was a betrayal of my club colors. But worse than that, I was truly afraid it would embroil the Kings and the Mafia in a war, because of me, and ultimately people I loved would get hurt.

I told myself I didn't love so my father had no one to hurt.

That was bullshit.

I loved.

If I didn't, what would I care if my club brothers fought and even died for me?

When my father had Lola killed, Piper told me the Kings would strike back. Not because of the dog, exactly; because of what it did to me. It was my choice. I chose not to. Because I saw what had happened to my father's enemies in the past.

How, so often, they just... disappeared.

I was raised to believe only the Mafia held sway over the Mafia. And the fact was the other bosses had never brought my father to heel. The Commission tolerated his evil. And the boss of all bosses, the so-called godfather, was in the wind; gone underground, years ago. My father said he was nothing but a spook story, a ghost; a shadow figure used to keep men in line. But even knowing that, the threat of that ghost did nothing to keep my father in line.

If there was anyone truly in a position of ultimate power, why would he let a mad dog run free?

There was no godfather. No one above my father, to rein him in.

I could defy him, sure. But that only risked getting other people hurt or killed because of it.

I knew running away with Talia would only mean never-ending danger for her.

But the longer I was with her, it only got harder—the thought of letting her go.

I could face my betrayal of my club, and risk punishment. Interrogation, beating, torture; these were all possibilities. The club was nothing if not a brotherhood, and I'd broken the code I shared with my brothers. Colors; brothers; chapter; club. I'd betrayed them all.

I could be voted out. My life, or just as bad, my life as a King, ended.

I'd been a King for a decade. My whole adult life. What would I be without them, even if I got away with my life?

As impossible as the choice was, I knew that if I wanted Talia safe, I either had to give myself up to the Kings or hand her over to the Kings and stand up to my father, somehow, alone. The choice was never going to be easy.

I'd been running from it, holding onto some boyish illusions of freedom, ever since I'd become a man. But I'd never be free until I faced who and what I really was. Until I faced the consequences of all my actions.

And found out if there was anything left for me on the other side.

So I pulled out my phone and called Jude.

He picked up after one ring. Silence greeted me, but I heard him breathing.

I could practically see him, sitting somewhere in the dark, not sleeping. Not smoking, not drinking. Just watching Roni sleep, maybe, bent on hunting me down and demanding answers, no matter how long it took.

"Jude," I said, so he'd know for sure it was me.

"I want to hear one thing outta you." He spoke slow and cold. "Do I need to start calling hospitals and morgues?"

I told him what I knew he wanted to hear. "Talia's unharmed." Luckily, it was truth. Mostly.

"I better see her soon, unharmed. That girl gets hurt, brother, you're gonna wish you never laid eyes on her."

Brother.

I knew he didn't use the word lightly.

I also had zero illusions that he actually meant it anymore. He was being as conversational with me as he could force himself to be, probably, so he didn't lose me. So I kept talking.

"She gets hurt," I told him, "I'll slit my throat myself."

"I'm holdin' you to that."

"Yeah. I know it." Now that that was out of the way, I got down to the reason I called. "The guy who took Roni, his name is Nico Barretti. You'll find him handcuffed to a bed in a house up in Burke Mountain. You want the exact address, you'll find my car at Grim's landscaping lot on the Number 7. My phone is in the glovebox. It's unlocked. The address is under Shane Madrigal's contact. It's his place. Shane and Grim had nothing to do with this and know nothing about it."

"Nico Barretti," he said slowly, probably trying to place the name of the man who'd taken his woman, looking for some motive.

"Yeah. He's my cousin on my father's side."

"And why," he said in a low, restrained voice, "would you be doin' dirty deeds with your cousin on your father's side? Your estranged, psycho Mafia boss father."

"I had nothing to do with taking Roni. That part was all Nico."

I heard his soft laugh. It was a terrible sound. I'd never tasted Jude's wrath, or even seen it in action. But I knew it would be brutal, where his woman was involved. "Right. You just abducted Talia."

I squeezed my eyes shut, dug deep to get through this. "Tell me one thing. Just promise me she'll be safe if I turn her over to you. You'll protect her."

"Yeah," he said darkly, "she'll be a hell of a lot safer than with a man who'd abduct her. I promise you that."

"You'll make sure she's safe."

"I'll make sure she's safe."

"Then you wanna come get us, we'll be waiting. We're at Dane and Devi's cabin. Jesse's been here, you can ask him or Katie for the address if you don't have it."

I hung up. Wasn't much more to be said over the phone.

My heart slammed blood and adrenaline and fear through my body. But what's done was done. I really couldn't run away from it even if I tried.

I'd done the right thing.

I had to turn Talia over to the Kings. It was the only smart move left to make. The only move.

The move I should've made when I gave Roni back. I never should've let Talia stay at Shane's house, waiting for me.

But then we wouldn't have had this time together, and I couldn't exactly regret that either.

It was time for me to stop being selfish, though.

I'd let the Kings take her home. And let them decide how to deal with me—and with my father.

Jagged as it was to swallow, the fact was it was never my place to try to handle him alone. That plan was always doomed to fail, someday.

Well, that day had come.

I'd fucking failed.

I thought I could handle my father. And maybe there was some stupid part of me that just *wanted* to handle it myself, because it was Talia.

But I'd fucked up. I'd failed her. In that way, I was just like him.

How many times did he fail me and Mom?

Countless.

Like him, maybe I was born to be bad. To ruin good things, like both of my parents always seemed so very capable of.

But all I could do about that now was make sure Talia was safe, and face the consequences of my mistakes.

This was the one thing I could do for her that my father was never able to do for my mom or for me, no matter if he ever really loved us or not.

I'd let her go.

Chapter Twenty-Eight

Talia

I woke up sometime in the night to an empty bed.

When I dragged myself upright, I saw the dark silhouette of a man through the billowy curtains that fluttered over the open doors to the balcony. I smelled sweet pot smoke and fresh air.

I slipped out of bed in Shane's hockey T-shirt. At this point, I figured I was keeping this thing and either sleeping in it for the rest of my life, to remind me of that time the love of my life and I shared a crazy couple of days while we fell madly in love, or burning it in a pyre while Al Green "How Can You Mend a Broken Heart" played on repeat and I guzzled peach schnapps from the bottle.

I padded out to the balcony and drifted open the curtain that felt like it was woven out of angels' wings.

Lex sat in the shadows. No shirt on, jeans undone, a joint in hand, gazing out over the forest. He looked up at me.

"Did I wake you?" His voice was soft and throaty in the night, and it made me shiver.

"No." I reached for the joint.

He handed it to me and I took a drag. I closed my eyes for a moment, letting the fresh air and marijuana smoke swirl in my mouth before exhaling. I handed it back to him. Our fingers brushed and an electric sizzle ran up my spine.

His hair fluttered a little in the breeze. I could barely see his face, just the basic landscape. Cheekbone, jawbone. Nose. Lip. He looked delicate and strong, beautiful and wild and human all at the same time. Breakable.

Real.

Bound by time and law and consequences like all the rest of us, and somehow ethereal, like he was part of the night.

I could still feel his hands all over my skin.

I took another breath of green, clean night air and looked out into the dark. Why couldn't it just be like this and never change?

Why did we have to answer to anyone?

I could remember when we were kids, his dad coming after him for something. Hiding in the trees between his summer house and mine. He knew he was in trouble. He held my hand and I wondered if he was scared.

Eventually, he'd told me to go home. He knew his dad wouldn't stop looking for him.

I knew he didn't want me to see him getting in trouble.

"I want to stay in this moment," I told him.

"Come sit with me." He patted the bench next to him and I sat down.

We sat looking out into the dark. There were a few stars through the wisps of cloud in the sky, so dark blue but not quite black. I could see the line of mountains on the horizon, low to the Earth, seeming so far away. "Is there really a world out there?"

"Theoretically."

"Have you figured out our escape plan?"

He didn't answer for a long moment. Then he held something out to me. It was my wallet, and a ring.

Carl's ring.

"Shit." I'd forgotten about the ring. Again. I took both items from his hand. "You found the ring, at Shane's place?"

"After I handcuffed Nico to the bed. I took a quick look around, make sure you didn't leave anything important behind. Found it on the side of the bathtub." He held the joint out for me and when I took a little drag, our eyes met. "Wasn't sure I was gonna give it back to you, or just flush it down the toilet."

"Well... thank you. You did the right thing."

"What happens to it now?"

I shrugged. I tucked the ring into my wallet to keep it safe and set it aside. "I guess I give it back. I'm not marrying him, Lex."

He said nothing. But I could tell he was relieved to hear those words.

"What happens to *us* now?" I asked him.

"Dane will come get us."

"Tonight?"

"Yeah. Soon." He didn't offer up more details.

We finished the joint in the dark. But I didn't feel relieved, exactly, just kinda more scared. Because I knew he wasn't off the hook, just like that.

"And then what? We call my dad?"

"I guess we'll see."

I considered that, and the helicopter pad on one side of the house, which I'd glimpsed from a window. "Will he come by car or helicopter? Or boat?"

"Does it matter?"

"Yes. I need to be prepared, in case you try to take off without me."

He looked into my eyes in the dark. "Why would I do that?"

"Because you're ridiculously heroic that way."

"You're delusional."

"Admit it. You'd still run if you thought it was what was best for me. You put yourself in danger to go against what your father told you to do and what the Kings expected of you, for me. Classic hero move."

Lex shook his head. "What are you preparing to do, say I did take off?"

"Well, if it's a car, easy enough to throw myself on the hood. Boat, trickier. Depends on the boat. Helicopter... I'd need to get the timing right, but if you tried to lift off without me, I'd definitely be grabbing onto one of the runner things like they do in the movies."

He stared at me. "You mean the landing skids?"

"Is that what they're called?"

"What are you, a stuntwoman now? You'd get yourself killed."

I shrugged. "Your fault. Shouldn't have tried to leave."

"I was trying to save your life."

I held his gaze. "I don't need a hero. I'd rather go down in flames with the villain."

"You don't mean that."

"If he's you, then yes I do."

I could feel his inaudible sigh in the dark. He looked out into the night.

He didn't say anything for a long time.

"You ever read *Romeo and Juliet*?"

I studied his hard profile. "Uh, sure. Eleventh grade English. Didn't everybody?"

He made a soft sound between a snicker and a growl. "Yeah. Because some educator decided it was a great idea to teach teenagers a love story where the hero and heroine kill themselves over each other."

"Huh. It never really hit me before how fucked-up that is."

He said nothing.

"Okay, you're worrying me. Why are you sitting out here thinking about teen suicide?"

"I'm not. I'm thinking about blood feuds and destiny, and falling in love with someone you'd rather die than be without, but who's probably gonna get you killed." He looked at me. "I can't let that shit happen to you because of me, Talia."

I took that in. I knew he meant it. I knew he'd tried to keep me from getting hurt.

But.

"You're doing a pretty typical dude thing here, Lex," I informed him. "Underestimating the heroine much? You're forgetting that Juliet was a total badass. 'That which we call a rose, by any other name would smell as sweet.' She didn't give a fuck that Romeo's last name was Montague."

"And where did that get her?"

"Right where she wanted to be," I said stubbornly. "With Romeo."

"Uh-huh. With his corpse."

"I mean, technically he thought she died first. The whole thing was kinda his mistake."

That observation did not go over well. He ran his tongue over his teeth, and I could practically feel him swallow back the growl. "Talia. You think my father's the only problem here? The Kings? It's not just *my* family that's the problem. What do you think your father would do to me right now if he could?"

Hmm. Good question.

Weirdly, I hadn't actually thought about that.

Lex's gaze drifted down to my mouth. "'Peace? I hate the word,'" he recited softly, "'as I hate hell, all Montagues, and thee.'"

I blinked at him, stunned. I couldn't quite place the quote. "Who said that? Juliet's mother?"

"Her cousin. Tybalt."

"You can quote *Romeo and Juliet*?" Of course he could. Just add that to his mile long list of panty-soaking qualities, somewhere up at the top, near the hot teeth.

"I wrote a paper in school about Tybalt Capulet as the personification of hate. I was overly fascinated with the dynamics of the blood feud, the war between the families."

"You have some experience with all of that," I said gently.

"Too much."

I bumped his shoulder gently with mine. "What's this about, Lex? I haven't swallowed any poison lately, and I don't intend to."

He took a deep, quiet breath. "I think your father and mine have some kind of grudge that goes deeper than a two million dollar ransom."

"How do you know?"

"I don't. It's just a feeling."

I could feel he was holding back, not telling me everything that was on his mind. Because he didn't want to scare me, or endanger me any more than he already had, maybe.

"Sometimes," he said thoughtfully, "what a man wants runs deeper than vengeance. Revenge only tastes sweet for a moment. A smart man prefers a compounding return on his power. Especially if he's greedy."

"What are you talking about?"

"It would've been so much simpler for my dad to just kill me," he mused. "But he's too greedy for that."

I slipped my arms around his waist and rested my chin on his shoulder, holding him close. "You're scared."

"'He jests at scars that never felt a wound.'"

I considered that quote carefully. "It's easy to make jokes about pain, about heartbreak, when you've never been hurt," I translated.

He met my eyes. "'I must be gone and live, or stay and die.'"

That one, I wasn't about to translate. I tightened my arms around him. He wasn't going anywhere. Over my dead body.

Well, damn; he was right. I was channeling some deep Juliet vibes right now.

I told him calmly, "If you keep quoting Romeo at me, I'm going to fall irreversibly in love with you, Lex Davenport."

"You've already done that," he said roughly. Our eyes held in the dark, like a solemn promise.

My heart constricted, along with my stomach, my lungs, and my throat.

"Yeah." I sighed a deep, shuddery breath. "Yeah, I have. Why do you have to be so damn right about that?"

"Because I know you." He ran his fingers along my jaw and cupped my face. "I always have. Little sweetheart with hair like spun gold and dark eyes that tell you her every secret, if you look close enough. Won't back down from a dare or danger. Always with something to prove. Hates to be underestimated..." He ran his thumb back and forth along my jaw. "Will give you her whole heart, even sign away her life to you and seal it with blood, to prove she's not afraid."

"Because she already knew you were the worst threat to her heart she'd ever come across. And despite every instinct she had to run like hell and never look back... she was all in."

"Tal, I was all in way before that. Remember when you jumped off your dad's boat because I dared you to? I jumped right in after you and my dad had to fish me out. And there you are, your dad fishing you out at the same time, and as soon as you stop coughing up water, you go and yell over at us—"

"I dared him to do it, Mr. Montanari!" I grinned.

Lex smiled back, halfway. "You took the credit, the blame and the fall. And you were so damn pleased with yourself."

"It was worth it, to see the look on your face."

"There," he said, brushing my cheek with his thumb and looking in my eyes. "There isn't a room on Earth the two of us have ever walked into where you didn't look at me with that spark in your eyes."

I swallowed. "Stupid eyes."

"You have zero poker face," he agreed. "Remind me to play poker with you sometime."

"Jerk."

He kissed me.

The kiss deepened as his hands slid under my T-shirt and mine roamed over his hard, naked chest. We got up slowly, still kissing, and my hands roamed down inside the back of his unbuttoned jeans to squeeze the perfect, muscled globes of his tight ass.

We stumbled into the bedroom as we undressed each other, and by the time we hit the mattress, we were naked, entwined. I licked his neck and scraped my fingernails over his back tattoo. He shuddered with restrained lust and plunged his tongue into my mouth. I hiked my leg up over his hip as we made out, and he pushed into me.

We fucked in the dark, a slow, desperate joining. Hands and mouths seeking out every sensitive place. Kissing. Clinging to each other. This intense, beautiful thing, splitting me open, my body taking his.

There wasn't enough of it to ever satisfy the hunger I had for him.

When I was with Lex, I could understand how with some people, it took a lifetime to get enough of their love. How you died, old, in each other's arms, still in love. Still falling.

We orgasmed together and I felt it in my chest, in my spine, in the marrow of my bones and the darkest places at the back of my mind, as much as I felt it pulsing in my core.

He bit my neck softly and kissed me there, whispering my name.

Natalia.

I wiped the tears away before he could see them.

Why did I ever think I was in love with Carl? Because he looked nice in a tie and opened doors for me and told me he loved me?

I'd take a drop of Lex's love over an ocean of Carl's. I'd die, parched on the shores as the tide of Lex's love receded from me, if it ever did, leaving me stranded. And I'd happily drown in his love again if the tide ever washed back in.

There were people you liked, people you loved, people you thought you'd lay down your life for... and people you'd actually lay down your life for.

Only right now did I know the actual difference.

We untangled ourselves slowly and lay side by side. Still catching my breath, I said, "You're skittish. I can still feel you thinking about walking away."

He met my eyes. "If I did that, promise you, I'd be running, not walking. I know you'd be up my ass with a knife."

I sighed. "I feel like I need to hold *you* captive now."

He snickered, tossing an arm over his eyes. "I've had so many nightmares about you, you have no idea."

I burst out laughing. "Wow. I don't know what to say to that. I had no idea I was so scary."

He didn't smile. "In every single one of them, I make you mine. And then I lose you. In some horrible way." His arm dropped and he met my eyes. "My father always comes for you."

"Lex. He's not going to take me away from you."

He shook his head slowly. "He can do anything. Trust me."

I propped myself up on an elbow, looking down at him. "You say that like he's a god or something. All-powerful."

"He's not a god, Talia. He's the Devil. And he's not all powerful. He's just unstoppable."

"How do you know that's true?"

"Because no one's stopped him yet."

"Maybe the Kings will."

He didn't say anything, but I could feel his hopelessness. Like he was certain the Kings were going to punish him if they ever got their hands on him.

But I had faith in Jude yet. And Roni.

"What should I tell them?" I asked him. "What should I tell Jude?" Because we both knew they'd have questions for me. At some point, they'd find us and there would be a conversation. A reckoning.

Jude would never let what happened to Roni go unanswered.

"Tell them everything."

"Really?"

"Lying to them won't help you. They'll find out the truth."

"The truth is I chose you." I ran my hand up his chest and caressed his throat with the backs of my fingers. "You tricked me. And I still chose you."

He inhaled, then exhaled slowly. "Then tell them that."

"And what should I tell my dad?"

"Tell him everything, too. If you want to."

I flopped next to him on the bed. "I don't even know what to tell him. He's gonna be so disappointed in me." I stared at the dark ceiling, realizing how little power that idea had over me. "Huh. I used to care about that, so fucking much."

"You don't anymore?"

I shrugged. "Maybe he'll disown me."

Lex drew closer to me. "Why would you say that?"

"Because." I sighed, uncomfortable with the memories that arose, so suddenly, out of the dark. "When I was a little girl, I thought he loved me unconditionally. I had no reason not to. He once told me, when I asked him why I didn't have a sister or a brother, that he already had the perfect child so he had no need of another one. It made me feel…" I thought back to that moment. I closed my eyes and really tried to feel it. It was so vivid in my chest, even now. "*Special.* And perfectly deserving of my dad's love. Like… I'd earned it by being so special." I opened my eyes to find Lex watching me intently. "But when you earn something from someone, they can take it away, right?"

He nodded a little, like he understood that, and I went on.

"My dad was away a lot, always working, but when he was around, he was a great dad. Committed. Loving. He made me feel cherished. But he was also really old school. Strict and protective. Hard. And because he was away a lot, I grew up with this unquantifiable feeling of worry. Insecurity, I guess. I used to hear my parents arguing about him being away all the time. I felt worried a lot, that they might get divorced and then he'd be gone for good."

"But he never left, right?"

"No. He didn't." I studied him, remembering our summers together as kids, and my dad's reaction to Lex. "He didn't like you."

"I know."

"Or at least, he didn't like me hanging around you. He told me to stay away from you. He told me your father was evil."

"He is," Lex agreed.

"When you dared me to jump off the boat and swim to shore, and I told our dads it was my idea, I didn't want to admit that you dared me to do it. I thought I was being so brave. Showing my dad that I wouldn't do something just because you told me to. It was a lie, of course. I thought he'd be proud of me. Instead, he got really mad." I thought back to that moment, too. To how I'd felt, knowing I'd disappointed my dad. "It was the first time I could remember him being so mad at me… it was almost scary. He was like this whole other person. He told me, when he grounded me, that your dad was in the Mafia. I didn't understand what that meant except that it was a dark thing. He said your dad was a criminal. And that like your father, you were bad." I could still hear my father's voice; feel his anger that day. "He told me that only a bad girl would tempt a bad boy."

You don't want to be a bad girl, do you? That was what he said to me, and it terrified me.

"That's fucked-up bullshit, Tal," Lex informed me.

"I know that. I mean…" I tried to be honest. "I think I know that. Now. But back then… I guess the way he spoke about you, and how angry he was… it made me feel like if I was bad, too, he wouldn't approve of me either. From that moment on, I tried so hard to be 'good.' Whatever the hell that is. I wanted to be deserving of my father's approval. I never wanted to see him angry like that, at me, again. I wanted him to love me so he wouldn't leave." I looked into Lex's eyes. "I spent all my life trying not to be a 'bad girl' so I wouldn't lose my father's love. Including marrying the man he wanted me to marry."

"You didn't marry him," he reminded me.

"Yeah. Thanks to you."

"You don't have to do that shit anymore," he told me. "You're an adult, Talia. You get to choose who you are and what you do. And who you choose to be with."

I studied him, wondering if he heard himself. Didn't he know the same things about himself?

"And what about your father?" I asked him. "What are you gonna tell him?"

"I don't know." He took a moment to gather his words. I thought he was gonna say more typical man stuff, like he'd figure something out. And tell me, again, not to worry. Instead he said, "He ripped out my teeth when I was eighteen."

I just stared at him, speechless.

Then I put my hand on his face, gently. He eyed me back, warily. I drifted my thumb over his lips, nudging them open. I ran my thumb lightly over his beautiful upper teeth. Tears burned in my eyes, but I blinked them back.

"This?" I whispered.

He nodded slightly.

"I thought they were veneers."

He took my hand and held it against his chest. "You can't put a veneer on something that doesn't exist. The fangs are implants and the rest is a bridge. Had to have surgery to repair what he took from me."

I heard what he said, but the words sank in slowly and painfully.

I knew, when he said it, that his father had taken so much more from him than teeth. Anyone could see that.

"Probably have to have more surgery in the future," he went on. "I got good work, but it won't last forever."

I stared at his face. I tried to picture him, a few years older than he was now, a few years hotter, and all mine. With his upper front teeth gone because they had to be taken out. And all I felt was devastated. I'd heard people poke fun at Lex's teeth, like they were on par with Nico's cheesy grill—like he'd purposefully gotten them as a vanity project, to be flashy and menacing.

When you knew the truth, kinda punched right through that idea, sucked all the air out of it.

"How could he do that to his own son?"

"He did a lot more." He gave a small grunt. "My father doesn't normally lift a finger to commit a crime. He gives an order to a guy, who gives it to a guy who gives it to a guy, and it's done. But he'd probably kill me with his bare hands, right now, if he could get them on me."

"Why?"

"Because," he said, with a small sigh of surrender, "I chose the Kings over him."

I wasn't sure what he meant by that. Did he mean when he patched into the club?

He squeezed my hand. Then he rolled onto his side, facing me, and put his other hand on the side of my face. "And I chose you over him, too."

I squeezed him back, rolling to face him. "I know. Last night, when you ran away with me instead of turning me over to collect the ransom. That was the bravest thing I've ever seen, by the way."

"Talia." He shook his head at me. "I chose you long before that."

"When?" I whispered. "When did you choose me?"

"I tried to, when we were kids. That's why I made you sign that pact. And when you came back into my life… I made you despise me so you'd never come near me."

"That was you choosing me?" I gave a small, skeptical laugh. But I was weirdly flattered.

"If I didn't," he said, running his thumb over my lip, "I would've been endangering you. Couldn't live with that. I had to keep you safe."

"That is some very twisted logic."

"Doesn't matter. I failed anyway." He brushed his lips over

mine, sending a warm thrill through my chest and deep into my core as he sighed… a sound of broken surrender that I knew I'd carry in my heart, for better or worse, for the rest of my days. "'Cause here you are."

"Yeah," I whispered, "here I am. With you. Right where I belong."

Chapter Twenty-Nine

Lex

I headed down to the kitchen to refill Talia's wine again. Figured I might as well get her drunk, make this whole thing as painless as possible. Neither of us could seem to sleep anyway.

Me, because I knew our time together was coming to an end, soon.

Her, maybe because she felt my unease, even when I lied to her and made her believe I wasn't leaving her.

I mean, I wasn't leaving her, exactly. But I knew I wasn't gonna get to keep her. There was no way Jude was gonna pick us up, drive us back to the city, congratulate us on our love, drop us off at home and tuck us into bed, wish us well and be on his way.

I wish.

I was pulling the wine bottle out of the fridge when I smelled it. Bike exhaust.

Leather. Woods.

Rage and cold metal.

"Shit," I muttered.

Then I felt the hard jab at my right temple and froze.

"Give me one reason," he said, from somewhere behind my right ear. Jude's voice was low and rough, like he'd hiked all the way up the mountain on foot just so he could kill me himself. And now I could hear him breathing, ragged with anger, yet creepily calm.

I didn't have to ask what he meant.

He wanted a reason not to paint the wall with my brains, right now.

Which meant I still had a chance to keep breathing. If only for a few more minutes.

I looked at the gun and he jammed it harder against my temple, crooking my head at an awkward angle. It was a Ruger Mark IV Lite with a suppressor, and his intent was clear. If he shot me right now, it would be no louder than a pebble tapping on the window.

I wasn't gonna kid myself that silencer was to save his ears. It was to save Talia.

So I'd be dead and gone, my body dragged out of here, before she even knew he was in the house. Hell, he'd probably even have time to wipe down the blood splatter before she wandered down, wondering what was taking me so damn long to get her a glass of wine.

I had the bottle in my hand and instinct kicked in, briefly. I considered turning and slamming it over Jude's—

Nope. Counterproductive. I'd be dead before I finished the thought.

"Talia's here," I said evenly, giving him his reason. "She's not hurt."

The gun left my skull. Not because I was out of the line of fire. Because the silencer at my temple was a warning. He was getting my attention.

And now he was backing up, somewhere behind me. Somewhere he could shoot me from, before I could make a move toward him. Somewhere I had no hope of knocking the gun away.

I had no idea if Jude Grayson had ever killed anyone. He wasn't the kind of guy to wear some biker patch or tattoo broadcasting the fact, or to go bragging about it, or even to let it slip to a brother over a few too many beers.

I had zero doubt, though, that he'd kill a man for what happened to Roni.

"Put the bottle down. Slowly."

"Yup." I slid it back into the fridge, slowly.

"Clasp your hands behind your lower back."

I did that.

"Back out of the fridge. Do it slow."

I backed up and the door swung softly shut.

"Where is she?" he said, his voice deadly low.

"Bedroom at the top of the stairs. She might be in the bathroom."

I heard movement. Not Jude. He was somewhere behind me and to my right, by the back door. This was a couple of people, at least. I heard soft footsteps on the carpeted stairs, going up.

"Don't hurt her," I said, automatically. They had no reason to hurt her. But I was freaking out. "She had nothing to do with this. With taking Roni."

Silence.

Then I heard a small squeal—definitely Talia—and muffled voices from upstairs. Men's voices. I started to turn, but someone grabbed my arms, twisting them behind my back—and a heavy body slammed me into the refrigerator.

My skull hit the cold stainless steel door, hard. I groaned as my head rolled back and forth against it. Somewhere, I could hear Talia's voice.

I pulled, but I felt the cold metal they clasped on my wrists. They'd handcuffed me. I heard a commotion, voices, people coming down the stairs.

"She's fine," I heard someone say. Maddox. "Coupla bruises. Nasty scratch on her head. She was changing the bandage…"

"Lex!" That was Talia, and I heard it when they caught her and jerked her back, preventing her from coming to me.

"Talia?" My voice was groggy. How hard did my head hit the fridge? My skull was ringing dully. Someone had me pressed against the fridge with his body. At least one person, maybe two.

Then hands grabbed my arms, the weight lifted away, and they jerked me around to face her.

But before I could see her, something black was yanked down over my head. A bag. At least it wasn't plastic. The rough fabric was scratchy and stiff, and I couldn't see through it. It smelled of dirt.

"Wait, what are you doing to him?"

"Take her outside." That was Jude. Low, even voice. Not fucking around.

"Maddox. Brother," I begged, whoever would listen. "Take care of her." I knew they wouldn't just let her go. Drop her off at home like nothing happened. There would be questions. They'd ask her questions until they were satisfied with her answers.

They'd probably keep her until they were satisfied with mine, too.

They'd have to debrief her. She'd seen too much, heard too much.

But they'd keep her safe. They'd keep her safer than I ever could.

"Jude?" I said, when no one answered me.

I could hear Talia struggling as she was taken outside. "He didn't hurt me!" she was yelling.

"Yeah?" Maddox muttered. "Where'd you get that cut on your head?"

"Wait. I want to see him!" she screamed, as whoever manhandled her out the door.

When I made that call to Jude in the night, I pretty much assumed I was gonna die. My club brothers could strip me of my colors and their protection, set me loose to be scooped up by my father. But they wouldn't do that.

I knew too much.

I'd lied to Talia to protect her. There was no conversation to be had, no chat that would get me out of this. The truth was the Kings would put me to ground themselves before this was over.

I knew it when not one of them spoke to me, as the black bag over my head was pulled tight around my throat.

Something sharp stabbed into my arm. A fucking needle.

"Jude..." I said, my tongue heavy in my mouth. "Jude... we should talk about this."

But then my eyelids grew heavy. My head and my limbs grew heavy. I didn't know which way was vertical anymore.

I couldn't feel my body.

Talia, I said, but it was only in my head.

Then I stopped feeling that, too.

Chapter Thirty

Lex

The walls and the floor were raw concrete. The ceiling was an open network of pipes, way too far overhead to be reached, even if I was standing on the battered metal chair that stood in front of me, empty. Water dripped in one of the moist corners of the cell, which smelled of wet concrete and mildew.

But I couldn't hear the water dripping anymore.

I'd regained consciousness while I was being chained to the grate in the floor. The water that dripped from the ceiling trickled across the floor, to the drain in the middle and through one of the holes in the iron grate. There was a thick iron loop in the middle of the grate, a chain attached to the loop, shackles locked around my ankles that attached to the chain.

The chain was short and heavy, and had me on my knees.

Another chain was attached to shackles on my wrists and disappeared somewhere in the ceiling, in the shadows beyond the pipes, stretching my arms above my head. My body felt heavy and weak. I couldn't stand up or lie down. I knelt on the concrete, the rough surface digging into my skin through my jeans.

I sagged in the wrist shackles, trying not to move at all. Moving only hurt.

I watched the thin, jagged stream of the water on the floor. But I couldn't hear it trickling into the drainage pipe below the grate anymore.

I knew exactly where I was.

They'd brought me to a place we called "the dump." A sprawling rural property owned by a retired King, scattered with random buildings, including this old, dilapidated work building. I was in a back room. I'd brought enough guys here for "questioning" over the years, it was familiar, even if I'd never been in this position before.

After they'd chained me here, they left. I didn't see who it was. They were behind my back when they pulled the bag off my head.

My vision was blurry for a while after I came to, the remnants of whatever they'd shot me up with.

After they left me, a metal door with a heavy lock clanked shut.

Then the music started playing out of the speakers that hung among the pipes up in the distant ceiling. It started out quiet and muffled at the start of the song, and I recognized it right away. Nine Inch Nails, "The Hand That Feeds."

Then it kicked in, loud.

When the song ended, it started right over again. It played again and again and again. I lost count of how many times it played until it was just going around and around; my head was ringing with it. And it wasn't lost on me, the song choice.

The hand that feeds…

The Kings.

I'd turned right around and bitten that hand.

I wondered if they knew I'd also bitten my father's.

And now, I was down on my knees.

How was I gonna get back up and face what I'd done?

And did I even have a choice about it?

Or were they just torturing me?

After what had to be hours of that song blaring on repeat, I didn't fucking know. I couldn't even think anymore with it going around and around.

Every time it ended, there were four seconds of ringing silence. And each time, in that ringing silence, I hoped to God it was done.

Then the song started over again.

―――――

I tried to think, and thoughts came, in slices, in the words between the song. I saw faces in the dark when I closed my eyes. My father. Maddox. Jude.

Talia.

I knew the Kings would take care of her. She was innocent. She was Roni's friend.

They'd return her to her father.

Jude would make sure she was safe.

But as the song kept playing, over and over, and the hours passed, I got fucking scared, all over again. Worried. I couldn't stop worrying about her.

Somehow, I didn't know that part would be so hard.

The hardest.

Why was no one coming?

In the Montanari family, you did wrong, you answered to my father. Joseph Montanari. A man who killed his own brother-in-law and sank his body in a lake. *No.* Who had his men kill his brother-in-law for him.

No one wrote the rules in that family but my father, and his father before him.

Who would the Kings send in to talk to me, to answer for my betrayal?

The waiting to find out was the worst part.

No. The song was the worst part.

Worrying about Talia was the worst part.

But Talia was safe.

That was the only thing that mattered.

I hung onto it even as my body ached in my shackles. And every time I nodded off, I dreamt that my ears were bleeding, as the song went around and around. As my father took Talia by the hand, and walked away with her into the dark.

———

If no one came, did that mean I wasn't even worth any final words?

———

Four seconds of ringing silence and then… nothing.

It took me a while to realize that nothing happened. No more song. I raised my aching head as the lock clanked and the door opened.

Not Jude.

That was all I could think. I didn't want to see Jude. I didn't want to have to look him in the eyes, see what I'd done to him. What I'd put him through when I had his woman handcuffed to a bed and he didn't know where she was.

But it was Blazer who walked in, followed by Jude's brother, Piper. They closed the door.

No Jude.

Blazer leaned against the far wall. The patch on his vest read *Secretary*, but Blazer was also one of our Enforcers. Deceptively clean-cut, hair combed back, he cracked his knuckles and looked blankly at me.

When the club needed someone to smile and look pretty for the cameras, make some public statement on behalf of the organization, Blazer was our guy. But you made a problem for the Kings? Good chance Blazer was one of the guys showing up at your door, and he wouldn't be smiling.

You caused a problem *within* the Kings? Good chance it was Blazer who'd be putting you in your place.

It was Jude's brother who walked right over to me, though. Big, blond, tattoos all down his arms, an old scar down one side of his face. A dead-eye look in his cool blue eyes that I knew well. It was the look he gave people who'd pissed him off—or who weren't worth his attention.

The chains rattled as I shifted on my knees, trying to sit up straighter. I tried not to flinch when my Vice President stood over me and reached for my hands.

He unlocked the shackles on my wrists and I instantly dropped to all fours. I had no strength left, barely any feeling in my limbs. I wavered on my hands and knees.

My wrists were raw and aching from chafing against the metal.

He unlocked the shackles on my ankles next.

Then he stood over me, looking down, and I instinctively wobbled to my feet. To look him in the eye. Accept whatever was coming, like a man, even as the pins and needles prickled all over my body and my head throbbed, as blood flowed back through my limbs.

Took me a minute to get fully upright.

When I did, Piper looked me square in the eye with a sort of intensity I'd seen many times, but never directed at me. In that moment, if he asked me if I thought he was gonna kiss me or kill me, I wouldn't have had an answer.

He took me abruptly by the head, big hands planted on both sides of my face, and kissed me on the lips. It wasn't affection. It wasn't a test of some kind. It was a message.

Way back, when outlaw MCs first became a thing, the members started kissing each other for the shock value. Back in the 1960s, kissing a club brother on the lips in public was about the most aggressively heterosexual thing you could do—because fuck anyone who dared say you couldn't, right? It was just another counter culture *fuck you* to the establishment. We did things our way. Always would.

Now, some brothers still did it, though less likely in public. It was more of a greeting in places like the clubhouse, biker rallies; kind of like a secret handshake, for members only. For brothers.

Now, Piper looked at me kind of like a father looking into the eyes of his wayward son. Piper had always looked out for me. He'd been my sponsor into the club. I would always be, in his mind, his responsibility.

I'd had many years, many opportunities to tell him what my father was doing to me. And I didn't.

That was what I saw in his eyes right now. Questions about my betrayal. And a wariness. He no longer knew if he could trust anything about me; if I was the man he always thought I was.

He released me, still looking me square in the eyes, and thrust a finger at the small bench against the wall. "Sit."

I sat, practically collapsing on the wooden bench, as Piper sat down in front of me on the lone chair.

I met Blazer's eyes, briefly. He remained against the wall, arms folded over his chest, watching. Giving me nothing to know what he was thinking. Blazer could come across as cold as a psychopath; it was kind of his specialty. But his love for the club and his brothers, his loyalty, ran deep.

I looked away.

Piper studied me as I carefully rubbed my wrists, getting the feeling back in my hands. He leaned forward, elbows to knees, and kept looking into my eyes. They could've done anything they wanted to; beaten me, strapped me to a polygraph. But Piper Grayson was probably just as effective at sussing out bullshit with a look.

"Enjoy the music selection?"

"Not bad," I said, my voice scratchy. I tried to clear my throat. I hadn't had anything to drink in hours, not since way back at Dane's cabin. What was that, last night? "Would be nice if there was a bit more of a selection. And some volume control."

"I'll take it up with management."

I waited for him to say more as he regarded me in silence. As our Vice President, Piper *was* management.

"You'll be fine," he said evenly. "I've been to louder concerts a hundred times. Ask Finn. Sure he can tell you exactly how much damage it takes to lose your hearing. No, wait. Finn was born half-deaf, isn't that right, Blaze?"

Blazer grunted an agreement.

I took a breath. "I'm sorry about Finn."

"Good. That was dirty shit to pull on a prospect who's worked so hard, harder than most guys, to get into the club, despite having what some would call a disability. And just when he's about to be patched in as a brother."

"Finn got patched in?"

"Nope. That shit needs a unanimous vote. Considering you're still a member, technically, can't hold that vote just now."

"I'm sorry I fucked him over like that." What else could I say? It was the truth. Wasn't proud of it, even when I did it.

I just didn't see another way to get to Talia.

"Yeah, I'd probably be feelin' like a real sack of shit about myself," Piper said, "if I were you. But of course, there's that other thing you shouldn't be feelin' too proud of either."

"I'm not," I said, carefully. "I want to tell Jude—"

"If you wondered why I'm here right now instead of him," he cut me off, "this isn't really my brother's scene. He'd take pity on you. I won't."

Yeah, I knew that. If Piper had an opportunity to step into a situation on his brother's behalf, he would.

"Or," he went on, "he might just snap and kill you, and I don't want that on his hands or his conscience. You're not worth it." He stared me down. "But given that you abducted his woman, and she's got his baby in her belly, it just might happen."

"I didn't know—"

"Never thought I cared too much about having kids myself, but when my baby brother comes to me, tells me his girl, who's just been abducted, is gonna have his baby, well, that does something to a man's heart. Even a man like me. And watching my brother sweat while you had his girl and that baby somewhere and he couldn't help them? That made me cold right down to my core. Made me feel like stomping your little rat head to blood and bits, so you tell me why I shouldn't do that right now."

I took another deep, shaky breath. I knew I had to fight for my life now. Plus, I owed them the truth.

So I told Piper everything.

"I didn't abduct Roni. That was Nico. Like I told Jude."

He said nothing.

"I borrowed my buddy Shane's car, took Talia from the hotel on her wedding day and drove her out of town, took her to Shane's place in the woods. Like ten minutes later, Nico shows up with Roni. He has her gagged and blindfolded. He says Roni saw me getting into the car with Talia, so he grabbed her."

"And why would you take Talia and hold her for ransom?"

I forced the words out. It was stunning, how much shame I felt in admitting them. "Because my father ordered me to do it."

Piper stared at me for a long moment. Then he laughed, a dark laugh with zero humor in it. "Your father. Joey Montanari."

"Yes."

His laughter was already gone, replaced with a look that could slice a man in half. "And why would Joey Montanari tell you to do that?"

"He said Talia's dad owes him money."

Piper held my gaze. His was cold, unflinching.

"And what the fuck does that have to do with you, Lex Davenport?"

Fuck. And here we were. The moment I'd never wanted to have, but feared someday I'd have to.

"I've been taking orders from him once a year, on my birthday. For the last nine years."

"For the last nine years," Piper said slowly, "you've been a fuckin' King."

I swallowed. "Yeah."

"Why? Why the fuck are you doing his bidding?" Piper's blue eyes darkened, sharpening. His gaze flicked down to my mouth. "Because of the teeth?"

I swallowed again, my throat parched. I glanced at Blazer. He hadn't moved, just watched me from where he stood.

I met Piper's eyes again. As far as I knew, Piper and King were the only Kings who knew the truth about what happened to my teeth. Dane knew, too, and I was pretty sure he'd told our grand-mother. Though he probably wasn't super detailed about it.

My mom knew, too.

But after the teeth, I really stopped talking to anyone about my father.

Piper and King knew about what he'd done to my dog. But not about what he'd done to Shane. Even Dane, and Shane himself, had no idea what really caused that car accident. That was my own darkest secret, something I'd been too ashamed to tell anyone.

Just Talia.

So for the first time, I told Piper the rest of it.

I confessed to him that when I'd told the Kings I had nothing to do with my father ever since Lola, it was a lie. I told him about what my father had done to Shane. And the annual penance he'd demanded. And as I unloaded all of it, I could still feel my father's grip over me. I could feel it in my gut like a fist around my organs, squeezing.

You'll never be free of what you are.

By the end of it, there were tears in my eyes. I willed myself to hold them back, but one or two spilled down my face.

Piper listened carefully to every word, but said nothing about what I'd just told him.

Instead he told me, "Every club brother knows, just like *you* know, that a threat against you is a threat against the entire club. We're a pack. We've got each other's backs. That's how this whole thing works."

I just nodded.

"So. Why didn't you tell us that your father was a threat to you?"

"Because. I knew you'd fight for me." My voice broke when I said it. So fucking regretful—that I'd never given them the chance to fight for me. That's probably what disappointed Piper the most of all. I could see it now, in his eyes.

And now, I'd no longer have the club protecting my back.

And it was my fault.

"And that's a problem?" he growled, when I didn't go on.

"Yeah. It's a problem." I cleared my throat. "Because if you launched a crusade against him, over me, my father would have a reason to kill you. You'd become a target."

Piper laughed again, a dark, unamused chuckle. "You think I'm afraid of Joey Montanari? Some sadistic Mafia boss out east?"

He glanced at Blazer. Blazer smiled. Chilling, that smile.

"What do you think, Blaze? Should I be scared of the Mafia Devil?"

"Dunno," Blazer said cooly. "Maybe? Lex seems to think he's something to be frightened of."

"You know what I think?" Piper skewered me with his cold blue eyes, his smile vanishing. He leaned in close. "I think your dad has fucked with your head for so long, he's convinced you he's more powerful than he is."

"It's not power that's the problem. It's what he's capable of."

Piper took that in. He got slowly to his feet and stood looking down at me. I looked up, meeting his eyes.

"They call him the Devil of the underworld, right?" he said. "Have you ever asked yourself, if that's true, then who the hell is God?"

I blinked at him. I didn't know what to say.

Piper flicked his chin at Blazer, and Blazer went to open the door. Neither of them said another word to me before they left. They didn't tell me how long I'd be in here or what would happen next.

I assumed they'd be looking into every word I said. Comparing notes with what I told Jude, and whatever Roni and Talia told them.

When the door shut behind them, I collapsed, curling up on the hard, cold bench. So fucking exhausted. Everything ached. I felt mildly nauseous.

Sleep pressed heavily on me as I fought it off, fought to keep thinking.

Maybe they were questioning Nico in a cell just like this one, right now.

Maybe they were torturing him.

Maybe I'd gotten off easy, so far.

At least they didn't turn the music back on.

———

I jerked awake when the door opened again. I'd passed out on the small wooden bench.

I had no idea how much time had passed.

Everything still ached. My joints hurt. Felt like I was coming down from the world's worst bender on rancid home-brew, during which I'd been slammed repeatedly against a brick wall.

Axel walked in as I dragged myself up to a sitting position, slumped against the wall. I blinked at my friend—or former friend. My virtual big brother.

I had no idea who I could call a friend, or a brother, anymore.

Maybe that was the most depressing thing of all. That I'd betrayed my friends.

The only real family I'd ever had.

People who *would've* died for me.

He was holding a bottle of water. He unscrewed the cap and held it out to me. I took it, my hand shaking, and drank some. I could feel the cool water trickling down through my body like rain trickling down a desert dune.

"Thank you," I croaked, looking up at him. "What the hell did you guys pump into me?"

Axel just smiled.

The club's Enforcers answered to the man standing in front of me; our Sergeant-at-Arms. But unlike Blazer, Axel was the last thing from clean cut. His clothes looked like they were in danger of splitting right open whenever his hulking muscles flexed. His skin was nearly covered in ink, throat to feet. His dark hair was buzzed short, shaved on the sides, and a tattooed script wound around the back of his head from temple to temple. *Property of West Coast Kings. Touch me and see.*

Honestly, I'd probably rank one of Axel's top qualities as "kind," but you'd never fucking know it to look at him.

And unless you were on his good side, you'd probably never see it at all.

Of course, I'd never been on his bad side before.

He spun the chair Piper had been sitting in, the back of it to me, and sat down, straddling it. It was Axel's job to protect the club. He kept us armed. He was responsible for the personal security of patched members and prospects. But he also ensured that the rules of the club were followed.

And he stripped the patches of members, when needed.

Right now, I didn't care about any of that.

"Where's Talia?" I asked him. "Is she safe?"

He didn't answer that, just scowled. "Everyone," he grunted, "and I mean everyone, is pissed at you."

"I know."

"But here's the thing about the club. We don't let a brother go down easy."

"Yeah." I swallowed. "Know that too." There was nothing about this that was easy. Maybe I should've been happy that they hadn't beaten the shit out of me. Yet.

But I wasn't happy.

"So. You been workin' for Joey Montanari all along? Spyin' on the Kings for the Mafia?"

"No."

"You tell me if you were?"

I swallowed again, my throat already dry. "No." No use lying to him. Axel was way too smart for that shit.

"Now, if you're me, do you believe a word outta your mouth, here on in?"

I answered that honestly, too, trying to take into account the years he'd known me and everything we'd been through as club brothers. And what I'd just told Piper in this room. I had no idea what I could say to keep them from punishing me, taking my patch, or worse. So I just told the truth. "I don't know."

"You waitin' on the music and the Twenty Questions to stop, the real torture to start?"

"Yes."

"Physical torture doesn't work," he informed me. "You know why?"

"Because you inflict enough pain," I said, as he'd told me, many times, "a person will tell you whatever you want them to, to get it to stop."

"That's right. And it doesn't make whatever they tell you true. No, you beat them because they deserve it. To make them suffer. But you want intel—" He reached over and tapped my skull. "You've gotta break someone in the mind. Or better yet, make them *want* to tell you the truth."

I swallowed. "I do."

"Good to hear. But if we wanted something from you you didn't give, you can trust me on this… we'd make sure you gave it."

I didn't say anything to that. I had no doubt he was right.

"You ever heard of the Valley Kings MC?"

"No."

He settled back, arms draped over the chair back in front of him. "When I got home from service, went home to the Okanagan Valley, there were no jobs awaitin' me. At least none that offered a lick of the excitement I got in the military. So I drove to the big city. Just outside Kamloops, I got a job bouncing in a bar on the highway, owned by members of the Valley Kings. Thought I had it made. Beer, power and pussy. What more could a guy want?"

His eyes moved slowly over my face, like he was making sure I was really listening.

I was.

"One day, these guys roll up, wavin' guns, say they're members of some Punjabi gang. Seemed they had a beef with the owners of the bar. They make a bunch of noise. Shots are fired, the place clears out. They demand money, make threats if they don't get it." He paused, studying me. "Now, you gonna guess what happens next?"

I wasn't totally sure where he was going with this, so I said nothing.

"Few days later," he went on, "a couple of Italians walk in the door, diamond rings glinting in the morning sun. Now, please tell me you know what these fuckers had to say."

That part wasn't hard to guess. "They wanted protection money."

"Bingo. They tell the Valley Kings they heard about their problem with the Punjabis, they've come to help. All the Valley Kings have to do is pay the Mafia, a much more reasonable amount of money, of course, once a month, and the Mafia will make the problem with the Punjabis go away. Unfortunately for these particular mafiosi scumbags, they didn't factor in that they were too new in town to know the lay of the land. Or that the Valley Kings were a West Coast Kings support club. You've never heard of the Valley Kings because they don't exist anymore. Because they got patched over as West Coast Kings, for their protection. But they still run the valley. So. What do you think happens, few weeks after that shake down, when the Italians show up to collect their payment?"

"I get it. The Mafia is into extortion."

"Not just into it. They get hard for it. Create a problem—send in your Punjabi friends to create a threat—then offer a solution. At a cost, of course. It's Mafia 101. Your father probably taught you this shit as a little kid over breakfast."

"He did."

"You should've seen this comin' a mile away. Even if it was comin' from your old man. No. Fuck that. *Especially* if. Since when do you start trusting that motherfucker?"

"I don't."

"Did it ever occur to you that this was all just part of his grand master plan to fuck with you?"

"Yeah," I said weakly. "It occurred to me."

"He created a problem and offered you the solution. Antonio De Santis owes him money. So the fuck what? He doesn't give a fuck about De Santis' money. He wants De Santis' territory. His *power*."

I looked up at him, listening. *Territory.* That word meant a whole lot of something in my father's eyes.

What territory was Axel talking about?

"He puts you in the middle," he went on, "to collect on that money. To set things right. But here's the thing. *He wins* either way it shakes down. And either way it shakes down, you lose."

I knew he was right about that. Because it sounded exactly like my father's MO.

"That sound like a good deal to you, Lex? Like loyalty, one hand lookin' out for the other?"

"No."

"And what have the brothers ever given you?"

"Loyalty," I said, my voice scratchy again. I swallowed, but I didn't reach for the bottle of water.

"And he got you to betray your brothers." Axel let that sink in before going on. "See, maybe this time when your old man fucks with you, he fucks with you just enough that the Kings kick you to the curb. Then you have nothing and no one, and crawl right back to the family."

"Yeah. I mean, *no*. I wouldn't have."

"But you fell for his shit."

I didn't really fall for anything, though. I knew my father was an evil prick who was only out for himself. I just didn't want anyone to get hurt. But Axel was still talking.

"You fucked up," he told me, and there was no away around the truth of it. He got to his feet. "But you did two things right."

I looked up at him. My eyes stung from the harsh light of the bare bulb that shone above him like a halo.

"One," he said. "And this is a big one. You brought Jude's woman back, unharmed. And two. You turned yourself in to the club. Make no mistake, those are the exact two reasons you're not dead yet."

I didn't say anything, because I didn't even know what to say anymore.

"You've got brothers here yet, Lex."

I could feel the tears burning in my eyes and this time I wiped them away. Guilt and relief. I felt stunned and grateful.

But that was way too easy.

I knew there would be more. A price to pay. They couldn't possibly let me off that easy.

No matter what, though, I knew I'd done the right thing—to protect Talia. I'd turned myself in for her. I couldn't regret that.

"You got anything you wanna say?" Axel asked me, his eyes assessing me darkly.

"Yeah. I want to know if Talia is okay. Can you just tell me she's okay?"

He stared at me for way too long before answering me. "That's out of my hands."

I tensed, every aching nerve sparking, as I struggled to understand what the fuck he just said. If the Kings had Talia, then she was in his hands. Her protection was literally his business. "Where is she?"

He looked me over, still assessing. "I can't tell you that."

I sat up straighter, a cold dread burning down my spine. "What do you mean? She's safe, right?"

Axel's eyes narrowed a little. "You don't even know who she is, do you."

"What do you mean?" I repeated.

He sighed a little. "She's the daughter of the most powerful Mafia boss in the country, Lex."

I stared at him, still not comprehending what the hell he was saying.

"That girl," he said, "is Mafia royalty and she doesn't even know it. You're not supposed to know it, either. Not many people do. So," he warned me, "you go spreading that around, I know exactly who it came from." He looked down at me with something like pity mixed with disappointment. "You stole her from her wedding, from the man her daddy approved for her to marry. Who do you think she's gonna marry now? You?"

I just gaped at him, said nothing.

Axel shook his head at me a little. Then he walked out, shutting the door with a clang. And I freaked the fuck out.

"Axel!" I staggered over, threw myself against the door, pounded on it with my aching fists. *"What the fuck?!"*

But he didn't come back.

The lights went out.

I felt my way through the darkness and collapsed on the bench. I couldn't answer any of the questions that bombarded me in the dark.

I pictured Axel going straight to Piper, to King, to the rest of the officers. I pictured them meeting about me, voting on my fate around the table in our sacred meeting room.

But that wasn't the end of it, was it?

Not if what Axel said was true.

She's the daughter of the most powerful Mafia boss in the country...

If that was true...

I imagined Piper and King, meeting with the leaders of other organizations. Trying to rewind the damage I'd done. Sending ripples throughout the underworld.

How deep did it go?

... the most powerful Mafia boss...

And what did Axel mean about me not spreading it around? How could I spread it around?

Did that mean they were letting me live? Go free?

I struggled to remember the names of the Nine Families of the Mafia. The members of the Commission. Was one of them De Santis?

No. No fucking way. I'd remember that. I would've connected those dots.

My father sat on the Commission.

And I wondered: who would make the decision about his fate?

It was a question I never thought to ask myself, all those years growing up in my father's shadow; I always thought he had all the power. But I realized with a strange kind of dread that even my father couldn't touch me in this cell.

I felt like a puppet with its strings cut, crumpled here in the dark and waiting for someone to come yank me up, tell me the final price, make me pay for my sins.

And it haunted me now: if it wasn't my father, who was actually in control of *my* fate?

They call him the Devil of the underworld, right?

Have you ever asked yourself, if that's true, then who the hell is God?

Chapter Thirty-One

King

We rolled into the gravel and mud clearing, not exactly a parking lot or anything at all. There were no lights out here but the ones provided by the headlights of the cars parked around us, some of them still running.

Shifty, the prospect who was driving me, pulled the Navigator to a stop. We were at the dump, as we so affectionately called it; it was after dusk and we'd parked in the clearing by the creepy, swampy creek that trickled through the field.

I sat in the passenger seat, even after Shifty got out, looking out at the dark wound of the creek that slashed across the Earth.

It was a bad day, all things considered. I had a brother sitting in a cell, and I'd either have to save him or let him hang. Or hang him myself.

I never liked days like these. Hadn't had many of them, but they ranked among the worst, generally speaking.

Axel, who was already waiting outside, opened my door for me when I didn't get out. I got out, slowly, and my Sergeant-at-Arms shut the door behind me and took his position at my back. To my left and right, a motorcade of parked cars, Harleys, and a cargo van, about a dozen of my club brothers standing watch.

Facing us was a similar lineup of vehicles, sedans, mostly. And a similar number of men, in dark suits and overcoats. One of them had opened the back door on a black Maserati Quattroporte, and out stepped a gray-haired man you'd probably never look at twice except maybe to notice his ride.

A man known to most by the name Antonio De Santis. Talia's father.

I knew him better by his real name: Domenico Bonacorso.

"You have the boy," Domenico said as we approached one another. It wasn't so much a question.

I wasn't even sure if he was referring to Lex, or Nico Barretti. Either way, the answer was the same.

"I do."

Domenico glanced past me, his dark eyes flickering over the vehicles at my back, as if he was expecting the corpse of one or both of them to be presented, like the evidence of a crime.

But this wasn't a trial.

I offered my hand and we shook briefly. Then we stood, flanked by our men.

"Nico Barretti," I said, observing his reaction to the name. He didn't give me one. "He says he was acting on orders. Didn't give up much else, though we really didn't push him very hard. Figured since he's one of yours, you'd want him back in one piece."

"He's not one of mine," Domenico said simply.

That might've been strictly true, but the kid was definitely Mafia.

I looked him over. It had been a few years since I'd stood face to face with the man in front of me. He'd aged, but then so had we all. His salt-and-pepper hair had gone completely gray. His shoulders looked thinner in his dark coat. But Domenico Bonacorso still had the soul of a bulldog and I could feel the growl beneath his words, even if he didn't bark.

"All the same. We've been gentle. Mostly. My boys might've gotten a little carried away on account of him abducting one of our member's old ladies. While pregnant."

"An upsetting situation," he agreed, but his tone was cool and removed.

"Walk with me, Antonio." I'd never address him as Domenico in front of anyone. Outing his identity would only ensure chaos in the underground—and a bullet in the back of my head.

Domenico Bonacorso was the godfather of the Canadian Mafia. But the fact that Antonio was Domenico was known only to a few; his underboss and his advisors, a few trusted allies. Most of the Mafia didn't know. Very likely, not even Antonio's wife or daughter knew his real identity.

Domenico had been deep underground, living as Antonio, for years. Only a shit show of this magnitude would bring him to an in-person meeting with me.

The two of us strolled down to the creekside alone, around the far side of the cargo van, to speak privately. One of Domenico's bodyguards walked down to the creek, out of earshot, to keep an eye on us. So did Axel, somewhere at my back.

"Seems the young ones are causing us trouble," Domenico said mildly, eying me again, once we had privacy. He was over twenty years my senior. Yet he spoke to me like a man who was his equal.

I wasn't his equal. I was everything he'd ever wanted to be.

Powerful. Visible. *Free.*

He needed me, whether he wanted to or not.

Unfortunately, we needed each other.

But *need* would only take us so far.

"Joey Montanari is not that young," I said neutrally. Montanari was older than me, in fact, by more than a decade. Which meant he should know better.

Way the fuck better.

"Yet he behaves like a spoiled boy," Domenico said.

"I can't disagree. And yet some of my officers say this whole problem is our fault. Because of our agreement with the Mafia. That we've allowed you too much power in Vancouver. That it's not worth it anymore. That you're too unstable, always infighting."

Domenico studied me cooly. His jaw flexed in the silence. His molars had to be grinding from that assessment.

"Is that so."

"I told them, of course, that the Nine Families are our allies," I went on. "That we have friends on the Commission. That Joey Montanari's actions won't stand."

He didn't address that. It was too early in the conversation to concede defeat.

Instead, he said, "I hope the boy, Nico, didn't cause you any trouble." He was fishing, of course, trying to determine if Barretti was still alive.

"Was no trouble at all."

"Your men are fast and effective."

"They are."

"And yet," he added with a hint of acid, "my daughter was taken right out from under the watch of her personal protection, which the Kings, my allies, were supposed to provide."

"We didn't exactly have all the facts," I said evenly. "If we knew she'd be a target, we would've been more... diligent."

Clearly, he didn't appreciate the implication of his blame in this, as no father would. I wasn't here to antagonize him, though, so I moved on.

"Interesting thing. The groom didn't seem all that broken up about his bride vanishing into the night. Much more concerned about how *you* were taking it. That was our first clue something was off. I'm thinking most men, on hearing that their bride disappeared minutes before walking down the aisle, are a little more concerned about where the fuck she is and if she's okay than what her daddy might think."

I studied him as he took this in, giving nothing away.

"Carl Caldwell," I mused. That was the groom's name. At least, that's what I'd been told—back when Jude came to me about a security check on Talia's new boyfriend, I ran it up to her father myself, and he gave the nod. And I didn't much like being lied to. "Or should I say… Giancarlo?" That was his real name, apparently; a name he'd given up, fast, when we took him into the Kings' "protective" custody as all hell broke loose at the wedding. "You plan on telling me who he is to you? And why one of my club brothers' old ladies was abducted from your daughter's wedding by one of your men?"

Domenico shook his head slowly, like he was deciding whether to be more annoyed or impressed with me. "You have Giancarlo, too, I expect."

"We've been providing room and board for a few days. He's been enjoying our basest hospitality. We're a little tight on space right now."

He eyed me, considering that. "You plan on handing him over?"

"No. Considering he's patched in as a Dead King, I'm feeling pretty inclined to keep him, for now." Domenico didn't seem to like that, but I didn't much care. "But maybe you can fill in the blanks of the story he told us. He was quick to let us know he was one of us. A brother. To save his own ass, of course. But on the rest of it, he went pretty mute."

Domenico gave a short, impatient sigh. "His name is Giancarlo Caldera. He's a nephew of Cesare Caldera."

Ah. I was getting the picture, gradually.

Cesare Caldera was the boss of the Caldera Mafia family, and as such, he was a member of the Commission.

"So, you're gonna explain to me why this Giancarlo, a Dead King, was marrying your daughter under a false identity? And why his bride running out on the wedding resulted in the abduction of one of my brothers' old ladies?"

Domenico eyed me again, but only to continue the illusion that he was in control. He was going to tell me.

Otherwise, why were we standing here?

"Cesare is one of my family's greatest allies. He ordered his nephew, on my behalf, to marry my daughter. It was an arranged marriage."

Yeah. I figured as much. The Italians loved their arranged marriages.

I would know.

"Did he know this order came from the godfather himself?"

Domenico made a bitter *tssk* sound. "You think I'd trust that kind of information to a boy like that?"

"Then why would you trust him to marry your daughter?"

He shook his head, like he was wondering that himself right about now. "Why does any arranged marriage come about?" He gave me a pointed look. "It seemed an ideal fit for them both. The marriage would strengthen the family connection. And Giancarlo would keep my daughter safe."

"Safe," I repeated.

He seemed to read my skepticism and felt the need to expand on that. "Giancarlo is unlikely to ever become boss of his family. He's not a made man. Cesare has sons who will take that role." He gave me a sharp look. "And my daughter was never to know about any of it. Giancarlo chose to patch in as a King, years ago."

As much as I didn't love to throw a fellow King under the bus, so to speak, it needed pointing out. "So you think a man who couldn't get her up the aisle without her being lured away by another man was going to protect her, 'til death do us part?"

"I want my daughter to continue to be shielded from Mafia life," he grit out. "Giancarlo was to keep that life a secret from Talia, as I have, all these years. He was told to court her, like a gentleman, not to steal her like a brute."

"Looks like he failed. Seeing as how she's pining away for one of my guys back at the clubhouse right now."

I saw his blood go up on that. His face turned a ruddy shade of offended.

If I were anyone else, I'd be dead at his feet with my head rolling across the dirt.

But he smoothed his suit jacket and reined his emotions in. He was answering my questions out of courtesy, playing nice. Because I had something he wanted. He hadn't asked me about her yet, though. He didn't want me to know how much it bothered him that I had his daughter and he didn't.

"They don't make men like they used to," he said calmly. "You're told to marry a beautiful woman, in service to the family, and you can't even get that right."

I said nothing as he eyed me. The predilection for arranged marriages within the Mafia wasn't one I shared. However, I had some experience with the subject myself. I could agree with him that it had its uses.

"No, he didn't," I agreed.

"I understand why you won't turn him over." He was assessing me, reading between the lines of everything I said. Was I still a friend, or was I becoming a foe right before his eyes? "We prefer to handle our family problems within the family."

"Of course."

"And *your* family." He raised a thick gray eyebrow. "I expect you'll be cleaning that mess up yourself?"

He meant Lex, not just Giancarlo. Both of whom I had locked away behind several walls and several dozen Kings, to his irritation.

"We will. But my family has a problem with yours and that can't continue."

"What do you propose?"

"I propose you hand over Joey Montanari."

Domenico chuckled softly. "An eye for an eye, a tooth for a tooth. I imagine you'd take that literally. Rip out his teeth, like he ripped out his son's."

"For starters. Then I'd put him down like the rabid dog he is."

"Sometimes dogs just need to be caged for a while. Tamed."

"I could hand over his nephew."

He considered that. "You'd trade him? After he abducted the pregnant girl?"

"If you hand over Montanari. We both know he's the root of the evil. I tear it out, less likely it grows back."

Domenico took a moment to respond, maybe considering that too. Maybe not. "Nico Barretti is nobody. He's not even been straightened out. He's of little value to me. You know I can't hand over Montanari."

"Can't or won't."

He studied me shrewdly. "A problem in the Mafia is our problem. It's our thing."

Yes. That was what they called the Mafia amongst themselves. Cosa Nostra. *Our thing.*

The 'Ndrangheta, out of Calabria, was now the most powerful Italian Mafia group in the world. They'd been trying to get a foothold in Canada for at least a decade. They'd made inroads. But the godfather, the boss of all bosses as they liked to call him, was Cosa Nostra—American/Sicilian Mafia—and he wasn't giving up ground.

"I let an outsider deal with a boss, the whole organization revolts against me. It's the same problem for you," he pointed out, "if you let me walk onto Kings' property and take vengeance on the boy who abducted my daughter."

"The way she tells it, she went with him willingly."

He knew as much. He'd spoken with Talia on the phone, several times.

"My daughter has always been... imaginative. Perhaps she saw something that wasn't there."

"She tells me it started when they were kids. That they agreed to get married. Some sort of blood pact. You're big on blood pacts in the Mafia, aren't you?"

They were. We both knew they were.

"And yet Joey's boy never took the oath," he reminded me.

"Maybe the man you selected to 'court' your daughter failed because she'd already found herself a better alliance."

At the word *better*, he took offense again. But he had to know he'd fucked up here.

"This isn't an MC/Mafia competition for breeding rights, Antonio. I just need your dog out of my backyard. Joey Montanari is out of control and he has been for a long time. You can't expect to keep letting him run off leash, sinking his teeth in wherever he likes and not eventually get bit back."

He said nothing, but he knew this was true. Domenico was a brilliant man. He'd held onto power, controlled the Mafia and the Nine families, the Commission, from the shadows, for almost two decades. Not any man could pull that off.

No man before him ever had.

He was silent for a long while before he spoke again. He looked off into the night, then studied me, that bulldog brain of his working in the silence.

"You know, *King*..." He said my name with slight derision. I knew it to be jealousy. "When my father was murdered by a rival family, I'd already started doing business on the west coast under the name Antonio De Santis. This was on my father's orders. He was a very smart man, a strategist. He saw the opportunity out west. No major families had ever settled in and taken territory here. My father was the first to try to accomplish it. Unfortunately, as you know, he didn't have the best timing. It was the 1990s and the Kings were seizing power in the underground, all across the country. So. How do you manage to hold any territory, thousands of miles from home?"

"I'm sure you'll tell me," I indulged him.

"You send an envoy. One who's smart enough not to get himself killed. One who's likable enough. You can never underestimate the value of a likable man. So many of us miss that lesson, try to rule by fear alone. And a man who knows how to make alliances and hold them, leave power in the hands of those who already have it—" he looked sharply at me again "—while still taking enough to satisfy his own higher-ups? Without getting greedy about it? Invaluable."

"And you did that."

He grunted an acknowledgment. "Behind the backs of the Commission. My father was ambitious, but too much so. It got him killed, in the end. It was the dawn of the new millennium and we were in a state of constant tension. Infighting had torn us apart, leaving my father and two other bosses dead." He eyed me sidelong. "The Kings were quickly becoming the first national organization of outlaws in the country, and right out in the open. Very cleverly, I might add, under your two names. The Dead Kings in the east and the West Coast Kings in the west. I knew, we would never survive our own inner turmoil if we didn't make external alliances. And I managed it. It was a feat no boss before me had achieved, negotiating that kind of alliance with the MC. Your father had as much to do with that as I did."

"And you gained the full support of the Commission. You'd earned the title of the first Mafia godfather in the country."

He shrugged that off. "I didn't want that title so much as I needed it. We needed it. It was the best thing for all of us. The only thing to keep us surviving, to keep us *together* as we reshaped ourselves in the wake of what became an all-out war. After I was forced to flee out west, to evade capture and prosecution, only a select few in my Administration and a few trusted associates had direct communication with me as the godfather. Even today, only a select few know my identity and whereabouts." He looked hard at me. "Joseph Montanari is not one of those people."

I heard what he was saying. Loud and clear.

Despite my own marriage, I was an outsider to the Mafia, and yet I knew things about the godfather—knew his secret identity—when many of the Nine, including Joey, did not.

"All the while I'm building a life out west," he went on, "the man who will prove my greatest threat is gradually gaining power. Joey Montanari was a soldier when I went underground, a decade younger than me, and yet we come from completely different worlds. Different schools of thought. He didn't respect the Commission or what we'd built. He didn't respect tradition. He'd never met me in person or even seen me. He started to question the godfather's existence, accusing my brothers of using me as a threat to keep control of the Commission, when in fact I no longer existed. He planted seeds of doubt as he rose to the position of boss of his family. The so-called Devil of the underworld." Domenico gave a low, scornful chuckle. "His reputation was earned and well-deserved. As long as it served the Nine and he was under his father's control, he was left to do business on his father's turf, his own way." He eyed me. "But now his father is gone. You see the problem I'm faced with?"

"I do."

Domenico looked out over the creek like he was looking back in time—and wished he could stab it in the balls. "Many years ago, Joey set his sights out west. My brother, my underboss, made an introduction, introducing me to Joey as Antonio De Santis. Let him know if he wanted to do business in Vancouver, he'd have to go through me. And he did. Until he didn't." He met my eyes again. "Over the years, I've watched Joey grow ever more ruthless, self-interested and power hungry. Now that he's boss, he senses weakness in my brothers. He still doubts the existence of the boss of all bosses. And he conspires to take the position for himself."

I considered that. It was hardly surprising, though it was almost disturbingly ambitious.

"He stirs rumors that I died years ago," Domenico said. "That my brother is using the ghost of me as a shadow figure to secretly control the Mafia himself. He's become bent on western expansion, where the Commission has less reach. No bosses live in Vancouver; just associates. Except of course, I live here."

We studied each other.

"So, Joey has decided Vancouver is *his* territory," I concluded.

"Maybe he thinks if he gains enough power here, he won't need the Commission anymore. He'll control business in Vancouver. As a consequence, he's decided that as a mere associate, Antonio De Santis will have to pay him tribute. Make no mistake. With his plan to kidnap my daughter, he planned to send me a message." His expression darkened, for the first time revealing both the anger and the powerlessness he'd felt over what happened—to his daughter. "That message is that he, Joey Montanari, has the power. That he'll make me pay tribute to him one way or another. That the west coast is now his."

He let that sit for a long moment. Of course, he and I both knew that there was no universe where anyone had territory on the west coast without the Kings' sanction.

And Joey Montanari had never come to me asking for a damn thing.

He'd only demanded it in sweat and blood, behind my back, from his son.

"Of course," Domenico added, "Joey knows I must have some sort of agreement with the Kings in order to operate here. Maybe he believes that once his son's betrayal of the Kings is revealed, after the kidnapping, Lex will have no other option but to finally come back to his father. Joey will have gained power over Antonio De Santis, an important strategic alliance with the Kings, and he'll finally have his son back." He paused. "Maybe Joey thinks that after that, he'll be able to smooth things over with the Kings by telling you that Lex orchestrated the kidnapping himself. He could twist the story however he likes. Joey is cunning like that, and Lex has motivation. *My daughter.* Joey will take the opportunity to seize control of my western territory, bringing the lowly Antonio De Santis underneath him… and negotiate a new deal for himself with the Kings."

Yeah. That all sounded perfectly plausible, if you were a greedy psycho like Joey Montanari.

"And yet," I said, "his rampant ego and greed vastly underestimated you. And the Kings."

"Yes. They did."

"The question is, what's to be done about it now?"

I knew Domenico was not a rash man. He was patient, calculating, and ruthless. He would take his time and get this done right.

He'd just laid out for me how Montanari threatened him, too. He didn't have to do that.

He was feeling me out. Making sure I had his back, maybe. Calling on that long-held alliance with the Kings.

"Your father and I had a certain respect," he reminded me. "We've had a strong alliance for many years. Become family ourselves." He studied me, waiting for a comment on that.

But our previous and current alliances had no meaning, no currency with me, if this problem kept being a problem. My loyalties lay with the Kings and the Kings alone. Others could always be severed. Replaced.

"We've been allies," I agreed. "But Montanari's... trespasses... can't continue."

"We're in agreement on that."

"I can call a meeting with him," I suggested. "Tell him we've brought Lex in, that we've stripped him of his patch and we're handing him over. It's what he wants to hear. We meet up, and instead we hand Montanari over to you. We keep it quick and quiet. No one has to know you're involved."

"No. It's *our thing*. We'll have a sit down and we'll work it out, our way."

Stubborn old bastard.

But I saw his position. I was in it myself. He was right; if I handed over a patched brother, even a Dead King like Giancarlo, to another organization for punishment, I'd lose the trust of my club, fast.

Still. He needed to know I'd go beyond the bounds of our alliance to keep *him* in his place, if it came to it.

"You should know, I've spoken with Mikhail."

At the name, Domenico bristled.

"And Donovan."

It was only fair to remind him that it wasn't only the Kings that Montanari had crossed. I had the Canadian head of the Russian Bratva on my side. And the Irish in Montreal. Among others. Joey Montanari, on the other hand, had been accruing enemies across the nation for many years.

"Is that a warning, old friend?" Domenico asked me mildly. "I thought we were playing nice."

"We were. But I've grown weary of playing nice with Montanari. Joey may be related to Lex by blood. He may have given him life. But loyalty is what makes family. Joey wants to come after my club brother, keep trying to suck him back into his filth, try to use a woman against him? That doesn't play well with me."

I gestured to Axel. He nodded to his brothers, Maddox and Hendrix, to open the back of the cargo van.

"Montanari likes blood pacts," I said, "here's one for him."

Maddox opened the doors and he and Hendrix hauled Nico Barretti from the van by his shirt and threw him, bound and bleeding, in the dirt. He was conscious, but barely.

I eyed Domenico as he looked down at the kid with marked disgust. At the prison tat of a spider web clinging to his temple.

Domenico made a gesture to his men, like, *Get this shit out of my sight*, and a couple of them mobilized, dragging Barretti away and stuffing him into the back of a car. Domenico listened for the sound of the door shutting behind him, then his dark eyes met mine again. "I appreciate you returning him intact. You always were much more... level-headed than your father."

"You might notice a few toes missing. Like I said, some of my boys might've gotten carried away."

We regarded each other in silence. He knew there would be an ask for this.

"I'm giving you more than I'm getting here," I pointed out. "Way I see it, I've more than paid, with that kid's life, for whatever inconvenience it causes you. I don't care how it impacts your organization—he ever contacts Lex again, Joey Montanari is dead."

I knew what that meant for Domenico. I knew the position I'd put him in and what needed to happen from here.

He needed to take this to his brother, his underboss, who sat on the Commission. Take it to the other heads of the Nine Families. Well, eight, because no doubt Joey Montanari would be left out of that particular sit down.

The Commission didn't rule the Mafia. It was a representative body. Not a government, but a means of consultation between the families, to settle disputes, agree on alliances, regulate the use of violence. They oversaw the control of territories. Matters were decided by majority agreement.

But in truth, as the boss of all bosses, Domenico maintained control through the alliances he'd carefully forged with many of the families. It was a wicked chess match, played in the shadows, decades long, and with only one victor. So far.

This was the way of the Mafia, and why there was so seldom a godfather. This one had to go into hiding to escape arrest, prosecution, overthrow and death. The fact that he'd survived as long as he had, quietly holding onto his power over the Nine and preventing all-out war within the ranks was a testament to his strength and his cunning. But it was a pressure cooker he ruled over, a volcano with roots that ran deep, and one day might blow his entire power structure sky-high.

So, I'd feel remiss if I didn't make my position perfectly clear.

"Out of respect, I'll tell you, Domenico. It's come to our attention that Montanari has been trying to lure his son back from the Kings, with violence and with money, for years. Nothing has worked yet, but obviously he believes that one day, it will. If it doesn't stop here, I'll put him to ground myself. Or let Lex do it, if he feels so inclined. *After* I rip out his teeth."

I had no illusions that the godfather was going to exterminate

Montanari. Not if he didn't have to. No one touched a boss. Even the boss of all bosses.

Instead, the Commission would likely dole out a punishment suitable to a boss who'd gone rogue: cutting off his balls, metaphorically of course, by decreasing his territory, his power. They'd make sure he felt it, but they wouldn't want to provoke retaliation. It was a delicate balance.

My father had made sure I understood these things, studying how other organizations worked, so that we could form alliances. You couldn't fight, or befriend, what you didn't understand. Not in this life. You'd rub the wrong person the wrong way—and be dead before you got a second chance.

Domenico knew enough to understand how I operated, too. How the club operated. "And what about my daughter?"

I almost laughed. "You've got a breathing Mafia body in that car. One who should be six-feet under. I suggest you drive away while we're more than even."

A lesser man would've done just that. Thanked me and begged my forgiveness and scuttled away with his tail between his legs.

But Domenico shook his head, slowly. "This situation with my daughter. Your club brother's involvement in this mess. I'll need reparations for that."

This time I did laugh, darkly. "What would you like me to do, throw her over my shoulder and bring her home to you? We offered her a ride here today. She chose not to come."

He took that in, jaw muscles twitching. "Seems she's waiting for Lexington Davenport to be released from whatever dark hole you've got him in."

"So it seems."

As a father myself, I knew that had to be hard for him to swallow. But short of storming the Kings' clubhouse and getting himself and his men slaughtered, there was nothing he could do about it but wait for word from me. So, here we were.

"If a woman wants one of my men," I told him evenly, "that's his business, not mine. If I intervened on behalf of every daddy or boyfriend who wanted their girl back after she followed one of my boys home, I'd never get anything else done."

Domenico's jaw flexed and I knew I was treading a line there. "Your boy ran off with my daughter. Ruined the wedding I'd ordered. He held my daughter for ransom. You think he just gets away with that?"

I considered that. "What if he doesn't get away with it?"

"I sense another proposal," he said dryly.

I knew the man felt affronted. It was a disrespect, what Lex had done. No matter if Talia wanted him to do it. But. Domenico was old school. He had a real hard-on for arranged marriages.

"What if he does right by her," I asked him, "and marries her? That wipe the slate clean for you?"

He chuckled, like it was a ridiculous idea.

But I could see I had him thinking.

"If he's what she wants… it puts a nice bow on this whole mess, don't you think?"

"You sound like an old man, King," he told me. "And more sentimental than I took you for."

I wasn't, on either count. Though I'd never been as young as Lex was, either. I'd never have tried to pull what he pulled behind the club's back, for any reason.

Even for a girl.

Domenico paced over to the edge of the creek. "I'm getting too old for all this shit," he muttered. "Sooner or later, it'll take me down. It's the way we go in this life. I want my daughter married and protected long before that happens. I want her secure. But you tell me." He turned to me. "You're a father. How do I trust a man who just abducted her?"

I joined him by the bank of the creek.

"Do you want her safe?" I asked him. "Or do you want her on your side?"

We looked at each other, hard.

"You want her out of Mafia life," I reminded him. "Yet you arranged to have her marry a Dead King without her knowledge."

He was silent a moment. Then: "Last year, I had a health scare."

"I'm sorry to hear that." I was. The Mafia would be plunged into chaos without him, very possibly, as families scrambled for power. It wouldn't be a good day for any of us.

"My daughter had turned twenty-five and she was unmarried," he went on. "I became concerned for her. What happens when I'm gone? I always thought I'd let her marry for love. That was naïve."

"Was it?"

"When my life flashed before my eyes, you know what I saw? My daughter. Alone in the world. In that moment, I got serious about marrying her to one of my allies. I've always shielded her from the life, and yet I knew she'd be safest with a man who's in the life. There's too much danger for her to be married to a common citizen. Especially if her father's real identity ever gets out. Who better than the nephew of an ally, and a member of the most powerful organization in the country? Cosa Nostra is a secret society. The Kings hide in plain sight."

"Plus, another marriage makes another bond between us." I wasn't naïve that that was a large part of his reasoning.

"If you were available and I wasn't so annoyed with you, I'd probably ask you to marry her yourself," he said grudgingly.

"I'm flattered," I said dryly.

"You should be."

"I won't make one of my brothers marry a woman. I can't promise you he will. But if he does, your problem with Lex is over."

Domenico looked out across the creek, into the dark. Then he sighed. "I won't make her marry him, either. That first arrangement didn't end so well. But if she chooses to say yes to his proposal... I'll allow it."

I considered that. The club was a true brotherhood. But there was a hierarchy, a rigid structure, for a reason. Our connections, our alliances and our code kept us strong. Loyalty was everything. The patch meant all. There was nothing that hurt us, or brought about retribution, like a brother betraying his patch.

I knew Lex would still follow an order from me.

I highly doubted he'd ever hesitate to follow an order in the future.

Lex was a good kid. I'd trust him with my daughter's life. He'd been a patched brother for a decade and I knew what he was made of. So that's why, when he took Domenico's daughter on her wedding day, it didn't add up. It wasn't something Lex would do.

Even if he wanted to stop her from marrying another man, he wouldn't do that shit without bringing it to the club. I knew there was something behind it, a reason he'd gone rogue on this. Something that was important enough to him to take that risk.

I thought it was his father. But after we questioned him, I realized—it was *her*. Talia.

He loved her.

He truly believed he was keeping her from harm.

"*If* he proposes," I said. "It'll be Lex's choice."

"Make sure he makes the right one. And you have my word." Domenico offered me his hand. "Joey Montanari is dead to you and to his son. It will be taken care of."

I shook his hand. "Respect, Domenico. I've always had it for you. Don't lose it now."

"And you, mine." His dark eyes flashed with a warning before we released hands. "You know of course, if you do strip Lexington of his patch, I'll be coming for him."

Yeah. I knew that.

"If you keep him in the club and he fails to propose to my daughter, or if she turns him down, I'll be coming for him."

I knew that, too.

Even so, I wouldn't force Lex on this. That was his father's way, not mine.

For so many of my club brothers, the club was it. The only

family they'd ever had. As family, I was in the rare position to give Lex what he truly needed, and the one thing that would earn his unfailing loyalty: a choice.

A choice so many of us never had in this life.

The choice I never had.

As Domenico turned to walk back to his awaiting car, I told him, "If Montanari causes any problems out east for the Dead Kings, I won't tell them to back off anymore. This rabid dog has been snapping at my heels for too long, Domenico. I've developed a severe allergy."

The godfather had turned back to me, his cold eyes locking on mine. "Say hello to your wife for me."

He got back into his car, and he and his men rolled out. I turned back to the creek and stood for a while.

No, they don't make men like they used to.

Which was why you bent over backwards to make deals with the good ones, like Domenico. If you didn't, then the rotten shits like Joey Montanari took over.

And when you found a good brother, you held onto him as long as you could.

There was no other way in the life. It was brotherhood or death.

Like it said on the patch over my ribs right now: *Kings Forever, Forever Kings*.

And I wasn't about to put a good brother to ground for his father's sins.

I'd addressed the club officers, yesterday. We'd already put it to a vote. I was proud of my brothers for their decision, to think rationally on this.

Even Jude. Though he was a Nomad and didn't get a vote, I knew he was working hard to forgive on this, to see a path forward.

I was a reasonable man who liked reasonable men in my club.

But Joey Montanari fucking with his son—one of my club brothers—behind my back, made my blood boil. He'd stepped way out of bounds on this. And to hear it'd been going on for years? Lex needed to answer for fucking up. But his father would answer, too. Because this would not stand.

It needed to end, and like I told Domenico, if he didn't handle it, I'd help Lex end it myself.

Whatever it took.

Montanari may have been the reputed Devil of the underworld. But he wasn't God.

Only one man held the position of ultimate power in the underworld. And I'd honor the position as long as I managed to hold onto it.

Power wasn't kept by crushing your enemies.

It was kept through your relationships.

Alliances were meant to be forged, and to be broken, when needed. And Domenico Bonacorso, the boss of all bosses, had better be ready to do right where Montanari was concerned, or the Kings' alliance with the Mafia might've been heading toward a bitter end.

Lex had already made his choice, where his father was concerned. Took him a dark minute, but he'd chosen.

He'd tried to protect the club.

He'd fallen in love with the wrong girl, sure. A girl he'd never be allowed to have if things hadn't gone down the way they did.

But better to fall in love with the wrong girl than never to fall in love at all. At least this love had a chance.

Maybe Domenico was right. Maybe I was getting sentimental.

Chapter Thirty-Two

Lex

S omething woke me in the dark. I'd been sleeping in another empty room with concrete walls, small and stuffy, but at least this one had a bed. And heat.

And a meal someone had left for me, a roast beef sandwich and a salad that I'd half-eaten before feeling mildly ill and falling asleep.

I was sore all over, bruised. Kneeling on cold concrete for hours on end while Nine Inch Nails raped my ears really sucked the life out of me.

I rolled over, slowly, to face the sound of the door as I heard the lock clunk and the latch disengage. The door opened slowly, the light flicked on, and as I blinked into the sting of the light… Talia stuck her head in.

She looked around, saw me, and freaked. "Lex!"

She rushed to me, tossing the door shut, and threw herself on me. I groaned, my arms going around her. Shit, that hurt.

"Babe! Are you okay?" She started running her hands all over me, squeezing my muscles like she was halfway feeling me up, halfway making sure I wasn't broken anywhere.

"Yeah. Good. Just... *ow*." I tried to sit up a bit, but she pushed me back down, her hands flat to my chest.

"Oh my God." She looked into my eyes, her blonde hair tumbling down around her as she hovered over me. Her hair was freshly washed, silky and soft and it smelled amazing, like fresh air. She had fresh clothes on, too. The scrape on her forehead had healed a lot.

She looked like a fucking angel.

She was whole and beautiful and unharmed.

I shuddered with relief. "You're okay."

She blinked at me. "*You're* okay."

"Yeah."

"*Shit*." She exhaled with relief.

Then she kissed me.

Sore as I was, I slid my arms around her. She sank against me, her tongue sliding into my mouth and lapping against mine. "Baby," she murmured between kisses. She sucked on my lip. Her hands slid up my neck and her fingers dug into my hair.

"Talia," I whispered, kissing my way along her jaw, then down her throat. Next thing, I was sliding up her shirt, dragging down her bra, and serving her tits into my mouth. I sucked each sweet nipple, then dragged my tongue around them in a slow circle. I was fucking addicted to those soft, hungry sounds she made whenever I touched her with my mouth.

How the fuck did I ever think I was supposed to give her up?

I couldn't. I wouldn't. I would've chased her down to the ends of the Earth, as long as I was still breathing.

She sighed, her breaths growing heavier as she shifted on top of me, seeking out my dick. Her crotch rubbed against mine, both of us wearing jeans... couldn't feel enough. I ground against her and she ground against me, my dick flexing as it stiffened.

She purred in her throat, an agonized, greedy sound of pure bliss, as I ground against her clit.

And I knew… she'd missed me, like I missed her.

She'd worried about me, like I'd worried about her.

She would've chased me down to the ends of the Earth, too.

Her body said it all.

Her fingers slid down my chest, my ribs… reaching down between us and popping the button on my jeans. I groaned.

Fast as fucking possible, I needed to be inside her.

I bucked my hips up, pushing my dick out of my jeans as she peeled them open. Same time, I sucked her nipple into my mouth and when she moaned in pleasure, I sank my teeth into her soft skin.

She cried out in gorgeous ecstasy.

The door opened and Talia squealed in surprise. She yanked her tits out of my face so fast she almost fell right off the bed, but I caught her. Maddox had strolled right in and shut the door.

"Oh," he said casually. "Shit." He turned away while she scrambled off me. "You decent yet?"

"No!"

He was already turning back around and pulling up a chair anyway, while she tucked her tits back into her bra and shirt. I zipped up my jeans. She gaped at me, like, *Your friend just saw my tits!*

I grinned at her and shrugged, like, *So? You've got beautiful tits, babe.*

She smacked my arm.

"Ouch."

"Maybe knock next time?" She was talking to Maddox but glared at me.

"No time for formalities, sweetheart. I've got pillow talk."

Talia looked confused.

"He means intel," I explained.

"Oh." She sat down on the bed, keen to be let in on this conversation, whatever it was. I pulled myself to a sitting position next to her, slowly, fucking stiff.

"This better be good," I informed him as we stared each other down.

Yes, this was the first time I'd seen Maddox since the whole abduction fiasco, and he wasn't beating my ass, so that was something.

But it was also the first time I'd seen him since he dragged Talia away from me and out the door of Dane's cabin—right before I was hauled away with a bag over my head. And more or less told by his brother, while I was locked in a cell, to never expect to see her again.

While I wanted his forgiveness and all for the whole betrayal aspect, I wasn't feeling too friendly now that my dick was up.

Plus, *he dragged Talia away from me.*

If I got between him and Élo, for any reason, he'd definitely beat my ass. At least.

"I'm here for King," he informed me. "He sent me to talk to you. Just relayin' orders. But first, I'm just gonna cut to the chase here." He eyed Talia. "So here it is. Your dad's the godfather of the Italian Mafia."

Talia blinked at him, like she was making sure he was talking to her. He was.

"Excuse me?" She looked from him to me. "What?"

I smeared a hand over my face. "*Shit.*" This was news to me, and yet I could hardly expect any less than *more* drama piled on top of everything else we'd just been through.

"This is *true*?" she demanded. "But—*what*—*how...?*" She spluttered for a minute in disbelief, then finally spat out, "My dad doesn't even speak Italian!"

I couldn't help smirking, amused. "That's the objection you're leading with?"

"No, sweetheart," Maddox said, "not the Italian Mafia, like in

Italy. In Canada. Those dudes haven't spoken Italian for generations, from what I hear."

"My dad," she regurgitated, stunned, "is the godfather. Of the Canadian Mafia."

"Uh-huh."

"*How?*"

"Dunno. You'd have to ask him. Anyhow, his real name is Domenico something. That's all I got. And he runs the whole show, the Nine families, the Commission. They're all out east, I think. Toronto, Montreal. Your dad's been deep underground for years. So deep, even most of the Mafia doesn't know exactly who or where he is."

"*Woah...*" Talia seemed to be taking this stunningly well. She blinked at Maddox, almost in wonder. "My daddy is the boss of all bosses?"

I frowned. "And how do you know that term?"

She gave me a vaguely dirty look. "I read shit."

"Yup." Maddox looked way less impressed than she was about it. "Godfather, don, boss of all bosses. All that shit. Those Italians are pretentious fuckers."

"Hey." Talia waved a thumb back and forth between her and me. "We're Italian."

"Allow me to correct myself. Those Mafia dicks are pretentious fuckers."

"Your boss is called 'King,'" she pointed out, with attitude. "Pretentious much?"

"First of all," Maddox drawled, "he didn't name himself that. It's a fuckin' road name. Second, he's not my 'boss.' And third, we're all Kings, baby." He flashed her a smile.

She rolled her eyes.

His eyes flicked to me, then back to her. "It is kinda sweet, though," he added, "how you're already defending the Mafia when you just found out two seconds ago you're related to them."

"Wait. If my dad's the godfather of the Mafia…" She blinked, putting it together. "Then that makes me…"

"The most valuable pussy in town," Maddox finished for her.

I shot him a look.

He shrugged. "What? King's daughter doesn't live around here. If she did, *she'd* be the most valuable pussy in town."

"Maybe you wanna rephrase that," I suggested, "and refrain from ever saying another word about my woman's anatomy."

"Sure. If you prefer, I believe the formal term would be 'Mafia princess.'"

Talia's eyes went wide.

"*Secret* Mafia princess," I corrected him.

"Holy shit," she breathed. "I'm such a badass!"

Maddox looked from her to me again, like, *She's adorable.* "Right. Look, I wasn't supposed to tell you any of that. I'm not even supposed to know. It's top secret. Like, your mom probably doesn't even know. I overheard some shit I shouldn't have heard, and King would flip if he knew I heard. But it wasn't exactly my fault the bug I planted on my van picked up some of his private conversation with the godfather."

I stared at him. "Why would you plant a bug on your van?"

"It's my fuckin' van," he reasoned. "I do what the fuck I want with it. And I wanna know if Hendrix is takin' it for joyrides."

Of course. I shook my head at him. "Please tell me you destroyed that bug and everything you got with it."

"Obviously. And you can't repeat any of this shit to anyone." He looked hard at Talia, who was still reeling over her newly discovered Mafia princess status. "I'm not even gonna ask you not to take that shit up with your dad, 'cause God knows if my old man kept something like that from me and I found out, I'd be knockin' his door down demandin' answers. But I will request that if you do take that shit up with your dad, you don't mention my name."

Talia nodded solemnly. "Absolutely. Understood. You can trust me."

"Good. It's in your best interest. He kept that shit secret for a reason. Which means he doesn't want it gettin' around."

Her eyes went wide again. "Right."

"Also." Maddox nailed me with his eyes. "And here's the part from King. You have to marry her or you're fucked."

"What?"

"What?" she echoed.

"Why?" I said.

Oops. Wrong fucking thing to say. Talia turned on me with the fires of hell flaming in her eyes. "Why *not.*"

"Something about alliances," Maddox answered me. "King wasn't detailed on that. And I couldn't hear it all through the bug."

"This came from King?" I said carefully.

"Yes."

"Did he speak with my father?"

"I don't know."

Talia slapped the mattress on either side of her. "Who cares? If this is a solution to the whole problem with your dad, and all we have to do is get married, you're telling me you have a problem with that?"

"Talia." I looked into her brown eyes, which were now burning at a low, resentful smolder—in my direction. "Think about it. Ask yourself why anyone would want me to marry you. Like for example, why *my father* might want me to marry you, after ordering me to abduct you to try to collect ransom from your dad."

"Because I'm a great catch!" She looked from me to Maddox and back, like, *Isn't it obvious?* "I'm almost literally a princess!"

Maddox sat back to enjoy this.

"He'd want me to marry you," I informed her, "so he can try to manipulate your dad, *through you,* for the rest of our natural lives."

"This came from King," Maddox informed me, "not your dad. He says the Mafia's hot for this whole arranged marriage thing. Turns out, the marriage to Carl was arranged. Behind her back."

Talia whirled back to him. "What?!!"

"Your fiancé's real name is Giancarlo Caldera. His uncle is boss of the Caldera crime family. Giancarlo's not Mafia, though. Not a made guy, anyway. But he is a King."

Talia's mouth dropped open.

"More eavesdropping?" I said dryly.

"Yup. Plus, Axel told me that shit himself. He had a few words with Giancarlo after the wedding. You know, security."

Beside me, Talia was in shock. "Carl... is a biker?"

"Yup. He's patched in with one of our clubs out east. The Dead Kings."

"Carl... was a *lie*? He doesn't exist?"

"Oh, he exists. He just failed to mention to you that he's a King, his whole family's Mafia, he probably gets a fat pay hike for marrying you and keeping you safe. And he was *ordered* to marry you. By your dad. The whole whirlwind, long distance romance thing was fake, though. At least, his side of it."

"That prick!"

"And get this," Maddox added with a way-too-happy grin in my direction. "His road name's Ripper. 'Cause back before he was patched in as a King, he was... wait for it... a fucking *stripper*."

Talia still hadn't recovered. "Jesus Christ..." Her voice faded out on a small squeak. "Oh, God. That explains *so much*."

"Don't tell me he stripped for you," I said flatly, trying to read that response.

"You can tell me." Maddox was still grinning, and I threw him a *shut up* look.

"Ew. No. I *knew* he'd have a hot bod under all those sweater vests, though..."

I frowned at her.

"I mean, I have a hard time picturing him as a biker. But as a stripper? Yeah. He was just so..."

"Smarmy," I finished for her. "I knew that guy was a smarmy shit."

Talia balked. "You did not."

"Totally sensed it."

"Bullshit. Why didn't you say so?"

"You were gonna listen?"

She glared at me. I raised an eyebrow right back.

She turned back to Maddox, pissed. "He didn't love me?"

"Hey, I dunno. He was really working those sweater vests and the 'Carl Caldwell, responsible businessman' vibes the couple times I met him. But I guess that was all part of the plan. You know, to seduce you and make you fall in love with him. Make you choose him. Very fairytale-come-true if you ask me. Dude has great hair. Sounds like your daddy wanted you to be happy."

"Wait. If he was sent to seduce me, why wouldn't he—" Talia clamped her mouth shut when we both looked at her.

"What?" I said.

"He wouldn't, you know…" She leaned in and whispered in my ear. "*Put it in.*"

My molars ground together at the mental image. Even though she just said he *didn't* fuck her… now I was halfway pissed *for* her and halfway pissed with the mental image of him putting it anywhere near her.

"I want way less details," I growled.

"Oh, shit." Maddox read my face. Or maybe Talia's. "He didn't lay that pipe."

Talia made an annoyed sound. "I thought he was being a gentleman! But if he didn't even love the cow, why not just take the milk? It was free!"

"Yeah…" Maddox scratched his head. "I mean, if I'm him and I don't want you to know who I am, I'm probably not taking off my clothes in front of you, so you don't see a bunch of biker tats. I'm thinkin' he was keeping those under wraps? There was… uh… also something mentioned about your dad being old school. Maybe he told Carl—Giancarlo—not to, you know, sour the milk until after he'd taken the cow back to his barn in holy matrimony?"

"Ugh. *Gross*, Dad," Talia muttered.

"Uh, according to what I heard," he added, "Giancarlo's pretty scared of your dad."

Talia went from annoyed with her dad to proud in a second flat. "Yeah. He's an old bulldog." Then she got teary eyed.

"Anyway, the godfather is supposed to keep *your* dad in line, Lex, but King had to offer him something to lock down that agreement. Which seems fair, negotiation wise, no?"

"Sure," Talia said.

"No," I said at the exact same time.

She shot me another fiery look. I was really making her happy today.

"So, what King suggested," Maddox went on, "is that a King marry his daughter. You know, another King, not Giancarlo. A King like you, Lex. And something about making an honest woman out of her, since you stole her from the wedding her father had planned?"

"Reasonable," Talia growled, tossing a resentful look at me.

"Also," Maddox added cautiously, like he didn't want those sparks shooting from her eyes turning on him, "everyone seems to think that Talia is into you—" he looked at me "—since she claims to have gone with you willingly."

"Starting to rethink that…" she muttered.

"Starting?" I said.

"I can't believe you don't even want to consider marrying me!"

I sighed. "I didn't say that. But you really want to be forced into yet another situation by a bunch of men calling the shots?"

"Oh, make no mistake. You are *not* calling the shots. You didn't even propose yet. Don't get ahead of yourself." She got up. "And by the way, I hated that diamond ring he gave me. No wonder I choked on it. My dad probably picked it out. I hope, for your sake, you can do much better."

With that, she left, slamming the door in her wake.

"Wow." Maddox chuckled. "Mafia princess, huh? Good luck with that."

Yeah. *Shit.*

Godfather?

Holy fuck.

Kinda felt like I was outta the frying pan here and into the fire.

"King really wants me to marry her?" I was trying to wrap my head around the implications of what that meant. King wasn't the kind of man to hook a brother up with a bride, far as I knew.

"Not what he said. He said to tell you that you should think about marrying her."

Well, that was clear as mud. "So, it's an order, or it's not?"

Maddox shrugged. "He says it's up to you. But basically something about you're dead if you don't? I guess the godfather expects you to make amends for ruining that wedding he paid for. And the way King made it sound, he only gets your dad off your back if he gets what he wants."

Right. Great.

Which meant that if Talia's dad didn't take care of my father, it would come down to the Kings to take care of him.

If they would.

Of course, if Talia's dad had already murdered me, not much incentive on that.

"Like I said." He gave me a very Maddox smirk. I'd only been gone a few days, but I kinda missed that smirk. "Good luck with that."

Then he got up to leave.

"Maddox." He paused at the door and met my eyes. "Thank you for telling us all this. I know you didn't have to." He'd used his knack for gathering intel to help me, when he didn't have to; it was a gesture. Of friendship, of forgiveness, or for old times' sake. Whatever his reason, it was selfless.

"You're welcome. And also, fuck you."

Yeah. I deserved that. "Any chance in hell we're still best friends?"

He sighed and turned to me. "Not gonna lie. My feelings were hurt you didn't come to me with any of this shit."

"I know. I'm sorry about that. It wasn't personal. It was—"

"I know. King told me about your dog. And about Shane." He let that sink in, like, *You could've told me about that, too.* "You thought if you get me involved, you play your hand on how much you love my ass, your dad somehow gets me killed."

"Yeah. Something like that."

"Forgiven. Don't even fuckin' think about pulling that shit again, though. I don't ever wanna have to doubt the guy who has my back."

I could see that he was pissed, but he didn't want to be pissed with me. He wanted me to be his brother. The brother he thought I was.

He wanted me to have his back.

"I have it," I promised him. "If you'll ever let me again."

He considered that. "Make me best man at your wedding, we'll see." He left, then popped his head back in. "I'm not wearing a fuckin' tux, though." He shut the door behind himself.

I got up, slowly, with a groan. I ached in the weirdest fucking places. Muscles I didn't know I had had been pushed to the limit in that cell.

Felt like I wanted to eat everything in the kitchen, then maybe throw up, sleep for a few days.

Instead, I went downstairs to the bar.

You want it, you fucking come and get it.

Shit, did she really expect me to give chase right now? Like I did in the woods? I couldn't have chased down a drunken sloth right now.

But for her, I'd fucking try.

———

When I dragged my sorry ass into the bar, there was no sign of Talia or Maddox or anyone else… except one man sitting alone at the bar.

Jude.

Fuck.

I went over to him, slowly. He didn't look up, but he knew I was there. He didn't immediately slam a fist into my face or pull out a gun either, so I sat down next to him.

We sat in silence, side by side, like brothers.

Never really thought I'd be in this position again.

After a moment, he picked up an empty glass on the bar, reached across to the tap, and poured a pint of ale. Then he slid it in front of me.

I appreciated the gesture, but if I even smelled a beer right now, I'd probably be sick.

There was one in front of him, too. Looked pretty untouched.

"Jude—"

"Not sure I'm ready for whatever you've gotta say."

Fair enough. If I were him, I wouldn't want to sit here listening to me explain myself, either. So I didn't try to explain.

I'd already explained to Piper. And every word that Piper thought Jude needed to hear, he'd have told him already. They were brothers, by patch *and* blood. For all I knew, they'd recorded my whole sad confession and Jude had already listened to it, word for word.

So instead, I told him, "I wouldn't hold it against you if you went to King and asked him to strip my patch."

"I did," he said bluntly. "Got voted down."

I swallowed that. And the fact that my club brothers had actually voted to keep me.

All of them.

"That vote's gotta be unanimous," I said, struggling to digest it.

"I'm not a Vancouver King," he growled. "Don't get a vote on this."

I knew that. And it had to be hard as shit to swallow, at a time like this.

It also meant Piper had voted for me; he was the Vancouver Kings' VP, and his vote sure as fuck counted. I considered what that meant.

"You and Piper come to blows?"

"Almost. Bad enough you had me fightin' with my own brother." Jude looked me dead in the eye for the first time since I sat down. "You fucked with my Roni."

"Yeah." I got choked up; didn't even know what to say. Could hardly force the words out. "I'll spend the rest of my life making up for it, Jude."

"Yeah. You fuckin' will. She had my baby ridin' shotgun."

"I didn't know that. I swear. I did everything I could to get her back to you. When Talia told me she was pregnant, I got her the fuck out of there. Talia almost ended up paying for it. It was a fucked-up mess, and it never should've happened."

He grunted. "Piper told me why you did it. He also told me what your dad did to your teeth." He glanced at my mouth. "I thought they were veneers."

"Yeah. Most people do."

His dark eyes met mine and held. "Why didn't you tell me? You could've told me that shit."

"Maybe. But I start telling people that shit, they start collecting reasons to make war with my father. And my father takes no prisoners."

"Yeah. Piper told me the whole story. Including how he manipulated you into kidnapping Talia."

"I noticed you didn't come for that story yourself."

"No, I didn't. I was in a killin' sorta mood for the last few days, kid."

Kid. That was what Jude tended to call guys of any age who he didn't hate but found some level of annoying. So that was something. Right about now, it was practically a term of endearment.

Relieved as I was to be having this conversation so fucking reasonably—and not at gunpoint or chained to a concrete floor—I wasn't sure I deserved it.

Jude had always been level-headed, though. He was a good man with a huge heart. Loyal. Steadfast. A true brother to anyone who had the fortune of getting close enough to him to be considered family.

I wasn't nearly as scared of him as I was broken up about how I'd hurt him. Roni was his fucking heart. Anyone who saw them together could see that.

I knew I had to earn back his trust, and the trust of everyone in my life. I had to pay penance for what I did. Make things right.

If that was even possible.

"The sound of you feelin' sorry for yourself right now is making my molars hurt."

Jude took a sip of his beer, and I cleared my throat. I tried not to feel sorry for myself. I didn't really have a right to.

"All I can promise you," I told him carefully, "is I would never have let her get hurt."

His dark eyes met mine again.

"We've got a code," I went on, "a way we live and breathe and die, and it's sacrosanct. We all know I betrayed it. And now you know why. But if it came down to it, I would've died to make sure Roni got home to you safe. I know you have no way of knowing that's true. I can only tell you, it's fucking true."

"If I didn't already fuckin' know that, Lex, you wouldn't be sitting here breathing right now."

Right. That was humbling.

And no doubt, very true.

"And you should know," he told me evenly, "the cost of brotherhood, for you, just went way the fuck up. You owe this club more than your life. And if I ever come calling, if any brother ever comes calling, you better heed that call. You put in a decade with this club and that's what's saved your ass. No one wants to see you go. Least of all my brother. But, Lex, you only get forgiven for this bullshit once."

"Understood."

"If any of that's a problem for you, you tell me, right the fuck now."

"It's not a problem." I could've said more to try to convince him. Gotten down on my knees and waxed poetic on how the club and the brotherhood were my life, and I'd spend every breath, for the rest of my days, making sure they knew it.

But talk was cheap.

Only time would prove to them that they hadn't made a mistake with me. My deeds meant far more than my words. And thank God I'd had ten years to show them who I really was, despite how I'd fucked up.

"I'm a King," I promised him. "As long as the club will have me."

"Good." He reached for something on the barstool to his other side. "Even though I didn't get a vote, they gave me this. For you." He tossed it at me and I caught it.

My cut.

I could hardly believe the King's colors were still on the back. He just told me they voted to keep me, but here was the hard proof, in my hands.

"Turn it over," he grunted.

I turned it over. There was a clean new patch on the chest. A name patch—with my new road name. *Joker.*

"Way I see it," Jude said, "every King needs a Queen, and a Joker. Wouldn't be the same around here without you crackin' jokes and making the brothers laugh. You make the brothers happy. That's got value. They're definitely not lookin' to a quiet bastard like me to make 'em laugh." I met his eyes. "You've got love here, brother."

I cleared my throat. "Jude—"

"Before you get cryin', check out the other one."

I looked for it, and there it was. On the ribs, opposite side from the KFFK patch that we all wore, *Kings Forever, Forever Kings...* there was another new patch. A skull and crossbones symbol. It was obviously custom made; the skull was wearing a black-and-white Joker hat.

To the West Coast Kings, the skull-and-crossbones meant one thing: I'd managed to survive a near-death experience.

I'd cheated death.

But under the circumstances, it meant something else, too. The club was giving me a second chance.

"I don't know what to say."

"Say you're never gonna forget who your brothers are again." I met Jude's eyes again as he spoke. "No matter what dark shit life throws at you. You don't wanna bring a war to the club's doorstep, too fuckin' bad. That's not your call. You tried to protect us, but you didn't give us a chance to protect you. Here on in, you got a problem, you bring it to the club. You go down, we go down with you. That's what brotherhood means."

"Yeah." I swallowed. "I get that now."

"Well, put it the fuck on, then."

I stood up and slid on my cut.

Jude stood up to go. He didn't give me a hug, which he normally would've done. For now, he seemed to have forgiven me. Maybe one day I'd regain hugging privileges.

Once he was sure his woman had forgiven me, too, maybe.

"I want to apologize," I told him before he could go. "To Roni. Whenever you think that's okay."

He took that in. "We'll see. For now, probably best you stay the fuck away from her. She's dealin' with hormones and you're not her favorite person." He eyed me. "But you should know, she did ask me to go easy on you. Considering how Talia feels about you... She thinks it's her job to look out for Tal, the two of them being so close, and Talia being younger. And so pretty and all."

"Right," I said quietly.

"I keep telling her, Talia's not as soft as she thinks. Have a feeling she handled herself with you just fine."

"She did," I admitted.

As Jude studied me, I felt like an asshole all over again, as he probably wondered what exactly went down between Talia and me in that house in the woods.

"Another thing," he said gruffly. "It's not okay with me, or with Roni, what you did to that girl, no matter if she held her own."

"I know."

"Good. I ever see you around Talia again, she better have a ring on her finger. *Your* ring. That's not a threat. It's a fact. You did her wrong. You need to make it right."

What the fuck?

I did not expect that. Not from Jude.

It was pretty much the same shit Maddox just said to me, though.

"Is this coming from King?"

"It's coming from me."

I wondered why. Jude wasn't married, or even engaged to his partner. "And the only way to make things right is to marry her?"

"No, Lex." He softened a little, like he almost felt sorry for me, for not getting it. "You either love her or you leave her alone."

With that, he turned and left the bar.

I sat at the bar alone, thinking over his words. He was right, of course. That was the only proper way to treat a woman you cared about, especially a woman like Talia. A princess. A future queen.

Thing was, I'd always loved her.

She loved me, too. I knew she did.

I also knew I'd never be able to leave her alone.

But I'd never force her to be with me, either.

I wasn't my father. I didn't fuck with other people's lives.

Which meant if I wanted her to be mine... I needed to finally step up. And offer her something that was worthy of her love.

Chapter Thirty-Three

Talia

I sat on the front porch of Dane and Devi's luxury cabin, the porch lights glowing over me and music pouring out from the small party inside. I could also hear the distant giggles and happy chirping of children's voices in the night.

It was Halloween, and it happened to be Sunday. After so many costume parties already this weekend, we'd decided to get out of the city. Lex and me, with his brother and a few friends.

I took a deep breath of the fresh forest air, the smell of smoke from wood-burning fireplaces wafting into the night. I decided I liked Halloween in the mountains. Especially when two grown men in fuzzy onesies walked up the drive with woven baskets slung over their arms. They were talking quietly about something, chuckling as they appeared between the trees and rounded the driveway loop to the front door.

I got to my feet, watching them approach. I wasn't in costume myself, but I appreciated their spirit.

Shane still had his dragon head/hood on, the metallic rainbow-colored spine down his tail glittering in the night as it dragged on the ground behind him. Lex's hair danced on the breeze as he smoked a joint. He'd pushed his horse hood down. He'd already told me he was "the Trojan horse." When I asked him if he meant the one that seized Troy or like a well-hung guy peddling condoms, he just rolled his eyes.

"Hey, Talia," Shane drawled, smirking up at me as they reached the bottom of the porch steps. "What're you doing out here all alone?"

"Just enjoying the night. Was it busy down there?" They'd gone down to the gate to hand out treats. I eyed their empty baskets. "You gave out all the candy."

Lex came up the steps toward me, slowly. "Seemed like the action was dying down, so we dumped what was left into the last few kids' bags." He set his empty basket down on the porch by my feet.

"Ah." I smiled. "Their parents will appreciate that."

"Halloween candy's for the kids, not the parents."

"Clearly."

He held out what was left of his joint to me, but instead of taking it from his hand, I leaned in close to suck on it a little as he held it, my gaze tangled up with his.

I barely noticed Shane slipping past us. "I'll, uh, see you two inside." He slapped Lex on the back and disappeared into the house. Voices and music wafted out into the night, then faded as the door closed behind him.

Lex didn't take his eyes off me, and after he dropped the roach on the step and crushed it under his boot, I leaned in until my mouth met his. And some more, until his arms went around me and pulled me tight against his body.

"What were you really doing out here all alone?" he murmured against my lips.

Thinking about you.

I wasn't about to say it. He really didn't need to know exactly how gone for him I was.

He probably already knew anyway.

"Just waiting around in case some hot dude in a costume came around, trick-or-treating."

"Yeah? You giving away tricks? Or treats?"

"Whichever you prefer."

A yummy noise rumbled through his chest, vibrating right through me as he kissed me again, deep.

"You know," I said when I came up for air, "you're very attractive when you do neighborly stuff like hand out candy to children in a cuddly horse costume."

"Yeah?"

"Yeah."

"Well, it was either this or my Jason costume," he said, as he started backing down the steps, taking me with him. "And the bloody-hockey-mask-and-machete combo would probably be a bit much. Considering most of the kids in this neighborhood look about seven years old, max." His arms went around my waist and he lifted me off the last step, hauling me into the trees at the edge of the driveway.

I giggled as he manhandled me, but my internal temperature went through the roof so fast, I thought I might combust. "Are we sneaking out of the party?" I heavy-breathed into his ear.

"Nope." He set me on my feet. "Just getting some air." Then he crushed his mouth to mine. And reached his hand between my legs.

"Mmm." I squirmed, backing up a little as he advanced, but kissing him back. "Is this how you treat a Mafia princess?"

"This is how I treat my Mafia princess," he said gruffly, pushing me up against a tree. He seized the zipper of my cozy sherpa jacket and unzipped in one long downward tug. Then he pushed it open, palming my breast through my tank top and bra. As he kissed his way down my neck, he pulled the tank top down, then buried his face between my breasts, licking my chest.

I groaned in happiness.

Then he grabbed my bra in both hands and yanked it down. My boobs spilled out and he latched onto a nipple, sucking hungrily.

My core clenched and I rubbed my body against his as he shoved one knee up between my thighs, grinding into me.

"Remember that time..." he said, kissing his way across my breast, then shoving the other one greedily into his mouth. His tongue lapped lazily over my taut nipple, making my toes curl in my shoes. "You came... on my gun?"

"Uh-huh," I sighed, as he latched onto my nipple again and sucked, deep, hungry pulls, until I was blind with lust.

His other hand slid back down and reached between my legs.

"If this is how you treat a princess," I said shakily, "imagine if I was a queen..." I laughed a little, almost choking when his fingers found my clit through my jeans and pressed.

Then his hand stopped. His mouth released my nipple, leaving me cold.

I blinked, looking into his eyes. He looked unfocused and faraway. But it wasn't exactly a lust-blind look.

"You okay?" I blinked. "What's wrong?"

"Nothing. Just thinking."

"I love it when you do that," I flirted.

He smiled a little. But he didn't keep sucking on my boobs. And there was literally nothing on Earth Lex liked doing better than sucking on my boobs, unless it was fucking me. Or sucking on my pussy.

Or nibbling on my clit with his teeth while I came.

Why was none of that happening right now?

Blood was thumping through my body, eradicating my ability to think straight. I took a breath, trying to clear my head. I touched his face.

"You just thought about... the Mafia? And it killed your hard-on?"

"It didn't kill my..." I reached down between us. He was still hard. But he stopped my hand and blew out a breath.

"Something's bothering you. Is it the meeting?" I knew he'd had a meeting today at the clubhouse, but I didn't know what it was about.

"How'd you know about the meeting?" he asked me warily.

"Roni."

"Ah. Well, Roni's got a big mouth." He closed my jacket gently, covering my chest.

Now I was worried.

"If it was a secret," I said carefully, "she wouldn't have told me. Jude wouldn't have told her."

"True."

"So, why didn't you tell me?"

"It's nothing you need to know about, Tal. Club business."

I frowned.

"Please trust me on this," he said seriously, taking my face in his hands. "It'll be best for you if you just accept, right now, that there are things about the MC and the Mafia that you'll never know."

I bristled at that. "Because I'm a girl?"

"Because you're not a member."

"And women can never be members, right?" I stared him down.

The corner of his mouth twitched. "You want to be a member, sweetheart?"

"No." I didn't. I just didn't like being told that I couldn't.

"My little badass," he said affectionately. He played with a lock of my hair, twirling it between his fingers. "Just so you know, even if you could, there's no way in hell I'd let you join."

I scoffed. "As if you'd get a say."

He smiled, like, *You know I would.* "Your dad wouldn't, either. You know that."

I rolled my eyes a little. "They call you godfather and you think you're some kind of deity, is that it?"

"I wouldn't know," he said seriously. "The only thing they ever called me was the Devil's son."

"And look how that went to your head," I muttered.

He laughed softly. Then he fixed me with a look that had so much love in it—or what I truly hoped was love—it made my stomach twirl. My knees felt a little wobbly. Good thing I was leaning on a tree.

"Whatever I don't tell you, Talia," he said soberly, "it's for your own protection. I don't share club business with Dane or Shane or anyone else outside the club, either."

I took that in with a deep breath. I didn't like it. Not at all.

But I understood.

The less I knew, the better for both of us. Roni already gave me the lay of that land, and as tough as it was to get my head around, I'd finally understood. It wasn't because he didn't want to share that part of his life with me. He just couldn't.

"Okay." I told him. "I don't like it. But I get it. And by the way, if you think for one second I'm ever telling you what we talk about when we have girls' nights, you've got another fucking thing coming."

He grinned slowly. "That's fair."

"It's really the bare minimum."

"So, what do you talk about? Dick size? Technique?" He ran his tongue gratuitously over his teeth. "Fetishes?"

"I guess you'll never know," I taunted.

His expression grew serious again. "I'll tell you this. I had a private talk with King a few days ago."

"You did?" I tried not to sound at all interested. But I knew King was the club President. Roni had brought me up to speed on the whole who-was-who, especially of the Vancouver chapter. Ranks, titles, and key names.

"It was about an agreement he made with your father," he said. He almost looked... nervous about it. "You know, that thing Maddox mentioned?"

"Oh?" I plucked a bit of lint from his horse onesie. "And?"

"And all I can tell you is that your father is gonna make sure that my father isn't a threat to us anymore. I mean, to you and me."

"Oh." I swallowed. Mention of his dad still made me nervous. Not so much for myself, but because of the hold he'd had over Lex for so long. I could see how it had damaged him. And how much better he was doing now that he felt free of it. "Well, that's good."

"Yeah. But also…" He cleared his throat. "Your father wants me to marry you. That part didn't just come from King."

"He…"

"Yeah," he said, when I just blinked at him, speechless. "I know."

Oh, no. No, he didn't know.

I was so fucking done with trying to please my dad.

Like, right around the time I found out who he really was.

I'd spent my entire life trying to be this sweet good girl and do everything my daddy said I should do, and in return he'd *lied* to me all that time. About who he was, about who I was… and definitely about the kind of man I should end up with. He'd told me Lex was *bad* when I met him—a ten-year-old boy—and that I should stay away from him.

And then he tried to arrange-marry me to another King—a former stripper, no less—behind my back?

"That motherfucking, meddling matchmaker," I muttered. "What the hell! What does he think I am, some sort of prize mare, to be auctioned off to his business contacts—" Lex shut me up by kissing me.

It was effective. I let him kiss me for a long, hot minute while I made grunty, protesting noises, then eventually gave in and just enjoyed it.

When we finally pulled apart, he rested his forehead on mine and we breathed together in the dark. "I'm not going to marry you because your father expects me to," he promised me.

"Good," I grumbled. "Serves him right. I am so giving him a talking to. He wants to keep his secret identity as the Mafia godfather from me all these years? Fine. But he's not getting away with this arranged marriage bullshit behind my back."

Lex lifted his head, raising an eyebrow at me.

"Okay, fine. So I let him get away with it *once*." It was true; I hadn't exactly given my dad any static about the whole Carl/Giancarlo thing. Yet. "What?" I gave him a little shove when he smirked at me. "I didn't want the confrontation. I hate it when my dad is mad at me."

"Uh-huh."

"But he's not getting away with this one. I mean, forcing you to marry me? Come on!" I made a weird, snorty, spluttery noise. "As if you're gonna be rushing to do that just because he said so. *Puh.* Yeah, Dad. Okay." I rolled my eyes, then stood staring into the dark among the trees with my arms crossed over my chest, steaming.

My eyes slid back to Lex, then away. He was watching me.

He tugged me against him again. "Talia."

"I mean, as if you'd marry any girl because some Mafia boss told you to." I looked anywhere but at his face.

"I'm not gonna marry you because anyone tells me to," he said softly.

"Obviously."

"Natalia. Look at me."

I chewed on my lip, trying to ignore the melty feeling in my stomach when he said my name like that. And finally met his eyes.

"The thing is…" he said. Then he took a deep breath. "This is new to me, Tal. I've never lived in a world where it was safe to love you."

I nodded a little, swallowing. "I know. Because of what happened to Shane. You loved him, and your dad…" I still shuddered every time I thought about it. Shane driving on that icy mountain road, the car sliding off and flipping into the trees. "He did that terrible thing to him."

"Yeah." He smoothed my hair back from my eyes and cupped my face. "But, Talia, the truth is I've loved you for a long time."

"You have?" I tried not to sound too over the moon about it.

He shook his head in wonder. "It's still hard to believe I can say that out loud to you now."

I bit my lip again.

"I love you," he said quietly, his voice a rough promise in the dark.

"Okay," I whispered.

Holy God. Did I just say "Okay" when he told me he loved me?
That was the stupidest thing I'd ever said to anyone, ever.

"I mean..." I cleared my throat. "That's good."

Okay, that was way, way stupider.

But Lex just smiled. "And I promise, we'll get engaged, get married... if you want to... when it's right for us. Okay?"

I nodded. "Okay."

"Good." Lex's eyes darkened as they slid down to my lips. He ran his finger down the front of my jacket and flicked it open, exposing one breast. My nipple instantly hardened in the cold night air—and in anticipation of the kindness it was about to receive. "You wanna keep going?"

"Fuck, yes."

"Good. 'Cause the Trojan horse is about to invade your fortress."

I tried not to smile too big as he kissed my neck.

"You know the Trojan horse wasn't real, right? It's a myth. Fiction..." I tried to remember what I was trying to say as he licked my throat and nibbled on my ear with his teeth. "It doesn't even make any sense. Like, a giant wooden horse appears outside a fortress and no one questions it, just rolls it on inside? Come on."

Lex paused what he was doing to look into my eyes. "You're telling me if I showed up on your doorstep like this, you wouldn't let me in?"

I pressed my hands flat to his chest and steered him backwards, up against a tree. "No, Lex. If *you* were inside, I'd tear open whatever gift you delivered yourself to me in." I unbuttoned every button down the plush front of his costume as I spoke, and spread it wide open.

Ugh. More clothes.

"Why do you have to wear so many layers, though?" I complained, as I pushed up his T-shirt and scraped my fingernails over his taut abs. He hissed in a breath; Lex liked a little pain. I didn't mind doling it out on occasion.

Especially when it made his dick so hard.

I raked the button on his jeans open and split the zipper open. No underwear. *My favorite.*

A few days ago, I'd forbidden him from wearing any, ever again.

Nice to see he was obeying orders.

I shoved him back against the tree again to show him I meant business. He raised his hands in surrender, a smirk on his lips.

I dropped down to my knees, and as I spread his jeans wide open, his hard dick jutted out. Right at my face, in the perfect position. I practically purred. Then I licked the swollen head, tasting his slightly salty pre-come as I flickered my tongue over the sensitive slit.

I loved giving him head.

Maybe because he loved it so much.

Lex groaned and relaxed back against the tree as I teased him with my tongue. Then he buried his hands gently in my hair, sending shivers down my back. "Yeah, Tal," he breathed, and warmth coursed through me.

I sucked his swollen cockhead into my mouth like yummy candy and savored the rush of doing this to him. Remembering how he'd denied me, stopped me that night outside the clubhouse—his birthday, no less. Wouldn't even let me touch his bare dick.

What a jerk.

With that memory in the front of my mind, I pushed my lips down his shaft, sucking the length of him into my mouth and down my throat.

Lex gave a garbled groan, and as I withdrew, scraping my teeth lightly along his rigid shaft, he said my name again in a soft hiss.

I did it again and again, taking him deep, swirling my tongue around… forcing his plump cockhead into the back of my throat. Then scraping my teeth along his length, dragging them over the ridges and veins… wondering, idly, if he had a teeth fetish like I did. I'd never thought to find out, yet.

When his cock flexed and grew impossibly harder, I figured I had my answer.

I slid a hand up to his balls. His ball sac was firm and heavy. I squeezed and pulled as I sucked him off, letting his pleasured groans guide me.

He stirred in response, flexing his hips, pushing into me every time I sucked him deep, his groan turning into a growl.

But before he could even think about coming, I pulled my mouth away and grabbed his hands. I tugged him down and gave him a little shove, made him lie down on the ground. "Don't move," I said as he lay back in his horse onesie, split open, his swollen, flushed dick jutting into the air. He watched me as I kicked off my shoes and wiggled out of my jeans and panties. "You look ridiculous," I gushed.

He laughed.

His hands went to my hips and squeezed as I straddled him, placing my knees on the plush fabric on either side of him.

"This is pretty comfy, though," I muttered as I angled my hips and lined up to take him. As I started to push down, Lex pushed up, filling me in a sudden, hot thrust.

I gasped and slapped my hands to his chest, pinning him with a look—telling him who was in charge.

Then I settled my weight on top of him. I dropped forward and kissed him as I started to ride him.

As I worked my hips up and down, devouring his cock with my pussy over and over again, our tongues battled in a slow, hungry dance. His hands slid up my body and cupped my breasts, squeezing. His fingers pinched my nipples, rolling the hard peaks between them.

Then he planted his boots in the dirt, bending his knees—and rammed his hips up from beneath me. Fucking me. *Hard.*

So much for being in charge.

His thrusts pushed me up, so our kiss broke. But my breasts quickly replaced my lips, meeting his mouth. He lapped his tongue over one nipple, then sucked the other one deep... and when his teeth slowly scraped the length of it, the incredible, tingling sensation—part pleasure, part pain—triggered a shattering response between my legs.

All my pent-up lust since last night—the last time he'd fucked me—exploded in a gushing wave. I fucked him harder and faster, meeting his thrusts with my own as I came. And while he nibbled and sucked on my breasts, he gave a satisfied groan. His hips snapped up in a final push.

He lifted me off the ground as he exploded inside me, our hands dragging over each other's bodies as the pleasure washed through us both.

Lex ran his hands up and down my spine, into my hair, down my throat... all the while sucking on my nipple. Even through his own orgasm, the man was all rhythm. Pulling, squeezing, coaxing every possible sensation from my flesh as I hyperventilated in ecstasy.

I tried to say his name, but my mouth wouldn't cooperate.

His hands were still skimming over me, under and over my clothes, raising small goosebumps in the cool night, as I finally collapsed on top of him. My face landed in his neck, where my lips pressed to the thudding pulse in his throat.

He held me like that for a long time, our hearts pounding against each other, and neither of us said a thing.

I love you, I wanted to say, *so much*, but that didn't come out, either.

Chapter Thirty-Four

Talia

We caught our breath, got our clothes back in place, and while we kissed for a few more minutes and Lex murmured sweet stuff against my skin like, *You're so beautiful* and *You taste so good*, I started getting cold.

So we made our way back up to the porch. Lex opened the front door for me and music spilled out into the night. He slipped into the house behind me. He squeezed my ass, gave me a sharp slap through my jeans, and growled a little *Mmmm* against my neck.

Then he headed into the kitchen, where Dane and Shane were talking, drinks in hand. I watched Lex walk over to them, peeling off the horse onesie as he went—revealing his tight butt in his faded black jeans, his black T-shirt skimming his lean, panther-like muscular frame and broad shoulders.

His eyes met mine across the room and he smiled a little, flashing his teeth when he caught me checking him out.

I took a quick look at the others. At the bar in the living room, Devi was playing DJ and making cocktails while chatting with Lex's friend, rock star Johnny O'Reilly, who sat on a barstool with his date in his lap. Lex had already told me not to bother remembering the girl's name because she was a "rando." To which I told him men were pigs.

Though I now realized I had forgotten her name. Oops. Carly? Karen?

I approached them on my way to the stairs, and Devi met my eyes. "Wow." A slow smile spread across her face. "You look high. Nice weed?"

I blinked at her. I'd barely had any weed.

"Oooh," Johnny's date purred from his lap, turning to look me up and down. "I didn't know we were having sex already."

"Huh?" I stopped dead. "I'm not sex. I mean, I'm not high. What?"

Shit. Maybe I was a little high.

Johnny's date smiled. She had an arm around Johnny and played seductively with his blond hair as he looked me over, too. I tried to discreetly make sure my jacket was sufficiently re-zipped. It was, mostly. No nipples were falling out. Did I look that recently screwed?

I met Devi's eyes again and she smirked. "My mistake. Guess I misread the, uh…" She wiggled her manicured fingers in the air, indicating my general condition.

"The glow you're giving off," Johnny's date finished for her.

Johnny smirked.

Heat bloomed in my cheeks; I knew Devi pretty well, but the others, not so much. "Be right back!" I dashed upstairs to clean up a little. You know, swap out the soaked panties for some clean ones and try to cool some of the post-sex glow.

I wondered if Lex was glowing.

As far as any of our friends knew—other than Roni and the Kings—I'd run out on my wedding to Carl for Lex. That was the official story. There was no abduction, to anyone's knowledge outside the Kings or the Mafia. And I hoped there never would be.

My friends had never really warmed to Carl; I shuddered to imagine what they'd think about Lex if they knew the whole story.

Well, I really was a runaway bride, but he also technically kidnapped me and held me for ransom. But don't worry, it's all good now.

Oh, and by the way, my dad is the secret godfather of the Mafia.

Nope. Uh-uh. I'd be taking some secrets to my grave one day, and those would be top two.

I grinned to myself as I shut the bedroom door behind me. Lex and I were staying overnight in the guest room at the top of the stairs. The same one we'd stayed in the last time we were here—when we were running away together. Or at least, I'd thought we were.

I looked around now, feeling grateful, relieved and a little nostalgic to be here again, so soon, as Dane and Devi's guest—with Lex.

Safe.

Because I now knew that the wrath of the West Coast Kings would come down on anyone who tried to hurt Lex again. Or hurt me.

Not to mention, you know, the wrath of my father, the Mafia godfather.

I was protected from up on high, and now all there was left to do was enjoy my life. Stop trying to be the good girl. And just *be*.

I went into the bathroom to freshen up and change my underwear, slip into my party dress. More party guests would be arriving later, and I wanted to be ready. I felt like I was already Dane and Devi's family now, unofficially. So in a way I was a guest, but I was also kind of a co-host. I wanted to show Devi—who might someday be my sister-in-law—that I took the position seriously.

And I wanted to show Lex: I was in this for forever after. Maybe I hadn't coughed up an official *I love you* yet, but I would.

I'd already admitted to him that I was in love with him, right here, that night. The words would come, when the time was right.

Like our engagement.

That thought thrilled through me as I stepped into my dress. It was pale-blue, sparkly, and fit my curves like I was glued into it while my boobs squished out the top. Since I rarely wore dresses, I figured if I was putting one on, I was going all out.

I touched up my glittery lipgloss and smoothed down my hair. It got a little tangled during the forest sex. There were some dried leaves in it. I grinned at myself in the mirror, wondering if anyone else had noticed.

Yeah. Definitely.

Oh, well. So Lex and I were in that groping-each-other-in-public, fucking-out-in-the-yard stage. Our friends would just have to deal with it.

Honestly, I'd never been in this stage before. With anyone. My other boyfriends had all been law-abiding, schedule-following, color-inside-the-lines guys. Fuck-you-on-the-bed-and-maybe-on-the-couch guys.

Not carry-you-off-into-the-woods-to-fuck-you-in-the-dirt guys.

Except maybe "Carl," the secret biker who was just following orders when he romanced me. The lying dick. I wanted to gag just thinking about it. It still made me feel sick, that I'd fallen for his lies.

And sucked his stupid dick.

And he didn't even make me come as a *Gee, thank you* in return. Not once. He never even rubbed up on my pussy.

Because his fear of my father was more intense than any love he ever had for me.

He'd already flown back to Toronto, without so much as in-person goodbye. His ring went with him; Jude had given it back to him for me. And I felt his fear, heard it loud and clear over the phone when I called him a few days ago, to hear what I could from his lips. He admitted nothing about his Mafia family, not that I'd outright asked, but he didn't deny that my father had arranged the marriage with his uncle.

He spent most of the very brief conversation stammering about how he hoped my parents weren't too upset about what happened, as if he was afraid my dad might have the line tapped.

Then he wished me well, about as politely yet impersonally as a ticket salesperson handing you a ticket to embark on a flight that meant they'd never see you again.

He said not one thing about us continuing our relationship. Clearly, he knew it was over. At least he was honest about that.

And you know what? I was no longer falling for anyone's lies. Including my own.

I looked myself in the eyes in the mirror, and let that sink in.

I, Natalia De Santis, was no one's good girl. I was whatever the fuck I wanted to be, from this second on.

I was a Mafia princess. A *secret* Mafia princess.

And I was madly in love with an outlaw biker.

I had an education. I had parents who loved me, a beautiful home, a great job, awesome friends, and a cute wardrobe. I had a boyfriend with a great dick who was more than willing to make me come in ways I'd never even known were possible.

And *nothing* had ever made me come harder than Lex Davenport fucking me in the woods while he left teeth marks on my skin.

And up against the wall in his room at the clubhouse.

And in his car, after cutting off my clothes with his knife.

He didn't treat me like I was too clean to get dirty. Or too precious to be touched.

Or bitten.

I loved it.

I loved the way he looked at me. Like he'd never stop trying to figure me out. He'd never back down from challenging me.

And most importantly, he'd never let anyone or anything keep him away from me, ever again.

When I strode back into the bedroom, Lex was just walking in. He shut the door behind himself with his foot—and when he saw me in my dress, he felt me up with his eyes so aggressively I actually stopped walking. I stumbled a little.

His eyes got stuck on my boobs and I smoothed my hands over them, plumping them up.

"You like?"

His gaze lifted, burning into mine. "Holy fuck. You are not wearing that in front of Shane."

"Yes. Actually, I am." I glanced at the two champagne flutes he held, half-filled with pale-gold bubbly. "Is one of those for me?"

He handed one to me, still taking me in. I spun slowly, giving him the full view. The back dipped low, revealing that I was braless.

"You wearing panties?" he asked in a low, gruff voice, and a thrill went through me. God, I was hungry for him again. Already.

"Yes." I finished my spin and locked eyes with him. "But only because you just came in me and I don't want to drip all over Devi's floor. You keep looking at me like that, though, you know I'm soaking right through these ones anyway."

He made a soft, growly sound deep in his throat, and raised his glass to me. "To you, Talia De Santis. And that dress."

"Okay." I grinned. "To me. Just kidding. To *us*." I tapped my glass against his.

"Just a sip," he ordered.

"Oh-kay," I said dramatically. "So bossy. Since when do you care if I get drunk? You know it just makes me slutty." He did know. The last week, we'd done very little with our clothes actually on. Except, well, fuck half-in and half-out of our clothes.

I took a small sip and he watched me with hawklike intensity as I did. "Good?" he asked.

"Yum."

"Take another one. Slowly."

I did, trying to make it look sexy as I wondered what he was thinking. Then something moved at the bottom of the glass. A flash of something—shiny.

I lifted the glass high, so the fancy ceiling light shone through.

"Lex!"

I pounded back the whole glass, using my teeth as a screen to make sure no foreign objects slipped through.

"Talia—" He laughed. "Jesus."

The engagement ring at the bottom of the glass hit my lips and I caught it carefully between my teeth. Then I grabbed it in my fingers, sucking the Champagne off of it. I looked at it.

Rose gold. With a delicate, glittery pavé band and a princess cut diamond. It was exactly what I wanted, the engagement ring of my dreams.

In fact... it was *the* engagement ring. The one I'd clipped and saved to my wedding scrapbook.

I met his eyes, disbelieving.

"I know," he said. "I stole Carl's move. What can I say. It was a dumbass move. But I figured you deserved getting through one where you didn't choke. And maybe this proposal could, I don't know, wipe that one from your memory?"

"But. How did you...?"

He shrugged. "Roni."

I blinked at him. "Roni told you about the ring I wanted?"

"She might've showed me the scrapbook you made with all your dreams in it." My mouth fell open, and he added quickly, "And I might've promised her I'd propose in return."

"You are absolutely kidding me."

"I'm not. Actually... I asked her for her permission to propose."

"You did not."

"Oh, I did. You think I'd get anywhere with you if she didn't approve at this point?" He sipped his Champagne while I stared at him, stunned. "I had to make sure we were all good. She's your best friend. Women protect their friends. Especially women like Roni Webber."

"And?"

He sighed a little. "She was chilly when I first approached her. You might say she's not a huge fan of yours truly these days. But she came around pretty quick when I told her I wanted to marry you. At least, enough to give me her blessing."

"Really?" I hopped up and down a little, thrilled that she'd forgiven Lex, at least enough to be happy for us on this.

"She said if I was serious about you and planned to protect you, she had no beef with me."

"I love that girl," I gushed.

"Yeah." His eyes softened. "She loves you, too."

I took a breath and said it. "I love you, Lex. I should've said that before, outside. I got nervous."

"Why?"

"Because. *I love you.*" This time, I put all the emotion I felt into it—and it kinda felt like I'd just ripped my own heart out of my chest and handed it over to him.

"I love you, too." A small smirk curved his lips as he moved closer to me. His eyes softened, kinda glistening as he gazed at my face. "Also. Will you marry me?"

My eyes misted right over. I blinked, trying to see him clearly, wiping at my eyes a bit. "I thought... I thought you said we'd do this when it was the right time."

"We will. We are."

"But..." I had no argument. I was just stunned. That he wanted this. Right now.

"You already said yes to me when you were ten," he reminded me softly, his eyes filled with a sweet nostalgia that brought back every stolen moment together when we were kids. "Don't change your answer on me now."

"The sad thing is," I said, with a little hitch in my breath, "I don't think it ever changed."

He wrapped his arms around me and pulled me against him. "So, you're telling me if I swaggered up to you when I was seventeen, or twenty-four, or the day of your wedding, and asked you to marry me, you would've said yes?"

"Probably. I've always been stupid for you like that."

"Talia. You're far from stupid. You just know who you are and what you want, and you're not afraid to go after it, no matter the consequences. I love that about you. I admire that about you."

I shook my head, still halfway in happy shock. "You make that sound so simple. But the crazy thing is… I've never been more of who I am than when I'm with you." I looked away, feeling ashamed of it for the first time. "I think I pretended I could be someone else, for Carl. And for my dad. For a long, long time."

"You don't have to pretend anymore." Lex laid his hand on the side of my neck and my eyes met his. "I see you, sweetheart."

I swallowed, my heart ripping open and blinding light pouring out as I looked into his eyes, almost knocking me over. I wavered a little on my feet.

"Babe?" He held me tighter against him.

"I'm having a moment."

"You wanna sit down?"

"No. I'm good."

He looked down at the ring in a death grip in my hand. "Will you put it on?" He actually sounded a bit worried. Like I wasn't into this whole idea of marrying him or something.

I'd never been more into anything in my life.

But I just stared at him, slowly blinking.

"I want to see it on your finger," he said slowly, studying me.

"Right." I looked at the ring in my hand. The very special, beautiful ring. Then I looked at him again. "I just realized I don't even know what you do for a living."

His eyebrow went up. He looked amused. "Is this really the time?"

"Fuck, yes. I already almost married a man it turns out I never really knew."

His expression grew somber. "Tal, he sold you a story that he was someone he wasn't. That wasn't your fault."

"And I believed it a little too eagerly."

"You know who I am. I might have to keep secrets sometimes, because of the club. But I'll never lie to you about who I am."

"So you'll tell me what you do for a living?" I pressed.

He considered his words carefully. "I make money."

"Very funny. Tell me *how* or I toss this ring into your drink and *you* can choke on it."

"You know I work on Jude's security crew," he hedged.

"Yeah. Sometimes. And I know what that pays. Don't tell me your part-time security gig pays for your restored classic car and your Harley. And all your leather, and your gun…"

"Guns."

I frowned. "Fine. Guns. Tell me how you pay for all that and a diamond ring? This is like… a fifty-thousand dollar ring, Lex."

His eyebrow went up.

"Oh, God. More?"

He said nothing, just teased his tongue along his teeth.

"Shit. Please do not tell me you stole it."

"I didn't steal it."

"Please tell me you bought it with money you earned legally."

I could see him turning that one over in his head. "That is a strange question for a Mafia princess to ask a man."

I narrowed my eyes. He touched the tip of his tongue to his canine tooth.

"Noted. And don't you dare try to be sexy in the middle of this."

His eyes sparked, enjoying this. "The middle of what?"

"This is a negotiation. Not a hostile takeover." I lifted my chin. "I get a choice."

"Of course you do."

"Then please tell me the government isn't going to come seize this ring one day."

"They aren't."

"And no psycho criminal thug is gonna come cut off my finger to collect it, either."

His smile disappeared. "Are you kidding me?"

"No. Tell me what else you do for work."

He sighed. "I have part ownership in a camera shop Axel owns."

"Cameras?"

"Surveillance cameras. That kind of thing."

"Oh." Okay. Well, that was more legit income. But what was it he said about the Mafia? They laundered their money through legit businesses? "What else? I know the Kings don't just exist to host parties and charity rides. I'm not actually the dumb blonde I sometimes pretend I am."

"I never thought you were dumb at all."

"Don't kiss ass."

He sighed again. "I work for King when he calls me. And Piper. And I'm pretty sure from here on in I'm gonna be Jude Grayson's personal bitch."

"Uh-huh. Doing what?"

"Whatever they ask me to do. Kinda like the guys who work for your father," he reminded me.

Yeah. I got that. And my daddy was not evil.

At least, I'd never be able to believe that he was. No matter what I found out about him.

"And that's all I'm getting?"

He seemed to choose his words carefully. "That's all I can give you. If I could give you more, I would."

Hmm.

I considered that, and how much my dad had given me. Far, far less of the truth about who he was. His life with me had been half-truth and half-lie. He loved me, but he never let me know who and what he really was.

Worse, he tried to make me be something different than I really was—to try to protect me from ending up like him.

Maybe he was never around enough to realize that there was

nothing he could do to stop me from being like him. In many ways, I was probably my father's daughter, more than I could ever know. But I wasn't ashamed of that.

Lex, though? He wasn't lying to me.

"So, you do anything they tell you to do?"

"No. Not anything. It doesn't work like that." He looked into my eyes, seeming to search for the words. "The MC is different from the Mafia. We're all independent, but we're together. If that makes sense. We're strong because we're together. There's mutual respect within the club, but it's not born out of fear. But the Mafia... it's a hierarchy of a different kind. You follow orders, period. I follow King's orders because I want to. But King doesn't order me around. I mean, he does and he doesn't."

"That's clear as shit."

"I could say no to King, or to Piper or Jude or any of my club brothers, and live. If I ever said no to my father, or to an order given to me by one of my father's men on his behalf... well, you know what happened."

Yeah. I knew.

Teeth. Shane.

Abducting me out of fear of even worse consequences for all involved.

I set down my forgotten champagne glass and took his hand. "My family and your club haven't always been... friendly," I reminded him tentatively. He'd been the one who told me as much. He'd also told me how much his father hated the Kings. And he'd told me what he knew of the complicated history between the Mafia and the MC. "What if one day they tell you not to be married to me?"

"Too late." He lifted my left hand and kissed it, then slid the engagement ring of my dreams onto my finger, his eyes locked onto mine. "Will you marry me, Talia? And fuck whatever our families have to say about it. We don't owe them anything anymore."

I gazed into his eyes and I loved him so fucking much in that moment.

"Yes. I'll marry you."

We kissed, celebrating the moment and marking it on one another's souls. Lex was going to be my husband. I was going to be his wife.

Neither of us would ask anyone for permission.

Okay, maybe just Roni.

"I'm so glad I got through this one without choking," I gushed.

"Me, too."

"You know this means you have to move out of the clubhouse, right?"

"Yup."

"I can kick out my roommates."

"You'd do that for me?" he teased.

"Happily."

"Nope. Can't do it. We're not living in a place owned by your father."

"Oh. Good point…"

"We're not living our lives how our fathers tell us to anymore."

"Agreed."

He smoothed his thumb over my cheek. "You know, all I ever wanted was freedom from my father."

"And now you have it."

"Yeah. Now I have it. But only because I made the ultimate sacrifice. Giving you up. I had to turn myself in to the Kings and face the consequences of all the shit I'd done, all my bad decisions, or we never would've gotten off the ground."

I liked that image and smiled at him softly. "Is that where we are now? Off the ground?"

"Yeah. Together." He kissed me softly, then pressed his forehead lightly to mine. "The thing is, considering I wanted out from under my father so bad… it was weirdly fucking hard to come to terms with the fact that it's not actually my father who holds the power in my life. And turning my back on him for good left this weird void. If he didn't hold the power in my world, who the fuck did?"

"I mean, you'd think that question would be easy to answer," I teased. But I understood what he was saying. I'd felt beholden to my dad and what he wanted from me all my life, too.

And he never almost murdered one of my friends.

"You'd think," he agreed.

"So. What's the answer to that question? Who holds the power in Lex Davenport's world?" I was half-teasing him to say me.

"Out there, in the world?" He tipped his head up to indicate the Earth and sky. "Honestly. King."

I laughed a little. "I know you mean that."

He put his fist to his chest. "But in here… that's mine."

"Yeah," I agreed softly.

Then he laid his hand on my chest. I pressed my hand to it, and I knew he could feel my heart thumping in there, double-time.

"I just had to decide what to do with it," he said softly. "Do I want to be my father's son? Or do I want to be something else? Something worthy of being loved by you."

I swallowed.

"I just need you to know that I chose this, Talia. I chose you. I'm not marrying you because they expect me to. I'm marrying you because I can't stand the thought of not being your man."

I bit my lip to keep the tears from spraying out the corners of my eyes, blinking furiously. *Keep it together, Tal. You can do this.*

"I've always cared about you," he rasped. "I didn't even know I could love you. It wasn't an option. That was how I saw it. But fuck that. I love you, Talia De Santis. But you and me, we're not pawns in their war."

My heart thumped as I took that in. It was scary and liberating. And so fucking romantic.

I knew he meant it. That he'd fight for me. That he'd never let my father—or his—try to control our lives again. But… "Tell them that," I teased gently. Because I was still a little scared, of both of our fathers.

How could I not be?

"Pretty sure King already did," he said seriously. "And if they don't get the message, babe, I'll tell them myself."

Ohhh. Badass Lex was making an appearance.

"Yeah?" he murmured, reading my poker face like I'd just flashed him with my Royal Flush. "You like that?" His voice seemed to get lower, deeper with each word.

"Mm," I made a noise that wasn't quite a word.

His hand squeezed lightly on the side of my throat. He ran his thumb over my jaw, looking into my eyes. "Who's your daddy now?"

Oh, God. *Wet panties.*

I'd never had a daddy fetish. Only bad girls with fucked-up father/daughter relationships had those, right?

Wait. Was I one of those girls?

"I feel like my whole self-understanding is splitting open and a whole lot of dark crap is pouring out."

Lex chuckled. "In a bad way?"

"No. I think… I think it might be very, very good."

"Good." His thumb drifted over my lip, then my chin, nudging my mouth open. "Because I'm gonna take you downstairs. We're gonna celebrate with our friends. You're gonna show off your new ring to Devi and have girl talk…"

"Uh-huh." I was mesmerized as his thumb played at my lip, holding my mouth open. His caramel eyes hit mine again.

"And later, Daddy's gonna drag you into the pantry and put you on your knees, then shove his cock in your sweet mouth. And once you've got it nice and wet, I'm gonna put you on your knees and bury it deep in your pussy and fuck you real slow."

"Okay…"

"You think you can be quiet while I do that?"

No.

"Um… yes?"

He smirked, like he saw right through that. "I guess we'll see."

I swallowed thickly, hypnotized by the desire in his caramel eyes. "How soon can we get married?"

He laughed. "Probably tomorrow, if you want to."

"Fuck me in the pantry first," I said, delirious with lust. "I like this new daddy thing."

"Yeah? Good thing, 'cause there's more where that came from."

More? What more?

I *needed* more.

I was so hooked on Lex Davenport, I needed to know what more there was. Right now.

"Oh, good," I gushed, as he pulled me toward the bedroom door, opening it so the music and our friends' voices drifted in. "Because I've got some more, too."

His eyes flashed at me over his shoulder, his tongue playing at a silver tooth as he paused.

"If you tell me yours," I whispered, "I'll tell you mine."

"Baby, what's the rush?" he teased.

I knew, from the way his eyes sparked, that he was dying to know what was on my mind, too. But he was willing to be patient if it meant driving me wild. He tugged me close and took my face in his hands, then kissed me, soft and hot.

"Don't you just want to…" I breathed hotly against his lips as he kissed me so patiently, "I don't know… tear me open to get at all the good stuff inside?" A generous two-thirds of me wanted to say *fuck the party* and just go fuck in the bathroom, right now.

"Nope." Lex shook his head, brushing his soft lips against mine. "I want to unwrap you piece by piece, and suck on you as you melt in my mouth."

I swooned, sagging against him as his words made my bones melt like chocolate in the sun.

"That's the only way to know you, Tal," he said seriously,

looking deep into my eyes. "And I'm just glad I have the rest of our lives to savor it."

Then he slid his hand into mine, laced our fingers together, and tugged me with him, into our future.

THE END

Thank you for reading!

Don't miss *Wicked Angel*,
the next book in the Vancity Villains series!

Need more of Lex and Talia's happily ever after?
Get the free bonus epilogue:
https://jainediamond.com/bonus-content/

Enjoy *Rebel Heir*? Have you read about Dane and Devi yet,
and Jude and Roni, and all the others?
Vancity Villains is a spinoff from my Dirty/Players series.

Books by Jaine Diamond

**For the most up-to-date list of Jaine Diamond's
published books and reading order please go to**
https://jainediamond.com/books/

Dirty Series

Dirty Like Me

Dirty Like Us

Dirty Like Brody

A Dirty Wedding Night

Dirty Like Seth

Dirty Like Dylan

Dirty Like Jude

Dirty Like Zane

Players Series

Hot Mess

Filthy Beautiful

Sweet Temptation

Lovely Madness

Flames and Flowers

Vancity Villains Series

Handsome Devil

Rebel Heir

Wicked Angel

<u>DEEP Duet</u>

DEEP (DEEP #1)

DEEPER (DEEP #2)

Never miss a book—join Jaine's **Diamond Club Newsletter**

at jainediamond.com to get new release info,

insider updates, giveaways and free bonus content.

Note to Readers / Acknowledgments

"Have you ever had that feeling you're being watched?" The moment Talia strolled in the door of Roni's apartment in *Dirty Like Jude,* making her entrance in the Dirtyverse—and telling Roni about the guy she'd seen eyeing her outside, a guy on a Harley with silver canines, and professing that he wasn't her type—there was a spark of utter magic in my mind. I knew Lex and Talia had a story and one day it would be a book. Like so many of my side characters' stories, theirs grew in the background throughout so many other books, and I'm so thrilled to finally get to share their love story.

I can't tell you how much fun I had writing this book. There is a part of me that loves the darker side of romance, where villains are the heroes, some criminals are hotter than they are truly evil, and good girls find out they aren't so "good"—and that's ok. I've long looked forward to writing more about the Kings and the darker side of the Dirtyverse. At the same time, I didn't want this book to stray too far from the tone of the other books in this world. I don't really consider it dark romance, but it definitely treads the line, and I hope you enjoyed the ride with me, Talia and Lex.

To my lovely PAs, Alyssa Giselbach and Siobhan Royle, thank you for all you do for me and for my readers. Thank you Alyssa for running the book club and making so many brilliant teasers.

Thank you to my wonderful narrators and the team at Brick Shop Audio for bringing these books to vivid life for my readers' ears.

To my vibrant, active readers group, Jaine Diamond's VIPs, thank you for being such a fun and lovely community, and sharing your passion for my books. To my incredible ARC Team, thank you for always being so enthusiastic about devouring my books in mere days and leaving such passionate reviews.

To everyone in the book community who has supported my work: it can be a very lonely and solitary thing to be a writer, so many hours spent alone, pouring out your heart and soul on paper; anyone who's reached out to connect and support me, I cherish you.

A note on Élo calling Maddox and his friends *mon petit méchant*. If you're a French-speaking person who read this and thought "she probably wouldn't say it like that," all I can say is that I am not fluent in French but I did research this. While it was difficult to get a consensus from the French speakers I spoke with on what Élo *would* say, I understand that this phrase is a literal translation though not particularly idiomatic in the French language. In the end I exercised creative authorial choice and went with the phrase that I felt fit the situation *and* read the best in the scene, in English. Thank you to everyone who weighed in on this!

To Mr. Diamond, you're the dark to my light and the light to my dark and everything in between. Without you I'd lose my shit trying to get all the things done. Thank you for being my partner in crime, as they say.

To my lovely, passionate, enthusiastic readers: THANK YOU for reading this book! I'm so honored that you chose to read this love story; my intent as a romance author is to spread love. As an independent author, I could not do what I do without you. If you've enjoyed Lex and Talia's story, please consider leaving a review and telling your friends about this book; your support means the world to me.

With love and gratitude,
Jaine

Playlist

After so many playlists, you might think I'd run out of songs, lol. But not so! This has to be one of my absolute favorite playlists so far—in the music selection itself, as well as how it helped me envision these characters' world and story.

As always, some of the songs on this playlist are mentioned in this book; others are songs that captured the feel of a certain scene or that I listened to while writing the book.

You'll find the links to the full playlists on Spotify and Apple Music here:
https://jainediamond.com/rebel-heir/

———

Sitting, Waiting, Wishing — Jack Johnson
*D Is for Dangerou*s — Arctic Monkeys
Soap — Melanie Martinez
Sinister Kid — The Black Keys

Local God — Everclear
Lost Cause — Black Pistol Fire
I WANNA BE YOUR SLAVE — Måneskin
I'm No Good — AWOLNATION
Black Holes (Solid Ground) — The Blue Stones
Back & Forth (feat. Vince Staples) — Emotional Oranges
Level — Black Pistol Fire
Afraid — The Neighbourhood
Pretty Bug (feat. James Vincent McMorrow) — Allan Rayman
Options — Hippie Sabotage
FOR YOUR LOVE — Måneskin
All the Pretty Faces — The Killers
DEVIL — Shinedown
Sick Muse — Metric
Look Alive — Black Pistol Fire
Just — Radiohead
I Think I'm OKAY — Machine Gun Kelly, YUNGBLUD & Travis Barker
Get High — Chet Faker
Call It Off — Tegan and Sara
You Get Me so High — The Neighbourhood
Dopamine — BØRNS
Whatever Tomorrow — Chet Faker
Time Is Running Out — Muse
Wolves — Garbage
MIDDLE OF THE NIGHT — Elley Duhé
Play with Fire (feat. Yacht Money) — Sam Tinnesz
Sweater Weather — The Neighbourhood
Holy Ghost — BØRNS
Talk Show Host — Radiohead
Karma Police — Radiohead
The Hand That Feeds — Nine Inch Nails
Evening On the Ground (Lilith's Song) — Iron & Wine

Smithereens — twenty one pilots
Wasting Time — Goody Grace
Electric Love — BØRNS
West Coast Love — Emotional Oranges

About the Author

Jaine Diamond is a Top 50 Amazon bestselling author of contemporary romance. She writes badass, swoon-worthy heroes endowed with massive hearts, strong heroines armed with sweetness and sass, and explosive, page-turning chemistry.

She lives on the beautiful west coast of Canada with her real-life romantic hero and daughter, where she reads, writes and makes extensive playlists for her books while binge drinking tea.

www.jainediamond.com

Join the readers' group Jaine Diamond's VIPs on Facebook
to chat with Jaine and other readers:
https://www.facebook.com/groups/jainediamondsVIPs/

Preview of Wicked Angel

Don't miss the next book in the Vancity Villains series,
Wicked Angel—Johnny and Angeline's story!

Wicked Angel is a sinfully hot enemies to lovers romance, about a seductive, a-hole (anti)hero on the brink of self-destruction and the quirky, kind-hearted heroine who discovers his darkest secret—and his heart.

———

PROLOGUE

Angeline

We all make mistakes.

We all fuck up royally from time to time.

We all harbor painful regrets, sorrows, and even secret shames.

Things we wish we never did.

And other things we only wish we never did because we know they're wrong, even if they felt right. Things we're so deeply confused about that the torment wedges deep inside, twisting like a knife between our ribs with every breath, until we fear that our boyfriend is about to find out.

Or, wait. Maybe that last part is just me?

Point is, we all make mistakes.

Some we hope to be forgiven for.

Some we don't deserve to be forgiven for because… if we could do it all again…

We'd still fuck up.

The night I fucked up, all I wanted was a quiet place to make a phone call in the middle of a loud house party. So I stepped outside and walked across the grass, away from the house into the dark, alone, for just a moment. But all it really takes is a moment for the world to crash into oncoming space junk.

"Hey, Angel."

I jumped a little at his voice floating out of the dark, a tidal wave of goosebumps running down my body. My heart lurched. My nipples pricked. My fingernails dug into my palm as I took a slow, deep breath and turned to find him sitting in the shadows.

"Hello," I said softly. I sounded like a young girl. A girl so much younger than I was. A girl who was deeply uncertain, suddenly, of the place where her feet met the earth. I was only twenty steps or so from my boyfriend. And from my older sister. Ten steps from a house full of friends. Any one of them would've saved me in that moment, if they could.

But the door was closed. No one could see me. Or him.

No one could see *us*.

Instead, it was all left up to me, and I fucked up.

Crimson and gold flared in the night as he clicked his lighter and firelight danced across his gorgeous face. His name was Johnny. He was the older brother of one of my best friends.

He was a mistake, long before anything ever happened between us.

Nothing had ever happened between us. But I'd crushed on him so hard and for so long, just the sight of his face, flickering in and out of the dark as that lighter sparked the joint in his hand, turned my stomach to a mass of snakes. Because I knew. I knew something very, very bad was about to happen.

And I was going to let it.

"Angeline Delacroix." He said my name slowly, like he was tasting it. Like he was really hearing it for the first time since we'd met, years ago. Every syllable so soft and sensuous on his lips in the dark.

Then he got to his feet, standing up to his full height, looming over me. I got a better look at his face in the moonlight. His eyes were wet with some emotion I couldn't identify. He looked high or drunk, or both.

He looked tormented.

It took my breath away.

His hands slid up around my bare neck, so suddenly I didn't even pull away. By the time his fingers had slid under my ponytail to cradle my skull, I'd gone almost limp. I dangled there in his hands as his watery eyes tripped into mine.

He was gone. Somewhere far away and somewhere deep inside me, all at once, as he looked into my eyes.

My heart fluttered like a trapped butterfly. My hands went to his waist, grabbing onto him, and his eyes flared. I didn't pull him to me or push him away. I just held on. I didn't even know what was happening except that in the utter chaos of this miraculous, fragile event called life, his orbit and mine had suddenly collided and locked together. And I couldn't move.

"Wh-why did you call me Angel?" My voice shook. My fingers dug deeper into his waist. I could feel his heat through his T-shirt.

Despite my name, no one had ever called me Angel.

His watery, dark-aquamarine eyes dropped to my lips. "First time I ever saw you…" he said, his voice rough and dark as sin, "you were wearing a shirt with a kitten on it. With wings. A fucking sequined kitten. You remember that?"

"No."

Yes.

But… he remembered what I was wearing the first time we met?

"And some short little shorts…" His eyes wandered down. "With bare legs. And high-heeled boots. And you know what I thought?"

I swallowed.

He leaned in, until his lips were so close to mine I could smell him—all his rough and ready maleness and his sweet-smoky after-shave and the alcohol on his breath. I could smell the joint burning down between his fingers, so close to my face. I could taste him in the air between us like an instantly addictive drug. "I thought, I bet she's even prettier when she begs."

I sucked in a breath. I knew he was about to kiss me.

I didn't move.

My core lit on sweet, heavenly fire as his lips met mine.

And yes, I kissed him back.

Because you know what? Life isn't easy.

We don't always get what we want.

We don't always want what we get.

Inside, we are nothing like what others think we are when they look at us.

We are deeply misunderstood.

And we are complicated. We are so many things; more things than we are not.

I *felt* so many things in that moment as Johnny O'Reilly kissed me in the dark, with only the moon and stars as witness to our seeking tongues, our pounding hearts.

He broke the kiss, abruptly, and I held my breath, reeling. My hands dropped away from him.

What the hell did I just do?

He turned my head in his hands and kissed my neck. "I'll take my time…" he rasped in my ear. "I'll make you purr." His tongue drifted up the curve of my ear and I shuddered.

"Don't," I whispered. I pressed my shaking hands to his chest and stepped back an inch.

"Don't... what?" He looked amused, maybe. And for a split second in the shifting moonlight through the trees, as his eyes met mine again, he looked broken.

I didn't feel amused. Or broken. I felt confused. I was reeling with emotions. So many feelings at once, I couldn't lock onto a single one of them.

But I knew I didn't owe him any explanation. I didn't owe him anything. I had no idea if he knew I had a boyfriend, but in the end, none of that was his responsibility.

I wrapped my arms around myself as his eyes dragged over me, slow.

Then his hands released me, gently. He brought the joint to my lips. I took a small, hesitant drag, breathing in the musky smoke. He took a drag, too, his eyes never leaving mine.

"You should go back in the house," he said softly, exhaling smoke into the air.

I should've. But for some reason, I lingered.

"I leave you out here all alone, in the dark..." He gestured into the darkness, his joint leaving a wisp of smoke and sparks in the air. "What kind of man would that make me?"

I wanted to tell him that I knew exactly what kind of man he was. But the words got choked up in my throat.

You kissed him.

It was sinking in, like teeth ripping into my heart. I cleared my throat and turned, forcing myself to walk back to the house as my body flushed with heat. And with hunger.

Guilt.

Shame.

"Good night, Angel," he breathed behind me, and a shiver ran down my back. I could hear the whisper of gratification beneath his words, and something strangely sad.

And for some reason, I felt bad about leaving him standing there all alone, in the dark. But I didn't turn back as my insides churned, my emotions still reeling in a chaotic tumult as the world spun around me, upside down and inside out.

You kissed him and you loved it.

In one sudden, unexpected moment, the entire trajectory of my life had subtly changed. Though I wouldn't know it until later.

I wouldn't say that it was that single, broken kiss that ended my relationship with my boyfriend, Flynn.

But I would say it was the spark that lit the fire, that in the end, burned our whole house down.